REASONS

THREE LIVES ONE SOUL

a novel

SHERRY DENBOER

First Trade Paperback Edition: 2022
ISBN paperback: 978-1-7779048-0-7
ISBN eBook: 978-1-7779048-2-1

Print book interior design by Sherry denBoer

The characters and incidents in this novel, although inspired by
actual events, have been fictionalized for dramatic purposes, and
are not intended to depict actual individuals or events.
Content advisory: This book contains intimate partner abuse.

Author website: www.sherrydenboerauthor.com
Twitter: @sherrydenboer
Facebook: Sherry denBoer author

Reasons is dedicated to
all the people who live their best life
despite, if not because of,
their challenges.

Gratitude

I am deeply grateful for all the people who cared and took the time to read and critique Reasons. A few people stand out: Mike Dodington, my neighbor, and my friend. Mike gave me his time and his knowledge and helped me take a messy first draft and turn it into something worthy. Thanks, Mike. You never complained when a few months turned into a couple of years. I'm forever grateful. Josh Templeton, an early critique partner who gave me his time, his writing wisdom, and ultimately, his friendship. Robert denBoer, my husband, who has listened to hours and hours of my thoughts and ideas, read and critiqued each page of Reasons, and cared about my writing experience more than anyone else. I love you, Robert. My love for you grows each day.

*"Biology is the understanding that
the stream of life, flowing out of
the dim past into the uncertain future,
is in reality a unified force,
though composed of an infinite number
and variety of separate lives."*

RACHEL CARSON, American Marine Biologist,
author, and conservationist.

1

the raven

The winter walk would do her good, or so she hoped as she reached down to retie loose laces. *Why now? What do they mean?* Rising, she kicked at the soft snow with the toe of her boot— her thoughts returning to the snippets of memories plaguing her as of late—razor-sharp, and alarmingly disconnected: William's hand pressed against her throat, the wood-splintering crash of a door kicked open, strobe lights, a fire escape.

Peaceful and picturesque, the snowflakes fell at a hypnotic pace, the winter storm vast and dense, and impressively soundless. On the hillside, Reason watched, and when an exceptionally large snowflake stood out from the others, she traced it until it disappeared into the seamless sea of white.

At thirty-five, Reason still grappled with her anxiety and anguished about the events of her past, ruminating about what she had done to cause them—often presenting a smile when what she secretly wanted was to confess the sense of dread she suffered daily.

She brushed the snow from her gloves, turning her attention to the nearby landscape, lifting her face to the wet, wintry freshness of the tumbling flakes. Basking within the seemingly protective, blanketing embrace of the falling snow, her troubling thoughts drifted away in a wave of unexpected contentment.

The early morning sun ascended as a hazy ball of light, hovering just above a prominent row of white pines, their tall trunks and flowing boughs cresting the hill opposite her. Reason scanned the small pond that sat frozen between her and the hill, her breath billowing about her face as she surveyed the scene with keen interest.

For her, the rugged terrain exemplified strength and calm and sparked in her a sense of peace and joy. She opened her arms wide, tilted her head back, and for a few moments basked in that feeling.

As she descended toward the pond, a movement caught her eye—a large black bird flying in the monochromatic sky. The bird swooped down and flew past where she stood.

Instantly entranced, Reason's gaze followed the bird as it sailed across the surface of the white, windswept pond. And when it broke from its glide, the beating of its powerful wings drummed into the silence—a slow, rhythmical sound like the repeated release of a measured column of air—exact and mesmerizing. "Aren't you splendid," she whispered.

The blackbird's flight was swift and decisive—an exquisite sight—a bold, black streak across the stippled milky-white. Reason raised her hands to her cheeks as the bird flew past—an unconscious reaction to a most peculiar feeling—a sense that the bird somehow expected her attention, and that it knew she was watching. Nearing the far end of the pond, it eased into a glide, its wings spread wide. Engrossed as she was, Reason took a quick step forward when the bird vanished into the forest, disappearing as if seized by the outstretched limbs of the trees. "Oh!" she blurted, surprising herself with the impulsiveness of her reaction.

With the bird's abrupt departure, the whole of the surrounding scene seemed changed. The snowfall had stopped. The sudden stillness of the landscape and the vastness of the slate-grey sky had become eerie and bleak. Reason shivered, wrapping her arms about herself, rubbing her hands up and down the sleeves of her parka. "There's nothing to be afraid of," she told herself. Yet she felt increasingly strange, lightheaded—and lost. "What's happening?" The sound of her own voice seemed distant. Her head ached, a dull, persistent throbbing at her temples. As a high-pitched ringing distorted her hearing, she teetered.

Lurching forward and then two steps to the side, she strived to steady both her posture and her thinking—her hands pressed against her temples to contain a rising sense of panic. Nothing had happened to cause the sudden change in her perspective, nothing but the black bird's appearance. Sensing that the bird must somehow be important, Reason searched the sky. But nothing above provided her with any sense of clarity. As she stood helplessly alone, she realized she could remember little before sighting the bird.

In a desperate attempt at self-control, curling her hands into fists and standing tall, she focused her search on the long, fluid limbs at the spot where the bird had disappeared—her eyes widening at an astonishing flash of memory. Where the bird had vanished, she had seen the trees move oddly, an incomprehensible bending and wavering. She cupped her hands to the top of her head—and mentally retraced the experience. *I can almost see it. Come on. Concentrate.* Feeling somehow altered, Reason vaguely sensed that something about her very existence may have changed.

In one swift motion, she dropped a glove and scooped up a handful of snow, pressing the icy crystals onto her neck, hoping that somehow the cold shock might help. "HEY!" she yelled on impulse, shouting at the impervious landscape, turning a full circle, hoping the bird had returned. "Where are you? Come back!" The sound of her voice seemed out of place in the icy silence, almost pathetic, and the scene unnervingly still and quiet. She waited, pushing her wet, bare hand into the armpit of her coat.

Out from the stillness came a powerful gust of wind, the cold burst of air revitalizing and strengthening Reason's resolve. She raised her arms and awkwardly boxed the cold air with two quick jabs, determined to find her way home, wherever that may be. Turning toward the ordinary snow-clad hills, lips pursed and eyes squinting, she fixed her mind on the vague details of what had happened. *I was watching the falling snow. The bird came from my left.* With her finger, she traced the bird's flight and when she got to the edge of the forest, she gasped.

Where the forest met the frozen edge of the pond, she had indeed seen the great pines shudder and then move unnaturally. And when they had, their thick trunks and long intermingling branches had blurred and distorted, and then they had formed a perfectly circular opening, one that the large bird had flown through with its wings spread wide. *For real? Did I see a kind of... doorway?* What she thought she remembered seemed highly doubtful, but the fresh memory was remarkably specific. Picking up her glove, Reason pulled it on, clasped both hands together at her chin, and then lowered them. *I saw it.* "Right there," she told herself, pointing to the now motionless trees that had altered so magically.

She laughed and slapped her thigh. Outrageous as the idea was, she was surprisingly certain of what she had seen, and that no normal force of nature had caused the spectacle. The flight of the bird, from its ordinary beginning to its exceptional end, had taken mere minutes, and when the bird had reached the trees, they had most definitely moved, and they had done so with swift and unusual agility. She cupped a hand over her mouth, trying to absorb the fantastic details, but still unsteady, and overcome with a persistent uneasiness, she sank to the ground, cushioned in the deep snow. *But why? What's happening to me?*

Mystified, Reason scanned the winter-bare branches of the trees that climbed the steep embankment across from where she sat. At the crest of the ridge, an impressive display of pines stood tall and graceful, their boughs far-reaching, staggered, shaped by the wind. Above them, the steel-grey sky hovered motionlessly. She returned her gaze to the magical forest and sighed at its current state of normality—shaking her head in dismay.

CB EO

Slouched on the bathroom floor, favoring her right hip and elbow, Reason carefully leaned forward, and pausing, caught her breath. Moving with meticulous care, she began pushing and pulling the damp, balled-up facecloth across the smooth surface of the tile. With each stroke, she labored to erase the memory of William's probing hands, the heat of his rancid breath, the stink of his sweat-soaked skin. But overcome with exhaustion, she slumped and stopped. Groaning, she squinted at the soiled floor, trying to focus on the drying remnants of vomit staining its stark whiteness. Starting up again, each of her movements painful and controlled, she wiped and scrubbed, striving to wash away the filth and the memories.

Moaning, supporting herself against the cold, outer edge of the tub, she struggled to her feet. Then shuffling to the washbasin and avoiding looking in the mirror, she pushed the stiff rubber plug into the rusty drain—and then rested. Sighing, her gaze fixed on the basin, she turned on the taps. With great care, Reason washed—the water turning pink in the sink. Shuddering, overcome by a perverse self-loathing, she dug her thumb deep into the softened soap and let the bar slide from her fingers. Her shame and the pain of her bruised and torn skin taunted her—both blatant reminders of the attack.

At the sound of shuffling footsteps, she grimaced and glanced at the closed bathroom door. The walking halted. "You in there, Reason?" asked her college roommate, her voice sleepy and muffled.

"Yeah," Reason managed, her voice thin.

"You gonna be long?" Reason stayed quiet, desperate for solitude, stalling. "Okay, whatever," said the loudly yawning girl. "No probs. I'll go downstairs. Musta been quite the party," she teased. Reason leaned against the door, listening to the footsteps receding.

Soon water was running through the pipes in the bathroom below. She relaxed, unrolled a large bath towel, and spread it out on the freshly cleaned floor. Carefully wrapping another towel about her battered body, and using one more for a makeshift pillow, she lay down.

Reason welcomed the hollowness growing within her. She wanted it to consume her—to make her go numb. She sank into its stiff embrace and waited to be alone in the house.

CR ₧

In the darkened hospital room, the two women exchanged a meaningful glance. One smiled somberly at the other and shook her head no. They touched hands in passing, a simple gesture of support. The morning nurse checked and recorded the old woman's vital signs. Returning the chart to its place, she turned to look out the window. Dawn was breaking pale yellow. It was time to let the light in.

"Reason is stable," said the night nurse, having paused at the doorway. "See you tonight," she added before exiting the room.

☙ ❧

"Wake up. I can see you stirring there. I said wake up! That's it. Open your eyes. It's time for a chat," oozed Pain.

No.

"You know you don't have a choice, right?" The words stung. Reason moaned. Now in her eightieth year, she was tired of fighting. "You're ridiculous, trying to be tough. You're weak," griped Pain. "And you're wasting your time if you think that the silent treatment will make a difference. How charming that you should try. Well, dearie, here's what I say to that: Go ahead. Try to ignore me. I'll keep talking. I enjoy talking." Reason sucked in air, wincing. "You must know by now that you cannot stifle me."

She gasped, holding back her tears as her leg muscles cramped and twisted in her flesh. *Go away. Let me be.*

"I will never leave you," screamed Pain. "I'll tear through your paltry resistance, and I'll do so with enormous pleasure. I'll burn within your flesh like the sizzling coals of a smoldering fire. And from there, my dear," Pain sneered, "I'll burrow into your blood and your bones, and every cell."

Reason curled her hands into tight fists. She lay on her back, in agony, willing herself to be stronger, to dig deeper, to resist the brutality of Pain. *You're a cruel beast and I despise you.*

"Yes. I am cruel. Cruelty is a specialty of mine. As is mercilessness. And with dazzling qualities such as these, I'll easily overwhelm the flimsy tissues that hold your fragile human essence." Pain leaned in close. Reason held her breath. "And if you don't learn how to be attentive to my needs, I'll gladly turn you inside out!"

Overwhelmed by Pain, she descended into its grip as if it were quicksand, and stuck there, struggled with thoughts of death—wishing for it—wondering when it would finally come. Lately, these dreadful thoughts had become more frequent and difficult to control. She had tried praying, appealing for a miracle, whispering her despair into the night, searching for God. She had prayed for endurance, for strength, for hope. But Pain was tenacious, and she, stuck in its grasp, had thought that if God existed, he had forsaken her.

Trapped in her failing body day after day, Reason languished. But lately, she had somehow discovered one singular saving grace. She had learned that if she focused on the flow of her breath, she could become rooted in the present—and the relentless chatter in her head dulled. So, in the midst of Pain's latest attack, Reason found the rhythm of her breath and slipped into a welcome stillness.

03 80

Reason slumped in the snow, her head bowed, cold seeping into her bones. She wrapped her arms about her knees and rocked back and forth. "Think," she whispered. *What do I do? Where do I go?*

Above, the Raven reappeared, flying in a slow circular pattern. "Craw, Craw."

Reason half leapt up. "I'm here. I'm here," she cried, thinking that the bird might be an ally.

"Craw, craw," came the bird's call again, seeming to urge her forward.

The Raven flew in slow circles, and with each rotation, it moved closer to the mysterious forest. Below, stumbling through the snow, Reason followed. The bird dove, plunging towards her, coming unusually close, its coat of black feathers glossy and smooth. As it passed, it seemed to look back and point its large curved bill in her direction. Then, with its voice deep and guttural, it drew her on.

03 80

The handset heavy in her hand, she listened to the man talk. His tone was firm and, to Reason's surprise, sympathetic. He had the voice of an airline pilot—precise, commanding, and calm. Still, she could not relax—instead rapidly tapping the fingers of her free hand against her forehead, unable to quell an overwhelming sense of dread and helplessness that seemed to be the substance of every thought.

A magazine lay open on the small table beside her, and as the man talked, Reason ceased her nervous tapping and thumbed listlessly through its pages. A headline caught her eye: "Thoughts on Belief". She pulled the magazine to her lap and read the highlighted portion in the middle of the page: "A tiny moment in one's life is like a child's building block—appearing almost meaningless on its own. But pile the moments up sequentially, and they'll build a tower of time that will reveal the true purpose of one's life—each moment full of great meaning and connected to the present. Nothing, and no one, is isolated." But here on the phone, right now, Reason felt horribly isolated. Her life was wildly out of control, and she knew it. She believed no one could understand the truth of her predicament. All she knew for sure was that William would eventually come for her, and when he found her, he just might kill her. She tossed the magazine aside.

The man on the phone had asked her a question. But she had kept quiet, unable to speak, his words somehow senseless.

She stared at the wallpaper just inches from her face and compulsively counted the tiny yellow flowers in its busy pattern. Clustered into small diamond shapes, the yellow flowers climbed the wall and seemed to fill every inch. A wave of nausea suddenly rose from Reason's belly. She pressed her forehead against the wall. The sound of the man's voice eased her back.

"Where is he, Reason? Where is William?"

She did not know William's whereabouts and squeezed her eyes shut, mildly comforted by this, grateful for it, because not knowing meant that she would not have to lie, and not knowing helped her cling to the wishful notion that William might be somewhere far away from her.

The man on the phone had introduced himself as Detective Newman. He seemed kind and unthreatening, but Reason had become suspicious of everyone.

"This is just you and me having a friendly conversation," said the detective. "Just you and me. So how about you help me find him?" Again, she said nothing. Overwhelmed by worry, Reason could not see past it. Her situation felt hopeless.

She listened to the detective's muffled voice as he covered the receiver and spoke to someone else, half-heartedly wondering if this exchange was about her. Then he was back. "Got a pen and paper? Write down my number. It's my personal line. Ok?" Reason hesitated and then picked up a stubby pencil and an old receipt from a dish of paperclips and abandoned keys, and scribbled down each number as the detective called it out.

"He's trouble. He's a thief. He'll take you down with him if he can. He doesn't care about you. It's all about him. It always has been. It always will be." He paused, and Reason heard what sounded like him sipping from a drink, slurping as if the liquid were hot. And then, as she agonized about William's motives, he added, "I think you know this. You know he cares only about himself. You're what... maybe eighteen? You've got your entire life ahead of you. Maybe you don't understand what that really means, but it means everything. Reason? Do you hear what I'm saying?"

The detective sighed with obvious frustration, his caring personality no match for her mistrust and fear. "You don't want to talk. I get that. But Reason, I'm on your side. I'm not your enemy." He waited for a reply. "Right. Okay. Call me when you decide you have something to say. I'm just a quick call away. Okay? Reason?"

Reason knew that she would not make that call. Convinced that no one would believe William's true nature, she was certain that no one truly cared. She picked at the curled edge of the magazine, living deep within her fear, a fear that kept her withdrawn and alone. "You don't understand," she said in a barely audible whisper.

"What? Reason?" She sat in the heavy silence, handset to her ear, retreating. "Talk to me," implored the detective. In stony silence, the muscles of her clenched jaw drawn tight—she listened to his breathing. He waited an excruciatingly long time, and then finally hung up. She had heard him sigh and clear his throat, and then he was gone. She waited to hear the blunt finality of the dial tone and then lowered her handset in its cradle.

"I'm so tired," she said to the wall of flowers.

In the townhouse where William had spent his childhood, and where his mother and two younger brothers still lived, Reason sat alone and pondered her pitiful circumstances. She and William had been sofa surfing for a very long time—having no place to call home.

But sometimes, at William's direction, they'd stay a few days at his mother's townhouse.

William's parents had divorced a few months ago. After the divorce, his father had returned to England and his mother had immediately begun her quest for another man. "Time to find a new husband! One who'll take care of my needs in a way that your ungrateful father never could." And fearing that potential suitors might be uninterested in the mother of three teenaged boys, she had asked that her sons cease to call her Mum, and instead, address her by her first name. "Start right away," she had insisted. "That way, you'll have it straight when we're out and about." Reason grimaced at the memory. She loathed William's mother.

The red light blinking at the base of the answering machine made Reason uneasy. She lifted her hand into the air above the machine, palm outward with splayed fingers—as if this physical gesture could block her compulsion to know if *he* had called. Dropping her hand to her thigh, she watched the flashing dot for a breath, and then looked away.

Ahead was the small kitchen with yesterday's dirty dishes. She had sat in the same spot back when William had unleashed one of his violent outbursts. During that argument, she had shown him defiance and had criticized him. "I don't care what you want from me. I just don't care anymore. I don't! You're... an idiot. You're an ass. You deserve whatever happened! You probably asked for it!" she had yelled, referring to his latest stint in jail. He had flown into a rage, and fuelled by her anger, she had not cowered. When he came at her, Reason had stayed seated and had moved too late—his kick coming as an appalling surprise—the heel of his foot striking her above her right eye.

Now, with no one expected home for hours, she stared at the spot where William had been that miserable day, his back to her, angrily turning the pages of a magazine, ripping them in his growing fury. He had turned his head with a slow, deliberate arrogance; his expression full of vile hatred. And in one swift move, he had slapped his hands onto the table, driven himself up and out of his seat, and charged her.

Reason winced at the vividness of the memory. *Where will I go?* She traced a yellow-flowered diamond with her finger; her expression grim as she wondered where William might be hiding. She did not know what he had done this time to warrant the police attention, but she surmised they would keep searching for him—and she hoped they would leave her alone. They did not know the things of which William was capable. But she knew, and knowing, terrified her.

CB ⅏

Go away. I was sleeping.

"But why?" snarled Pain. "You know all too well you'll never get away from me just by sleeping. So why try? But you must tell me, dearie, when you drift off, where do you go?"

Go away!

"No. Answer me. Do you go somewhere?"

No. I go nowhere.

"Whatever do you mean? I can find out, you know. And I'll tag along. So, you might as well tell me now. Where do you go when you close your eyes?"

You don't understand the importance of my time.

"Oh, but you are wrong. I do. And I know exactly what I'll do with it."

I'll resist...

"Ridiculous! Now, tell me. Where do you go?"

I told you. I go nowhere.

"Fine. Be stubborn. You're a petulant child. Do you think I don't know how to play your little game? Because I do. So, you might as well tell me. What do you do there, at your precious nowhere?"

Are you daft?

"Whatever do you mean?"

What do you think I do?

"You probably do nothing. How very annoying."

That's right, my friend.

"Oh, so now we're friends?"

Leave me alone!

"So be it. Go to your useless nothing. But I warn you, I won't be far away. I'll haunt your dreams and I'll be right here when you wake up."

Tormented by Pain, Reason moaned with exhaustion, but she felt the magnificent Raven pulling her back. She was so sure of the bird's presence that she sank comfortably into sleep—and left Pain behind.

ങ ဟ

With her feet planted squarely in the deep snow, and her hands on her hips, Reason faced the line of trees that edged the pond, their branches thick, low and impenetrable. "Craw, Craw," called the bird from behind her. It flew in a wide arc, moving away from the forest, and then turning back, rapidly picked up speed. With growing excitement, she watched as its great wings drummed the air, beating swiftly and effortlessly.

When the bird closed in on the blockade of trees, she held her breath in anticipation. And when it was upon them, as she had seen before, the trees distorted, opened wide, and the bird disappeared. But this time, the trees stayed parted, the center of the magical opening shimmering and wavering. "Craw, Craw," called the Raven from somewhere on the inside.

"Now!" Reason shouted, and she scrambled through the great coniferous doorway. Snow cascaded from the treetops, falling all around her, but she entered the forest untouched by a single bough. Inside, she extended her arms protectively and peered into the shadows.

"Oook, oook, oook," croaked the Raven, beckoning her forward. Moving cautiously, Reason followed the sound.

Just inside the dense forest, a large grouping of evergreen trees stood tall and intimidating, giant forest guards ominously peering down. Beyond them, the snow had miraculously disappeared. Instead, dry leaves and pine needles scattered the ground. And nearby, a few leafless trees stood strangely ornamented with plump beads of water. When pale sunlight breached the forest canopy, filtering down in blinking sheets of dusty white, the large droplets lit up brightly and glittered like jewels.

"Oook, oook, oook," cooed the Raven again, its call softening, flowing down from somewhere high in the darkened canopy.

Reason searched the treetops. She glimpsed the bird's silhouette passing through a collection of long, thin shafts of light. And once more she followed, moving deeper into the woods, her childlike love of the forest not easily subdued—the thrilling mystery of the wilderness always sparking vivid images like hooded thieves in the shadows or young queens on white horses. "Where are we going, Mr. Raven?" she wondered. "And where has all the snow gone?" She picked up a handful of dry leaves and then let them fall from her fingers.

Feeling energized and breathing in the earthy freshness, Reason could not help but think that if the color green had an aroma, its scent would be this: plant matter, damp soil, pine, and spicy cedar. But the serenity of her moment did not last. William's smirking face flashed before her, wavering amongst the leaves, his voice conspicuous and menacing, "I've got it all planned out." She gasped and stumbled backwards. The leaves on the nearest trees rustled and a tremendous cracking cut through the quiet of the forest.

Reason dropped to the ground. As she shuddered and looked on, the branches of nearby trees bent and then snapped, and to her right, a giant evergreen came crashing to the ground. The tree settled quickly, and the forest once again became quiet. She stood and took a nervous step toward the fallen tree, but from somewhere behind, a twig snapped. She froze. "Is someone there?" she cried, the tiny hairs on her arms rising. And then in a hushed voice to herself, "What... is... happening?"

Near her feet, leaves and dirt jumped and skipped as the ground beneath them began to quake and rumble. Nearby, the pines trembled and then swayed. Struck dumb with fear, Reason stood mesmerized. Ahead, in the direction that she had been traveling, the trees shook convulsively and, disturbed by some unseen force that seemed to move towards her, one by one they lifted and fell to the ground. When a powerful spray of dirt showered her, Reason came to life. She fled mindlessly into the woods, stumbling through the tangled undergrowth. A ghastly cry tore through the forest behind her. She spun around, but no horrifying beast reared its ugly head or charged forth from the shadows. She turned and kept fleeing. Ahead, the ground cracked and heaved and the shrieking grew louder. Forced to her knees, Reason clamped her hands over her ears and screamed—fear rising like bile—bringing with it the sting of a long-familiar and anguished helplessness.

In every direction, loose debris swirled up from the forest floor; the bits and pieces gathering and spinning as funnel-shaped clouds. Then, all at once, the newly uprooted trees rose from the ground, ascending at a fixed pace, rising as a group, ten feet, twenty feet, then halting, floating within the blustery chaos. Large branches broke from the hovering trees—and then stayed floating alongside them. Smaller branches dropped to the ground and snaked about, some wriggling towards Reason. She rushed away, stumbling backwards as the slithering branches disintegrated into powdery ash. Then, in an intensifying and terrifying roar, all the floating pieces split, and twisted, and weaved together. Having fallen, Reason hesitated as her mind grappled with an engrained and surreal habit of reflexive detachment. Coming to her senses, she turned from the madness, rose to her feet, and staggered away.

Ducking and zigzagging, she fell onto a soggy, rotten log. The decayed wood crumbled. Her hands sank into the stinky, wet muck below. Clambering to her feet, she spotted a wedge of rock jutting out from the forest floor like a broken bone. Lunging for it, she squeezed herself between it and the rumbling ground. Stealing a glance at the violently changing forest, she shuddered and turned away—large chunks of organic matter pummelling the nearby ground in loud thwacks. Reason shouted—her incoherent cry lost in the uproar. And then, as abruptly as the whole disturbance had begun, it ended—the unnerving quiet that followed, eerily punctuated by the occasional dull thump of falling debris.

In the core of the wild scene stood a frightening tunnel-like structure constructed entirely from the uprooted trees. Reason shivered and stared, terrified that the hideous thing might twist its gaping mouth in her direction and snatch her into its ragged wooden jaws.

The cavernous creation reached far into the forest, snaking out of sight. She summoned her courage and dared to lean forward and peer into its massive throat. Inside was an ominous black void and from the blackness oozed a low, sinister hum. Breathless and shaking, she imagined a beastly creature lurking within the darkness, sneering, watching, waiting to pounce. But nothing more happened.

She eased out from under the ledge of rock and jumped up to flee. But her legs seemed weighted down. Pushing against the stone and grasping at nearby branches, Reason mustered all of her strength into wrenching herself free. But the tunnel seemed to pull on her, drawing her in. And to her horror, she realized she had a dark desire to enter it, a temptation to give in. *No. No! Pull away!*

When at last she had dragged herself to what she hoped was a safe distance, the ground beneath her feet shook and rumbled again. "What now?" she yelled into a rising din, and once more she cowered panic-stricken as more trees, great and small, were swept into a large mass of churning organic matter. And when the chaos had finally settled, a second tunnel had formed, facing the first, the two gaping mouths so close together, the tunnels appeared to be ready to battle one another.

A creepy chattering poured out from the entrance of the second tunnel—as if many voices were whispering at once. And as with the pull of the first tunnel, Reason had to drag herself away.

"Craw, Craw," cried the Raven, breaking the horror of the moment.

Relieved to hear the bird, Reason searched for it. It called out again, confirming its presence. She hurried toward the sound, eying the treetops, but a bellowing voice stopped her cold. "There you are," it said. "I've been waiting for you. Come. Join me. We must talk about William."

The disembodied voice engulfed the forest like floodwater, out of place and rushing into a space it did not belong. Reason dropped to the ground and then scrambled to hide behind the nearest tree. Eyes darting about, her mind reeled. *Chat? William? What?*

Her breath coming in short bursts, every muscle rigid, Reason waited, pressed against the tree. The bark bit sharply into the palms of her hands. Agonizing moments passed. She laughed—a quiet, nervous giggle—shaking her head in a jerky little burst of astonishment. Then, forcing her limbs to move, she peered around the tree. "Who's there?" Nothing but silence. She sat back, and again she waited. Then she stood, her back against the tree, indecisive, second-guessing what she had heard, stealing a glance at the tunnels. *But those horrible things are bloody real! What are they?*

Dry leaves shot into the air at her feet. She yelped. A chipmunk scurried past, undaunted by the hideous change in its surroundings. Her fingers pressed to her heart as if to contain it, Reason stepped out from behind the tree. The booming voice spoke again. "No need to be afraid," it said. "You're quite safe with me."

A surge of panic sent white sparks into her vision and pins and needles to her fingertips. She darted back behind the tree. "Where are you? What do you want?"

"I'm here, in the library. My name, young lady, is Edward."

"What?" she mouthed in amazement. *Have I gone completely mad?* She pressed her forehead against the rough bark, took a deep breath, and once again stepped out from behind the tree. She blinked in disbelief. Before her, in the wild remoteness of the woods, stood an enormous, tilting building. And above its old and weather-beaten front entrance was a cracked and faded sign—LIBRARY.

"I see I confuse you. I understand. Come. Allow me to explain," said the voice in a softer, compassionate tone. "You are safe. Come inside. Have a cup of tea with me." The door to the library opened and out walked an oddly dressed man—his smile wide, toothy, and disarming. He walked to the top step of the building's front porch and, stopping there, leaned against one of its four round wooden columns. Without knowing why, Reason felt comforted by his presence.

The frozen pond she had so recently left behind seemed to exist in a completely different universe from the one in which Reason now

16

found herself. But here, deep within the forest, in a terrifying but wondrous new world, as the twin tunnels of doom hummed and buzzed behind her, Reason strangely felt safe. She smiled and sighed, acutely aware of the sudden and significant elimination of her fear. Then she accepted an invitation to tea from a bizarre stranger who, standing on the porch of a mysterious library, smiled gregariously and beckoned her forward.

2

the librarian

Faced with relentless Pain, Reason lay unmoving, but she struggled with dark, disheartening thoughts. Her mind screamed for relief as she probed it for a solution, for a way out. Yet even when her antagonist was most agitated, when it frightened her with its brute force and constant attacks, she had come to realize that a marvelous phenomenon could occur. And when it did, it tamed the obsessive chatter in her head.

Her transformation from panic to peace always started with a sleepy sensation, a sort of drowsy acceptance that would wash over her just when she felt she could take no more. When this happened, her mind would rest. And at rest, basking in a blissful state of stillness, Reason had discovered a whole other world. In it, extraordinary and exciting things were happening, and with them, she had found hope. All she needed now, to keep this hope alive, was to figure out how to keep Pain from interfering...

"Welcome back. I woke you just exactly the way I like to. And my, oh my, I had fun."

You're a bully. I hate you.

"Oh, that's too bad. But you know, dearie, without me—you're nothing. You and me, we are the same."

We are not. I'm not you.

"You're foolish and funny. Too funny."

I'll keep fighting you. And one day, I'll...

"Idiotic creature! You bore me with your nonsense."

Shhh. Do you hear that?

"Hear what? How vulgar. I was talking..."

Isn't it beautiful?

"What are you blathering about?"

Must go...

"What? I'll not let you!"

❧ ❧

"Oook, oook, oook," sang the Raven from a nearby branch. And as more of the forest creatures recovered from the tumultuous creation of the tunnels, birdsong trickled down through the many tiers of tree boughs.

Inside the transformed forest, the air had become hot and humid. Reason unzipped her coat, removed her winter boots, and pulled her socks from her feet. Ahead, a pathway of thick, flowering thyme led to the front steps of the library. With her boots tucked under her arm, she walked down the path, the plants soft and cool beneath her feet. *It feels so real.*

The tunnels stood a reassuring distance behind her, their eerie sounds almost silenced. She glanced back, wide-eyed and wary, and then to the peculiar man called Edward for further reassurance. He appeared curiously unbothered by the recent creation of the terrifying structures—his shoulders relaxed; his smile unchanged.

"Join me," he encouraged. "Join me in the revered halls of the library. Come in—and tell me about William."

What? I don't understand. And... "What about those things?" she said, gesturing over her shoulder.

"Give them nothing. Do not look at them. Come inside."

Reason fought the temptation to give the tunnels one last look—her mind ablaze, each step forward placed as if the ground might shift and give way. Tightening her grip on her boots, she tried to quiet her thoughts. *What are those horrible things? And... William? For the love of... why him?* And just in case Edward might offer her a clue, she stopped and gave him a desperate, inquisitive stare. But the strange man simply flashed a toothy smile. Incredulous, she asked, "Who *are* you?"

"Please, come inside." His eyes seemed to twinkle with the wise calm of someone who has not a care in the world.

"Why?"

"So that you can begin your journey."

"Journey?" she squeezed out. She waved her free hand in a wait-a-second gesture, adding, "Here? Now? But I was just out for a... I was... there was a bird and..." But her rebuttal, now meaningless, vanished along with her memory.

"Yes. Come in, and I'll tell you all about it."

Along with his charming smile, Edward wore a navy-blue Porkpie hat. Fastened above its flat brim was the ornamental eyespot of a peacock's feather. Buttoned to his chin, he wore a purple shirt with ruffles. The ruffles fell in soft curly waves to a pale-yellow cummerbund. On top of the flamboyant, blousy shirt he wore a navy coat with tails, the purple fabric spilling out from the cuffs of the fancy jacket. His trousers were dark and formal but strangely rolled up to just below his knees. Reason eyed him doubtfully. He smiled pleasantly, leaning casually against the column, his bare feet crossed one over the other, his arms loosely folded across his chest.

"Come," he beamed. "Follow me." He beckoned her forward with a leisurely swing of his arm and then pushed off from the column and disappeared into the building. And as he walked away, she noticed an embroidered line of yellow-flowered diamond shapes that traveled the full length of his coat, from collar to tail.

Reason ventured onto the faded steps leading to the front porch— pausing at the top. The smooth surface of a marble floor gleamed pink inside the open door. Squaring her shoulders, she walked inside. As she moved deeper into the entranceway, the natural light of the forest receded and gave way to the golden hue of flickering candlelight. Reason stopped again, mesmerized by the dark shadows dancing on the walls of the foyer. Then, in an onrush of adrenalin and a quick push through uncertainty, she pointed her chin upward, adjusted the boots under her arm, and darted into the room beyond—relieved that the fear she had succumbed to only moments earlier had transformed into a notable sense of well-being. To her surprise, she bristled with excitement.

Much larger than the narrow entry had implied, and in strong contrast to the building's rustic exterior, the foyer opened into a vast and extravagant room. And centered within this large space lavished a broad, curving staircase, its steps clad in a royal-blue carpet, plush and striking even in the soft glow of the candlelight.

As it ascended, the staircase curved toward the windowless wall to Reason's right. There, it narrowed, climbed to a second level, and then doubled back across the room. Halfway across, it merged with an upper balcony, where, perpendicular to this balcony, a wide hallway retreated into darkness.

Curiously drawn to the darkened hallway, Reason searched the shadows there—the depthless black, riveting—and dizzying. Despite its puzzling allure, she pulled her attention free and returned it to the climb of the staircase and its continuation up the wall to her left.

Having wrapped around the entire room, the flight of stairs turned one last time and ended at a tiny landing above her head. *How strange. A dead end? Pretty grand for... nothing.*

Lost in wonder, Reason strolled to the bottom of the stairs, where an elaborate banister began. Carved wooden vines, leaves, and plump roses climbed the handrail all the way to the tiny landing high above. She ran her fingers over a rose in full bloom. Above, an opulent chandelier hung in the center of the space, and against the infinite depth of the pitch-black ceiling, the flickering candles hovered like a cluster of shimmering stars.

Reason's gaze returned to the darkened hallway above. She began climbing the stairs, but soon halted at the sound of a faint noise coming from beyond them. She peeked over the railing. On the far side of the room, an exceptionally long corridor lit up. Its marble floor glistened in a magnificent tartan pattern of indigo, alabaster, teal, and mauve. And at the far end of the corridor stood Edward. "Please," he exulted. "This way my friend."

He removed his hat with dramatic flair, raising it high above his head and holding it there by its brim. Then with exaggerated care, he placed the hat on a nearby table, and as if it was a living creature, bent down and stroked it. Finally, he turned toward Reason, patting and fussing about his head to tame his wandering white curls. She took a few steps towards him and then stopped. Edward had abruptly straightened, and tilted his head as if he was listening intently to a faraway sound. Reason listened too, but she heard nothing. She continued along the corridor, her pace slow and steady. As she neared him, Edward visibly relaxed and tapped the table. "Your winter garments are of no use to you now. I suggest you leave them here." Bending forward, he performed an elaborate bow, rising slowly, eyes on Reason. For a moment, he seemed to study her with fierce intensity. Then he smiled. "It's time for our tea!" he declared. "That, and a nice little chat." Then he disappeared into a side passageway and Reason quickly followed, brimming with curiosity.

The main hall of the library was marvelous, its vastness even more surprising than the room with the grand staircase. Edward stood just inside, and with a wink and a sweep of his arm, he ushered her in. Reason entered timidly, skimming the room, brows lifting at the disorderly extravagance of the large space.

The room smelled of old textiles, damp paper, and lamp oil—vintage and musky, and infused with the rich chocolaty coffee scent of ancient books. In jumbled lots, the books and bundled manuscripts lay scattered about, piled high in unruly stacks atop haphazardly placed chairs and tables. Loose sheets of paper, discolored buttery-brown and curling at their edges, lay strewn about the many tabletops or hung precariously from wall ledges and bookshelves. And at the opposite end of the room sat the principal attraction—an enormous, handsome writing desk. A magnificent floor-to-ceiling window framed the desk, and beyond the window, the lush green forest presented like an enormous work of art. Reason glanced at Edward and seeing that he still smiled in a calm, kindly, and patient manner, she moved past him and navigated through the clutter to the opposite end of the room.

The shiny, uncluttered surface of the desk stood in striking contrast to the rest of the room. An old-fashioned lamp sat at the corner of the desk, and lined up in a tidy row beside it stood three glass ink wells. These appeared to contain even amounts of ink—each well labeled in a beautiful script: Crimson, Cobalt, Ebony. And placed neatly beside each well was an exquisite glass pen. Reason ran her hand over the glossy surface of the desk and then reached toward a pen, but stopped short of touching it. She turned.

A woolly layer of dust seemed to cover almost everything but the writing desk and the few articles that it held. Edward had moved to the center of the room and stood grinning—his thumbs hooked into his cummerbund. She started towards him.

Near Edward was an ornate urn. It sat on a mirrored tray atop a pink marble plinth. Hot vapor rose into the air above the urn. Beside it sat a small round table set with a gold tray. The tray contained two white porcelain dishes, one filled with sugar cubes, the other milk. At the foot of the plinth, the wood-plank flooring sagged into a shallow depression.

Reason slowed, eying an eclectic but cozy grouping of chairs surrounding the urn: a red sofa, a brown leather armchair, and two cushioned benches—each draped with a blanket. The scene looked warm and inviting, but she turned away, bringing her palms together, raising her hands, and tapping her linked fingers against the point of her chin. She squeezed her eyes shut—delaying, trying to gather her thoughts, and then again, turned from Edward.

A collection of lit oil lamps sat randomly placed about the library—their flames curiously unwavering. Reason looked from their steady brightness to the still black shadows cast onto the paintings hung high on the walls. Opposite the writing desk, an impressive bookcase ran from the floor to the ceiling—countless books and trinkets lining its many shelves. Beside it, a massive, austere fireplace loomed. In it, a low bed of coals glowed orange-red.

Reason blew out a long column of air, unsure what Edward wanted of her in this strange place and wondering how she might continue to stall. A squeeze at her elbow caused her to spin around in panic. Only the stillness of the library stood before her. She turned back to Edward's even gaze, her hand on her elbow where the touch still lingered. Her heart gradually regained its even rhythm as intrusive thoughts of William subsided. Her lips parted in a surge of doubt and then closed at the sight of a moving mobile of Earth's solar system.

The large mobile revolved silently—the smooth movement hypnotizing. She veered towards it, watching as the celestial objects ambled in their orbits about the sun—Mercury, Venus, Earth, and the others, the whole of the planetary system represented within this strange, otherworldly library. The sight of the mobile calmed Reason. Her anxiety retreated. Behind her, Edward nodded in silent approval.

To Reason's thinking, the solar system embodied a wonderful vastness of being—a sort of cosmic testimony to the existence of a higher power, one that had also created humankind. For her, the solar system was celestial evidence of the connectedness of all things, including her. It provided her with a sense of balance and belonging. She had often taken the time to watch the sky, imagining herself as a speck upon the Earth's surface, closing her eyes, concentrating, trying to visualize the great planet turning on its axis and tracing its elliptical orbit. The practice was soothing. She imagined herself a part of the Earth's cosmic greatness, and the connection made her feel safe. So, here and now, standing below the mobile as it moved with such smooth precision, she relaxed.

Edward sensed Reason's contentment. He had watched with keen interest as she had explored the library. When she had found the rotating globe of Earth, and her gaze had softened, he knew she was ready to begin her journey. She turned and faced him. "Who are you?"

"I am Edward."

"Yes. You said that already. But who are you to this forest? To this place?" She spread her arms wide and then pointed to herself. "Who are you to me?"

"I have many roles, as do you." He cocked his head and grinned mischievously.

"But..."

Edward raised his hand in a gentle but firm gesture that requested silence. "I am the Librarian. I am the keeper of a vast collection of wonderful resources. I am the custodian of records and the protector of knowledge." He lowered his chin, eyes fixed on Reason.

He seems kind enough. But what does he want? "And... what's at the top of that grandiose staircase at the entrance? For a moment there, I thought I was supposed to... climb it. But at the top, it seems it travels to nowhere... and then there's that dark hallway...." She stopped speaking—and shivered.

"Ah yes. The Stairway to Limbo. It leads to a place for those individuals whose situations remain... uncertain."

Reason's brow furrowed. She wanted to hear more, but Edward's cautious expression suggested a reluctance to continue. She waited. He remained silent. She decided to pursue his strange need to talk about William and managed a casual tone. "Why do you want to know about William? Why is he, of all people, so important?"

"I don't know," said Edward with quiet frankness, turning and calmly pouring a cup of tea.

"What could he possibly have to do with this... crazy place? Or with you? I haven't seen William, or spoken with him or about him, for years. I don't care to talk about him now." Reason stiffened, irritated and perplexed by the inclusion of William into this peculiar experience; uncomfortable at the thought of revisiting her troubled past.

"Your mind will be put at ease once you've become more acquainted with where you are," Edward offered in a carefree and unhurried tone. "Now, shall I pour your tea?"

As he prepared Reason's tea, Edward launched into a description of the opulent device he was using to make it. "This," he said pointing, "is a Samovar." Giving in to his eccentricity, Reason begrudgingly looked at the urn. The appliance was large and ornate, with a cylindrical body. Edward explained that its handles, faucet, and fixtures were all, "exquisitely crafted from an elegant blend of copper, silver, and gold." From a faucet near the bottom of the large metal container, he dispensed liquid and described how he was diluting the strong concentration of tea with boiled water. "Come," he announced.

"As we gather about the Samovar and drink our tea as the Russians do, I'll tell you about this extraordinary place."

"Are you Russian?"

Edward laughed. "No. This is a gift from a previous visitor."

Reason squinted at this information, but remained quiet.

Edward closed his eyes and for a moment appeared as if he was remembering some past pleasure. Then, with a quick shake of his head, he returned to the present and offered Reason a cup of steaming tea. She did not especially want the tea and hesitated. But Edward stood with his arm outstretched, waiting. She took the cup and saucer, glanced at the liquid inside, and then watched Edward drink from his own cup. She leaned in for a teeny sip. The tea was delicious, with traces of cinnamon and cloves.

"Please," said Edward. "Sit." Reason chose the brown armchair, its soft leather fissured by age. "No one arrives here understanding why," began Edward. "Understanding comes with being here. No two visitors tell the same story. Each of you is unique, just as your experience here will be." Reason listened intently, wanting very much to understand and to make sense of what Edward expected of her. "Before you think of asking me what your particular experience will be, I must inform you that no matter how much you may want me to tell you, I cannot. Not because I don't want to. Not because I'm not permitted to. No. I cannot tell you because I have no way of knowing. Besides," Edward paused and sipped his tea, "the process, your process, is not my business. The result is my business. But don't ask me about that either, because I'll not know it until you, yourself, do."

As Edward spoke, tea in hand, he paced slowly, occasionally glancing at Reason. Suddenly he stopped, and turned to face her directly. His eyes seemed to grow dark. His ever-present smile had vanished. Reason started and sat forward. "It's important for you to remember that each being's experience contains a recurring element, a distinct symbol, a unique pattern. This pattern is the heart of your experience, the hub, tying everything together. Its presence signifies that all is as it should be, that every event, every person, and each thing in your story, no matter who or what, no matter what happens, however brief or long-lasting—is meant to be—and is connected." He bent toward Reason, pulling his cup and saucer tight to the ruffles of his blouse. "If you are careful and mindful, you might sense the presence of your particular pattern. And if you do, the sensation will be one of momentary clarity. And this, young lady, this flash of awareness, will reassure you that you are on the right track, no matter," he paused, "how unsettling your course."

Reason abandoned her tea to a nearby table and slid to the edge of her seat. The old leather squawked as she prepared to stand. But with his eyes fixed upon hers, Edward leaned in closer still. Reason sat back. "I can see that you are in doubt," he said. "Such concern is... normal, but do not fret. Please... follow me."

He spun around, pivoting on his shoeless feet, his coattails taking flight and skimming Reason's knees. He moved swiftly toward a large wooden door near the fireplace. She glanced about the room, but nothing could convince her to stay where she was. So, she followed— and stood close by as Edward blew dust from a large rusty deadbolt and then unlocked the door. He stepped back from the thick, arched door, and together they watched it open—on its own—hinges creaking. Cool air rushed into the library, washing across their faces, carrying with it the sweet, heady scent of roses. Edward motioned Reason forward, and side by side, they crossed over the threshold and stepped outside.

"Stay near to me," he cautioned, and with a tilt of his head and a quick nod, he led the way down a narrow path. Reason shot an anxious glance at the closing door and then turned back to Edward in time to see him disappear around a bend. She rushed to catch up.

A beautiful lush arbor sheltered the path, white clematis and pale blue roses winding throughout its latticed framework. Sunlight cast a skewed, shaded image of the flourishing arbor onto the dirt path below, and now and again, through the greenery, Reason glimpsed blue sky. *No forest?*

They traveled in silence, and after rounding a particularly long bend, the covered path ended at an open meadow. Edward stopped. Reason stopped beside him. To their right, tall grasses with feathery plumes the color of milky tea swished serenely. To their left, a field of purple lavender dazzled in the sunlight. Ahead, grassy hills rolled on boundlessly, the strong breeze blowing the short grass into great sheets of silver and green.

Edward clasped his hands together and twirled to face Reason. "Along the way, indicators will appear. Signs, if you will. These signs will guide you from place to place. For some of our... visitors, they require very little participation to advance. For others, much more must occur before they can proceed. Nevertheless, regardless of the length or complexity of one's overall experience, a reckoning always occurs, a test of sorts. So, be alert. But do not fret. For if you feel lost or confused, or should trouble arise, the Raven is always nearby and will assist you."

A reckoning? Trouble? The Raven? Reason had forgotten about the bird, and in that moment of heady relief, she searched the sky.

"The Raven will respond only when you have a genuine need," added Edward perceptively. And with a reassuring smile, he directed Reason to a nearby bench. She sat. He seemed to linger in his thoughts while he watched her. Then he sat beside her and took her hand into his own. "This meadow contains your first sign."

Reason's impulse was to stand and look about. But for as long as Edward held her hand, she stayed seated by his side.

"Finding all of your signs, whether many or few, is critical. Otherwise, young traveler, you cannot move on."

Biting her lower lip, Reason tried to absorb the meaning of Edward's words.

"Do you understand?" he asked.

She felt fragile and incompetent and shook her head. No. She did not understand, not in the least. Edward gave her hand a quick squeeze and then let it go.

"Is this some sort of game?" she asked.

"Your life is never a game," he answered, the teeniest hint of dismay showing in the momentary narrowing of his eyes.

"Am I dreaming then?"

"No."

"No?"

"No."

"You're saying that all of this is... real?" She waved her hand in disbelief.

He paused, eyeing her thoughtfully. "Don't be discouraged. You have more understanding than you might think. In fact, you may have already sensed your first sign as it draws you nearer. The first sign is often the most important one. It summons you through your memories, memories that you've contemplated both in your sleep and while awake. But you've been too absent of mind and too preoccupied with doubt and shame to be open to the full meaning of these memories—too lost in thought to realize the truth within them. But this, young lady, is about to change."

"Please—stop talking in riddles. Speak plainly. Help me understand what's expected of me. What am I supposed to *do*?"

"It is not for me to say. A voyage of discovery awaits you." Edward smiled warmly and pointed across the meadow. A large solitary tree stood in the distance. "Look for your first sign at The Tree of New Beginnings." The tall grasses swooshed, filling the silence between them.

Reason peered at the tree, seeing no answers in its seemingly lonely existence. She turned her attention back to Edward. "But what am I supposed *to do*?"

"Trust that you will find your sign. Touch it and it will lead you." Edward stretched out his chin, pushed his shoulders back, and stood tall—towering over Reason. "But, before you can go, before you can begin your adventure, you must tell me about William. You must tell me who he is to you. Nothing more. Nothing less. Along the way, more detail will be required. But for me, I need only to be told who he is to you. As the librarian, I must catalog this information. Then, Reason, your journey can truly begin."

"But, I'm not ready." Reason stood, and at that moment William's face closed in on hers; his eyes black; his lips stretched into a wide, misshapen grin. Instantly, she felt lightheaded and unnaturally tall, as if the ground beneath her was falling away. A throbbing erupted within her head, the same aching pain that she had experienced at the pond. She stumbled to the side. Edward moved quickly, guiding her back to her seat.

"You are feeling the pull of the tunnels," he warned.

Remembering the horror of the two tunnels, Reason stared imploringly at Edward. "I feel sick," she exclaimed. "I think I may throw up." Aghast, she put a hand to her mouth and turned away.

"You're experiencing the power of the emotions that created the tunnels. Whenever you feel those particular emotions, the tunnels grow stronger, and, like powerful magnets, they will attract you. They will try to pull you in. You must resist. The tunnels need you for their very survival."

"What are you saying?"

"They feed on your fear and worry. So, you must be calm. Use your breath for focus. Breathe in... Good. Now exhale... That's it. Think only of your breath. In. Out." Reason tried to focus on her breathing, but the nausea was too great. She pitched forward and retched, the sour taste of bile hot and burning. Her face pale, she grew hot, sweat prickling her brow. "Reason, you must try harder! It seems too much, but it will get easier. You must concentrate!"

Edward kneeled before her and placed his hands upon her head. She lifted her gaze and his eyes instantly soothed her. She breathed— in, out, slowly, mindfully. Her muscles relaxed. The nausea abated.

Edward's gold-flecked, violet eyes glistened like hypnotic pools, willing Reason to be still. His large, warm hands covered her ears, muffling the external noises and emphasizing the sound of her own breathing. With their eyes locked, Reason eased into a renewed sense of calm. Her fear subsided, and in its place, as the realization of the power of the tunnels sunk in, a wild frustration overcame her. She pulled Edward's hands from her ears and carefully stood. "How could you wait so long to warn me about the tunnels? I... I could see that they were odd and I could feel that they were powerful but, but..." Reason clamped her hands to her head. "How could I possibly know how dangerous they are? Why didn't you warn me sooner?" She turned to face Edward, her stare both incredulous and appealing for his help. "And what—exactly—do you mean when you say the tunnels *need* me?"

Edward clasped his hands behind his back. "Well," he began, "some people are extra sensitive to the emotions of their surroundings, absorbing much of the energy swirling about them. And in their need to understand *fully*, and to be both helpful and content, they constantly try...," he paused and waved his hands in mock exasperation, "to do the right thing—always striving to live up to what they think others expect of them, despite not always being sure of what that is. And while constantly trying so very hard to solve endless problems, they suffer greatly when they fail. Why do they put themselves through such trials? Well...," he peered intently at Reason, "so that they can heal the world of course. Those who are healers of hearts continually strive to preserve some sort of balance—and when they cannot, they fall into a state of instability. And instability, my dear Reason, is a great facilitator of worry and fear." Despite her desire for a simpler and more comforting explanation, Reason knew that Edward was describing her—and the profound realization kept her silent. "The tunnels feed on worry and fear, specifically *your* worry and fear—which they need for their very survival."

"Feed?" she whispered, dropping her shoulders and groaning. "Are you telling me that whenever I feel worried or frightened, the tunnels will somehow know and grow?"

"Not exactly..."

"Then... what?"

"Your fear and worry will physically strengthen the tunnels, and with their increased power, they will become more intent on pulling you inside."

"What happens if I enter one? Not that I plan on doing that, but what happens if I do?"

"You may never get back out," Edward grimaced.

Dumbstruck, Reason sat heavily, dropping her head into the heels of her hands. She laughed—a bewildered, strangled chuckle. "How can I possibly be expected to avoid feelings of worry and fear? Particularly here? In this strange place?"

"The key to your success is not in avoidance. You will, of course, experience fear and worry. They must not overcome you."

"But how do I manage that?"

"Feel the emotions without letting them consume and control you, without letting them drive your decisions... and the tunnels will lose their power over you. They will try to regain it. They will pester and distract you, but you can defeat them. Remain true to what you know best."

"And what is that?"

"Love—kindness—honesty. They have steered you in the past. They will do so again. They are powerful and crucial to your survival here—as crucial as the blood running through your veins. Use them to find your way. Let your intentions speak your truth. Do this, and you will succeed."

Edward turned away. She waited. He remained silent. "Edward?"

"I am listening for the tunnels."

Reason became still and quiet and did the same. The meadow was full of sounds. The grasses swept back and forth, a comforting ebb and flow like distant ocean waves, a calming contrast to Reason's heightened nerves. Large-winged insects, some flying over the field, produced a persistent high-pitched whine. The more Reason listened, the louder all the sounds became. Beside her, she heard the broken buzzing of a bee, but she could hear nothing of the tunnels.

"They are quiet. This is good," said Edward. He held his hands as if in prayer, the tips of his fingers touching his chin. Nodding and smiling, he turned to face Reason. "They are dormant once more." He ran his hand through his hair. "And yes, of course, my duty is to tell you about the tunnels. My preference was to do so before they became active. But alas, things do not always unfold the way we would like. Tell me, do you remember the sounds that the tunnels make?"

"Of course, I do. How could I forget?"

"Good."

"What could be *good* about that?"

"Good... because you will hear the tunnels when they come for you. And this will allow you to execute an escape."

REASONS | Sherry denBoer

"When they come for me? An escape? Escape to where? I don't have a clue where I am, let alone where I might escape to!"

"Escape does not always mean that one must physically flee. Remember, your emotions fuel the tunnels."

"Are you suggesting that I'll be planning an escape from my emotions? Because that's impossible." Reason's brow wrinkled as she stared at Edward, her thumbnail now wedged into the tiny gap between her two front teeth. Runaway emotions had always been her downfall, reckless and overwhelming even when she was deep in denial and disconnected from her badly broken life.

"Awareness will remove your doubt. You are more than capable of noticing when feelings of fear and worry arise. And when they do, you can notice them with a sense of purposeful detachment—a skill essential to your success. You must journey with care. Be primed and ready at all times. You can do it. You must believe that you will." As a gesture of encouragement, Edward offered his hand to Reason. She took it. He smiled affectionately. "The time has come for us to part." He gently squeezed her hand. "You must tell me who William is."

Reason pulled her hand from the comfort of Edward's touch. She stood, her mind reaching back into the darkness that was William. "I was very young when I met him. I was crazy about him. All the girls were. We all thought he was very handsome." She bowed her head. "I was so proud—elated that he had chosen me. William... was my boyfriend."

A crack of thunder detonated in the distance. The sky had darkened and was now brimming with rapidly billowing storm clouds. "What's happening?" Reason turned to Edward. He was nowhere to be seen. "Edward? Edward!"

She was alone. A storm was brewing and moving in on a fierce wind. In the distance, the branches of the solitary tree swayed and billowed, and in a moment of frantic desperation, Reason bolted, rushing breathlessly toward the promise of a sign.

3

a significant sign

❝ You're a curious little thing, aren't you? Trying so hard to avoid me."

I'll not just try. I will.

"Nonsense. You must know by now that I am stronger than you, much stronger. You're a pitiful creature."

Reason's eyes twitched behind her pale pink eyelids. Tiny beads of sweat glazed her brow and clustered above her upper lip. Her eyes flickered and opened, her gaze wandering over the room—unable to resolve its fuzzy details. *I'm tired. I don't care.*

"Well, you will care, dearie, because I merely require your pumping heart and working mind to make you care. I'll never give in to your cries for mercy. And your pathetic attempts at indifference will never sway me." Pain sneered and descended. "And whenever I choose to, I'll expose your spirit for what it is—thin and weak—and then, you wretched little twit, I'll crush you!"

At the peak of Pain's rant, Reason surrendered, relinquishing control, and in doing so, drifted into the blissful oblivion of sleep.

଼ ଼

Like forcing a door closed against a strong, gusting wind, Reason struggled to contain her anxiety—knowing that she must do so to avoid the tunnels. She raced toward the large lone tree. *Stay calm. Focus. Eyes—on—the—tree.* Dressed in blue jeans and a light sweater over a white t-shirt, her bare feet pounded the dirt path. Overhead, thunder unfurled and rolled across the sky. As the wind picked up, bits of loose debris lifted from the ground and twirled across her path.

Ahead, the tree shone like a beacon of hope—its enormous, shimmering canopy billowing and rose pink—its roots plentiful, visible above the ground and spreading in all directions around its gigantic trunk.

As she ran, Reason took darting glances at the yellow-tinged purple madness above. The dark sky suddenly lit up, and a deafening boom erupted. A deep rumbling followed and then crackled—a fracture breaking far and wide.

The raindrops came intermittently at first, splatting here and there onto the dusty ground. Reason's legs grew heavy. She looked down at her thin, dirty feet, focusing on their steady movement—ignoring her fatigue. Again, thunder detonated. *Keep running. Stay calm. Don't give in to the fear. Don't give in. Just get to the tree...*

Straining to listen for the terrifying sounds of the tunnels, she could hear nothing above the storm. The meadow grasses flattened, weighed down by the now heavy downpour. Beyond the tree, a lightning bolt flashed in the bruised sky, a skeletal arm reaching to the ground. The thunder that followed seemed to cackle in sinister approval.

Lurching across the last few yards, Reason burst through the tree's low-hanging branches and stumbled to the ground, the dirt beneath her hands still dusty-dry. In frequent flashes of white, lightning lit the battered landscape all around the tree. She rose to her knees, breathless and shivering, and shouted into the uproar, "What now? Where is the sign?"

As if in answer, a tiny glimmer caught her eye, an object hanging from the tree and gently oscillating. Teeth chattering, she moved towards it. A delicate gold chain dangled from the root-twisted trunk. Reason gasped as she recognized it.

With a trembling hand, she reached for the chain—and a ghostly vision of William raced past her—his arm outstretched, his hand reaching for the necklace. Reason cried out in protest, and the vision vanished. When her fingers made contact with the dangling chain, her world went silent and black.

35

 CR ৪০

Reason stared into impenetrable blackness, the sound of her breathing seeming oddly detached, as if her breaths were floating alongside her, not hers at all. Edward's words came back to her: "Breathe, Reason. Breathe."

She heard a faint click—and then a low hum, and then she covered her face as bright light poured into her eyes. Peering through her fingers, Reason could see nothing in the blinding white. She stood with a slightly forward lean, as if ready to launch into a run, clutching the gold chain, listening to what sounded like the hum of fluorescent light fixtures. As her vision improved, she straightened—patting her head, her shoulders, her arms—astonished to discover that she was completely dry and clean.

Blinking, she found herself in what appeared to be a warehouse— an enormous square space with a high ceiling of exposed steel beams. The entire room, and everything in it, was white. Filling it wall to wall were rectangular white tables arranged in immaculate rows, a white high-backed chair neatly tucked in at each one. And upon the surface of each table sat a shiny white telephone. The phones were bulky and wedge-shaped, each with a rotary dial pad. Reason walked to the nearest phone and touched it. She scanned the many rows of tables and then the walls and the ceiling, seeing no windows, no doors—and no people. A phone rang, the shrill tone piercing the heavy silence. Startled, she looked wildly from phone to phone. From among the hundreds, one phone rang: briiing, briiing... briiing, briiing. *Which one is it? Do I... answer it?*

Trying to pinpoint the ringing phone, Reason gripped the necklace so tightly, its small round clasp imprinted into the flesh of her palm. Remembering that she held it, she fastened the chain about her neck. Wearing the necklace seemed to give her courage, and courage gave her focus. With new determination, she stepped toward the sound of the ringing phone.

God-like, a woman's voice boomed through the large space. "No sense in taking your time. Answer the phone, my dear." Reason yelped and spun around. Bracing against the closest table, she gaped at a portly, middle-aged woman who, dressed entirely in red, sat on a high-backed red chair behind a large, red table. Her stare fixed on Reason, she held the handset of a red phone to her ear, the fingers of her free hand drumming the glossy surface of the table.

The ringing phone was unsettling, but Reason stayed still and quiet, mouth open, staring at the woman, unsure of what to do next. The woman waved a dismissive hand. "Never mind me. Answer the phone."

Reason came alive, turning her attention again to locating the ringing phone, making her way into the rows of tables. But the ringing changed location and now seemed to come from where she had been. Reason hurried toward the new location, but as she did, the ringing promptly bounced elsewhere within the massive space. Turning back, she was startled to see that many of the tables, chairs, and phones had vanished. She glanced uncertainly at the woman in red, who shrugged her shoulders and smiled placidly.

Reason pressed on, tracking the ringing, and each time she turned in a new direction, in random batches, the tables, chairs, and telephones disappeared. At last only one phone remained, and it sat near the woman in red. Winded, Reason snatched up the handset. "Hello?" she said more loudly than intended. The voice on the phone spoke in unison with the moving lips of the woman in red.

"Well, that certainly took some time," the woman said in jest. "Please, tell me your name."

Perplexed, Reason moved to lower the handset and talk directly to the woman, but shaking her head, the woman said, "No, my dear. You must speak to me using the phone."

"But why? We're in the same room... and you're right there."

The woman did not reply. Reason hesitated and then obliged, raising the handset to her ear.

"I understand I may confuse you, but I am in charge here," said the woman. She was smiling, but her tone was sobering. "I know where we are. You do not. I know what must happen, how it must happen, and why it must happen in a certain way. You don't need to understand how this place works, but you do need to find a balance between trust and resistance." She paused and examined her red-painted fingernails. "Knowledge and understanding are best gained with patience. Please, tell me your name."

"Reason. My name is Reason."

"Well, Reason, let's get started." The woman hung up her handset and stood, and despite her short, wide stature, she carried herself imposingly. "Follow me," she said, and with a quick tug at the hem of her jacket, she turned to face the wall of the warehouse. Reaching into her pocket, she retrieved a bundle of keys.

Reason looked at the handset in her own hand and, shaking her head, placed it back onto its base—almost falling over when at the moment the handset landed in its cradle, the phone, the table, and the chair vanished.

The woman in red pushed a large key into the white wall where no door was visible. Her back to Reason, she spoke. "It's in your best interest to hurry because once I go through this door..." she paused and glanced over her shoulder, "it will soon disappear."

Reason ran toward the woman, who had pushed a portion of the wall forward and disappeared into a darkness beyond it—into a blackness that the closing panel was rapidly eclipsing. Reason leapt at the wall. A sliver of black was all that remained when she got her hand braced against the door. She stopped, holding the door ajar, peering into the darkness ahead. "You can do this," she whispered, and pushing forward, she passed over the threshold.

A pale, yellow glow infused the dark, and as her sight adjusted, Reason saw that from where she stood, to either side of her, the wall curved forward. The appearance of the new room was in utter contrast to the methodical and stark layout of the white warehouse. The furnishings of this new circular space were informal and colorful and seemed almost charmed by a magical quality. Lulled by the sight, Reason wandered deeper into the space. On a circular purple carpet in the center of the room sat two enormous beanbag chairs—one red, the other orange. Strewn about them were many brightly colored cushions. Reason turned a full circle. She ran her hand over a silk brocade that hung from the ceiling—one of the many hanging works of art in the room. "It's all so lovely," she whispered, unsure of what she should say or do. The woman stood nearby, seeming to smile in agreement.

High on the wall, narrow rectangular openings shed thin beams of platinum light into the space, creating a broken ring of hazy illumination around a ceiling fan turning silently above their heads. The fresh woody scent of sandalwood permeated the air and the ember of an incense stick glowed on a low table nearby. Reason breathed a visible sigh of relief, settling into the calm of the room.

The woman peered stern-faced at a closed door opposite her. Reason looked at the same door, and then back at the woman, who shook her head before moving to the red beanbag chair. With surprising agility, she lowered her plump body into the chair and once settled, for a moment did nothing but watch Reason. Then, eyes still fixed on Reason, she pointed to the orange chair. "Please, have a seat." Lined up in a neat semi-circle near the woman's feet sat several telephones, wedge-shaped like those in the white warehouse, but here they were in a rainbow of colors.

Reason fit herself into the soft chair, and as she did, muffled sounds came from beyond the closed door. The woman in red was watching it again. Reason held her breath, pressing her fingers into the chair, wondering what the woman was waiting for. Muted laughter came from behind the door, and then an object thumped against it—a quick, dull thud. Reason fidgeted, her eyes darting to the door. Nothing more happened. She turned back to the woman—who returned Reason's puzzled gaze with a mildly apologetic smile.

Frantic whispering erupted on the other side of the door. Two more dull thuds ensued. A burst of laughter followed. The woman in red winced. Suddenly, the door opened a crack. Reason sat forward. The woman in red forced a smile as through the narrow opening animated voices grew louder.

"You go."

"No, you go."

"I insist *you* go."

"*No*, you go."

"Shall we go together?"

"Yes. Good idea. Together!"

"Count of three?"

"Yes, on the count of three."

"Who will count?"

"I will count."

"Ok."

"Ready?"

"Yes. No. Wait!"

"What?"

"Nothing. Go ahead. Count."

"Are you sure?"

"Yes!"

"Ok then. One, two, three, GO!"

The door swung open. Reason jumped in her seat and the woman in red sighed. Two strange and identical creatures virtually fell into the room, wobbling and teetering. One creature laughed. The other reached out its skinny little arm and covered the mouth of its tittering partner. Soon they were both laughing while covering each other's mouth with a furry, paw-like hand. Then, each stole a glance at the other, and unable to contain their delight, their arms dropped to their sides and they burst into hearty bouts of laughter. Reason could not help but smile. The creatures seemed harmless little things, their antics silly. The woman in red labored to sit forward in her chair, her flushed cheeks scrunched up with impatience. "Enough!" she scolded.

The creatures stared at the woman, and then at each other. Odd-looking, they stood about four feet tall and had rounded faces and portly bodies. Their long, skinny arms and short legs protruded rigidly from their plump figures, jutting out at wide angles like the stick limbs of a snowman. Androgynous, they wore no clothing but had long thick fur that covered their bodies and tapered to a velvet fuzz on their faces, hands, and feet. Watching them, Reason gasped, and almost clapped, as their furry bodies suddenly changed color. Upon entering the room, they had been the color of light lavender, but now, laughing hysterically, both creatures transformed into a bright shade of red.

"Enough." repeated the woman. "Settle down. The two of you are hopelessly impertinent. What an excruciating display of improper behavior. Restrain yourselves." She scolded them, but she did so affectionately. The two creatures turned away from one another, one holding its head in its hands and the other holding its belly. Little by little, their laughter dwindled, and as they quieted, they turned a beautiful sea blue. "The two of you, come. Meet our guest."

Reason sat up straighter.

"Reason," said the woman with an air of authority, "allow me to introduce you to Mr. Up and Mr. Down." She fanned her arm toward the two furry creatures.

Up and Down? Really?

"And my name is Ruby," added the woman in red.

Right, of course it is.

As shy children might, Mr. Up and Mr. Down playfully shoved each other, and then together they moved toward Ruby, who leaned back into her seat, the chair groaning. The creatures skipped in behind her and stood straight and rigid, like chubby little soldiers.

"Welcome to the Communications Center," said Ruby. "Don't let the relaxed mood fool you. Our role here is very important. The function of this room is at odds with its appearance and stands as a good example of how easily we can misinterpret our environment." Ruby opened her arms wide. "There's an important lesson here, one of great value." She rested her hands on her belly and continued. "As creatures of habit, and often, of obsessive thinking, we frequently live unaware of what is truly going on inside our minds." She tapped a red-polished fingernail against her temple. "We are often quite oblivious to the countless thoughts and emotions that run amok in there, and we are ignorant of their effect upon our conduct." Pausing, she gave Reason a thoughtful look, her eyes kind and attentive. "Perception is central to your experience here, because what you notice and how you understand it will affect your progress. Your impressions, whether they are fleeting and passive or long-lasting and

41

intense, will have a powerful influence on what happens here." And as if to lend credence to her words, she lowered her voice and spoke more slowly. "But if you can learn how to become still within—to be present and wide awake to any moment... well, my dear, you'll get much closer to the truth. And the truth can enrich your life."

For a moment Ruby stared into space; a pause of peaceful bliss—and then closing her eyes, said, "Living mindfully is a blessing, a lovely blessing." She returned her attention to Reason. "Learn how to be present, and it just may save your life."

Save my life? "But how do I...?"

A wave of the woman's hand silenced Reason. "You may worry that you don't know how to be mindful, but you do. You were born with a keen awareness and you can rediscover this inherent quality. All I ask of you—at this moment, is to be in it. Don't judge it. Observe. Be present—in every moment—and you'll give yourself the best opportunity to succeed. Trust in that."

"Okay...," Reason managed, narrowing her eyes, bringing one finger to her chin, and then dropping her hand into her lap—focusing on the word trust.

"Now then," said Ruby, "I shall properly introduce myself and my associates. I am the Chief Operator of Communications. Mr. Up and Mr. Down are operators in training. While you continue your journey, we'll be here at the phones, tracking your progress." She pointed to the floor at her feet. "These phones look rather clunky and old-fashioned, don't they? They do. But they are powerful instruments, much more so than you might think—and they will aid us tremendously in tracking your adventure. But you need not worry yourself about the details." Ruby grinned—a smile that seemed to find only her lips—as if the seriousness of her words would not allow more. "We were aware of the moment you touched your first sign." Mr. Up and Mr. Down fidgeted excitedly and giggled in unison. The woman acknowledged their outburst with a sideways glance. The two operators shrunk back down, working hard at suppressing their enthusiasm. "The necklace was your first sign," continued Ruby in a solemn tone. "Although we can't see you during your excursion, we can detect when you've connected physically with a sign." She raised her hands, palms curved upward as if she held an invisible sphere. "All things exist within a constant movement of creation and communication. Stories develop and change, and new pathways make way for fresh opportunities. Your signs," she said, pausing, her smile finding its way back to her eyes, "are the connecting dots within your unique story. And from here at the Communications Center, we will track each one." She winked at the little operators. They giggled. "We will know if you miss a sign, and a connection is lost. So, you see, we have a very important job."

"A lost connection? That sounds alarming."

"Things lost can be found," said Ruby with an encouraging nod.

"But how will I..."

"Trust the process, Reason. We may not interfere. But we're here to reassure you we will observe your progress. And," she lowered her head, raising her eyes only, locking them on Reason, "one way or another, everyone eventually gets where they need to be."

As Mr. Up and Mr. Down listened, they watched Ruby with obvious admiration—nodding their heads enthusiastically at the bits of her discourse that excited them. And like tiny bursts of fireworks, explosions of color coursed through their fur-covered bodies.

Ruby wriggled up and out of her chair. "While Mr. Up and Mr. Down may seem... distracted," she said with a hint of amusement, "again—I counsel you to withhold judgment." She faced the two creatures. "My apprentices are smart and eager and well into their training. They perform their duties with meticulous care." Up and Down puffed up with pride, their fur standing on end and turning hot pink.

When Ruby turned back to Reason, her expression had noticeably softened and her posture had relaxed. "I have another important role. I am also known as an Experience Guide—one of many. You'll meet others along the way. As guides, we can provide encouragement if a particular experience becomes too... overwhelming. And as your first guide, it is with me you must begin sharing the details of your life with William. So, shall we begin?"

43

Ruby moved to a jeweled stand and retrieved a small golden box. Mr. Up and Mr. Down squealed in delight and then embraced one another. Ruby put the mysterious box onto the palm of her hand, held it in the air, turned, and holding the box out ahead of her, walked back to Reason. "Let's start with the item contained within this box."

Reason leaned away from Ruby's approach, too nervous to touch the tiny container held aloft like a precious jewel. Paying no attention to Reason's doubt, Ruby reached for her hand. She placed the little golden box onto Reason's palm and curled her fingers down upon it. A smiling, furry face moved close to Reason's ear. "It's OK, Miss Reason. It's OK. Look inside. Look inside the box." Reason turned toward the creature and the little beast stepped back—its ginger-colored fur fluttering where it fell in thick, long ringlets from its plump belly. As Reason considered its caring expression and twinkling eyes, the fuzz on the creature's face shimmered. And from head to toe, the creature turned a dark shade of plum. Pointing to the small golden box, it mouthed, "Open it."

Ruby raised her hand. Up and Down at once became hushed and reverent, a new color cascading over their bodies, diluting the plum to peach and then the peach to pale yellow. Reason took in a deep breath. She raised the lid. Inside, coiled on a bed of blue silk, lay a fine gold chain. She put her hand to her throat, feeling for her necklace. To her surprise, her throat was bare. *I don't understand.* The necklace in the box was the same gold chain that she had discovered hanging from the solitary tree. She took it up in her palm and scrutinized it. Near its round clasp dangled a wee leaf and a tiny gold heart, and as she remembered, a delicately scrolled R engraved on the heart. But where the pendant normally hung was instead a large, basic gold link. This simple link was new, added to the chain since Reason had last seen it.

Tears welled in her eyes as old memories brought feelings of pain, regret, and shame. And seeing her discomfort, the little round operators instantly lost their composure and their pale, yellow hue. They viewed Reason through sad, glistening eyes—droplets of muddy-blue cascading through their furry bodies.

REASONS | Sherry denBoer

"But I was wearing this," Reason managed, holding the necklace up for Ruby to see. "I know I was wearing this necklace. I put it on in that big white room." She pointed to the wall where the door had been, staring at its blankness as if the answer might turn up there. "And the pendant... where is it? I know there used to be a pendant, but... I can't remember what it looked like. Why can't I remember? I used to wear this necklace *all the time*." She looked at Ruby, her expression enquiring and grave.

"The large link has replaced the missing pendant. But do not fret. The simple link is temporary. Your memory of the original pendant will return when the time is right. What's important now... is that you understand the necklace has come back into your life because it has significance to a past event with which you have yet to make peace."

"The necklace was a gift from my parents... for my birthday," said Reason, holding back more tears and passing the tiny links of the chain between her fingers.

Mr. Up and Mr. Down waddled to Reason's side and began stroking her hair. "It's OK. It's OK," they consoled. She found it impossible to not smile at their childlike sincerity. The creatures responded by smiling at one another, nodding their heads in unison, and turning an exquisite sea blue.

"All is well, Reason," said Ruby in a quiet voice. "The pendant is nearby and will soon be back in place. Your memory of it will come back to you in its own time and in its own way. And now, because you know the significance of the necklace, you may wear it." Ruby took the chain and fastened it around Reason's neck. "You've experienced a considerable shift in everything you thought you understood. Our world is one of many surprises. You need time to adjust. For now, we'll take a break—have a nice long rest—and then your journey will continue. Come."

Reason readily complied as Ruby led her to the door through which the two creatures had entered earlier. Mauve and giggling, the creatures ran ahead. They opened the door and then all four moved into a narrow hallway beyond. Ruby took up the rear and behind them, the door to the round room slowly closed.

Candles in simple glass sconces lit their way. Mr. Up and Mr. Down skipped ahead, their feet thumping on the stone floor—their large button-like tails bouncing on their fuzzy rumps. The long passageway ended at the bottom of a spiral staircase. In single file, they ascended. Reaching the top, they stepped one by one into an open, airy space where a large skylight revealed a clear blue sky. "Which room, Ruby? Which room?" squealed Up and Down; circling Ruby and Reason and vigorously pointing at various doors. "This room?" exclaimed one. "That door?" hollered the other. Along the walls on either side of the large wide hall were tall arched doors—all of them closed.

"Patience," said Ruby as she walked them all to the far end of the hall, chose a key from a large ring, and unlocked a door. "You'll be comfortable here," she offered, and with an encouraging smile, she stepped out of the way and nodded for Reason to enter. Too weary to ask more questions or to object to the craziness of the moment, Reason entered the room. The door closed behind her. She was alone—the sudden quiet and stillness substantial.

She stood in a beautiful and spacious bedroom; the furnishings minimal but inviting. A large four-poster bed stood against a wall of white-washed wood, and on the lightly stained wood floor, two rugs lay like pools of frothy white foam. Reason moved to the bed and ran her hand over the downy softness of the thick white bedding. She pressed her fingers into one of the four plump pillows resting against the bed's scalloped headboard. And then, feeling the full weight of her exhaustion, she crawled into the bed fully dressed and pondered the incredible events of the day. Overwhelmed by the craziness of the whole magical experience so far, Reason brought her palms to her eyes and held them there—wondering about this journey she was supposed to be on, what was expected of her, and fretting that she might fail.

She rolled onto her side, hugging a pillow. At the far side of the room, through a window that seemed hung on the wall like a painting, was a square patch of blue sky with one cottony, pink-tinged cloud. Reason brought her fingers to the large link of the necklace, marveling at its mystery and at its ability to bring her both joy and sorrow. A breath before she sank into the glorious embrace of sleep, she saw the black silhouette of the Raven fly past the window.

4

nurturing the truth

W hen Reason awoke, night had fallen. With heavy-eyed curiosity, she stared at an unfamiliar bedside table. A single oil lamp burned there, its flame wavering fitfully and emitting a thin curling trail of black smoke. She rolled onto her back. Silver moonlight spilled across the ceiling. Reason had slept well, a deep, intoxicating sleep. Drowsy and disoriented, she sat up.

The necklace slipped from her collarbone. She reached up, her fingers finding the large plain link. Bits and pieces of the previous day came rushing back—the snowy landscape and the Raven, the tunnels and Edward. She recalled the library, the garden path, the loud booming of the thunder—the solitary tree. She relived the stark white of the warehouse, the piercing ring of the telephone—Ruby's comforting voice. In sleepy wonder, Reason smiled—remembering the silly antics of Mr. Up and Mr. Down. *What comes next? Will I remember everything I was told?* As fascinating as the memories were, she felt weariness reclaiming her. Sleep drew her back, sank her down, and subdued her once again. And when Reason next opened her eyes, daylight was streaming in through the open window and a breeze played with the long gauzy curtains. She raised herself onto her elbows and inhaled the fresh air.

On the bed at her feet lay a tidy pile of clothing. Reason pulled the small stack closer. On top was a white linen blouse. Along with the blouse, she found a tank top, undergarments, a lightweight vest, and beige linen pants. She held the articles of clothing in the air, the sizing of each garment curiously accurate—and wondered who had brought them into the room. Remembering the lit oil lamp, she looked to the bedside table. The wick no longer burned. Rested and strengthened, she laughed aloud at the thought of the two little operators tiptoeing into the room and endeavoring to be quiet while she slept.

Eager to get on with the day, Reason swung her legs out from beneath the covers. The air was crisp. On the floor beside the bed sat a pair of flat, brown sandals. With the bundle of clothing held to her chest, Reason slipped her feet into the shoes, the leather soles smooth and cool, a comfortable fit. She stood and listened for any sign of life outside in the hall, hearing only the soft fluttering of the drapery as the sheer fabric waved and flapped in the breeze.

Reason moved to the unscreened window and reached through the slit between the curtains; the stone surface of the sill cool to the touch. A powerful gust of wind made the fabric billow and cleave to her legs. She pulled it free and stepped forward.

In deepening shades of blue, the gently sloping curves of broad-based mountains rolled towards the horizon. And below the snowy mountain peaks, lingering pools of pale pink mist hovered and swirled. Closer to Reason's vantage point, a blue-tinged haze flowed as a fast-moving fog that thinned every so often to reveal a lush green valley far, far below. She stood on the tips of her toes and leaned into the opening. The stone wall ascended high above her and plunged into a milky mist below. The air smelled of damp soil. Just then, the sound of shuffling feet and suppressed laughter preceded a soft tapping on the bedroom door. "Who's there?" she asked.

"Breakfast, Miss Reason. Breakfast!" one of the little round operators announced gleefully.

She opened the door and the two creatures burst into the room, bright red and laughing. One held a steaming mug of coffee. The other balanced a tray of food in its outstretched arms.

"Steady as she goes!" exclaimed the coffee-carrier.

"It's OK. It's OK. I've got it. I've got it!" squealed the tray-holder, its round face scrunched into a ball of concentration. "I've got it!"

Reason laughed and tossed the bundle of clothing onto the bed. She grabbed a small table and slid it forward. "Put it here!" she cried. "That's it. Be careful! There you go." The tray landed with a whack, and they all looked from it to each other, and then erupted into hearty laughter. For Reason to laugh so spiritedly was a wonderful feeling, timely, and enormously uplifting.

"Does Miss Reason wish anything else?" inquired one creature, huffing and puffing, and slowly gathering its composure.

"Anything else at all?" asked the other.

Both creatures now stood at exaggerated attention, their plump bellies protruding comically. Screwing up their faces, they appeared to struggle at containing their wild merriment. And failing to remain serious for long, each one fell back into uncontrolled giggling.

"You two are too funny," laughed Reason, plucking a strawberry from the rescued breakfast tray and popping it into her mouth. "Which one of you is Up and which one is Down?"

"I am Mr. Up," answered the one on her right.

"I am Mr. Down," replied the one on her left.

"But how can I tell you apart?" she asked while eying the buttered toast, quartered oranges, and black coffee. She reached for the hot drink but stopped when Mr. Up and Mr. Down unexpectedly dropped to the floor. They poked at each other, laughing, straightening their legs, and thrusting their feet in the air. On their soles were arrows, green arrows pointing at the heel on one, and brown arrows pointing at the toe on the other. "So, the only way I can tell you apart is if I can see the soles of your feet? That will not work too well," said Reason.

Up and Down rolled onto their stomachs, pushed their chubby bodies up onto their knees, and rose to stand. They brushed off each other's furry backside and then turned to face Reason. "Mr. Up has green eyes," stated Down.

"And Mr. Down has brown," added Up.

Reason peered into their eyes. "So, green means up and brown means down."

"That's right, Miss Reason. That's right," said Down.

"I see," said Reason, standing back, bringing the coffee to her nose, then taking a sip.

"We have a message from Miss Ruby," the creatures suddenly declared in unison.

"Miss Ruby would like you to join her downstairs," said Up.

"Yes, she would. All the way downstairs," cried Down.

"She's in the greenhouse!" they exclaimed in unison.

"Without a doubt, she's in the seedling greenhouse," said Down, a little more composed.

"After you've eaten, of course," said Up with a wink.

"That, and changed your clothes," added Down.

"Naturally," they agreed in unison.

And then, as if remembering something of great importance, Mr. Up leaned into Mr. Down and whispered excitedly. Down's eyes widened. "Oh, yes indeed. Most important," he exclaimed and then scurried out of the room, momentarily disappearing before returning with a leather bag.

"Miss Ruby says you'll need this to carry your things," explained Down.

"What things?"

"You'll see. You'll see!" they giggled in unison. Then Mr. Down proudly presented the bag to Reason—a soft leather satchel with a buckled shoulder strap. Reason took the bag and examined it, flipping open the large outside flap and putting her hand inside one of two ample interior compartments.

"It's beautiful," she whispered.

"Furthermore," said Up.

"Yes, quite so," agreed Down.

"We have a piece of advice for you," continued Up.

"Indeed, we have excellent advice," piped in Down.

And then together they proclaimed, "Go through the bathroom to get to the greenhouse." And with that said, the operators promptly scooted from the room and the bedroom door closed with a soft click.

What?

CR ℇ०

With the satchel strapped across her chest, Reason touched her necklace for good luck and ventured into the bathroom. The room, a small windowless space, contained a shower stall, a toilet, and a pedestal sink with a mirrored cabinet hanging above it. Reason examined the walls, the floor, and the ceiling, but she saw no sign of a trap door—or unusual handle—or secret button. She turned her attention to the little towel closet and, removing the linens, reached into the dark cubby. At the top back corner, her groping fingers finally found a tiny hook and eye. She unfastened the hook and the back wall of the closet sprang open a crack. Holding her breath, Reason pushed the panel all the way open. Behind it, a soft light revealed a narrow spiral stairwell. *Now that's a secret staircase!*

Looking inside, she saw curved stone walls following the spiral of the staircase—the walls decorated with tiny pieces of framed floral artwork. The descent was steep but looked manageable. Reason removed the emptied shelves, and then holding the satchel close and turning her body sideways, she stepped into the passageway. Confined within the tight spiral, as she descended, Reason grimaced—experiencing a trace of claustrophobia, looking down constantly as she went—the stairs descending into the eeriness of gloomy shadow. The steep descent required her to use her hands to brace herself against the icy-cold wall, and as she went, she could see ahead only a few steps. Twenty steps down, she came upon a square opening in the outside wall. Grateful for the fresh air, Reason stopped to breathe it in and to peer outside. The opening was tiny, and the wall so thick that she could see only a diminutive patch of pale blue sky. She hesitated before continuing down, becoming increasingly anxious about leaving the fresh air behind. And worrying about the depth of the stairwell, she grew more and more afraid of the confinement.

Two more steps down, she felt the heat of human flesh suddenly pinning her hand against the stone. A puff of air brushed her cheek, then the moisture of hot breath against her neck. The unmistakable villainy of William's voice entered her ear: "No matter where you go...." A surge of dread coursed through her. Her fear intensified. An ominous hum, increasing in volume and swift as the wind, plunged down from above. The door to the bathroom slammed shut. Reason wrenched her hand free and scurried down the next few steps. Then, shaking her head, she stopped and looked up at the empty stairwell behind her. *Shit.* Deliberately closing her eyes, she focused on her breathing. *Don't think about the tunnels. Don't think about him. Just count the stairs.* "Thirty-two, thirty-three," she muttered in a trembling voice, stepping with care.

Refusing to give in to the sense that someone or something pursued her, and ignoring the chill deep in her bones, she took a breath and stoically pressed on. A blast of fresh air suddenly wafted up from below. Quickening her step; *forty-nine, fifty;* she arrived at a small landing where air flowed generously through a large opening in the wall. She dared to stop, breathing in the fresh air, persuading herself to remain calm. Through the window, Reason saw the outer edge of a terrace several feet below. Her heartbeats slowed. The chills dissipated. She turned and continued down. Arriving at last at a small wooden door, she burst through it.

A magnificent terrace sprawled before her; the immense structure reaching far into the distance. It appeared to protrude from the vast precipice from which she had just descended. Reason slowed to a halt, turned, and looked up. The enormous rock face ascended into a thick mist. Moving to a railing near the terrace edge, she looked down. Far below, the snowcapped mountains that she had seen from her room above flanked a lush green basin. Forests of dark green coniferous trees climbed the sides of the mountains, gradually giving way to a barren terrain of rock, snow, and ice. In the valley, a rapidly moving river traveled the length of the deep cut, vanishing into a thick ground fog at either end. Reason breathed in the earthy dampness, and for a few precious moments, experienced a joyful lightness of spirit—a sense of being freed from any burdens.

Turning from the railing, the weight of her current circumstances returned, and she looked about for Ruby, soon locating her in a glass greenhouse at the far side of the terrace. The greenhouse was large and opulent and appeared to be floating a few inches above the terrace floor. Inside, Ruby straightened, stretched, and then massaged the small of her back. Spotting Reason, she poked her head out an open window and hollered, "Feeling refreshed? Ready for your day?"

"I hope so," shouted Reason, taking a step toward the floating structure.

"Stay where you are. I'll come to you," offered Ruby cheerfully. Reaching forward, she appeared to enter some sort of command into a pedestaled control panel, and the structure rose an additional five or six inches. It began coasting toward Reason, coming to a stop close to where she stood. It whirred and lowered and then hung motionless a few inches above the terrace. Looking pleased, Ruby motioned for Reason to step inside.

Under the weight of her steps, the structure remained steady. "Amazing," said Reason, taking in the scent of fresh soil. Inside, the air was warm and moist. To either side of a wide center aisle, fine sprays of mist produced a soft hiss—the water raining down upon rows of small plants, collecting in the hollows of the tiny shimmering petals and leaves, pooling in shallow basins that had formed in the rich dark soil.

"These are seedlings destined for the Garden of Lost and Found," said Ruby, fanning a gloved hand above a colorful patch of tiny, sprouting plantlets. "Tending to them is a hobby for me," she beamed. "With a transportable greenhouse, my hobby is wherever I am." She reached down and touched a seedling. "Each day I'm amazed at how they've changed, grown stronger, budded, and blossomed." Ruby turned to Reason. "We've many gardeners all over this land. They nurture acres of seedlings just like these, cultivating them for the Garden of Lost and Found. Look at these beauties," she said, returning her gaze to the seedlings. "They have the radiance of jewels."

"They do," said Reason, gazing in amazement at the tiny plants. Brilliant as rubies, emeralds, and sapphires, their tiny fragile stems stooped under the weight of the vibrant, twinkling buds. After a moment she turned to Ruby. "What is the Garden of Lost and Found?"

Ruby brought a small container to her nose. Within it, on a slender stalk, a blue sapphire bud grew above three topaz leaves. Ruby breathed in the flowery scent and then passed the fragile seedling under Reason's nose. It smelled of wet soil and berries. "You'll learn about the garden soon enough," she said casually. "For now, we must address more immediate needs. You must tell me about William."

Reason again recoiled at the mention of William's name. She stared at her hands, wringing them, and then reluctantly, she raised her gaze to meet Ruby's. "Thinking of William is dreadful. The very thought of actually discussing my life with him is sickening. I'm embarrassed... and ashamed." She lowered her eyes, fidgeting impulsively with the buckle on the satchel's wide shoulder strap.

"Well now," said Ruby, "all the more reason to talk about him, to come to terms with those memories, to put them to rest." Carrying forward a tall stool, she set it down alongside another and gestured for Reason to join her.

"William was a disaster. The details of my time with him are ugly." Reason turned her face away.

"Could there be something more beyond the ugliness?" asked Ruby, removing her garden gloves and arranging them neatly on her lap.

"That's impossible," said Reason, irritated by Ruby's persistence.

"Is it?"

Carried away by a flood of memories, Reason began experiencing the familiar degrading and suffocating darkness that was William. She shivered. "The ugliness was too great," she retorted, frowning and reflexively clenching her fists.

"Perhaps," said Ruby, leaning down and picking up a small watering can and, from her seated position, sprinkling water onto a nearby flat of seedlings.

"No. For certain," insisted Reason.

"Perhaps," repeated Ruby.

"Not *perhaps*. Most definitely!" said Reason impatiently, staring at the floor.

"That's quite a judgment. Are you certain that the entire story will be ugly?" inquired Ruby, unaffected by Reason's noticeable irritation.

"Yes, because I lived it. It's ugly. Hideous," muttered Reason.

"Even the ending?" coaxed Ruby.

"What?" Reason looked up.

"The ending, is it ugly?" Ruby continued to water the seedlings, appearing only casually attentive to Reason.

"What ending?"

"It's your story to tell..." Ruby said, setting the watering can down and peering amiably at Reason.

"There never was an actual *ending*. Over the years, the whole experience just... sort of... faded away. Never completely. Never truly gone from my mind. The memories can still torment me... in flashbacks and nightmares." She slumped her shoulders and dropped her gaze. "I don't think this kind of thing ever *really ends*."

"That's interesting. Tell me about that."

Again, the two women met each other's gaze, and Reason wondered if she could, for the first time in her life, and so many years later, speak frankly to someone else about her life with William. She sighed—and gave in—the words suddenly spilling out. "For the years I was with him, and for a long time after, I felt I wasn't worthy of life. I would think that a deserving person must be far more intelligent and valuable than me."

"Why?" Ruby asked, her eyes bright with confidence. "Because you will always be worthy."

Reason shook her head, frowning. She slipped from her stool and turned away. "I'm still so ashamed," she mumbled.

Ruby stood. "Shame paves the path to worthlessness," she said. "But no one will judge you here. Let's walk—and you can tell me more."

Ruby led Reason from the greenhouse. Out in the open, the breeze had picked up. Together, and in silence, they walked along the palatial span of the terrace, stopping at an ornate metal railing. In the distance, the Raven flew. "Craw, Craw," rang out its call. Reason watched the bird, and then tightly gripping the cold, twisted metal of the railing, began to tell Ruby the story of her life with William.

CR &O

Miss A. Macy Grace sat in a small chair beside Reason's bed. She looked up from her book when Reason moaned, and then she stood, book in hand—and watched as Reason winced in her sleep. Macy reached down and touched her arm. Reason's body trembled, and in her fitful sleep, she lifted her hand and swiped at the air. Macy guided the frail waving hand back down by Reason's side, and then with the care and tenderness of a mother to a child, she bent forward and whispered, "Sleep, dearest Reason, sleep."

5

first flight

66 That's it. Come on. Here I am. Return to me."

Why are you always interfering—always in my way?

"I'm not in your way. I *am* your way."

Leave—me—alone.

"That, little dearie, will never happen."

I'll fight you.

"You can try," mocked Pain.

Reason grimaced and rolled onto her side. She had shifted woozily from sleep into hazy wakefulness, and sensing a subtle movement of the air about her, became vaguely aware that someone had entered the room. The person moved past her and then lingered at what appeared to be a window. She struggled to see more clearly, but exhaustion took her once more into sleepy oblivion.

Miss A. Macy Grace turned and faced the bed, watching Reason's features soften as she slipped once more into the tranquility of slumber.

ೞ

Except for a thin shade of grey light spraying a portion of the small front porch in a milky hue, the house sat cloaked in darkness. Inside, in a windowless bathroom, Reason waited. She had entered the small room in a rush, and now, in the dark, stood with her back against the door, grateful for how the pitch-black seemed to swallow her whole. Closing her eyes, she held her breath and listened. Water leaked from the tap at the sink, dripping in a slow steady measure into the drain below.

Reason wrung her hands together, thinking it unlikely that William had pursued her. Nonetheless, she knew that with him it was a possibility. He had already broken many of the rules of the halfway house—without a single supervisor or counselor appearing to notice. She knew, fueled by his rage, he could have followed her. He could have slipped out unseen. With this possibility looming, she remained still and alert to every sound.

As dawn emerged, and the sun spread its glow into the other rooms of the house, the thin line of light at the bottom of the bathroom door grew brighter—and Reason considered that she might be safe. She slid to the floor, wincing at her stiff, sore muscles, old tears evidenced in the chalky lines marking her swollen cheeks. Her shame was so intense, she could taste it in the bitterness of the blood crusting the corners of her mouth. She bowed her head, exhausted—thinking that by now William might be fast asleep—sprawled on his bed in the bedroom he and another felon shared in the halfway house across town; in the very room from which she had escaped a few short hours earlier.

Reason knew that she would eventually have to lift her battered body off the floor. She also knew that she would inevitably turn on the light and look in the mirror. But utterly defeated, and dreading the inescapable examination of her wounds, she could not yet bring herself to move. She knew from experience that to view her battered face was disturbing, the reflection in the mirror a ghastly stranger until she recognized the frightened and ashamed eyes staring back. She sighed—not needing a mirror to understand the damage done to her face. She reached up, gingerly touching the ballooned eyelid of her right eye. Beneath her probing fingers, the contours of her flesh felt unfamiliar—jelly-like. Her face bulged grotesquely. Congealed blood clogged her nostrils—a metallic taste lingering. Her fingers traced her burning jawline, finding a bloody split on her upper lip. The cut prickled and stung. Her lips too swollen to close fully, she gently pressed her fingers to the corners of her mouth and eased her lower jaw from side to side.

She leaned her head against the door and winced—reaching behind gingerly—feeling a walnut-sized lump protruding from a patch of blood-matted hair. She shifted her position—and in doing so, discovered a tender area of flesh behind the buckle of her belt. And at that moment, a burning pain scorched the skin on her inner thighs, reaching to her core, gutting her. She balled her hands into fists, feeling it all, every bit of her wounded self.

Her blouse hung open at her side, the sleeve missing—her scraped breast exposed. In the dark, Reason reached for the tattered material, and in a sudden need to cover her nakedness, pulled the fabric up against her shoulder and held it there. Shifting her position to ease the increasing pain, she found that her right foot was bare and that the sock on her left was wet. Wearily, she pulled the damp sock from her foot and tossed it aside.

Staring into the dark, Reason's thoughts went to the horrors she had just suffered. She could not be sure, but she guessed that the entire ordeal had lasted for six hours, maybe more. During the attack, she had pushed her emotions aside, doing so for the sake of her survival. But now they advanced unchecked, bringing nausea and additional misery. She shivered and cried quietly, grateful for having survived, and for the moment, for feeling safe.

In the stillness of predawn, Reason had escaped William—running frantically through the deserted town, reluctantly stopping to catch her breath or to quit the exposure of the open street to flee into the shadows—searching the silent, empty streets for any sign that he had followed. But here, in the dark and quiet stillness of the bathroom, she could finally let go, and in doing so, Reason felt the full impact of the experience. Nausea erupted unrestrained. She leaned to the side and vomited.

Balling her hands into fists, Reason brought them together at her chest. *How did I ever think I could hope for a better life? He'll always fucking find me.* Then she dragged herself up from the floor—every muscle objecting. Finding the light switch, she let her fingers linger on it, leaning against the wall, delaying the inevitable. She inhaled quickly and exhaled slowly. Then flicking the light on, through a blinking eye, she fixed her gaze on the white porcelain sink. Her vision adjusting, she focused on the pinhead-sized water droplets lining the circular chrome ring of the drain. And then Reason raised her face to the mirror. And as she did, a strange thought came to her mind, moving into her psyche as if someone had whispered into her ear: "*It's extraordinary how resilient the human body is, more so than the mind, less so than the soul.*"

CR &wc;

Gasping for air, Reason staggered from the railing. She spun around and stared wild-eyed at Ruby. A moment later, having remembered where she was, she cried, "What the hell was that? I was there! I was *actually there!*" She brought her trembling hand to her face, held it in the air for a moment, and then briefly cupped it over her mouth. "At first, I was here... on this terrace, holding this railing." She gripped the railing. "And then... and then I was there! I was there as my younger self!" She turned to Ruby, who appeared perplexingly untroubled. "How can you be so calm? I feel sick. Why was I there? Why was I backwards in time, in that... shitty horror story?" She stared in disbelief at Ruby, who stood poised and seemingly unaffected. "Don't you understand what I'm telling you? I relived that nightmare, detail after awful detail, experiencing it just as I had before. I could smell that stinking bathroom. I could taste the blood and feel the pain!" Reason held onto the railing, bending forward, lowering her head, trying hard not to be ill.

Ruby took a step toward her, one hand extended as if to console. "Breathe, Reason. It's alright. I understand. I understand more than you'll ever know. Your reaction is rather expected and frankly, normal."

Peering over her shoulder, Reason gasped at Ruby. "What? How is being back in that hell... or any of this... fantasy land," she waved a hand in the air, "normal?"

Ruby smiled and then looked past Reason, beyond the railing and into the distance, where a lavender mist had merged with the pale blue of the sky. "We have granted you a chance at an extraordinary journey," she explained. "And when you tell us your personal story, openly voicing its most private details, you'll spontaneously transport into that story precisely to relive it. We use this re-experiencing technique to separate fact from fiction, because an inauthentic story will prove quite useless," she counseled.

"What?" Reason tapped the railing with a fist. "I can't do that! Look how sick it makes me. I feel horrible." Exhausted and ailing, she rested her head on her arms and the empty satchel silently slid toward the railing.

"The nausea will pass," offered Ruby.

"But I don't understand. Why must I do this? It's hard enough talking about the experience, but to relive it! You can't expect me to do that... I just can't!" Reason braced against the railing and then stood and faced Ruby, expressing her horror, disturbed by this woman's remarkable composure in the face of her own enormous discomfort.

Ruby pursed her lips, watching Reason, and then once again she looked out over the valley. And after a few calming breaths, despite her trepidation, Reason gained a new perspective. She thought about Ruby's role in this fantasy world of adventure and personal journeys. She soon realized that Ruby had probably had this very discussion many times before, calmly and patiently explaining the process to former shocked *visitors*. And she, Reason, was Ruby's latest guest, no different from the others. The rules will not change for her. She sighed heavily, and smiling weakly at Ruby, settled in to listen.

"For you to realize your highest truth, you must take part in the *full* experience. A memory is fragile. But, as you have said, you could feel, smell, and even taste the experience. This sensory involvement elevates the memory, which on its own is just a precarious understanding of past events. Reliving your story creates a necessary separation between fact and fiction. Your story is therefore told authentically—and the experience unfolds as it actually happened." Ruby smiled reassuringly. "Come now, dear. Trust the process." And taking Reason's hand, Ruby led her toward an opening in the railing, where a stone staircase led to a lower terrace.

The two women descended side by side. They walked slowly and Reason, consumed with thoughts of her repulsive past with William, was finding it hard to settle her nerves. "Ruby, for so many years, I tried to come to terms with that time in my life. I can't imagine being there again. My God, being back in that bathroom..."

Ruby stopped walking, turning to face Reason. "You can return. Yes, you'll be revisiting the experience as it happened, but you'll do so with fresh awareness. You'll do so as a *witness*. And once the initial shock subsides, you will be fine. You are here because you are ready."

"But it was such a shock—a terrible, terrible shock! Why didn't you prepare me?" Frustrated and not waiting for an answer, Reason turned away and continued down the stairs. Ruby followed.

"If I had forewarned you, you may have been too afraid to even begin. But you have begun. You have been there, in the past, and you are here now. So again, I ask you to be patient and to trust in the process."

The stairs ended at a circular terrace. Just ahead, a fountain of teal-tinted water tumbled into a large round pool. Lush, variegated ivies spilled over the low stone wall that contained the water. A sculpture of giant hyacinths sprung up from the center of the fountain, and on the terrace surrounding it, large basins teemed with a rainbow of live hyacinths—their sweet springtime scent pleasant in the air.

Ruby moved to a stone bench near the fountain and sat. Reason joined her. Behind them, beyond the railing and level with the terrace floor, a thick purple mist swirled. "Why am I here?" asked Reason. "What's the purpose of all of this? Edward and you... you both speak of me beginning a journey—some kind of rite of passage, but I'm struggling to understand."

"I expect you are hoping for a tidy answer," said Ruby. "But such an answer does not exist. You're not the first to visit us and you'll not be the last. No one, *no one* adjusts immediately. In the beginning, the experience of this place is too difficult for the mind to absorb. There's nothing in your earthly understanding to which you can compare this experience. So be patient. You'll adapt. The process takes time. Your unique purpose for being here will eventually be revealed. For now, know that you being here is deemed necessary." Ruby spoke tenderly and passionately.

"By whom?"

"Well, *some* believe that their journey here is God's will—or that of some higher power. Others argue against such beliefs." Ruby smiled, her eyes smiling too. "Despite our differences, love binds all of us—because love doesn't discriminate. Love brings you here, my dear, to what we call the Flight of the Soul." She raised her hands, holding them open as if they cradled an invisible object. "This journey is about reconciliation—and all you need—is a little courage, and a heap of inspiration."

The tumbling water filled the silence that followed, and Reason, surprised that to some extent she found Ruby's explanation comforting, shrugged her shoulders. "I've never really practised a religion. God has... come and gone in my life. And yes, I also believe in the power of love." She looked about. "All of this... the beauty and the wonder, you, Edward, Mr. Up and Mr. Down... the mystery... it's all so strange and overwhelming. Yet, I feel I'm... meant to be here." She held her hands in a gesture of helplessness. "But revisiting the past? Reliving it? Ruby, that's genuinely horrifying. It'll be impossible for me not to worry. And how will I contain my fear? How will I hold off the tunnels?"

"All the experiences of your life are available here. Yes, you will experience the fear, worry, and sorrow associated with your past. But you'll also experience courage, serenity, and joy. The love that brought you here will guide you. And when you feel afraid, remember that your fear cannot exist without you also knowing courage and calm." Ruby spoke patiently. "Inner balance, Reason, is always possible. Remember, here at the Communications Centre we'll always know where you are. We'll be right here tracking you. Try not to anticipate the moments yet to come. Be here and now. And as you journey, be mindful of your true intentions because they will guide you too." Ruby smiled reassuringly. "So, please, continue to tell me your story. Start at the beginning. Tell me how you and William met."

ᏣᏁᏬ

"Hey, what did ya get for your birthday?" asked Cara, leaning toward a mirror and applying a thin line of black eyeliner across the lids of her pale blue eyes.

Reason combed through Cara's closet. A pile of clothing, tried and discarded, lay strewn across the bed. "Can I wear your brown cords tonight?" she asked.

"Yeah, go ahead. Can I wear your opal earrings? So, what did ya get?"

"Hang on. I'll show you in a second." Reason stripped off her jeans, kicking them from her feet, pulling on Cara's light brown corduroys, posing in front of the full-length mirror. She tucked in her blouse, unfastened the top button, re-buttoned it, and tugged at the shirt's collar. "I got this," she said, pulling a dainty gold chain forward from her neck, holding it by its pendant. "This necklace."

"Cool. I can't really see it though. Move your fingers. Is that a locket?" Cara, applying a sheer pink lip gloss, peered at Reason in the mirror.

Just then, Cara's mother's voice streamed up from the front hallway below. "Girls? Ivy is here." Eager to get on with their night, Cara and Reason each grabbed their purses and matching jean jackets and rushed out of the bedroom.

Ivy drove her older brother's sky blue, two-door, '78 Chevy Nova. The car wasn't all that old, but his foolhardy driving had left it in rough shape—and a constant source of embarrassment for the girls. But the freedom of driving around town on their own more than made up for the dents and rust. Cara slid into the backseat while Reason sat up front. The car seemed to float atop the hot summer asphalt, all the windows down, the air blowing hot and blustery. Reason glanced at the speedometer, surprised that it read little more than the posted speed. Ivy was often a distracted driver, sometimes speeding while fumbling through her purse for cigarettes, lipstick, or a cassette tape. This evening, on their way to the weekend hayride, from the car radio the band *Kansas* blasted *Carry on, Wayward Son,* and the girls sang along.

Ivy passed a lit cigarette over her shoulder. "My Mom found my cigarettes the other day," shouted Cara from the backseat, taking the shared cigarette, holding it low near her lap to avoid the wind.

"Shit!" replied Ivy.

"And?" asked Reason, looking over her shoulder into the backseat, her long hair blowing wildly about her face.

"She took 'em from me. That's all. She knows if I'm going to quit, it won't be because she's yelling at me."

"Are you gonna quit?" asked Reason.

"Yes, when YOU do!" laughed Cara, leaning forward between the two front seats to flick ashes into a dashboard tray.

"Just not today!" Reason shot back.

A golden-pink sun simmered low in the sky by the time the girls arrived at the hayride, an outdoor party held every Saturday night during the summer months, and rarely chaperoned.

The Chevy bobbed up and down as it negotiated the rutted field. Ivy turned off the engine and a mix of shouting voices, laughter, and music drifted across the field toward them. Of the three of them, Cara was the most popular. She was a blue-eyed blond, vibrant and a little crazy, the kind of friend who Reason laughed with regularly, but also felt most obligated to keep in check. Reason was considered the most unruffled and poised of the three, while Ivy suffered considerable self-consciousness and constantly strove for Cara's pluckiness and Reason's praise.

Ivy retrieved a flashlight from the car's glove compartment and a wine canteen from the trunk. Cara snatched up the canteen, holding it above her head like a trophy. She kissed it and then guffawed. Reason also laughed, shaking her head at her friend's silly antics before turning to lead the way through a row of prickly brambles.

The sky ahead had deepened to a rich indigo and the trees lining the farmer's field had become one long, dark shadow. A few of the brightest stars were showing, and the mosquitos and crickets were coming alive in the twilight. The girls waited on a path where two hard-packed tracks lined a center patch of flattened brown grass. They heard the tractor's motor before seeing its headlight, jerky and yellow, cross the field as the vehicle chugged out from behind a row of trees. The old vehicle towed a flatbed and eventually came to a fitful stop in front of the girls, bringing with it the pungent smell of farm animals and the woody scent of fresh hay. They all hopped on, sitting shoulder to shoulder on one bale of hay, Cara in the middle as she often was. As the tractor jerked into motion, Ivy toppled off her seat, landing clumsily on the hay-scattered bed. "Hey, how embarrassing!" teased Cara, reaching down and giving Ivy a playful shove.

"Do you think they'll be here tonight?" ventured Reason, plucking a cigarette from Cara's jean jacket pocket. "Share a smoke?" she asked as the big wheels of the tractor trundled on.

"They're always at these things, aren't they?" said Ivy, reaching over to light the cigarette, the ember burning brightly. The girls went silent, each thinking about the possibility of seeing the boys and anticipating the fun that lay ahead.

Within a half-hour of reaching the bonfire—the blazing centerpiece of the party—the girls had finished their small canteen of wine and had begun canvassing the crowd for someone willing to share a beer or two. The light of the fire wavered in a golden glow on the carefree faces surrounding it. The girls mingled and moved through the partygoers, searching for the two boys, William and Baker. They soon spotted them.

Reason pretended otherwise, but her full attention was on William. She watched him as he passed on the far side of the fire. They had never spoken, but she hoped maybe they might this evening. Through the tall dancing flames, she watched with keen interest as he stopped and talked to a pretty girl with long, blonde hair. The girl wore a boxy, cropped jacket with long leather fringes hanging from the sleeves. William moved in very close to the girl, appearing to hug her. Then, with a beer in his right hand, he stepped back, spread his arms wide, and shrugged his shoulders. Reason watched the girl shake her head while William waved his arm dismissively and took a swig of beer. He turned from the girl, leaving her standing alone, and walked away to a nearby hillside and sat. The girl appeared to hesitate, and then she turned and walked away. William's gaze never returned to her. He sat far enough from the fire to be partially obscured in the shadows. Reason thought little about what she had just witnessed between William and the girl, and buoyed by wine-inspired courage, she crossed the distance between them and sat down on the hillside beside him.

"Hey," she said. "Nice fire."

He did not look at her and she felt immediately foolish. *Nice fire? Idiot.*

William broke the excruciating silence. "I've seen you around. What's your name?"

He's seen me around! Reclining on the hillside, William lay on his back, his hands behind his head, his feet crossed, his beer bottle propped up by his side. "Reason," she said, relaxing—feeling a little more confident.

"What kind of name is that?"

"It's a *reasonable* name," she offered, her customary answer.

Straightaway, he asked, "Wanna smoke a joint?"

She looked at him. He stared at the night sky. Taken aback, Reason feigned calm and for a moment wondered if she should try getting high, always somehow having avoided doing so up until now. "No... thanks."

He rolled onto his side to face her. "Why not? It'll be fun." Their eyes met.

"Just don't need any more tonight," she lied.

As he stared at her, she turned away and pretended to be interested in a group of partiers walking nearby. "Where are your friends?" he asked.

"Somewhere over there," Reason gestured nonchalantly, feigning composure. She scanned the area on the far side of the leaping flames, easily found Ivy and Cara, and watched them. Cara was laughing as she moved through the crowd—Ivy trailing behind her.

"Want to take off?" asked William unexpectedly.

Reason hesitated, picking up a pebble and tossing it into the darkness, dismissing an uncomfortable fluttering in the pit of her stomach. Avoiding the question, she asked, "Who was the blond girl you were talking to?"

"No one," William answered—rolling away from her.

To Reason's dismay, he seemed annoyed by her question. For months she had dreamed about meeting William. All spring she and the girls had schemed to run into the two boys, planning outings in town to places where William and his friend were likely to be. The scheming had all been in fun. They had not expected to get a chance to meet the boys. But alone with William now, and the night growing long, Reason did not want to mess up the opportunity to make her intentions known. "No. I mean... I can't go with you tonight. Maybe another time?" She looked at his face; its handsome details lit in the golden glow. At eighteen, William had striking features, long blond hair, steel-blue eyes, and a charming smile. Reason was love-struck.

"Maybe," he said. "Gimme your number. I'll call you." He remained on his back, hands behind his head.

Reason reached into her purse. *Are you kidding me? Is this really happening?* Pretending to be calm, she searched through the small leather bag and found a pen and a gum wrapper. She jotted down her parents' telephone number. William rolled over to face her. She passed him the paper. He took it, glanced at it, smiled at her, and stood. Then he picked up his beer, and using it, saluted her before walking away.

OH MY GOD! Reason was hard-pressed to contain her elation. Restraining her pace and expression, inwardly bursting with joy, she made her way back to Cara and Ivy to share her amazing news.

CR ⯑

Reason opened her eyes to feathery slips of cloud drifting in a pale blue sky.

"Welcome back," said Ruby.

Reason raised to her elbows and then sat up. "It's like waking from another life...." She reached for her necklace, still unable to remember the pendant. "Being there again, at the beginning of it all, being able to feel those moments as they occurred... it was *so* strange.

And Cara and Ivy, I loved them very much." She smiled at the memories of her teenage girlfriends and wiped a tear from her cheek. "I was extremely nervous sitting there beside him—and remarkably naïve. His self-absorbed attitude is obvious to me now." She laughed dejectedly. "I had a gut feeling that I was in over my head, that something wasn't right, but I ignored it. I thought William was handsome. I mean *really* handsome and... better than me. I felt lucky that he was interested in me at all." She stood. "For a long time, I wanted to believe that in the beginning, we were happy—that things were once good between us. In fact, for a while, I convinced myself of that. But sitting beside him on that hillside, talking with him that first time, my gut said something was off. I didn't listen. I sensed that being with him was somehow wrong, but I didn't seem to care. I went out with him, anyway. Not that night—later that week, and in the end, I became his... pathetic possession." Reason found Ruby's gaze and held it. "Ruby, I thought that my shame had surfaced much later in my relationship with William—much, much later. But the shame was already brewing right there on that hillside. I didn't know... back then, what shame felt like. I didn't recognize it. I do now... I do now." Reason held her head in her hands and drew in a long breath.

Ruby smiled, walked to the terrace railing, and peered over. "Come, Reason. Look." Reason hung back, burdened by her despair. "Come or you'll miss them." She joined Ruby at the railing. "They fly to the Garden of Lost and Found," said Ruby. "With the passing of each day, they follow others, like you Reason, who have gone on their own journey, and found their way to the Garden."

Reason followed Ruby's gaze. Hundreds of dragonflies flew where moments earlier a thick purple mist had billowed. Flying swiftly, the massive swarm clinked and glistened like millions of tiny pieces of tumbling crystal. Every so often a lone dragonfly would fly up to the height of the terrace, hover there, and then abruptly nosedive to rejoin the swarm. As Reason leaned forward for a closer look, an exceptionally large dragonfly rose from the group and alighted upon the railing near to her. She gasped and took a small step backward.

In awe, she studied the creature, wholly fascinated. A fine webbing of tiny black veins filled the dragonfly's four long, narrow, pink-tinged wings—the delicate wings gently curving inward at their rounded tips and twitching repeatedly. The wingspan must have been at least the length of Reason's hand. The beautiful creature's iridescent body shimmered bright blue—tapering to a tail that curled upward to a pointed tip marked with two tiny red hearts. And set in its large head, itself a glistening green orb, large glossy eyes reflected the cloud-streaked sky.

As the swarm passed and thinned, the tinkling decreased. The dragonfly on the railing lifted. It hung in the air momentarily, and then darted close to Ruby's face. She nodded once and the stunning creature reversed and dipped sideways toward Reason, who started and laughed. It hovered at her eye level. She stood still—captivated—feeling a mysterious sense of connection with the creature. Then it tilted its busy wings and swooped away—disappearing into the departing swarm. "So beautiful. What's their purpose?" Reason walked along the terrace, tracing the cool metal surface of the railing beneath her fingers, watching the purple mist roll back in.

"The dragonfly signifies change. It symbolizes the transition from illusion to clarity," offered Ruby. She strolled casually behind Reason; her hands loosely clasped across her bosom. "Through its ability to present itself in a multitude of colors, through the iridescence of its body and its wings, the dragonfly represents the many possibilities of being. It represents change in perception and celebrates the soul's advancement from the confines of illusion to the freedom of clarity. And clarity, Reason, provides a path through life and death without fear." Ruby moved to the fountain and put her hand into the falling water. She splayed her fingers, the water falling from them in thick spirals. "The dragonflies rejoice with those who have found their way to the Garden of Lost and Found." Ruby moved to the bench and sat. "Come sit. Continue your story. Tell me about the first time you experienced William's dark side."

Reason sighed and stared into the purple mist. "Like you said, Ruby, memory is fragile. It has an ebb and flow to it. And mostly, my memory of those dark years has ebbed more than it's flowed... a survival instinct, I suppose, a way of trying to get on with my life as undamaged as possible. I have, however, never forgotten the details of the very first time he hit me." Reason lowered her gaze as she circled the fountain. "I never thought I would speak of it to anyone." The tranquility of the cascading water did little to subdue the disturbance stirring within her.

"Meticulous memory is not a necessity. Authenticity is," offered Ruby candidly. "Authenticity will lead the way."

Ω ∝

The old grandfather clock dutifully chimed half-past three in the morning as Reason opened the front door of her parents' house. To her left, silver moonlight and the pale yellow of the streetlight shone through the bay window—casting a grid of skewed shadows across the living room floor. With her back pressed against the door, she leaned into it, closing it with a gentle push. She stood still to listen. The house was quiet, her parents apparently asleep. Reason made her way to the stairs and up to her bedroom—her father's snore pushing through his closed bedroom door.

Moving past her parents' bedroom, she entered her own, shutting the door without making a sound. Relieved to have snuck through the house successfully, Reason slipped off her jacket and turned on the bedside lamp. She was feeling sad and insignificant—a misfit, an imposter in her own life. Wishing things were different but stifled by the weight of her unhappiness, she turned toward her bed, looking forward to sleeping her troubles away. A white envelope lying on her pillow stopped her cold. On the front of the envelope, in her father's handwriting, was her full given name. Her heart sank. She shrugged her jacket back over her shoulders and stared bleakly at the envelope, knowing it contained bad news and that she was, to some extent, responsible for its contents.

In recent years, Reason had witnessed the slow deterioration of her parents' relationship. At times, the emotional separation between them had become extreme—and they both had started drinking too much, her father drinking openly and her mother failing in her attempts to conceal it. The alcohol seemed to enhance the frequency and intensity of their arguments—with both her parents enduring their individual disappointments in conspicuous stretches of stony silence. To Reason, they appeared to have fallen away from one another to the extent that she wondered why they remained together at all. Their troubles, added to her own rapidly growing sense of isolation, had caused a breakdown in the communication between them all. And lately, disturbingly, at unusual times in the night, Reason had encountered her father acting strangely. She would find him standing alone in the darkened kitchen, staring straight ahead, or sitting on the edge of his bed, his head bowed, his arms hanging limply. The first time she had come across him in this way, she had quietly called his name, but his expression had remained unchanged and he had stared through her, consumed by some overwhelming gloom. Ultimately, she had learned to leave him alone when he was in this state—and without fail the following morning, he would act as if nothing had happened.

Reason sighed and took the envelope from her pillow. Inside was a letter from her father, and he had written it on paper she recognized—a bittersweet recognition.

As a young girl visiting her father's place of work, his large hand wrapped around hers as they walked through his offices, she was honored to be his special little guest—in awe as the adding machines clicked, the phones rang, and the people chatted. She had liked the distinct smells of carbon paper and something else that she could never quite identify, which reminded her faintly of the glue she used in her art classes. She was calmed by the orderliness of her dad's office and delighted by his name sitting boldly on a placard on his desk. The same brand of paper which she now held in her hands, she had once proudly used to scribble her childish fragmented sentences, trying to imitate her dad, looking for his approval, and back then—always getting it.

The letter contained the news that she had somehow expected. Her father was requesting that she move out of the house. Reason could sense the anger in his words: "You are far too insolent to live under my roof." She felt terribly misunderstood, but also angry and ashamed of how her life had spiraled into its current state of gloomy insignificance. In business-like detail, the letter's four pages described how her parents could no longer tolerate her rebellious behavior—or her presumed use of drugs—or her frequent choice to stay out past her curfew. It said that they "had done all that they could to open her eyes to becoming a responsible young lady"—the word "all" heavily traced and underlined. Her father had ended the letter with the declaration that the time had come for Reason to face the consequences of her unfortunate choices. He had given her one week to get her things in order and to move out. She was seventeen.

A single sheet of paper separated and floated to the bedroom floor, landing face-up near her feet. It contained three brief sentences she could read from where she stood. "The situation has become unendurable. I have changed my mind. I want you to leave now." Reason felt certain that her father had been waiting for her that evening, his anger building—and likely fueled by whiskey. She imagined he scrawled these last words in haste, and tiring, slipped the additional page into the envelope before going to bed.

Caught in the clutches of her own problems, the thought did not enter Reason's mind that her mother and father might still love her or worry about her. What her mother might have been thinking while her father composed the letter, Reason could only guess. *Had she read it? Did she approve? Did she even know about it?*

Despite her weariness, the sudden alienation gave Reason new determination. Defiantly, she retrieved the single sheet of paper from the floor, folded it, and pushed it and the rest of the letter into her jacket pocket. She moved to her bedroom window and pulled back the curtain. The night was still and quiet, the street empty of traffic. She leaned forward to look at the moon; the glass pressed cool against her cheek. The sight of the full moon somehow comforted her and gave her courage. Turning from the window, she saw a bookmark that her mother had given her many years earlier—a simple rectangular bookmark of tiny yellow flowers clustered into a chain of small diamond shapes. On impulse, Reason picked it up and put it in her pocket with the letter. She switched off the bedside lamp, walked boldly out of her bedroom, down the stairs, and out the front door.

C8 80

William and Reason sat side by side in the backseat of Baker's car, their knees touching—their first date. Reason held a joint between her index finger and thumb, passed to her over the shoulder of an unfamiliar girl sitting in the front seat. Not knowing what to expect, she put it to her lips and inhaled. The pot had an earthy taste and smelled both sweet and skunky—the end of the joint held pinched between her lips, unpleasantly limp and wet with saliva. The smoke burned her lungs. Coughing, she passed the joint to William without looking at him. On their way to the movie theatre, between the four people in the car, the joint passed through Reason's fingers three more times.

Flying high, her mouth parched, she watched anxiously as William purchased tickets for a film called *The Exorcist*. He pushed the paper ticket into her hand and she stared at it as if it was a living creature—her buzz really kicking in. Inside the theatre, Reason's heavy stone and the film's horror proved to be an excruciating mix. She spent a large part of the movie with her eyes fixed upon the back of the red vinyl seat in front of her, her heart racing, her mind in an unrelenting and terrifying flutter. She cringed as disembodied voices and frenzied sounds exploded from the speakers, filling the theatre with shrieks and inhuman snarls. All around her, the horrified screams of the movie-goers added to her terror.

In Reason's life, she had many times witnessed various drugs being bought, sold, or swapped. Finding one's drug of choice was relatively easy, but a fortunate innocence and a healthy fear had, until this point, kept Reason from partaking. But here, on her first date with William, she had felt compelled to fit in, to appear experienced in order to keep both his attention and affection. So, she had put the joint to her lips and become overwhelmingly high and unnervingly paranoid. She gripped the seat of the theatre chair, determined to regain some control.

In the months before this first date, feeling disenchanted with her life at home, Reason had become more and more adrift. As her relationship with her parents had deteriorated, her siblings, all older, had either moved away from home or, as Reason believed, seemed to want little to do with her. She had become withdrawn and detached, and had plunged into the isolating gloom of self-worthlessness. Her father's letter had come as no surprise. And although she knew it must have pained him to write it, and that it must have upset her mother to know of it, the letter had left her feeling defeated. Her future seemed so bleak that she preferred to ignore it—to let it unfold as it may—to face its misery grimly and alone. Thus, walking out of her parents' home that night, Reason's fear, disguised as anger and bravado, caused her to run troubled, unraveling, and utterly unprepared into William's controlling world.

C33 80

Almost eight months had passed since Reason had first met William at the summer hayride. And still innocently infatuated by his charisma, she lived in the glow of her first love. But she often wondered how it was that William had chosen her, believing that William could have any girl that he wanted.

One afternoon on the living room floor in his mother's townhouse, William and Reason wrestled playfully. Reason, growing tired, asked him to stop. But William became more aggressive. Pinned to the floor, his knees digging painfully into her elbows, she winced and looked up at his face, seeing a strange and unfamiliar scowl. Squirming to get free, she yelled, "Stop, William! Stop! You're hurting me! It's not funny. STOP IT!" He straddled her, his hands pinning her wrists to the floor above her head. The pain in her elbows had become excruciating. He grunted and thrust his face down at hers, his long blond hair falling into her eyes. His weight heavy upon her chest, Reason could not breathe. She panicked. "GET OFF ME!" she squeezed out, and bringing her leg up, kneed him hard. William rolled forward over her head. She sat up, her back to him, rubbing her elbows. "That hurt, William. That *really* hurt!"

Angry, Reason stood. She turned to face William, glimpsing his incoming fist before it hit her squarely in the jaw. Her head spun. She teetered, stunned. The second blow took her down.

Falling hard onto the sharpness of the arm of the couch, Reason brought both hands to her face, trying to contain the pain. In a daze, she lowered her trembling hands and stared at them. William came at her again. She scrambled up onto the couch, recoiling, instinctively covering her head with her arms. But William landed upon his knees at her feet. "I'm sorry. I'm sorry," he whimpered, looking up at her, his body quivering. "I don't know why... I didn't mean it!" He tugged at her legs, attempting to hug them. "I'm sorry," he repeated.

With his body leaning heavily against her legs, he dropped his forehead onto her knees. Dumbfounded, she stared down at the top of his head, not wanting to touch him. He looked up, eyes wide and apologetic. Reason pulled her legs out from beneath his grasp—his hands sliding down the full length of her calves.

William slumped to the floor, and almost immediately, Reason felt as if she had somehow caused the entire event—that she may have overreacted—that she may have hurt him first. Perhaps he had never intended to hurt her. Perhaps it was an accident. She leaned forward and laid a trembling hand on his down-turned head. "William...," she managed, "it's... okay."

They sat like this for some time, her hand on his head, Reason stunned into silence and William shaking and whimpering. She comforted him, the thought never occurring to her that he had not once attempted to comfort her.

6

burden of shame

❝ Wham bam! And just like that, I've crushed your spirit," snickered Pain.

Don't be so sure. I can still fight... I'll...

"Shut up. You're an insolent, annoying creature!"

Macy watched Reason's eyelids flutter and her breathing quicken. Then she bent down, placed her hand on Reason's shoulder, and whispered something for Reason's ears only.

༄ ༅

Shuddering, sweeping her hands across her thighs, Reason attempted to brush away the lingering sensation of William's touch. She held her breath, waiting for the disturbing feelings to settle, trying to focus on the sky above where wispy clouds fanned in a progressively widening wake. Gradually she returned to the present where Ruby, trustworthy and encouraging, waited patiently by her side.

"I can still feel him," she whispered. "I can feel his body shaking against my legs." Reason rubbed her thighs and jabbed at her calves. "So many years have gone by since that miserable day. Many times, I've thought about what happened. I've tried to justify why I accepted his apology. I've tried to understand why I didn't leave him then and there." Reason hung her head. "I've always been embarrassed... ashamed of my choice to stay."

"Don't get caught up in the shame, Reason. Carry on, dear. Carry on."

"Experiencing that time as it was, being there again... I was so young and naïve. But now I think I can understand my younger self from... a wider perspective." She paused, leaned her head back, and closed her eyes. "I can understand how I tried to process that moment—to pocket it. I can see, all these years later, how at that age I couldn't deal with that kind of shock and betrayal. It happened so fast, and my denial was practically immediate. I think I accepted his apology because I'd already taken the blame for what happened. I saw what he did as if it was something I caused." Reason shook her head. "But that reasoning... on its own... isn't enough. There's more to it." She looked at Ruby. "I couldn't get my head around the fact that anyone could be so cruel to me. I wanted him to love me." She smiled a little, pleased that she was finding a new understanding. "When I was younger, I think even starting as young as maybe seven or eight, I was such a perfectionist—and always looking for approval. I wanted to do what I thought was right and keep everyone happy. I used to think I was pretty good at it. But facing rejection or listening to criticism was something I didn't deal with well. So, when I couldn't avoid it, I'd just take the blame... and then work on fixing what was wrong with me." She groaned. "Being in that moment again, when he hit me for the first time... taking blame for what he did was second nature for me. Taking blame felt like taking control. All I wanted was for the whole shameful experience to go away like it never happened at all." An expression of surprise and recognition lifted her features. "I feel as if I can see it so clearly now. Taking blame was my first step down a long road of denial." She clasped her hands tightly and brought them to her chin. "And I remember how thoroughly I believed I had nowhere else to go. I couldn't bear the idea of my parents knowing my world had become so pathetic, and, at the time, I was pretty sure they didn't care."

"Denial can spread like an infection—contaminating everything in its path," said Ruby.

"Yes," admitted Reason. "Denial is like a shitty tattoo. You can cover it up or paint over it to try to make it something else, but it's never really gone. It's always right there just under the surface, making some sort of negative statement and reminding you of your poor decision." Reason eyed Ruby. "Do you know what I mean?"

Ruby nodded.

"It's easier to see the truth now," continued Reason. "Back then, I was too young and inexperienced. I didn't understand what was happening. I never understood why I thought so little of myself or why I accepted blame so readily. I think I see why now. I see that I had little self-esteem long before I met William. But back then, I didn't know. If only I'd been more aware." Reason felt a sudden surge of sadness. "I believed wholeheartedly that I had provoked William. I even thought that maybe I had meant to hurt him... because he was hurting me and I was angry. I thought I deserved what he did. What a ridiculous thing to believe. He hit me. His behavior was completely inappropriate. It should've been as simple as that."

"Do you think you judge yourself too harshly?" asked Ruby.

"Maybe. But the harsh judgment is because I'm still appalled that I didn't immediately leave him. I ought to have known I deserved better, but I felt inferior. I felt as if I wasn't good enough or pretty enough or smart enough. Crazy, isn't it, that kind of thinking?" Reason sighed in defeat. "So, here I am, sitting here with you in this strange place and revisiting the past." She put her hands to her head. "Is all this remembering supposed to make me feel less shame? Because if it is, it's not working." She hung her head. "Oh Ruby, I've so many horrible, miserable memories. Why didn't I demand better for myself?"

Ruby raised her chin and hands simultaneously, clapping her hands once. "Well, Reason, you've more work to do. Don't let the gravity of a perceived defeat get in your way. You've only just begun. You're already making progress." She took Reason's hands into her own. "Take a deep breath and tell me more."

○彡 ⌥

William's violent outburst had become their unspoken secret. Reason fully believed that the terrible experience would never happen again. After the incident, William had become very attentive—and extra affectionate at the slightest of misunderstandings. He had made Reason feel important to him, keeping track of where she was in the house, in the neighborhood, in the town. "Your shift ends at four-thirty, right?" he would confirm. "Yes," she would reply as he walked her to work. And with a squeeze of his hand, he would pull her close and add, "See you no later than four-forty-five. I'll be waiting." Life went on, and Reason believed that William's intentions were good. Oblivious to his growing control over her, she did not notice that he was methodically stripping her of her individuality and independence.

Masking his behavior as devotion, he began monitoring her constantly—systematically coaching Reason and gradually imposing more and more rules on her. William rarely left her alone, and in time, he no longer approved of her visiting with her friends, Cara and Ivy—convincing her they were jealous of her. "They want to break us apart."

"William, I...,"

"Listen to me. I know. They're jealous. I don't want to lose you. We don't need them. We only need each other."

Over time, she lost contact with her friends altogether. To cope with her loneliness, Reason began using drugs regularly—preferring an ongoing high to distract her from a heightening sense of self-disgust.

Before long William began regulating how Reason dressed—and even how she wore her hair. He began warning her to be careful about her clothing choices—grabbing at the waist of her jeans or tugging at her blouse and expressing his disapproval. With growing frequency, he began taking it upon himself to decide what she would wear—reserving certain articles of clothing for himself, holding them up in the air, closing in for a kiss, and whispering, "Wear this later, for me." In time, Reason became obsessed with her clothing, often scrutinizing her selections for anything that might garner William's criticism. And in these moments, seeing her face in the mirror, she would sometimes glimpse sadness. At first, this recognition would catch her off guard, and she would stare at her reflection as if she was looking at a stranger. But as she learned how to endure her life with William, and how to close herself off to feeling anything, she saw her sadness less and less.

Despite the overwhelming evidence confirming the devastating negatives in William's personality, Reason was caught in a raging current of her fear and denial. Instead of sensing a need to leave the unhealthy relationship, she remained bound to making right all the wrongs she perceived she had committed against it. With quiet determination, she sincerely believed she could wait out this awful spell, and that once again William's love would match her own.

But William had steadily become more aggressive, sometimes shoving her or grabbing her by her arm. He listened critically to what she said and how she said it, often disapproving of her tone. And on one occasion, when they had been sitting at his mother's kitchen table with his brother and his brother's friends, William's scowling face had lunged near to hers. He had seized her by her hair and snarled, "Move your fucking arm!" She had been casually resting her arm on the top edge of the chair beside her, a chair on which his younger brother sat. "You with him, or me?" he had hissed, while everyone at the table had shifted into a moment of uneasy quiet. Soon after, when she was leaving for her work, William's brother, younger than William by one year, followed her outside. As he approached, he appeared apologetic, shaking his head, raising his hands in exasperation, opening his mouth to speak. But before he could utter a word, William burst through the front door and hurled himself at his brother. The violent scuffle was brief but frightening. William's brother, who had not fought back, stood, brushed himself off, and without saying a word, walked back into the house. Albeit tenuous and futile, that occasion had been the only time that anyone had come to Reason's defense.

William's increasing violence, his cruelty toward Reason, and his control over her life—had her sink deeper into the wretchedness of her shame. Isolated and scared, she believed she had no options—and no one to turn to for help. Chronically anxious and often exhausted, she had built a mental barrier against all feeling, and despite the ongoing stress of William's growing abuse, Reason had become mired in a murky existence of mind-numbing endurance. Now and then, when the fog briefly lifted, instead of thinking that she deserved better, Reason often thought about what she was doing wrong in the relationship, how she could improve herself, and maybe, just maybe, win back William's love and respect.

CR &O

At midnight on an unusually sultry spring night in 1980, a break-in took place at a local fitness club. During the investigation the next morning, police found empty Orange Crush pop cans scattered throughout the facility. One can lay on the floor near the juice bar. The perpetrators left another one at the foot of a locker in the men's changing room. And in the hallway outside the manager's office, they left more cans at the end of a trail of orange-stained carpet. And one more, a full, unopened can, the culprits left atop the large and otherwise bare reception desk—the desk where Reason spent her working hours as the club's receptionist.

Orange Crush was William's favorite drink. When Reason saw the empty cans of pop strewn about, she was sure they were evidence of his involvement—and she was certain that she knew the purpose of the full can left on her desk. He meant for it to be a warning—a threat—left there to provoke a sense in her that she too was guilty of the break-in, and that she had better keep her mouth shut. While the police investigated, she had waited with the other employees, obsessing about the cans of pop, worrying that just by looking at them, her connection would become apparent. She fixed her gaze on the floor and tried not to fidget.

The facility kept the club's safe secured in a room on a locked floor, one story up from the main entry. When William had realized that he could not get to the safe, he had resorted to trashing the manager's office—and in the end, had stolen nothing but a few personal effects. Reason, who knew nothing of his plan to break in, had arrived for work that morning as usual, escorted by William. Agitated, he had parted from her much farther from the building than was his habit. She had walked by herself to the employee entrance at the rear, climbed the metal staircase, reached for the door, and paused when she saw that the normally locked door was ajar. Reason stood momentarily confused when the door had opened fully and a uniformed police officer had stepped out. She listened distractedly as the officer spoke. "Are you an employee?"

"Yes..."

"Your name?"

She said her name. He checked a list.

"Come in, but touch nothing."

"What? Why?" she stammered.

"There's been a break-in."

She moved past the police officer; her stomach twisted at the sight of the damaged door. With slow, sickening certainty, Reason sensed William's involvement. She said nothing about her suspicions. The police did not question her and simply sent her home along with the other employees. They never caught William for the break-in. And, by connecting Reason to it through her feelings of guilt, he had further secured his control over her.

☙ ❧

A fall chill hung in the air when William broke into the local department store at two o'clock in the morning. Thinking his plan ingenious, he and a friend had climbed in through an accessible unlocked rooftop vent, and then down through the paneled ceiling directly below. From there, they had dropped into the menswear department. But before their feet hit the floor, they had set off the store's security system. Store video captured it all and made for an easy conviction. And because William had served probation for an earlier offence, this time the presiding judge thought it time for a stiffer punishment—sentencing him to two years less a day in a minimum-security penitentiary. But three factors came into play to alter the actual time he served: The first was that minor offenders got released early because of an overcrowded jail. The second was that William received credit for time served while awaiting trial. And thirdly the court required offenders to serve only three-quarters of their full sentence.

REASONS | Sherry denBoer

During the trial and his time in prison, Reason lived at William's mother's house, moving through its rooms like a ghost. No one in the house paid her much attention, and she had not minded. Every day, she worried about William's release, fearing being with him again, wanting to escape. But she had proven herself to be a fool. She had let everybody down—her family, her friends—everyone. She couldn't face them, and she was certain they would turn her away, anyway. So, still very much under William's control—having little money and thinking that she had no one to turn to for help—she could think of nowhere to go.

William had made it clear to Reason that he expected her to visit him regularly at the penitentiary. Fear made her comply. During the visits, he harassed her—demanding that she smuggle acid into the prison. "You know what happens when you say no to me." While she avoided giving in to his demands by using several excuses, she knew that upon his release, she would pay the price for her noncompliance. And when she occasionally missed a visit, William accused her of cheating. "Where were you last week? Did you take the bus here today? Did someone drive you? Who? You fucking him?" He threatened her imagined lover with violence, and even promised harm to members of her own family. He made these threats vehemently, and Reason knew that he could absolutely follow through. So, she visited him obediently almost every Sunday and became reluctantly familiar with the cool authority of the prison guards—the reverberating clang of bolts and latches—and the somber droning of the facility's many electronic doors.

The prison visits were always difficult and depressing. Once inside the prison walls, at the third of three visitor checkpoints, Reason endured the "person, package, and purse inspection". She would watch silently and awkwardly as the guards dumped out the contents of her purse and searched through every item—emptying her change purse—opening her cosmetics case, twirling out her lipstick, dumping out her tampons. Then came the frisking as the guard patted his hand up under her skirt or pushed it deep into her pants pocket. Feeling insignificant and violated, Reason would hold her breath and stoically comply—knowing that a guard could execute his right to call for a full strip search.

With the series of unsettling inspections completed, Reason would join the other visitors as the guards led them through a sequence of long hallways fitted with several reinforced doors. Eventually, she and the others entered into a large, bleak room with unadorned walls of concrete block painted a sterile white. Within it was a reinforced, windowed cubicle that housed two additional guards. Each visitor would take a seat on a chair at a table bolted to the cement floor. And there they would wait—lost in thought—some solemnly, others eagerly watching the door from which the inmates would appear. Reason's gaze would wander to the visiting families, and sometimes, she would envy the innocence of the excited children, who cared only that they were about to see their daddy.

The journey to the penitentiary was long and dismal. Each Sunday before sunrise, Reason would join a group of women—the sisters, wives, girlfriends, daughters, mothers, and grandmothers of the prisoners—all gathered like a reluctant congregation in the side chapel of an inner-city church. The church workers required each visitor to recite her name, and the name of the incarcerated she was going to visit, and then move single file into a long white van.

In the stifling heat of mid-summer, windows open mere inches, the van lumbered down the highway with its lackluster occupants riding in stony silence. Tightly packed, the sweat-soaked passengers bounced in unison on worn bench seats, the silence between them broken now and again by a mother quieting her child, a cough, or the stifled sob of a passenger making the trip for the first time.

With little outward emotion, Reason tolerated the grim journey. But without fail, and most often just as the van wheeled out of the church parking lot, she would become preoccupied with her clothing choices—nervously examining the cut of her blouse or the length of her skirt, wondering whether William would praise or admonish her. Her obsessive fussing would last for the first twenty minutes of the trip, and then sighing resignedly, Reason would gaze out the window, and welcome the distraction of the fast-moving landscape.

Two hours later, nearing the prison, she would begin mentally preparing herself for the visit, closing her eyes at the thought of William sliding to the edge of his chair—as he did each visit—and despite her silent protests, reaching to slip his hand inside her blouse. Often the other inmates would stare and snicker, and then curse and heckle when the prison guard would catch on and shout, "NO PHYSICAL CONTACT!" Stuck inside the sweltering van and thinking of these things, Reason would bow her head and try to tame her growing anxiety.

For Reason, the months of William's incarceration passed far too quickly. And then, once again complying with his order, she was present to meet him upon his release. She stood alone—steeling herself for the sight of the dark green prison van that would pull into the parking lot and drop him off. When it did, he stepped from the small bus, walked directly to her, put his arms about her, pulled away, and ripped open her blouse. Stunned and horrified, Reason gasped and clutched the fabric closed. William pushed his face uncomfortably close to hers. "No fucking bra?" And then he pressed his lips against her ear. "No fucking drugs?" She stood stamped in place—humiliated, heart pounding, watching in a daze as he smirked, turned, and walked away.

Petite and small-breasted, Reason often went without a bra. She could do so discreetly. William had never complained. But on this day, he had chosen a public place to chastise and humiliate her because she had refused him drugs in jail. She was, of course, expected to follow him as he sauntered off, and afraid of what might happen if she did not, she did so in a despondent haze. Walking behind him, gripping the fabric of her torn blouse, all the downtown noises went quiet.

C3 80

Reason opened her eyes, visibly troubled. Ruby took her hand. "You're completely safe here with me," she said firmly. "You're doing fine. Releasing those buried memories will free you from their power." She squeezed Reason's hand again. "Remember that you're not really there with William, where your light was so methodically dimmed. And you're revisiting a tiny piece of your full life. All the pieces are valuable, no matter what they entail. Each moment is a consequence of the one before. You are here, Reason, because you were there." Ruby smiled, her gaze direct and compassionate. "Somewhere along your life journey, you began to carry the burden of shame. Since then you could not shake it, thinking that you deserved it. Sometime along your journey, you noticed the weight of this shame and wanted to escape its burden, but you didn't know how. Eventually, you realized the value of letting shame go and you became driven to find a way. Remember that fact. And in moments of overwhelming despair, remember that the truth awaits and that there's always more to learn and discover." Ruby sat back, pausing, smiling tenderly. "To be released from your shame, you must face its source head-on. When you do, you'll understand that shame and your time with William have served a purpose. You'll learn to accept this purpose with an open heart, and by doing so, free yourself of shame's control. Acceptance is the key to letting go. So, go on dear, go on and see yourself for all that you are."

"I'll try, Ruby. I'll try my best. But please, don't leave me," whispered Reason.

"You are never alone," said Ruby reassuringly.

Reason closed her eyes.

7

a little piece at a time

At fourteen, Reason watched with a mild but growing envy as her girlfriends blossomed before her eyes, maturing much earlier than her, and buying new clothes to suit their changing bodies. At sixteen, she remained disappointed, her figure still vexingly boyish. And because people often assumed that she was several years younger than her actual age, Reason felt limited and frustrated by her undeveloped figure and girlish features. At last, just before her seventeenth birthday, Reason moved into womanhood. Her mother had educated her on the facts of menstruation, but she had mentioned nothing about sex and the feelings and choices faced by a teenager new to that kind of intimacy. Reason was a virgin when she met William, just a few weeks after that seventeenth birthday.

On the afternoon that Reason lost her virginity, she had wondered why people called it a loss of innocence or purity. The word loss made her feel that she was somehow at fault, and the phrase, loss of innocence and purity, made her feel that she had somehow become spoiled. For Reason, losing her virginity had felt more like a violation, the experience very different from the way she had imagined.

The sun shone brightly that afternoon. But once its light had filtered through the dirt-smudged window of the high-rise apartment, and passed through the slit in the pulled curtains, its brightness was significantly subdued and the apartment remained dull and grey. William and Reason had been dating for three months when, in that darkened room—lustful, hell-bent—and showing little regard for Reason's feelings, William's hands hungrily groped her body. He heaved himself on top of her, his pants pulled down below his knees. His body heavy, he pressed her thin frame into the worn springs of an

89

old couch, his breath hot on her neck. And at the sudden stinging pain that radiated up from below, her body tensed and she instinctively pulled away. But William pulled her back and kept moving, raising himself so that his chest swayed back and forth a few inches above her face.

As her body moved under the thrusting motion of his, for a few seconds Reason wondered when the love-making would feel tender and passionate. Lost in this thought, she stared blankly at the muted television screen opposite her, where some woman was smiling amiably into the camera. The woman on the television chattered endlessly and pointed at a painting of tiny yellow flowers clustered into diamond shapes and traveling in a single vertical line up the center of a blue canvas. William adjusted his position, moved his arm, and blocked her view. Reason waited for it to be over.

She had protested, albeit weakly. No, she didn't want to have sex. Earlier, on the couch, she had kissed and hugged him, testing the water, not wanting to disappoint him, unsure of what to do. But William had persuaded her onto her back and moved his body on top of her. He had responded to her reluctance by pressing his hand lightly over her mouth. It smelled of nicotine. He put a finger to his lips. "Shh," he said, and kissed her. "I've waited a long time," he whispered, unzipping his fly.

When finished, neither attentive nor loving, William rolled off Reason and onto the floor. She felt miserable. Regret surged forth in waves. She watched him move to turn up the volume on the television, his pants still bunched around his ankles. She felt disgusted and embarrassed by his nakedness, and by her own. He sat back and kicked off his pants, and with his back to her, lit a cigarette. "Wanna smoke?" he asked, not bothering to look at her, merely holding the cigarette pack over his head.

Reason had been too upset to answer—with a sickening feeling growing in the pit of her stomach as she watched William shrug his shoulders and drop the pack of cigarettes to the floor. Behind him, she pulled on her underwear and straightened her t-shirt, holding back her tears. As William smoked and watched the television, she moved past him and into the bathroom where, closing the door, she clamped her hand over her mouth to stifle the sound of her weeping.

ɔʒ ɛo

Tacked to the white-tiled ceiling was a poster of a doctor. The young doctor grinned down at Reason, but even with his wide, toothy smile, he seemed to scold her. In his outstretched hand, he held a pink pamphlet about birth control. She shifted on the hard surface of the table and the thin sheet of paper beneath her ripped. Another stiff sheet of paper floated on top of her—and was no comfort at all. Cold metal stirrups bit into the soles of her feet where the clinic doctor, a man in his mid-forties, sat on a rolling stool. Silent tears slid from the corners of Reason's eyes. She was eight weeks pregnant.

Through the ever-present grapevine, Cara had heard about Reason's pregnancy and had taken it upon herself to call Reason's mother. And later that day, with her mother waiting in the apartment lobby, Reason had stood staring at the intercom, fighting to find a trace of courage, stunned that her mother had found her, and relieved that she had found her alone. Leaving the apartment, her mother had driven them to a park, to a local lookout point which they had often visited as a family. Side by side, Reason and her mother had sat and stared at the lively view of the harbor, the world seeming light and lovely everywhere but inside the car.

"The choice is yours," her mother explained, her tone soft yet resolute. Unable to stop crying, Reason could not respond. "Please... look at me," urged her mother, reaching over and laying her hand on top of Reason's, but Reason could not make herself turn her head. "You're so young. A baby will be very difficult to take care of with no money and no experience. You're so..." Her mother made a stifled noise. Reason stole a glance her way and thought that she might be crying. Her mother looked out the side window and then rolled it all the way down. Cold air rushed into the car. "You're so young," she said out the open window. "But it's your choice, and I'll support whatever you choose. And," her mother paused. Reason stared straight ahead. "It's okay if you want an abortion. You've so little life experience. Your future...." Her voice trailed off. She was clearly crying. She looked at her hands, closed her eyes, and then returned her gaze to Reason. And when Reason saw her mother's tear-streaked face, shame overcame her. In her mother's expression seemed to be the loss of the future that she had dreamed for Reason, and dying with it was her mother's hope. All Reason could think was that she wanted her mother's pain to end.

She chose to terminate the pregnancy. The week leading up to the procedure was full of fear, anxiety, and uncertainty. But when the whole sordid affair was over, Reason began immediately to bury the experience—and make it her dark secret. Allowed back into her parents' home to begin her convalescence, she was recuperating on the family room couch when her father arrived home. But she could not look at him, closing her eyes tightly when he bent to her and kissed her forehead. Neither of them said a word.

For many months now, Reason had found the events in her life to be distressingly overwhelming. At barely seventeen, she had experienced her first period, met William, been told to leave her parents' home, been homeless, had sex thrust upon her, and had endured the agonizing complexities of an abortion. Her self-reproach seemed well deserved.

Five weeks passed before William showed up banging on her parents' front door, her father at work, her mother at one of her many volunteer jobs. Reason's life back at home had been going well, all things considered. They weren't talking all that much, but when they did, the conversation between Reason and her parents was positive. The fighting between them had stopped. "Been long enough," William said, holding the screen door open.

"William, I..."

He slapped his hand against the brick wall. "What did I tell you?" he snarled.

"William, please. I want to stay here."

"Well, you fucking can't!" He yelled and grabbed her by the arm. The family dog, a small terrier tied up in the unfenced backyard and disturbed by the shouting, barked and whined. "Do I need to quiet that fucking dog—right fucking now—or are you coming?" he hissed.

Reason gathered her meager belongings and left her parents a scribbled note: "Thanks, Mom. Love you both, Reason."

No one in the family spoke of the pregnancy ever again. Her parents seemed to have ceased to acknowledge it just a few short days after the procedure. Whether her siblings knew of it, Reason did not know. No one asked her about it. No one asked her how she was. No one said how they felt. Everyone carried on as if the ended pregnancy had never happened. Reason felt certain that the silence was because it was so shameful. Such an act, like so many things she had experienced, did not deserve the light of day.

CB BO

As time went on, alone and vulnerable, Reason's routine became surviving each day and making ends meet financially. She had not made a conscious choice to stay with William. She had simply believed that leaving him was impossible. And despite everything, desperate for a sense of closeness and connection, she maintained an insufferable belief that she could fix their relationship and regain his love.

CB BO

The stone bench cold against her back, Reason shivered. The air had dampened, and twilight was closing in. Sitting up, she suppressed an urge to run, to escape her dismal memories. Mortified, ashamed of her past, and shocked by her own story, she dreaded the thought of continuing it. She stared at Ruby, expecting outrage. But Ruby tilted her head and smiled, her expression one of compassion and love—and once again she urged Reason to continue.

CB BO

After a long night at her job counting inventory, Reason had arrived back at the apartment and fallen into a deep sleep on the living room couch. A loud thudding roused her. Opening her eyes, she saw morning light behind the long brown curtains at the balcony window. And caught between a dream state and wakefulness, she became easily transfixed by a white shaft of light penetrating the dark room. It streamed in through a narrow crack in the curtains, falling like a laser beam upon a single white daisy set atop a nearby table. A little wilted, the flower's thin stem arched out from a clear glass vase. Lit as it was, it appeared almost heavenly.

Reason had received the flower from a homeless man. He had been sitting on the grimy sidewalk—feet bare—pants rolled up to his knees. Having little money, she had given him a handful of change scrounged from her pants pocket. His eyes had been extraordinary—large and kind, the color of purple twilight. And for a split second, as she received the flower from his hand, she had felt a sudden wonderful sensation of contentment. Staring at the daisy now, she felt a faint sense of hope.

A banging at the apartment door shattered her moment of calm. William's hushed but irritated voice sounded from the hallway, "Open the damn door!" Startled out of her sleepy haze, she stumbled from the couch, and the moment the door became unlocked, it sprang open and smashed into her shoulder. The physical pain, like what she often endured at William's hand, barely fazed her anymore. He pushed her aside. Then he and a man she did not recognize barged into the apartment, each of them hauling an overstuffed garbage bag. They dragged the bags through the narrow doorway and into the tiny kitchen opposite.

Reason glanced at the clock on the stove—10:23. And then she watched with weary indifference as the two men dumped the contents of the bags. Boxes of cigarettes, bags of candies and cookies, pairs of jeans, deodorant, jewelry, and other items spilled out onto the kitchen floor. William sifted through the mess and picked up a bracelet made of tiny green and white beads. He passed it to her. "We did it right this time," he said with a smirk. "Take it. It's for you." Reason reluctantly took the bracelet. Later that day, she flushed it down the toilet.

❧ ❦

In the bleak days that followed the robbery, Reason had suffered tremendously—enduring bouts of crippling anxiety and mounting fear—and fighting back despairing thoughts as she planned her escape while pretending that nothing had changed, stashing away a few dollars here and there, the bit of her spending money that William did not control. But even in the face of her appalling situation, a spark of life had managed to survive. A tiny piece of her old spirit was breaking through the haze and was telling her she deserved better. Despite William's threats to her life, she decided she would rather die than live as she was. She began to plan how she would leave, knowing that she must be patient. She needed time to put some money aside, and to plan where she would go—knowing that she would have to go into hiding and move out of town.

Early in her planning, she and William attended a wedding with his mother and his mother's boyfriend. Reason was loath to go, but she knew she must keep up appearances. The event would ultimately lead to an incident that would set her plan in motion.

They all sat together, a seemingly happy family. William, handsome and charming, spent most of the reception flirting with the single girls or smoking joints outside the service entry. Charismatic, he easily hid his dark side, and the few who had witnessed his violence maintained their silence. He treated Reason like a possession, and she felt like one. She looked around at the surrounding tables and wondered how many of the faces there concealed their own sorrows. Closing her eyes, she listened to the din of tinkling cutlery and mingling voices, and found the sounds to be soothing. Dreamily, she imagined herself walking to the exit and disappearing. Loud music boomed. She opened her eyes. The disc jockey was beginning his set. She watched a crowd of cheerful people file onto the dancefloor. Then, miserable and picking at her food, she eyed the clock and waited for the evening to end.

During her time with William, she had learned to obey him. She had lost contact with all her friends and all of her family. Living in fear, she had tried to please William, but she had learned that there was no pleasing him. Despite the danger, she wanted her life back.

She wanted her life to have some meaning. Gradually, she had felt capable of starting a new life without him. Thinking of this, sitting at their table at the wedding reception, she had felt stifled and suffocated, and was finding it difficult to suppress her desire to bolt.

Reason was nineteen.

A tap on her shoulder startled her. Instinctively, she glanced at William. His head turned away; he was busy talking with his mother. Over Reason's shoulder, a young man stood smiling down at her. He pointed toward the dance floor and mouthed, "Wanna dance?" Understanding the likely consequence of doing so, she got up from the table and followed the young man to the dance floor. William had not noticed.

They danced to a slow song. "I ain't missing you at all..." Reason sang quietly into the young man's shoulder.

"You like John Waite?" he asked.

"I like this song," said Reason. They danced close together, his hands placed lightly on her lower back and hers around his neck. He danced stiffly and self-consciously. She liked the feel of being held by someone she did not fear. She danced freely, closing her eyes and imagining that this moment was one from her new life. For two glorious minutes, Reason felt transported to another place.

And then, without warning, William yanked her away by her elbow and held on. He shouted at the young man who, looking shocked, took a step back, and then disappeared into the crowd. Then William turned to Reason. With both hands, he shoved her in the chest. She fell awkwardly, and from the floor, watched him walk away. No one came to help her to her feet. The music changed tempo. A disco ball twirled overhead. White balls of light slid across the floor, scaled the walls, and skittered across the ceiling. And in a rush of adrenalin, anger burned through her embarrassment. Lifting herself from the pulsating dance floor, she brushed off her clothes and stood defiantly. Fury drove her as she marched back to their table. At long last, Reason wanted more than merely to survive William's wrath; she wanted to thrive with him knowing it. She stopped behind his chair, and ready for whatever might happen, calmly planted her hand firmly at the base of his neck. He flinched for an instant, but remained facing forward. His skin was sweaty. She leaned toward his ear and pressed her nails into his flesh. "Never treat me like that again. You do not own me. I am not yours. Not anymore." She took her seat next to him as he delivered her a long, cold stare. She felt an unfamiliar emotion filling her up like an elixir. It felt like pride.

Reason endured the rest of the reception with a new, calm dignity. On the drive home, William's mother sat in the passenger seat and talked incessantly, while William sat in stony silence beside Reason in the back seat. She blocked out the sound of his mother's voice and stared out the side window.

Rain glazed slippery black on the asphalt where the street lights glared in large shimmering patches of blurry white. The windshield wipers swiped back and forth, back and forth, their repetitive tempo a soothing sound to Reason. Dreading what lay ahead, she concentrated on their beat, hearing in it a rhythmical composition: "Aheeek, thunk... aheeek, thunk..." She watched the tiny raindrops slide along the glass, band together, and then stream off into the darkness—and imagined herself spilling out into the blackness too—freed. Sitting next to William, she could sense his simmering rage. She turned and faced him, refusing him her fear. He smiled a slow, sickening grin. They were to spend that night at his mother's boyfriend's house, so boldly looking him in the eye, Reason felt hopeful that she would be safe for at least this one night—and then, in the morning, she would find a way to escape.

When they arrived back at the house, Reason slipped into the bedroom—seeking solitude. The room was cold, and the rain smacked the darkened window in blustery sheets. She stood holding an oversized t-shirt in her hands, about to pull it over her head, when William entered the room. He stared at her and then turned, moving in stiff increments to face the door. Pressing it closed, for an agonizing moment, he remained there, unmoving and silent.

"William...,"

"Shut the fuck up," he spewed in an angry whisper.

"Leave me al..." He lunged, snatching the t-shirt from her hands. "Give me the shirt, William!" she demanded, desperate to cover her nakedness. He tossed the t-shirt to the floor and charged, seizing her by her arm, wrenching it up over her head. Grabbing a handful of her hair, William yanked Reason off her feet. Searing pain ripped through her scalp. She reached up, but thrown sideways, folded her arm across her chest to minimize her impact with the bed—crying out when she crashed against it. William let go of her arm, but held her by her hair a moment longer. Reason screamed out in pain, and when he let go, she crumpled in a heap. But William immediately reached down and hauled her up by both wrists. Her skin burned beneath his grasp. Hanging awkwardly, Reason kicked at William's legs. He released one of her arms and she grabbed at his face, but he punched her below her ribs. The air left her body in a guttural holler. He released her other arm, and she fell forward, retching and moaning. The next blow came down from above, landing on her temple. A screeching whine filled her head. She swiped at William, finding only air. He kicked her into the wall, her knee and ankle hitting first, her chin and elbow next. She collapsed to the floor, hanging on, fighting fiercely for focus. Like a wild animal, through the strands of her long hair, Reason glared up at William—loathing him. His face was purple-red. He sprang at her again, but the bedroom door swung open so quickly that it slammed against the wall. William stopped mid lunge and turned to confront the intruder.

His mother's boyfriend rushed in and then stopped and stared at William—looking angry, then surprised, and then fearful as he took in William's demeanor. He took a step backward and looked from William to Reason crouched on the floor, bleeding and bruised. He stared at her nakedness. She felt disgusted and pathetic, but grateful for the intrusion. "Keep the fucking noise down," the boyfriend muttered, his gaze lingering on Reason. And then, to her horror, he merely backed out of the room, leaving the door open—a small mercy. William sucked in his cheeks, gathered spit, and hurled it at Reason. She did not flinch. The interruption was enough to end the beating.

William undressed, sat on the bed, and scowled at her. "Get up. Get into bed." She said nothing and crawled to the farthest corner—naked, shaking, and cold. Dreading that he might drag her to the bed, Reason held her breath—but William left her alone. She waited until he had fallen asleep and then reached for her t-shirt—remaining curled up on the floor, her back against the wall. And there she stayed—awake and trembling through the long hours of the night.

In the morning, Reason pretended to be asleep when William got up from the bed. He walked across the floor and stood over her for some minutes before leaving the room. She dressed to the sounds of him and his mother talking and laughing in the kitchen down the hall. His mother had always turned away from his dark side, denying its existence even when he aimed it at her.

Later that day, at the first safe chance she received, Reason made her way to a payphone. She dialed Detective Newman, told him about the garbage bags full of loot, and where he could find them.

8

the cowboy

" Why are you always blocking the light?"
"Because I like the dark."
"I want you to leave."
"I don't care about what you want."
"You're cruel. But I'll... change that."
"Well, dearie," scoffed Pain, "you can always dream."

Lying on her back, eyes closed, as she waited for sleep to take her away, Reason felt a strange sensation. She clutched onto the bedsheet as an odd feeling took hold. She had an uncanny sense that she existed in two places at once. Eager to explore the feeling further, she pushed aside Pain's incessant squawking and drew in a long breath—releasing the air slowly. Pain's voice became a low mutter. And before she had fully inhaled for the second time, Reason remembered her recent dreams—dreams so vivid that they felt real. She wanted to return to them. She wanted to know what they meant.

She relaxed. Pain went quiet. Sleep came.

ଔ ଓ

Pleased with Reason's progress, after watching her for some minutes, Miss A. Macy Grace held Reason's hand and then took care to tuck the blankets around her shoulders. Then, with her book in hand, Macy moved to her chair by the window. For a long while, she watched the traffic, and then she smiled and resumed reading.

ଔଓ

REASONS | Sherry denBoer

The sky was especially brilliant; the sun shining bright white. Reason shielded her eyes to get a better look. *Him again?* She had first noticed the man in the cowboy hat about three weeks before. He had entered a downtown café just as she had exited. He was hard to miss— a bigger-than-life sort of fellow, standing out from the crowd, easy to remember, wearing what appeared to be genuine western attire from head to toe. Reason had seen him three times in the last two weeks, and this time, the fourth time, he tipped his hat and addressed her. "Hello, darlin'."

Hello, darlin'? Who talks like that? She found the cowboy's behavior amusing and acknowledged him with a quick smile. Pushing open the large glass door, she moved past him into the college foyer. But at that moment, a sudden surge of anxiety rippled through her, and a few paces into the large open entrance hall, she stopped to look back. To her surprise, and causing her instant alarm, outside the closing door, the cowboy stood facing her. He tipped his hat again and then turned and walked away. Reason looked behind her. No one else was nearby. She turned back. The cowboy had disappeared. She put her face close to the glass and peered out. He was nowhere to be seen. *Relax,* she thought, dropping her hands from the cool, smooth surface of the window. *You're safe. You're perfectly safe.* She looked outside again, and then turned and made her way to her first class.

挅 挆

Detective Newman had come in person to make the arrest. William was eventually found guilty and handed his sentence by the same judge who had presided over his previous conviction. And this time, the judge had ordered that William would serve his full term.

After the arrest, life had brightened considerably for Reason. She had moved to a new town, enrolled in college, and was well into the first year of a three-year business course. One month after William's arrest, while living in her new town, she had met with a professor at the local college. He was a meticulous and kindhearted man, who, with a grandfatherly air and a compassionate smile, had encouraged her to enroll.

Returning to school had not been a straightforward decision. Although Reason's first two years of high school had been exciting, and she had found it easy to excel, by grade thirteen, discouraged with her studies and having just begun dating William, she had quit halfway through the school year. She had been away from formal classes for four years and would return as a mature student. All this considered, she had wondered if she could find her way back to the success that she had once known. Profoundly grateful for the second chance, when permitted a grant and a loan, she enrolled, worked hard, and soon thrived academically.

During the arrest, everyone had gathered in the narrow front hallway of the small apartment. Seeing her cuts and bruises, Detective Newman had shot Reason an anguished look, and then returned his attention to William and forcefully fit the cuffs onto his wrists.

Uncertainty filled the hours after the arrest. When the elevator doors had closed, with the detective having taken William away in handcuffs, Reason had slipped into the bedroom, slumped to the floor, and wrestled with her anxiety. Fearing that the charges might not stick, she waited nervously for news—worrying that William would find out that it had been she who had tipped off the police. But Detective Newman, a man of his word, did not reveal Reason's involvement.

With William gone, Reason was free to walk away—and she found this new feeling of liberation extremely unfamiliar. Before she lost the opportunity, she bundled her meager belongings together and, without saying a word, left. On her first evening of independence, curled up on a narrow cot at the local YMCA, she waited for sleep—savoring the new sense of relief, hardly believing it, but settling into the calm of being free. She lay in a somber room full of strangers, and yet Reason overflowed with contentment. The thin blanket pulled to her chin, and her small case of belongings safely tucked between her back and the wall, she made a promise to herself. She resolved to prove, to herself and to the people with whom she had lost contact, that she could do better, and be a better person. She would work long and hard to redeem herself and maybe one day, if she could prove herself worthy, her family would accept her back.

Meanwhile, despite his incarceration, William was devising his own plans for Reason's future.

CB ත

Heavy-eyed, Reason stirred. Above her, a face hovered, its features resisting definition before coming into focus. The face was Ruby's. She smiled and then moved away. And as her face slid off to one side, Reason saw the night sky—a dazzling spray of stars surrounding a breathtaking, multicolored galaxy. She gasped.

"Impressive, isn't it?" said Ruby in a soft voice, her face reverent as she stared upward at the boundless celestial display.

The fathomless night sky tugged at Reason. It seemed to draw her in. She felt as if she was falling into its vastness, and the sensation became so convincing it unnerved her. She sat up. "Whoa! I felt as if I was about to... drop into all of those stars. At first the feeling was so peaceful, then I... well, then I thought I was falling—and it scared me."

"Letting go of the rational mind can be wonderful—and that's what you experienced. You felt the limitlessness of the sky because you let go of thought and gave yourself over to your senses. Your experience was fleeting, but for a few exquisite seconds, you were strictly an observer and connected to the boundless splendor of the universe. Until your rational mind intruded," said Ruby matter-of-factly.

With the stars lacing the night sky, and the moonlight washing the land in shades of blue-grey and mauve, Reason settled back onto the stone bench, hoping to find her way back to the sky's hypnotic magic. But the memories of her story rushed forth and she sat upright. "I left him," she whispered—a tinge of sadness in her voice.

"Yes. You did."

She pressed the heel of her hand to her forehead. "I feel like I should be happy to tell you that. But I feel so empty, as if the shame of it all has tainted everything good."

"Revisiting your past will not immediately rid you of shame," said Ruby. "But being present in your own story will bring you closer to the truth, and the truth will lead you to the root of your shame and from there, to acceptance. My dear Reason, try not to agonize at every step. Just be present as you take it."

Ruby pointed to the sky. "Look. Do you see?" In the distance, flying toward one another, two tiny spheres of white light moved across the night sky. As they came together, in unison, they suddenly plunged straight down and then swung in a wide-sweeping arc toward the terrace.

"What are they?" Reason asked, wide-eyed at the sight.

"Carriers—transportation that will take us to a quiet place where you can rest before continuing your story."

"Wait. We're about to fly?" Reason stepped toward the railing. The white orbs drew nearer, growing larger.

"We are indeed."

The spheres, moving at a tremendous speed, quickly neared the terrace. Reason stepped back from the railing, watching in amazement as the machines slowed to a crawl and crossed over her head. Together, the carriers lowered to the terrace where they hovered and hummed. Inside each one, a dark shape hung abstract and shadow-like. "Come," said Ruby, moving toward the two suspended balls of light.

The idling carriers glowed—each one round, but with indistinct edges that seemed almost woolly in appearance. And visible inside each machine, wavering fluid-like, was a shadowy silhouette resembling the shape of an angel's wings. "Do as I do," said Ruby, stepping inside the nearest machine. She moved effortlessly into the glowing matter, and once fully inside, turned to face Reason. She stood with her legs slightly parted, and her arms raised as if they rested on invisible supports. Reason moved toward the unoccupied orb, holding her breath, her cheeks bulging. Ruby laughed. "It's not liquid, dear. No need to hold your breath." Her voice was distant but clear. "There's nothing to it. Come now, step inside."

Reason stepped into the glow. She felt immediately warmed as the inner shadowy substance adapted to her shape and embraced her from head to toe. She found she could move with ease and breathe without difficulty. She bent her knees and extended her elbows, the substance swelling, and folding, and accommodating her every movement. She raised her arms as she had seen Ruby do. The inner material guided them, lowering each arm until it was in a horizontal position and resting comfortably. And as the shadowy substance continued to fit Reason within it, appearing to harness her in place, Ruby spoke again, her voice clear and crisp and streaming into Reason's ears as if through a headset.

"Although we mostly program these machines with predetermined itineraries, for our journey, I will pilot both using voice recognition. While in flight, you'll hear my voice only when I am addressing you. You'll hear my voice exactly as you hear it now, and if you choose to, you can talk back. Look down to your feet. Do you see the pink dot? If you want to talk to me, step on it and speak." Ruby watched Reason locate the pink dot.

"Can you hear me?" Reason asked eagerly.

"I can."

Am I really going to do this?

As if in answer to Reason's unspoken question, Ruby asked, "Ready for takeoff?"

"Right now? Already? I..."

"Relax. You'll be fine. It'll be fun."

Reason smiled weakly. "I guess I'm as ready as I'll ever be. Are we going far? Can we land somewhere if I become panicky? Can you really pilot my carrier too?"

"Take a deep breath, Reason. Our trip is relatively short and we can land whenever and wherever we choose. But I prefer to stick to the plan. You'll be fine. Trust me. Piloting the two carriers is a straightforward task. Now, are you ready?"

Reason clutched anxiously at the substance surrounding her. "It feels strange having nothing completely solid to grab onto. Okay... fine; I'm ready. Let's just get on with it."

105

Ruby's calm, confident voice sounded within Reason's carrier. "Command carrier one. Tag carrier two. Destination Buoyant..." Her voice faded. Reason moaned as her carrier responded to the command; the machine's low drone rising in pitch. The carrier moved across the terrace and then lifting, climbed alongside the railing. Reason held her breath as it moved beyond the railing and hovered. She looked down. The carrier dropped. Her body lifted, and the substance held on. She screamed. The shadowy substance gripped her and held her firmly in place. The craft dropped mercilessly and then finally eased into a horizontal trajectory. Reason squealed as the sudden change in the direction pushed her backward and the shadowy harness pulled her back into position. She laughed, childlike. In the distance, hurtling through the sky like a shooting star, Ruby's carrier led the way.

Fearing that the distance between them had grown too great, Reason glanced apprehensively at the pink dot at her feet. But Ruby's carrier soon grew larger, and in a few quick seconds, Reason's had caught up. Together, the two carriers slowed and eventually stopped—hovering side by side, the luminous galaxy glimmering above, a mauve mist swirling below.

"How do you like the ride so far?" came Ruby's voice from the twin orb.

"Unbelievable. It's crazy!"

"Let's have some more fun, shall we?"

Before Reason could respond, the two carriers sunk into the mist below—a thick purple haze that promptly engulfed them both. Eyes wide, she strained to see into the dense fog—gasping as her carrier cleared the purple mist and continued its descent, rushing toward a river far below. Settling into the intense downward motion, Reason squealed with delight as her craft slowed, changed direction, and then raced forward, skimming over the glassy surface of the water.

Bright starlight shed a buttery glow on the scene ahead. The two crafts navigated the meandering course of the river—their shadows skittering across the rugged mountainside—mountains so steep they flanked the waterway like skyscrapers lining a narrow city street.

Reason's carrier slowed and stopped—hovering above the water—the machine's glowing exterior softly pulsating.

Reason's excited gaze wandered over everything. Beneath her, and below the calm water, was a pristine riverbed of luminous white sand. Above, the thick mauve mist had dissipated. And ahead, the surface of the river wore an impeccable reflection of the mountains and the starry night sky. A large fish suddenly jumped from the water. Reason glimpsed its glistening yellow form before it disappeared into a whisper of a splash, leaving behind one round ripple of water. She watched the circular wave of water expand. And then all at once fish were everywhere—bright flashes of color wriggling and darting, all swimming toward the narrowing channel ahead. Reason stepped on the pink dot. "What a beautiful sight! And the water... the reflection is perfect." Ahead, as a large school of fish swam beneath it, the celestial image reflected on the water swelled, and then it quivered with the movement. And when the last of the fish had disappeared, the river returned to a state of glassy-smooth tranquility.

"Yes, the river is beautiful. And almost always serene," said Ruby. "Day and night, no matter the activity above or below, its mysterious properties always return it to a wonderful state of tranquility. The river reflects all that it observes. It is suitably called the River of Reflection. It serves as a reminder to us that stillness within is always possible. And that no matter how uncertain or troubling an experience may at first appear, the ability to observe it from a place of clarity and calm, is possible."

"How lovely."

"Indeed," said Ruby. "And now, dear Reason, we move on."

"Okay. Part of me hates to leave this place."

"We must go. But you can use this feeling of calm for what comes next." Reason shot Ruby a quizzical eye. "Don't worry about a thing. Just follow my instructions." Reason relaxed a little. "Keeping your arms where they are, use your hands and firmly squeeze twice—two quick consecutive squeezes. Like this." Ruby demonstrated. The shadow inside her carrier flashed. "You must do this to instruct your carrier to hold you more securely."

Reason did as she was told, feeling the shadowy substance embrace her more snuggly. "Okay. Done. But why, Ruby? Where are we going that we need more..." Reason's voice faded and her eyes widened. Ahead, where the river significantly narrowed, it also appeared to end. "Is that... a waterfall?" Reason's stomach tightened.

"You'll be fine," said Ruby. "The carrier will keep you safe. Falling with the water is part of this journey, and a powerful experience."

"Seriously? No. I don't think so. I can't do that! How big is it? What kind of drop, Ruby?"

"Don't anticipate the fall, dear. Go with the flow of the river and ride the water. Now, give your carrier another command. This time, squeeze three times." Again, Ruby demonstrated. The shadowy image in her carrier flickered and then glowed bright orange. "Orange signifies maximum protection."

Of course, it does. "Why can't we fly *over* the waterfall? Why must we go down it?" Eager to be properly secured, Reason squeezed and quickly found herself enveloped in an orange glow.

"Trust in what the experience will offer you. And trust in yourself," said Ruby. "Close your eyes, Reason. Be still. Be quiet. Listen to the surrounding sounds." Again, Reason did as she was told. Her carrier lowered to the water. Then it shut down. The quiet that followed was wonderfully impressive. She smiled, sinking into the gentle rhythm of the water lapping against the exterior of her machine, transfixed. "Here we go!" said Ruby, breaking the spell. Reason gasped and opened her eyes.

The carriers moved steadily and inescapably towards the water's edge. Not far ahead, Ruby's carrier dropped out of sight. Reason cried out. "Shit. SHIT!" For a breath, her carrier seemed to balance precariously on the brink, and a moment before it tumbled over, she saw a large pink fish leap into the air and then disappear. Then a frothy wall consumed everything, and for a moment Reason felt suspended in the milky white. But the falling motion soon registered, and as her carrier plummeted, she screamed into the deafening roar of the falling water.

Reason's howling lasted until her carrier plunged into the churning water at the base of the falls. The vehicle rolled deep into the frothy pool, the crashing above becoming a low-pitched, muted rumble. An intense vibration shook the craft as thousands of tiny bubbles streamed up its exterior. Reason held her breath. Her carrier burst through the surface of the water and she again heard the full blast of the roaring falls. Suspended in the air briefly, the craft dropped, bobbed, and rolled. And then finally it settled upright and drifted toward calmer waters. Relieved and invigorated, Reason trembled with excitement. She laughed wildly; her joy uncontainable. "Bloody unbelievable!" She stepped on the pink button. "Ruby, you were right. I feel amazing. That was... electrifying!"

Ruby grinned. "Falling with the water gives one a reprieve from heavier matters. The waterfall plunge is very good for that."

Reason's carrier lifted. It skimmed along the surface and stopped alongside Ruby's. "Flying and falling—this entire experience is crazy. Crazy exciting! I feel like a kid. I feel... more alive."

"Being fully present will do that for you," said Ruby. "But now we continue." Contrary to her cheerful voice, Ruby exemplified authority. Her strength and confidence gave Reason courage and made her feel safe.

In unison, the carriers lifted and Reason's machine zipped in behind Ruby's. In a broad sweep, they soared into the shimmering night sky. Nearing the mountainside, they continued to climb, tracing its rugged profile—layers of red, white, and ebony scrolling by in long, fluttering ribbons of color.

Reason squealed with delight as her carrier cleared the mountain top, the terrain dropping away so suddenly that she pitched forward. Seconds later the machine swooped down, and following close to Ruby's, raced along the mountaintop's rocky landscape.

Ruby's carrier made a sharp turn to the right and Reason's pursued it. Together they sped above a barren terrain dappled with single evergreens. The sprinkling of trees soon thickened into a large, dense forest—a dark green blur rushing beneath Reason until she flew beyond it and over the brink of a vast cliff.

Ruby's carrier disappeared into a sea of cottony clouds. Reason's followed. Through gauzy patches of white, a dark form took shape, and soon an immense wedge of land emerged. It hovered in the air as if it had somehow severed from the planet below and had floated away to become an island in the sky. Its craggy, grassy terrain overhung its tattered edges—the sides of the strange landmass plunging deep into the misty blue below. "Welcome to Buoyant Island," announced Ruby.

Drawing nearer, rectangular shapes came into view, tiny rooftops, six of them clustered together on a patch of bright green. The two carriers hovered above them and then lowered in a precise vertical descent, coming to rest side by side.

C3 80

The night air had cooled substantially. Reason pulled her vest tighter and hugged the satchel to her body. "That was incredible, Ruby. I'll never forget it. Never! How could I?" She backed away from the carrier, its shadowy interior fading to a pale ginger. And then, through the soft leather of the satchel, she felt an object. "What's this?" She pulled back the satchel's wide flap and felt inside. "It's a stone. No. Wait. A seed maybe?" Brown in color, one end of the small round object was darker than the other, as if someone had dipped it in black paint. Lightweight, glossy, and heart-shaped, it fit nicely in her palm. She closed her fingers around it. "It feels nice. I don't know what it is. Maybe a seed?" Reason held her hand out to Ruby. "Do you know?"

Ruby looked pleased. "It's a mindfulness bean, and you've earned it."

"A mindfulness bean?"

"Yes. I'll tell you all about it, but let's get inside first." Ruby gestured toward one of the small buildings. "Inside, there's a meal waiting for us. And you'll need your rest. We've much to do. In the morning, you'll continue your story, and your journey." Ruby's plump figure walked away along a narrow boardwalk that led to the door of a small stone cottage. Reason followed.

Inside the one-room cabin, a fire glowed. The burning wood popped and crackled, and bright embers rose in its heat. Opposite the fireplace were two beds, each one neatly made up with checkered quilts and plump pillows. At the foot of one bed, a table held the evening's dinner. Seeing the food, Reason realized her hunger. She lay her satchel on the nearest bed and walked to the table. A wooden platter held a small block of cheese, a loaf of bread, some sliced meats, and a pot of jam.

Ruby tended to the oil lamps burning in the small cabin, their quivering flames casting a soft light in the room, but leaving dark shadows in the corners. "We've no electricity or running water," she said, moving to the table and pouring red wine into one of two goblets. "Will you have some wine?"

"Yes. Thank you."

"We have water if you prefer."

"No, please, the wine is perfect."

"We have plenty of water." Ruby pointed over Reason's shoulder. "There, in the large wooden casks along the back wall. That's more than we'll ever need for a one-night stay."

Ruby moved to the fireplace. With a long black poker, she jabbed at the burning wood, flattening and then spreading the bed of hot coals. Using the poker, she pointed at the back wall of the cabin. "Back there, you'll also find the door to the outdoor toilet." She leaned the poker against the wall, added a log to the fire, and then sat down at the table. "Sit. Eat." She tore off a piece of bread and then passed the loaf to Reason.

"Everything is so... well prepared. Thank you." Reason needed no coaxing to eat.

"Being provided for is never a worry for us." Ruby emptied her goblet and then poured herself more wine. "Now then, the mindfulness bean. I'll tell you about its purpose, and then we will sleep—because tomorrow is a big day."

Bigger than today? Reason popped a piece of bread into her mouth.

"The mindfulness bean is a gift of exceptional value. Carry it with you always." Ruby sipped from her goblet. "It will remind you to become aware and present. Being present is useful, because left unnoticed, a runaway mind can make a real mess of things. But with the bean in your possession, you'll learn to become aware and present more and more—no matter when or where you find yourself. And you'll discover that you can observe what exists without being overwhelmed or consumed by it—and without the need to judge. This will benefit you on this journey. Do you understand?"

"I think so. The bean is a reminder of sorts, a kind of tool, right? A tool for... creating a kind of inner stillness."

"Well said. The bean is indeed a tool, one that will help you become more mindful of your thoughts, and more aware of how those thoughts affect your perception. The mindfulness bean encourages acceptance and hope." Ruby put her goblet down and leaned forward, her arms on the table, her hands clasped. "You earned it Reason. With the bean's help, you can now learn how to turn a daunting challenge into a great opportunity."

Reason rolled the bean through her fingers and then tucked it safely away.

❧ ❧

The moonlight threw a pale silver light through the cabin's two front windows—the slanted beams stretching across the dark floor and over each of the beds. Reason felt calm and safe and more protected than she had been for years. Beside her in the other bed, Ruby snored. Reason smiled at the joy of meeting such a remarkable woman.

A firefly landed on the windowpane, and as Reason watched, it crawled across the glass, its bright glow flickering. *Sleep will never come. Can I handle what tomorrow will bring?*

But sleep came, and in the morning, Reason opened her eyes to a sunlit room and the smell of fresh coffee. The morning air was cool, the cabin door wide open and framing a glorious day. Reason slipped out from the warmth of her bed.

Standing at the open door, she shaded her eyes. In the pasture near the parked carriers, Ruby sat in a garden chair—sipping her coffee. She wore a fresh red suit with thin gold trim on its lapels and cuffs. Seeing Reason, she sat forward in her chair and waved. "You're awake! Grab yourself a bite to eat and come join me. There's hot coffee by the fire." She patted the empty chair beside her.

Feeling energized, Reason dressed. She poured herself a cup of coffee and filled a small plate with strawberries, a biscuit with honey, and some cheese. And then, with her satchel over her shoulder and giving the cozy interior of the cabin a final look, she left to join Ruby in the garden.

At the end of the cottage boardwalk, a thick rose bush bloomed. It teemed with fat pink roses that pulled long arched stems toward the ground. A small sign, partially hidden in the blooming greenery, read: "Cottage of Content." The night before, Reason had noticed neither the rose bush nor the sign. Now she grinned at the accuracy of the name.

The pasture grass shimmered under the white light of an early morning sun, and wisps of mist lingered at the tops of the tall trees that lined it. The two women sat side by side, slips of steam rising from their mugs. Reason wondered what this day might bring. She wished she could get to the point of her journey without having to tell her story. But expecting the opposite, she peeked over her mug at Ruby. "What happens now?"

"Well, my dear, after you've eaten, you tell me more about that cowboy."

Reason sighed. Ruby put her mug on the ground and moved forward in her chair, her arms on her knees, her hands clasped as if in prayer. "If things become unmanageable along the way," she explained, "remember the mindfulness bean. Breathe mindfully. Stillness will bring you awareness. Awareness will bring you clarity."

Reason twisted in her chair and eyed Ruby suspiciously. "If things become unmanageable?"

Ruby lowered her chin, tilted her head, and leaned forward. "Sometimes what you perceive to be your reality, is misleading." She paused and smiled shrewdly. "You can make a situation unmanageable simply by thinking it so. But you· can always change the way you perceive your circumstances." She pointed to Reason's satchel. "The bean will remind you to become present. And then you'll have a chance to create a wider perspective, to see new opportunities, to make the unmanageable—manageable." She sat back in her chair. "That's all," she said decisively. "Remember this and you'll be fine."

Reason felt the mindfulness bean through the soft leather of the satchel and wondered if she would remember Ruby's advice during any upcoming "unmanageable" moments.

⋘ ⋙

The students crowded the cafeteria tables, some having skipped their classes to take turns playing Euchre and to watch music videos on the large wall-mounted TV. They laughed and shouted over the loud music, many of the young students living away from home for the first time and excited by their newly found freedom.

Even in a large crowd, the cowboy stood out. Taller than most and well over thirty years old, he did not look like a typical student. He was an unusual character, not only because of his flashy western attire, but also because he was always alone. Since leaving William, Reason had learned to be alert, aware of her surroundings and of the people around her. So, when she noticed the cowboy leaning against the far wall and staring at her, she faked having somewhere she needed to be and excused herself from the card game.

Leaving the cafeteria, she chose an exit where a wide and often congested staircase led to washrooms and a lecture hall. Climbing the stairs, Reason squeezed through a mob of students traveling in the opposite direction. Reaching the top, she turned to look back. Students jostled back and forth below, but she did not see the cowboy. Relieved, she slipped into the washroom.

Exiting through a second door on the far side, Reason moved directly into a large lecture hall. There she found some classmates preparing for class, one that she had intended to skip but would now attend. She slipped into her usual seat and settled in.

The rest of Reason's afternoon unfolded uneventfully, but the unsettling thoughts brought on by the cowboy had not diminished. After class, a nagging anxiety plagued her as she rounded a corner to walk the short corridor that led to her locker. At the far end of the hall stood the cowboy. Momentarily stunned, she stopped. Their eyes locked. The corridor was hopelessly quiet and deserted. She turned to leave.

"Wait." His voice resonated in the empty hall. Reason froze. "As you might have guessed, darlin', I'm here because of William. But there's no need to be afraid of me. We can work this thing out." He spoke deliberately, his voice deep, surprisingly unintimidating, almost compassionate.

Work what out? Fuck! Reason hung her head, her heart pounding. Turning, she steadied herself against a bank of lockers. The cowboy walked unhurriedly, closing the gap between them, his boots loud on the polished floor. Reason stood her ground and forced herself to make eye contact. Her fists clenching, she prepared for the worst. Stopping within a few feet, the cowboy lifted his arm. Reason tensed reflexively, but he only tipped his hat.

"We shared a cell," he offered benignly.

"What?"

"I was his cellmate, darlin'."

Reason chose not to respond, remaining still, and she hoped, unreadable.

"He told me all about you. Told me how he expects you to wait for him. Asked me to be sure that you do. Told me just how to make sure." The cowboy smiled. Reason felt sick.

So. There it is. The ugly truth. How could I think my life would be any different? He'll never let me go. Her courage faltered, but she managed an even tone. "We *were* in a relationship. We no longer are and never will be again. He lied to you." Reason kept her gaze steady on the cowboy's, dismayed by his grin.

"I'm not surprised, Reason. Not in the least. Not after hearin' him brag on and on about how he treated you as if it was his God-given right. Nevertheless darlin', a deal *is* a deal, and I have an arrangement

115

with him, a promise that I intend to keep." The cowboy backed away and leaned against the bank of lockers on the opposite wall—lowering his head and crossing his arms casually as a group of students entered the corridor. The big hat obscured his face. Chatting and laughing, the students paid no attention to Reason or the cowboy, and passed by without incident.

"I reckon your classes are finished for the day." The cowboy pulled his hat from his head and ran his fingers through his curly blond hair.

Reason could feel her heart beating as if it might burst. She was frightened and sickened by this strange man. The thought of reporting the cowboy's actions crossed her mind. But, she thought, who would she tell? What would she say? That she thinks someone is following her? That she's afraid of unwanted attention? That she feels harassed? No one did that. Who would care? As far as Reason knew, she was alone in this threatening situation. To show the cowboy some defiance, and even though she had started to tremble, she answered boldly, "Don't be so sure. What do you know? You know nothing about me!"

"I know your classes are done for the day. Call it an educational guess. You and me... we have things to talk about. We could talk here, but darlin', I'd really like a cold brew."

"The word is educated," Reason offered, immediately feeling ridiculous for correcting him.

"What's that, darlin'?" His head bowed, his back against the lockers, the cowboy casually examined his fingernails.

"Nothing," she said weakly.

He pressed the heel of his boot into the bank of lockers and pushed himself away. The thin metal bent and then popped back into place. Reason's palms were sweaty, her mouth parched. "I'm not going anywhere with you," she managed.

Her muscles rigid, she moved past him to her locker. The short distance seemed dramatically lengthened. With shaking hands, she reached for her combination lock, hoping not to fumble it. The chunky metal unlocked with a clunk. The locker door squealed open. Reason retrieved her jacket, pulling it out from the narrow compartment. The zipper clanged against the metal. Time seemed halted, sounds heightened. She shut the locker and pushed the round, heavy base of the lock into its broad u-ring. Reason squeezed her eyes shut, took a deliberate breath, and then turned to confront the cowboy. He spoke first.

"I get it. I scare you. So, here's my offer, darlin'. Take the night to think about things." The cowboy pulled something from his jean jacket pocket. Clasped between two nicotine-stained fingers, he held a matchbook. He offered it to her.

"I don't want that," Reason blurted, feeling frantic. The cowboy moved closer. She stepped to the side. He did the same and blocked her way. She glanced at the exit and moved again, but again he shifted in front of her. He raised his hand. Reason fought the urge to push him. Standing too close, but not touching her, he put his hand against the wall of lockers near her head. He smelled faintly of sweat and old cologne. The sleeve of his jacket brushed against her cheek. Reason shook. Her chest tightened. She struggled to breathe. "I'll scream," she sniped. "Don't touch me. People will come. I'll fight you. Get the fuck away from me!"

The cowboy laughed and then moved uncomfortably close; his breath hot on her face. "I'm not fixin' to hurt you. I've no intention of ever touching you. But you will meet with me. I made a deal with that jerk boyfriend of yours and I intend to keep up my end." Bringing the matchbook close to her face, he let it fall. It hit her in the chest and then skittered across the floor. "Look at the matchbook," he whispered, and then in a louder voice, "Meet me there tomorrow mornin' at ten." He stepped back, tipped his hat, turned, and walked away. When Reason could no longer hear the echo of his boots, she slumped to the floor.

Two students entered the hallway and walked past her. One of them inadvertently kicked the matchbook across the floor. He looked down at what he had kicked and then continued walking. His friend looked back as they passed, giving Reason a curious glance. But, locked in her fear, she did not fully register their presence, and was soon alone again, the matchbook tormenting her. Horrified by the sight of it, and by the misery it represented, she buried her face in the fabric of her jacket, suppressed her need to scream, and slowly pounded her fist on the floor.

9

offer of protection

R eason spent the long hours of the night in fitful slumber, swinging between nightmares full of awful people doing dreadful things, and lying awake ruminating. The exchange with the cowboy had kept her from sleeping. *What the hell does he want from me? For God's sake, what's the point of trying?*

In the distance, a train's haunting wail swept across the countryside. Reason glanced at her bedroom window, waiting to hear the sound again. A cool night, she drew the covers to her chin and imagined the train plowing into the darkness. Again the sound of the train's horn spurred the lonely night, and despite its melancholy cry, it comforted Reason. She rolled onto her side, feeling a little less alone.

CзахꙘ

When Reason left William, her broad plan was to embark on a new and worthy life. Attending college was a solid step in that direction. Not so long ago, the idea of returning to school had seemed impossible. When it became a reality, she gratefully and genuinely cherished the academic environment. She maintained good marks, and her firm commitment and work ethic made her somewhat of an inspiration among her friends.

Withholding the details of her earlier life had not been a part of the larger plan, but the longer Reason kept her shameful past quiet, the more she believed it had no business in her new life. Honored by her friends' desire to seek her out for advice or companionship, she valued and enjoyed the new kinship. She wanted her classmates to need and respect her, and they did. And yet, because she feared disappointing her new friends, and because she believed her past to be too disgusting and humiliating to share, she kept it a secret.

After a while, suppressing the truth about her past caused Reason some unexpected problems. While caught in a web of her obsessive thoughts, she became convinced that she was betraying her friends, believing that the new and worthy Reason that they all admired was merely a thin disguise for the part of her that was appalling and shameful. Now and then, overwhelmed by this conflict—and craving love—she would become reckless and plunge into bouts of binge drinking and promiscuity. And afterward, while paying the price of a nasty hangover, she would suffer gloomy episodes of self-loathing and regret. And sometimes, often when she was out in public and doing rather ordinary things, she would suddenly suffer a crippling panic attack—her heart racing, her palms sweaty, her mouth parched. She kept these episodes secret too.

In particularly lonely moments, when Reason longed for comfort, she imagined telling someone about her violent past—anyone—if only to unload the burden. But broaching the subject seemed impossible. She had become convinced that revealing her past would serve only to expose her for being deceitful and vulnerable and unworthy of respect.

Having never expected that her painful past would haunt her in such disturbing ways, Reason endured its wrath in stoic silence—and kept people at arm's length.

CB EO

Reason jumped over a puddle of murky water as the rain pelted the city streets. All night long the rain had fallen in a steady drizzle, and by morning it had become a heavy downpour. Water gushed curbside, fell raucously into sewers, and poured from awnings and rooftops. She ducked into the recessed entryway of a candy store and, under its cover, waited there for the rain to let up.

On either side of the store's front door, French windows rose to an old tin ceiling. On the tall windows were images of red candy apples, thick slices of fudge, stacks of peanut brittle, and a mouthwatering assortment of truffles. Reason turned away. The pictures portrayed a cheerful happiness that did not exist in her life. The sight of them made her feel lonely. She stuffed her hands into the shallow pockets of her jeans, her fingers finding the cowboy's matchbook. She turned it over twice and then pulled it out to look at it. Black letters on its cover read, "Kelly's Kitchen", and on the back, "Ribs and Chicken" underlined by a row of tiny yellow flowers clustered into diamond shapes. Reason flipped open the folded matchbook; half of the matches were missing. She cupped her hands to the window and peered inside. A wall clock read 10:04. She was late. The rain was not slowing. She sighed, and with her head bowed, ran the final two blocks to the diner.

In a booth at the rear of the narrow restaurant, the cowboy sat facing away from the entrance, his hat peeking up above the high-backed seat. Reason stiffened at the sight of the conspicuous hat and, clenching her fists absentmindedly, moved towards it. To her right were seven booths, mostly empty, and on her left, a long sit-down bar ran the depth of the restaurant. A man and a woman sat at the bar. A young waitress poured each of them a coffee. As Reason passed by, the man asked for two pieces of cherry pie and the woman discreetly checked her lipstick in a compact mirror.

With what she hoped was a neutral expression, Reason stopped near the cowboy's booth and waited for him to notice her. He raised his head, but his gaze was across the table. "Have a seat, darlin'," he said, sliding his hand along the glossy surface of the table and gesturing opposite him. Reason sat. "It's good you came," he said casually, looking her in the eye and smiling. For a second she could not breathe.

"Did I have a choice?" she said with a frown, tossing the matchbook across the table. The cowboy caught it before it slid over the edge.

"You made the best choice you could've, darlin'. I'm not lookin' to hurt you. You'll have to trust me on that. He wanted me to, that nauseatin' boyfriend of yours. He's a piece of work alright. He paid me to keep you in line, but I never intended to follow through with that part." The cowboy flipped the matchbook between his fingers and then put his hands under the table and sat up straight. "I'd never treat a woman that way. Never. Ever." He relaxed his shoulders and pushed his hat farther back on his head, more of his face coming out from under its shadow. "A woman is to be respected. She's to be enjoyed, appreciated, cared for... loved." And then, as if he was generously sharing some delicious secret, with a wide grin he added in a low voice, "Because she's a treasure of pleasure!" He tossed the matchbook onto the table and then methodically rolled back his shirtsleeves, revealing heavily tanned and tattooed forearms. Reason was unimpressed and wished only that he would get on with whatever he wanted. "I have a need and it's one your boyfriend can satisfy," he said coolly. "You and I darlin', we need to get along." He waved to the waitress, tipped his hat, smiled flirtatiously, and then addressed her. "Sarah, be a darlin' and bring us a couple of coffees."

Sarah smiled and, with the coffee pot in hand and her hips swaying, strutted a path to their table. The coffee smelled fresh. Reason welcomed the hot drink. "Cream or milk?" asked Sarah, beaming at the cowboy, clearly enamored.

He reached out and affectionately closed his hand around hers, jeweled rings adorning each one of his fingers. "Milk is for tea, darlin'. But I can see just by lookin' at you, you've got plenty of sugar."

Sarah gave the cowboy her best silky smile. "You sure are fine looking, but you're gonna have to work harder than that," she teased, bending toward him, her low-cut blouse emphasizing her ample cleavage. "You want white or brown sugar, honey?"

Annoyed and restless, Reason shifted in her seat and shot them both an angry glance.

"Well now, I sure do like you," raved the cowboy.

Sarah reached into her apron and pulled out a mixture of brown and white sugar packets and tossed them onto the table. "We'll see about that," she said, turning and sashaying back behind the bar. The cowboy watched her every step, tipping his hat, sucking in a column of air through puckered lips.

"What do you want from me?" asked Reason, speaking more loudly than she had intended. She plucked up a creamer and testily tapped its small plastic base against the chrome edge of the table.

"Just your company, darlin', nothing more," replied the cowboy, his attention now on his coffee.

Reason was both puzzled and alarmed by his answer. She pulled back the lid from the little cream container and poured its contents into her coffee. The thick, white liquid sank and then ascended in a swirl. She dropped her spoon into the brown porcelain mug and stirred, buying time, waiting to regain her composure. "What does that mean?" she asked in a hard-fought-for, even tone.

"The deal, darlin', is William gives me what I want if he knows that you're behaving. His word, not mine. He wants proof that you're loyal and waitin' for him."

Reason's stomach flip-flopped. "He knows where I am?" she blurted. *Of course, he knows where I am.* She lowered her head.

"I guess you know the answer to that," said the cowboy. "And darlin', he's getting out in two months, maybe even less." Reaching for the small pile of sugar packets, the cowboy kept his gaze on Reason.

Knowing that she must look shaken, she lifted her mug from the table. Her mind raced. The hot liquid quivered. She felt chilled. "He's not supposed to be released for another six months," she managed, glancing at the cowboy, who looked at her with unexpected compassion.

"He's applied to serve the rest of his sentence in a halfway house," said the cowboy. He paused, gauging Reason's reaction. "That's my current situation. For the balance of my sentence, I'll be livin' like a king at the halfway house here, in this little-bitty ole town." He stacked four sugar packets one atop the other, picked them up by their ends, and smacked them against the edge of the table. Reason waited patiently as he ripped open all four at once and poured the white granules into his black coffee. Through her growing panic, she tried to concentrate on what he was telling her. "The transfer is supposed to be a way of integratin' us depraved convicts back into the good graces of society. William has applied to the same halfway house... the same one that I'm in now." He sipped his coffee. "We don't always get what we want," he continued, folding the empty sugar packets into tiny squares. "It's mandatory to apply to more than one, and we don't know which town we're headin' to, 'til a few days before they ship us out. So, who knows? William might not get into this one, darlin'." He reached across the table, attempting to take hold of her hand. She flinched and pulled away.

William's voice suddenly screamed into Reason's head. He had her pinned up against a wall, his spittle spraying her face, his hand seizing her by the chin, forcing her to face him. "Never think of leaving me. No one else will ever have you. You're mine or you're fucked. Screw around and I'll know. I'll find him. Then I'll find you." His threat had come after he realized she had changed, that she had become less compliant and more defiant. And he was determined to force her into submission. She cringed with fear then, and felt that same fear now, certain that he would make her suffer.

Reason stared past the cowboy. *What do I do? Where do I go? The cops? They'll do nothing. It's my word against his. Useless.* She blew out a slow column of air, desperate for shelter—for a safe place to hide. She knew of no such place.

"All we have to do, is show him proof," said the cowboy. "Proof that I've contacted you, and soon after that, it'll all be over. I'll owe him nothing more. He'll keep his end of the deal, and you and me, darlin', we'll be strangers once again. He'll never know that we worked together."

What? Reason looked at the cowboy, wanting to object, but too panicked to speak, she merely blinked despairingly.

"He won't know that I'm not beating you, and when he moves here, if he does, I'll be here too... at least for a little while, anyway. So, darlin', I can watch over you."

As Reason's panic grew, so did the noise in the diner. The cowboy's voice became distant and tinny. From behind the counter, cutlery clanged, hand dried by Sarah, and dropped one by one into a metal bin. The front door screeched open. A group of shouting students entered, and for a brief moment, they brought the din of the street with them. Reason resisted the urge to clamp her hands over her ears as the unfamiliar students unexpectedly reminded her of her friends. *Why is this happening? What about school? Shit! My friends... what will they think? I can't let them see me with this idiot. Make a damned plan. Think. Damn it, think!* Reason looked up, reacting to the cowboy who appeared to be trying to get her attention.

"HEY!" he shouted, waving his hands. The couple at the bar turned to stare. "Hey, Reason. Where'd you go, darlin'? Look at me." He had got hold of her hand. She snatched it away. "At least you got some warning, right?" He leaned back, smiling weakly, watching her.

Reason felt paralyzed. She gaped at the cowboy, confused by his smile. But all at once his idiotic grin angered her, and she found her voice. "What good does a warning do me?" she hissed. "Why can't you both just leave me alone? William is conniving and cruel. His obsession with me, his plotting against me... it's because he wants revenge... because I left him. He's a monster and a coward. He sees me as a thing to own and control. I think it thrills him to be a... a fucking bully. Prison hasn't changed him, not one bit. In fact, I think he might be worse. Do you think he enjoys being an asshole?" Reason took a deep breath and went silent, fuming and shaking.

"Yes," said the cowboy. "I think he does. I reckon that he feels like a big tough guy when he hits you. But he's a repulsive, little man. And yes, he's obsessed with keeping you as his... property." The cowboy looked stern-faced and grim, even a little awkward. He sat back and then forward, adjusted his hat, and adjusted it again. He appeared to be struggling with some kind of stubborn inner conflict. He exhaled through a loosely clenched fist, then leaned his arms on the table, cupped his coffee mug with both hands, and shook his head in a visible display of quitting the mental battle.

Exhausted, Reason put her face in her hands and stared through the slits between her fingers. In a low, subdued voice, she asked, "What does William have that is so damned important to you?"

"Straight up?" he asked. Reason sat back and frowned. "Drugs," said the cowboy. "I'm an addict, darlin'—for more than half my life. In a few months, I'll be at court-ordered rehab—again. I'll give it a go, but sobriety hasn't stuck yet. Seems I'm a lost cause." He sat up, straightening his back and raising his chin as if readying himself for a challenge. "In the meantime, see this?" The cowboy held out his hands, palms down, fingers spread, trembling and twitching. "Withdrawal," he said somberly. "William had cash waiting for me, hidden, for when I got out. Don't know how he got it there. Don't care. It paid for my first few hits. His payment to me is in drugs, enough to do me until rehab. Again, don't know how he gets it, and I don't care." The cowboy seemed to slump in resignation. "Not sure I'll ever kick the habit. Not sure I want to. Done too much for too long; it'll probably be the death of me, darlin'." And then with his voice gentle, maybe even apologetic, he added, "I won't touch you, Reason. I can promise you that. But he's got my drugs, and you're the key to me getting them."

Reason shivered as if an icy wound at her core had opened and was spreading. The reality of the cowboy and his awful need was undeniable and overwhelmingly real. Not knowing what to do, she played along, at least until she could plan something better. "What do I have to do?" she asked drearily. "I won't do anything illegal. I'm finally turning my life around. I've met some great people. They see good in me as if my past with William never existed. I'm finally becoming the person I want to be. Please don't screw that up."

"I don't mean to mess up your life, darlin'," he said. "But I've got no money and no contacts here. I know you're on to something good. I can see that. I've been watching you for weeks and I can see that you're happy." Reason flinched at the thought of being watched, and more so at not having noticed. "But I'm a junky that's found a way to get his fix. Plain and simple." He reached into his jacket pocket and pulled out a green pack of Export "A" cigarettes. "Want one?" he asked.

Reason took a cigarette. Being angry almost always heightened her desire to smoke. The cowboy struck a match. Sulfur scented the air and the little flame burned off in a tiny puff of grey smoke. With his hand cupped around the match, he lit her cigarette. They sat in silence, with Reason holding her cigarette over the ashtray—now and again tapping it against the thin metal. "You still haven't told me what I have to do," she said resentfully, folding her cigarette into the ashtray and sitting back in frustration.

"Just spend a little time with me... and write William a letter." The cowboy kept his head down as he spoke, raising his eyelids only when he mentioned the letter, watching Reason from beneath the brim of his hat.

"What?" Reason asked in disbelief. "And say what? Hope you rot in hell? Should I write that?" Shocked at the request and repulsed by the idea, she glared at the cowboy.

Thick white smoke curled from his mouth and nose. "I hear ya," he said. "But it's what I need. I need you to write to him and tell him we met the hard way. Beyond that, tell him he's a lowlife asshole. Be creative. I don't care. But you *have to write to him*. Because he needs to believe that I've scared you, that I've hit you. If he believes that... then I get my drugs and you get my protection."

Reason clenched her jaw, suppressing an urge to yell. "Your protection?" she asked in mock surprise, and then in a sedate, bleak tone, "I didn't ask for your stupid protection. And even if you could protect me, which you can't, what happens after you leave? Who'll protect me then? I can't count on anyone, but me. And you... you don't know what he's capable of. No one does. He's clever at hiding who he really is. No one understands that part. *You* certainly don't. He's threatened my family; I have to keep them safe. No one can protect me. No one. I can't go to the police. They won't do anything, not until they see that he's actually hurt me." She paused, shaking her head in frustration, containing her anger. "And what you really don't understand, is that if William gets to me this time, he could very well kill me." Eyes glistening, lips trembling, Reason glared at the cowboy. He raised his chin but said nothing. She continued. "You know, I used to fight back. But I soon learned that the more I fought, the worse the beating." She drew an audible breath, struggling to hold back her tears. "When I began to cower, to raise my hands only for protection... that's when I became unrecognizable even to myself. I became completely worthless. I became invisible." Reason gripped the

127

chrome-banded edge of the table. "But, despite that hellish experience, I made my way back to the land of the living, to self-respect, to people who know their worth and who strive to be their best." Reason clenched her fists. "I'll never cower again. If it costs me my life, I'll *always* fight back. I won't let anyone have that kind of control over me ever again. So if William finds me, I'll go down fighting. But don't you dare tell me you can protect me when we both know that you can't."

Reason slid out from the booth and started for the door. The cowboy grabbed her arm, and then let it go. "McKenzie," he said.

"What?" she spat out in amazed contempt.

"My name. It's McKenzie."

Reason stared incredulously at the cowboy's upturned face, and then turned away, and walked out of the diner into the pouring rain.

CB ∞

The next day was sunny, but the sunshine did little to improve Reason's gloomy state of mind. And although she had wished and prayed that the cowboy would disappear, McKenzie was waiting for her at the end of her school day. Expecting his appearance, she had prepared excuses for her friends, making up plausible explanations for her need to be alone. But her lies weighed heavily, her deception and the cowboy's presence seeming to be the disturbing proof that she was merely a visitor in her new life, the old one having never really ended.

Struggling to conceal her anxiety, she left her last class with her shoulders raised and her textbooks held tightly to her chest. She entered the corridor that led to her locker, and to her dismay, with his hands in his pockets and his hat pulled down, the cowboy stood leaning against the bank of lockers that contained her own. She slowed as she neared him. "I don't plan on hanging out with you," she announced. "I've got a good life here, and it doesn't have any room in it for people like you." The cowboy adjusted his hat and raised his head.

"People like me..." McKenzie drawled, emphasizing each syllable. Then he chuckled dispassionately, and added in a mildly dejected tone, "Well then, your new life is a smart one, darlin'." He stood in Reason's way, then slid sideways, permitting her to get to her locker. "Meet me at the diner at noon tomorrow," he said. "We've got plans to discuss." And without waiting for a reply, McKenzie turned and left Reason standing alone. She never saw him at the college again.

The diner became their meeting place, and during their third meeting, McKenzie strolled into the restaurant with unusual, nervous energy, eyes darting about, grinning incessantly, his pupils dilated. "I'm having a grand day, darlin'," he announced brazenly, standing too close to Reason. And when she stared back in silence, he twirled around, swaggered to the counter, swooped in behind it, and put his arms around Sarah.

McKenzie was a petty hustler who had wandered through most of his days in a perpetual state of intoxication, drifting through many a small town, leaving behind young broken hearts and occasionally a warrant for his arrest. Reason was cautious when she was with him, but she was not afraid, and she found that on some days, she even liked him. Despite his addiction, which he mostly hid from her, and in spite of his connection to William, Reason found that McKenzie was friendly, and although his behavior was quite eccentric, he seemed genuine. But on that day, he had been pathetic, making Reason feel both angry and sad. She hated how her world had collided with his.

Sitting in their customary booth, Reason faced the entrance, moderately satisfied with the small measure of privacy the high-backed seats provided. Annoyed, she watched McKenzie who, loud-mouthed and obnoxious, flirted with Sarah. And Sarah, who struggled to move him out from behind the counter, smiled when McKenzie took her into his arms, not deliberately meaning to spur him on, but doing so nonetheless. As Reason and the other patrons watched, McKenzie finally shimmied his way out from behind the counter and lifted his hat in a polite farewell, his blond curls flowing. He performed an elaborate, albeit wobbly, bow, causing his hat to slip from his grip. He plucked it from the floor, almost losing his balance, then brushed the dirt from its wide brim and plunked the big hat back in place. Spinning around, he spotted Reason. "There's my darlin'. My jewel, my path to perfection, my purse!"

What? Shit. Shut up! Reason cringed and shrank back in her seat. She had planned to talk to McKenzie about the letter, the letter she was going to refuse to write. But with growing disappointment, she realized that that conversation would not happen today. And unsure how to respond to McKenzie's stoned stupidity, she merely groaned irritably. She knew what it felt like to be high, to be drunk, but McKenzie's behavior was extreme and went far beyond her limited experience. She decided she would stand up and leave. But McKenzie ambushed her, blocking her way. She waited impatiently as he rambled on, his usual calm manner absent. She considered trying to interject, to slow him down, but that idea right away seemed pointless. Unimpressed, and having lost what little patience she had left, Reason raised her voice. "Stop it, McKenzie! You're impossible like this. What are you on? Whatever it is, it makes you ridiculous."

To her surprise, McKenzie became silent. He sat down heavily, opened his mouth to speak, but made no sound. Then, after a brief convulsive twisting of his lips, he burst into laughter. But his moment of giddy absurdity was fleeting, and once more he became sullen and silent. Minutes passed. Reason reached out to touch him, but thought better of it. She left him sitting in his stupor. Before she exited the diner, she glanced back. He had not stirred.

CS EO

For three days, Reason saw no sign of McKenzie. She wanted to believe that he had changed his mind and given up on her. But on the fourth day, she found a folded paper note taped to her locker. In neat block letters, it read:

> "SORRY. WON'T HAPPEN AGAIN. I'LL BE AT 222 RIVERSIDE DRIVE TOMORROW AT SIX. BUZZ 60 AND I'LL LET YOU IN."

She crumpled the piece of paper, clutched it to her chest, and pressed her forehead against the hard surface of her locker.

ೞ ೲ

The thought of meeting McKenzie in a private setting unnerved Reason. Already on edge, she stepped from the city bus and walked the remaining three blocks in a daze of apprehension. Arriving fifteen minutes early, she stood looking up at an old, but relatively clean and tidy, high-rise building. Near the front door was a small, well-maintained garden with two benches. Reason sat and wondered glumly if she had misread McKenzie. She began preparing herself for the genuine possibility of a confrontation and, for the first time, realized that he might not be alone.

At precisely six o'clock, she entered the building and found the number sixty on the foyer directory. Beside it was the name: "A. Browning". *I thought he didn't know anyone.* She hesitated and then pressed the buttons on the worn pad. Almost instantly, a loud electronic ringing filled the small, overheated vestibule. Instinctively, she counted the rings. After four ring tones, a thin, crackling static preceded a man's voice. "Sixty," said the voice. It was definitely McKenzie's.

"It's me... Reason."

The glass door beside her clicked. "Six-nineteen," said McKenzie. He sounded tired.

Reason moved into the lobby. A mixture of disinfectant and citrus hung in the air. She pressed the elevator button, and a low, monotone droning signaled its advancement. Her heart raced. A large scratch crossed the full width of the closed elevator doors, ascending from left to right. *A battle scar*, thought Reason. The doors opened, slicing the old wound in two. She stared at the plain interior of the empty car, needing more time to calm her hopelessly overstrung nerves. But knowing that she must tell the cowboy her decision not to write the letter, with her fingers pumping with nervous energy, she stepped inside.

The door to apartment six-nineteen was about halfway between the elevators and a stairwell exit at the other end of the long hallway. Reason made a mental note of the exit location. McKenzie opened the door before she arrived. Minus his customary hat, he looked strange, just an ordinary guy. "Come on in, darlin'," he said with a smile. Reason stayed put. "What?" he asked. "It's OK. It's my lady friend's place. She knows I'm here. She's at work."

Reason took her hands out of her pockets, where they had been balled into fists ever since she had stepped off the elevator. She moved past the cowboy, who closed the door behind her. On full alert and anxious, she looked about. The cowboy's boots sat on the floor near the front door, distinct and oddly abandoned. Beyond the boots, parquet flooring ran the length of the entrance hallway and continued into the living and dining room area. To Reason's right, off the front hallway, was a small kitchen. Through the kitchen, she could see another hallway, one that she knew typically led to one or more bedrooms and a washroom. The entire apartment was uncomfortably hot, but not wanting to stay any longer than was necessary, she kept her jacket on.

"Back in a minute, darlin'," said McKenzie. "Go on in." When McKenzie disappeared into the back hallway, Reason, without moving, surveyed the living room. Two dirty ashtrays full of cigarette butts and a plate of partially eaten pizza sat on a round, glass-topped coffee table. Behind the coffee table was a fat, black leather sofa. Beside the sofa, on a small side table, was a spoon, along with a small foil packet, a pack of cigarettes, and an open bottle of beer. Reason took a step into the room, not wanting to sit on or touch anything. The toilet flushed, and McKenzie returned.

"You ought to know by now that I don't bite, darlin'. Have a seat," said McKenzie, entering the room while adjusting his shirt. He picked up the plate of pizza, dumped the contents of one ashtray into the other, and then carried the whole mess into the kitchen. Returning, he sat on the couch and took out a cigarette. With the unlit cigarette jutting from between his teeth, he leaned back, crossed his feet on the coffee table, closed his lips around the cigarette, and looked expectantly at Reason. "Ya got that letter for me, darlin'?" he asked, the cigarette bobbing as he spoke. McKenzie put his hands behind his head and leaned back. "Sit," he said.

"Why are we here?" Reason asked defiantly.

McKenzie patted the sofa beside him. "Sit," he said again. She hated his presumptuousness.

"I don't want to sit, McKenzie. I don't want to be here." She stepped toward the door. He dropped his feet to the floor and sat forward.

"I'm not hittin' on ya, Reason," said McKenzie, softening his tone and using her name unexpectedly. "Take it easy. Sit wherever you'd like or stay standing." Reason stood her ground. McKenzie shrugged his shoulders and continued. "This apartment is where I keep my stash. That's all. Nothing more. I asked you here because it's convenient. I obviously can't have drugs at the halfway house and I've got strict curfews. I come here every day and I'm back at the house before ten o'clock each night. For the next couple of months, this is my life." He lit his cigarette and then deftly flipped the cigarette lighter back and forth between his fingers.

"I can't write the letter, McKenzie," blurted Reason. "I won't write it. I want nothing to do with William. I'm trying very hard to get away from... all of this." She gestured half-heartedly. "I haven't got everything worked out, but for sure my plans don't include him." She paused, attempting to gauge the cowboy's reaction. "Because of William, a part of me is forever damaged. I'm... broken. The me that used to dream, that used to trust people, that laughed freely... he killed all of that. And for me to have any chance at reclaiming who I was before him... I had to escape. I had to run. And I did. I escaped. And now? Now, I hide. Forever." McKenzie watched Reason, but his expression was flat and too impassive to read. "I'm someone else now. I'm finally becoming who I want and need to be. I can finally dare to believe in my future, a future that's only just begun. But because of what he did to me, I fight feelings of anger every single day. I trust no one. My heart is hardened. But here, in school, where my story is whatever I want it to be, whatever I can dream, I'm free." She raised her voice. "I'm sorry, but McKenzie, you represent everything I don't want to be. Your way of life is ugly, and it scares me. This apartment scares me." Reason huffed, her anger growing. "This place takes me back to being with him. I don't want any part of this life. It disgusts me to be here. You disgust me!" Breathless and trembling, she leaned against the wall.

McKenzie took a long drag from his cigarette, and then he took another. His prolonged silence infuriated Reason. She squinted at the door, contemplating a quick exit, but she stayed where she was and waited. A nearby clock ticked. The fridge hummed. A car horn blasted from below. Finally, McKenzie spoke. "Well," he stated plainly, clearing his throat. "I figured you might not write the letter, darlin'. But I sure didn't expect the personal thrashing." He stubbed out his cigarette. Tiny red embers broke away and scattered in the ashtray.

Reason felt a sudden and unexpected sadness for McKenzie, and for her harsh words. "I..," she fumbled.

"Save it. I don't want your pity," he said, pinching a piece of tobacco from the tip of his tongue. "I know what I am. I know what I'm not. Maybe I'll kick this shitty habit, maybe I won't. Who knows? Had some of that conviction of yours when I was your age, but I was already a junky by then. I've been drifting for so long... it's all I know. Hell, I've hit rock bottom so many times... with all the chances that I've had... if it was gonna happen... I should've been clean years ago." He looked away, unseeing, lost in thought. "It's a shitty life, but it's the one I've got. Every minute awake is about my next fix." He shook his head and looked at Reason, his expression like someone caught in a lie and ready to tell the whole truth. "The addict sees what he wants to see. He hears what he wants to hear. He does things he never imagined just to get his fix, and then immediately he plans for the next one. Addicts hurt the ones they love and then pretend it never happened—because that kind of darkness, darlin', results from being deep inside the belly of addiction." McKenzie stood, blew out a heavy-weighted sigh, and then sauntered to the large living room window and looked out. Without his hat and boots, he seemed small and vulnerable.

Reason did not know what to say or do. She could think only of getting away, but McKenzie suddenly turned and faced her. "I need the drugs, Reason. I knew I wouldn't get a letter out of you. So, I wrote one myself." Reason stared at McKenzie, silenced by the shock of onrushing fear. "He'll know it's from me, of course, but that doesn't matter. I told William that we're getting along famously. You doing what I tell you, being that I've been keeping you in line and all, teaching you how to behave. Gave him just enough detail to keep it convincing. Prisoners' letters are not private. Guards open and read them. So, I picked my words carefully. He'll understand. The point is... he thinks I'm roughing you up, sick bastard that he is. Me, I'm a different kind of sick bastard, but I'd never hurt you, not like that." McKenzie ran his fingers through his hair. "In a day or two, I'll have what I need. And that, darlin'... is my news for you." And then in a quiet voice, almost a whisper, he said, "I'm truly sorry for what you've been through, but I wrote the letter and mailed it."

Exhausted, and with the beginnings of a headache beating at her temples, Reason slumped onto the wide arm of the couch. "Do you know if he's coming here?" she asked in the low, hopeless tone of a person defeated.

"Don't know," said McKenzie, sounding sympathetic. But instead of comforting her, he looked angry with himself and snatched up the spoon and the small packet of foil and walked from the room. Reason followed him into the kitchen. On the counter were bottles of vinegar, rubbing alcohol, and a knife. Reason watched as McKenzie dissolved some drug; crack cocaine, she guessed. He held the spoon in one hand and heated its contents using a cigarette lighter. Reason wanted to ask him to stop, but shock and awkwardness kept her speechless. She longed to leave, but McKenzie turned and walked past her and back into the living room, syringe in hand. He sat down on the sofa. Reason felt sick—nausea gumming into a thick ball in her throat.

To object to McKenzie's blatant display of self-indulgence seemed pointless. Remaining quiet, she watched as he rolled up his sleeve and with his free hand and his teeth, tied an elastic strap around his bicep. He closed his fist and dabbed alcohol on the inside of his forearm. Then positioning the needle, he pushed the sharp point into his skin. Reason cringed and turned away, looking back when the syringe hit the glass top of the coffee table.

McKenzie sat slumped with his eyes closed, his head lolling backwards. Then he shuddered and moaned, and his head came forward. His eyes white slits, he smiled garishly, momentarily soothed by the onrushing effects of the drug. Reason could not bear to look at him. She rushed to the door and ran from the apartment.

10

daleel

❝ I'll not allow you to *endure* me. You must suffer!" howled Pain. But Reason was becoming more familiar with Pain's surly nature and persistent outbursts. And she learned that she too was persistent— and capable of not giving in to its wrath.

"You're not so mean and tough."

"What? Oh, really…" Pain snarled. "Shall I prove you wrong?"

"I'm beginning to see through your prickly disguise."

"I AM PAIN! I am your enemy. You WILL fear me!"

Reason winced, but Pain became uncharacteristically quiet. Knowing that her moment of peace would be short-lived, she hoped that sleep would come quickly.

CS ℘

The curtains fluttered at the open window, every so often billowing into the room. When the wind settled, they fell straight and flat and still. Outside, in the deepening twilight, a lone cricket chirped a lazy song.

Reason moaned in her sleep. Macy, who stood by her bedside, bent down to her. "You're brave, my dear, and you're making progress." Reason stirred, thinking that she had heard the divine whisper of an angel.

CS ℘

Surveying the halfway house seemed the logical thing to do, if only to learn exactly where William might be living. Approaching from the opposite side of the street, Reason stopped behind a bushy hedge where she could view the house more discreetly. An old century home, it was on a wide and impersonal street. Even the few trees that lined the boulevard seemed abandoned and starved.

The house—a sterile, white stucco cube—stagnated on the bleak and barren ground as if long forgotten. With shabby brown trim at the doors and windows, and little vegetation to soften its stark exterior, the two-story building seemed vacant. A narrow cement sidewalk sliced through the center of its patchy front lawn and led to a windowless front door—beige drapes drawn closed at each of the tall, narrow windows that flanked the door.

The house was deeper than it was wide. On one side, and in striking contrast, a small, tidy red-brick bungalow seemed almost to cower. On the other side, paved tight to the wall of the house, a crumbling parking lot sat rife with tall weeds growing through its many cracks. Reason studied the house, counting three large windows along the upper level. Towards the rear, a black metal balcony served as a fire escape, its retractable ladder deployed, the bottom rung hanging a manageable step above the asphalt. On the same wall, on the lower level, were two mid-sized windows near the front of the house, one large bay window in the middle, and then a tiny window, likely a bathroom, nearest the rear. The inhabitants had drawn dreary beige curtains closed at each window.

On the greying asphalt, leaning up against the house, were two white plastic chairs. A third chair lay on its side, near a black metal railing enclosing a cement staircase that led below ground. The house was utterly unwelcoming, and its drabness was exactly what Reason thought William deserved. She wondered which window belonged to McKenzie, and which could become William's. The thought was unnerving and caused her to look about as if William were already there, following her, waiting to pounce. Other than discovering its location and appearance, Reason had gained little by visiting the halfway house. "What was I expecting?" she said to no one.

 C8 80

Two months had passed since Reason had left the cowboy in his drug-induced euphoria. She had not seen him since that day, but she had felt his presence and had found evidence that he had been nearby. Yellow matchbooks appeared on her doorstep or wedged into her locker with the words "all clear" printed inside the little flap.

Reason somehow knew that William would be assigned to the local halfway house and resigned herself to the notion that his looming arrival was the awful way of an unfair world. Wondering if she could somehow prepare for the dreaded day, she thought about contacting McKenzie. But she could think of no truly useful reason to do so. With nothing to do but wait, she grew more and more anxious.

ଔ ฺ๛

"Welcome back, my dear," said Ruby, sitting forward in her chair.

Having once again returned to Ruby's world, Reason discovered a stranger standing beside them. She wondered how long the man had been there, and how much of her story he had heard. Shifting from the trance of storytelling to the reality of this magical world had become less and less jarring for her, each transition easier than the one before. But seeing the man standing there was nonetheless surprising.

"This is Daleel," said Ruby. The stranger said nothing, but closed his eyes for a breath and nodded. "Daleel is most interested in hearing more about the cowboy," Ruby explained patiently.

Daleel was old, his features kind—whittled by time. The outside corners of his eyelids drooped, giving him a look of perpetual sadness. He wore a white cloth headdress held in place by a slim, black headband. The fabric fell to well below his shoulders and fluttered in the breeze. His beard and mustache were also white, as was his ankle-length garment, the dazzling white contrasting and emphasizing his dark skin and brown eyes. His hands, one placed upon the other, rested atop a waist-high stick. Thinking of his age and wanting to be polite, Reason addressed him. "Do you want to sit?"

The man's mustache widened as his lips formed a smile. "Kind of you to ask," said Ruby, "but Daleel does not require a seat. He joined us while you were telling your story. He is your next Experience Guide, and he will soon lead you from the island."

"But what about you, Ruby? Does this mean you'll be leaving me?" Reason had become accustomed to Ruby's comforting presence, and the idea of losing her was alarming.

"Don't worry, my dear. You're in expert hands with Daleel. You can trust him as you have trusted me. Like me, he is interested in your story and he is keen to hear more about the cowboy."

Reason, perplexed, glanced at Daleel. "What can I say about the cowboy that you don't already know? What more is there?" she asked.

"Many people come and go during a life experience," replied Ruby. "Some encounters are fleeting, people passing almost unnoticed. Other encounters are longer and sometimes last a lifetime. Some people, like McKenzie, are not long in one's life, but their presence is powerful, often more than we know. So, tell us, what did you think of him?"

Reason looked from Ruby to Daleel. Ruby was still smiling, but Daleel gazed down solemnly. "I don't know," she said. "He made me sad... and sometimes he made me mad. He scared me. Well, not him exactly... his addiction, his lifestyle, and his connection to William. And yet I guess I believed that underneath all that misery and embellishment was a kind-hearted man." Reason looked once more at Daleel; nothing in his countenance had changed. "I don't think that I ever would have guessed it, but over the years I've maintained a soft spot for McKenzie, and I've wondered about him from time to time. I've wondered if he got straight or even if he's still alive. I hope he is. But I've always felt guilty and ashamed to... well, to have liked him." Reason squinted at Daleel. He moved very slightly, blocking the sun, which shone halo-like behind the wavering fabric of his headdress.

"Why feel guilty about sensing the good in someone?" asked Ruby.

"I don't know, I... I was embarrassed by him. It appalled me how he linked me to William, and to my past, a past I hated. I was embarrassed by his garishness and his sad life." Reason shook her head. She laughed sadly. "I was ashamed to know him."

"Ah, but there is alvays more to discover," said Daleel. He sounded out each syllable distinctly—his voice gentle, deep and flowing.

Reason blinked and cocked her head, confused by Daleel's comment but reassured by his gentle manner. "What more is there to discover about McKenzie? He was an addict. What more is there to know than that?"

"There is alvays more," said Daleel with a hint of mystery. He walked a short distance away and then stopped, his stick in one hand, his free arm out to his side and parallel to the ground.

"Craw, Craw," called the Raven.

Reason looked toward the sound, pleasantly surprised at the bird's return, and comforted by its loyalty. From a stand of glistening blue-tinged evergreens, she watched the bird swoop down, and with wings flapping, pull itself up into the air. As it neared, the sound of its powerfully beating wings became distinct. Having closed the gap between them, its talons flashed forward, its body angled back, and in a flurry of feathers, it landed atop Daleel's outstretched arm. Cocking its head, blinking, lifting its feet one at a time, the Raven was a stunning vision.

"Please, place your hand on mine," said Daleel, his free hand holding the top of the stick, which he held out toward Reason.

"Wait, what about Ruby? Where's..." But Reason sensed that Ruby had left them. She glanced at the Raven, encouraged by its presence. Then she sighed, turned to Daleel, reached out, and put her hand on top of his.

CS &O

Reason's surroundings became blindingly bright, and the ground beneath her feet went soft. She shaded her blinking eyes, looking about at a startling view of a barren desert. The air was stifling and the sun a fiery white ball in a cloudless sky. The vast, open space was overwhelming. She felt disoriented. "Where are we?" she asked, hearing nothing in return but the roaring wind. "Daleel?" She was alone.

Her fingers groped for and then found the mindfulness bean. She pulled it from her pocket. *Use the bean. Focus. Breathe.* Feeling lightheaded, she kneeled in the hot sand. *Don't panic. He'll show up. He won't leave me alone.* She was thirsty. *It's so damned hot.* Struggling to understand, she stripped down to her T-shirt and tied her blouse around her head. *What am I supposed to do here?*

Windswept dunes rolled to the horizon—an endless line of golden sand rippling against a flawless blue sky. Reason passed the bean through her fingers, squinting into the distance, staring at a prominent sand peak that stood out from the rest. The giant dune rose from the desolate landscape in the shape of a pyramid—sand blowing in dusty waves over its long angular edges. *What do I do? Go there? It's so far...*

Amid her uncertainty, Reason remembered the Raven—and Edward's words. "The Raven will come when I need him," she whispered aloud, feeling hopeful. "Raven!" she shouted. "I... I need you. I need you now!" Nothing happened. The relentless wind blew in loud gusts. Climbing to her feet, she shaded her eyes.

From beyond the massive, triangular mound of sand, a black dot appeared. Reason soon became certain that the moving dot was the bird, and with the mindfulness bean held to her chest, she called out excitedly, "Over here! Over here!"

"Craw, craw," came the bird's call.

Relieved and somewhat reassured, Reason laughed hesitantly, and copying Daleel, raised her arm out to her side. When she could hear the beat of the bird's wings, she squeezed her eyes shut, let out a tiny squeal, and waited nervously to feel its talons grip into the flesh of her bare arm. When the sound of its beating wings stopped, she did not move. She waited... and waited. And when she finally opened her eyes, the Raven was pacing in the sand less than a yard away. She dropped her arm. "Well, how was I supposed to know?" she said with an awkward chuckle, half expecting the bird to answer. But all it did was take a couple of quick hops in the sand.

What now? Happy for the company, but a little dismayed that for the moment the bird did not seem to offer anything helpful, Reason continued to search the desert for some kind of answer. In the direction from which the bird had come, a sudden shimmering caught her eye—a speck flickering just enough to summon her. She took a step forward, and as she did, the Raven lifted from the ground. They traveled together, the bird flying ahead, and every so often, circling back as if to check on her.

The wind blew blisteringly hot. To shield her face from both it and the sun, Reason pulled the fluttering material of her makeshift headscarf forward. Her exposed skin prickled in the heat. The shimmering thing in the distance turned out to be much farther away than she had first thought. The walk was taxing. Her feet kept slipping back in the sand. She struggled to focus on her goal ahead, and not on the endless desert stretching in every direction—avoiding dwelling on her thirst, or her exhaustion, or the thin layer of courage striving to keep her fear at bay.

Finally reaching the shimmering object half buried in a rising drift of sand, Reason dropped to her knees beside it. Pushing some sand away, she saw a tin container about the size of a shoebox. Twisting it free, she brushed the sand from its surface. Reason read the words etched into the lid: "Set Yourself Free". Spying what could be a latch on the side of the container, she slid it sideways and the underside of the tin box swung down. A book fell out. *Impossible!* Reason recognized the book as a journal from her past. She stared at it, unable to pick it up right away, its appearance a shock. "I burned you. I know I did," she muttered to the small book lying in the sand.

The Raven skittered toward her. It pecked at the pink leather binding of the journal, as if coaxing her to open it. She closed the empty tin box. "Oook, oook, oook," cooed the Raven. Reason brought the diary to her lap. Her clothes stuck to her clammy skin. She reached for the journal, pausing before touching it, then quickly flipped it open. Inside, a corner of one page was significantly dog-eared. She opened to the marked page and read the entry aloud.

"I had a dream about William last night. He
was nice to me—so strange. We were laughing and

143

dancing. He looked handsome and was kind. How weird is that? When I woke up... I wanted to go back into the dream. I wanted to feel more of that from him. I was missing him. WHAT'S WRONG WITH ME? The dream made me feel as if all the shitty stuff that happened... maybe didn't happen at all. If only for a few minutes, that's really how I felt. And I wanted to be back with him—back in his arms. But now, I'm just stupid embarrassed. I'm disgusted by my wanting him. It was just a dream, not at all the truth, and I KNOW THIS. And still, I missed him. And worse than that... I liked, no, I wanted him and that feeling lingers. I'm so ashamed. Why couldn't he have loved me like that in real life? Thank God no one will ever read this entry. P.S. Did I make him hate me?"

Reason hated how the entry ended with such a pathetic question. She closed the journal, not wanting to read any more—wondering why she had to read it at all, and particularly now, so many years later. *And here? In the desert? It's too absurd!* She remembered vividly when she had written the entry. It had been after she had started college, just a few months in, and a few short days before the cowboy had entered her life. Reason sighed, embarrassed by her own words. She re-read the inscription on the metal box, doubting that the discovery of her journal would lead her to any sense of newly found freedom.

The Raven suddenly lifted from the ground. Reason started, then hastily slipped the journal into her satchel, plucked up the tin box, and stood. "Wait!" The bird flew low to the ground, swiftly moving away. "Wait!" she shouted again. It flew toward the great sand pyramid, rising higher into the sky as it went. Reason kept her eyes on the Raven, dismayed by the distance growing between them. When the bird cleared the tip of the pyramid, it swooped down beyond it and disappeared. She tried to run, but hindered by the soft footing and the scorching heat, slowed to a measured, tedious pace—tired, thirsty, and hungry. *Where is Daleel? Where am I?*

The heat poured down from above and radiated up from below. Hot and blustery, the wind seemed to attack her from all sides. As Reason closed in on the pyramid, it loomed above her, many stories tall. She rested at the lowest point of the immense dune, staring up at it. To go around its wide base would mean a long struggle, but to climb its steep sides seemed impossible. From somewhere beyond it, the Raven called out, urging her on. Reason pushed forward, choosing a partial climb over the slow rise at the pyramid's base. Her calf muscles ached. Her arms were turning pink. She wiped the back of her hand across her parched mouth.

"Craw, Craw," called the Raven again. Reason focused on the bird's cry, pushing to get around the great mountain of sand, desperately hoping that she would find something more than miles of sandy dunes on the other side, knowing that she could not bear the sight of an endless stretch of desert. She stumbled, sending clumps of sand scattering down the steep slope. But she pressed on, and when she finally neared the angled crest of the mammoth dune, an astonishing view beyond emerged—a welcoming scene that revealed itself incrementally with each step that she took.

Nestled in a little green oasis, tall palm trees edged a rippling pool of bright blue. Lush, feathery fronds waved high above the water, crowning the leaning trunks like unruly tufts of hair. Enormous boulders, unusually oval and smooth, lined the pond—and around their broad bases, spreading like giant wine stains, were beautiful, low-lying red-flowering cacti. Daleel stood beside one boulder, his shoulders reaching half its height. And beside him, statue-still as if subjects in a painting, stood two camels.

Daleel faced away from Reason, looking skyward. A huge planet bearing an uncanny resemblance to Earth hovered there. The planet's immensity and looming proximity made Reason feel she could almost reach out and touch it. One half of its magnificent splendor hovered clearly detailed, while the other half faded into the ether. Cosmic white clouds, thin like pulled cotton, hovered above the planet's

145

titanic bodies of blue-black water and vast brownish-green landmasses. Reason stood stunned, her discomforts all but forgotten. Daleel turned to face her. "Takes your breath avay, does it not?" he said, rolling his R into a soft purr. Reason was silent, the scene before her rendering her speechless. "You did not think I vould leave you alone in the desert, did you? You must be thirsty." He beckoned Reason forward. She could then smell the camels—urine and manure carried to her on the hot wind. Pulling her gaze from the sky, she moved past the large animals, and past a pink-tinged boulder three times her height. Beyond the boulder, a tent came into view.

Daleel passed Reason an animal-skin pouch. The water was warm, but she drank eagerly, the blouse on her head fluttering in the wind. She wiped the wet from her lips. "That planet... what is it?" she asked. "It's beautiful." She swayed, tired and overheated.

"Come," said Daleel, taking her by the hand. He led her to the tent, a round and colorful structure, its fabric buffeting in the wind. Elaborate designs of strange flowers, animals, and fruits, exquisitely embroidered the tent from base to peak. Once inside, Reason dropped her chin to her chest in relief, right away cooled. She pulled the blouse from her head, her hair wet with sweat. The sudden change from the bright sun to the dark interior caused a gauzy grey veil to obscure her vision briefly—but she could smell the fresh fragrances of mint and coriander.

The tent rose in a draping curve above their heads, to a peaked center held aloft by a thick wooden pole. On the sand floor near the pole lay a neat pile of folded blankets, and close to the tent wall stood a table loaded with food. A cloth, woven in the rich hues of orange, purple, and gold, fell from the sides of the food table and rippled in the breeze flowing through the structure's large screened windows.

"Are you hungry? Vill you join me in a meal?" asked Daleel, approaching the table. He began filling a plate with food, piling it high, nibbling as he went, making sounds of approval with each mouthful. Reason was extremely hungry. She found dates and cheese, bread, mutton and goat, yogurt, fresh fruit, and cold barley and pumpkin salad. The selections looked and smelled delicious, and she was prepared to try a bit of each dish.

Daleel gestured to two large goblets of hot tea. Spiced with cardamom, the tea smelled delicious. "The planet is called Giabella," he said. "She looks a bit like your Earth." He pointed to the pile of blankets. "Please. Take one. Sit and eat. Giabella is not important to your journey, but she is, eh, a thrilling vision to be sure. The sight of her is common to me, but to you, I imagine she is, eh, extraordinary. She never ceases to please the eye."

Reason nodded, enjoying the textures and tastes of her food, the flavors mingling perfectly. She sipped the delicious tea, wondering whether the magnificence of this magical place could ever diminish. *Until now, I think I've been wandering through life, not really paying attention. But every bit of life is a marvel.* She smiled, remembering childhood games she used to play in the fields behind her house. *I knew back then that life was a wonder—a grand adventure. I knew it before I grew up and became... afraid of failure and judgment. Back then, each day was a miracle. And for all the years that have passed since, all I've ever had to do to realize that miracle again, was to stop, look, and listen.* Through the tent window, Giabella hovered gloriously. *All I had to do was to look at the sky. Or stop long enough to realize the miracle of the planet beneath my feet.* She closed her eyes. *Or to listen to any beating heart. I'm so grateful for the reminder now—reminded to pay attention and to notice the great wonders of life.* Reason nodded her head thoughtfully, satisfied by this simple insight.

"Tell me, vhat have you discovered so far about the cowboy?" asked Daleel, his voice plucking her from her thoughts. "Are you ready to tell me how he inspired you?" He had abandoned his plate of food and now walked stick in hand, his posture slightly bent, his robe stretching and hugging the contours of his legs.

"Inspired me?" Reason sat puzzled by the question, wondering how the cowboy could be the least bit inspiring.

"Yes, did you never think that he vas capable of such a thing?"

"I can tell you I certainly never thought about him in that way."

"And vhat do you think now?"

Reason remembered the journal. The satchel lay by her side. She put her hand on it. "When I was around McKenzie, he reminded me of... thoughts and feelings I had pushed aside. I didn't like the reminder then." She glanced at the satchel. "I'm not thrilled about the reminder now."

"Feelings are never truly pushed aside," said Daleel. "They simply, eh, lie in vaiting. Tell me about these thoughts and feelings that the cowboy avakened in you." He had stopped pacing and now stood peering down at her. She gave him a curious look. He looked wise, his eyes twinkling ever so slightly. Reason thought of the entry in her journal, and the confession within it. "It is okay, my dear," said Daleel in a soft voice. "There vill be no judgment by me, only, eh, consideration and guidance." He lowered himself to the ground and sat on a folded blanket in front of Reason. Despite his age, he sat cross-legged. "Please continue," he said.

"Before McKenzie contacted me," said Reason, "I had a dream about William. After McKenzie entered my life, I dreamt that same dream repeatedly." Reason pulled the journal from the satchel, leaving it unopened on her lap. Daleel did not acknowledge it; his gaze remained fixed on her. "I remember thinking that McKenzie was somehow responsible for the reoccurrence of my dream—ridiculous, I know. But every time I saw him, he reminded me of my dream and of the feelings it had provoked, feelings I was ashamed and afraid of." Reason put her hand on the soft, pink leather of the journal, still too ill at ease to open it. Daleel blinked his sad eyes, and with an almost imperceptible nod of his head, encouraged her to continue. "The dream was not exactly the same every time, but the situation was, with William and I being together as a happy couple. In those dreams, he treated me kindly and with respect. He was wonderful, caring, and loving." She suddenly wondered if Daleel knew about William and asked him.

"Yes, my dear, I know all about Villiam. Please, continue your story."

"Well then, you will know that what I have to say next is... repulsive."

"It is my duty to guide you. I listen. I do not judge."

Curious about Daleel, Reason asked, "What is your job here? I mean, you know, what do you do? Edward is the Librarian. Ruby is the Communications Director. What about you? What do you do?"

"Ah yes, titles and duties. I can tell you that Edward is more than the Librarian and Ruby is more than the Communications Director. These are their roles, yes, but roles alone do not define the person. People are much more than the roles they execute."

Reason nodded hesitantly. She wanted a clearer answer. "Yes, okay, that's true, but do you have something special that you... execute?"

"I am the Keeper of the Portals. As you have seen, vee do not alvays travel from one place to another conventionally. From time to time, vee use special doorvays. It is my responsibility to ensure that these doorvays are vorking properly, and it is my great pleasure to do so." His sad eyes twinkled, momentarily merry.

"Have I already used one of these doorways?" asked Reason. "It seems I'm in one place one moment and then, just like that, I'm in another."

"Although you have traveled from here to there vhile you have been visiting vith us, you have not done so through a Portal. A Portal takes you to a very special place. Vhether you pass through it or not vill depend upon vhere your story and your discoveries lead you." Daleel raised his right hand as if ready to take an oath. "Meeting me is a good sign that a Portal is nearby. But to get to it, you must tell me more. So, vhat do you have to tell me that is so, as you say, repulsive?"

Telling anyone this humiliating part of her story felt like jumping off a cliff. Reason could try to prepare herself, try to calm her nerves, but in the end, the telling of it meant pushing her fear aside and leaping. "I missed him. When I awoke from those ridiculous dreams, I missed William. And if I'm being brutally honest, I wanted to be in his arms. I wanted *that* kind of love from him." Reason peered sheepishly at Daleel. He said nothing, looking at her with kindness. "Do you understand what kind of person I was missing and wanting?"

"Yes."

"Doesn't that shock you?"

"And vhy should it shock me?"

Reason groaned. "How could I miss him? How could I want him? What was wrong with me? I've never confessed this to anyone before. Back then, I thought my wanting him meant I deserved how he treated me." Reason picked up a handful of sand and let it run through her fingers, waiting for Daleel to speak. He remained quiet. She continued. "Those damned dreams were to blame. In them, he was always good to me. This goodness must have confused me, right? I didn't want to be back with him. He terrified me. But, waking from my dream, a part of me seemed always to be missing him, and wanting him to... love me the way he did in my dreams." Reason could not sit still. She stood and moved to the table of food, staring absentmindedly at its contents. "Before McKenzie came around, I dreamt of William only once and I thought I could forget about that dream, forget about the shameful feelings it incited. I thought it was a one-time thing, one dream, one regrettable reaction. But after McKenzie entered my life, the dreams kept coming. The feeling of wanting William became like a fire that I couldn't extinguish, a passion I was ashamed of. Why would I ever want someone who had treated me with such hate and cruelty?" Reason looked at Daleel, wondering how he could abstain from judging her now. "What wise words do you have for me now?" she asked self-consciously.

"Sit."

"Sit? That's it? Aren't you appalled?"

"Sit, my dear. I am an old man, happy to be discussing these matters from a place of comfort. Please sit, back vhere you vere, here," he pointed a crooked finger to the ground, "in front of me."

Reason sat, their knees almost touching. Daleel reached forward and placed the open palm of his hand near her face, his rough, dry fingertips touching her chin. "Fire is a good vay to describe your passion, but you must understand that your perception vas limited by the hard truth of the relationship itself. You are vise, Reason, avare of the control of the abuser over the abused, no?"

"Well yes, but..."

Daleel waved a hand to silence her. "It is sometimes many years before the mistreated is free from such all-encompassing control. Such deeply rooted conditioning leaves an open and bleeding vound. It bleeds like an oil spill, black, slick, and spreading. And like the black oil that chokes the life out of the sea, Villiam's control and your resulting deep vound did the same to you. Avakening from your dream, you thought you vanted him, but it vas not him you vanted. You missed and desired the idea of love. But you desired a love that never existed, and yet, albeit imaginary, a love you vere not villing to let go. This is vhat brought you shame. But the truth, my dear, is nothing to be ashamed of." Daleel pushed his shoulders back and clasped his hands together. "Denial is a tool the ill-treated sometimes use for survival, but it is useful only for a brief time. Life must be observed for vhat it truly is, and be accepted for better or for vorse, before it can be truly lived."

Reason smiled reluctantly. "It's very hard to acknowledge that I was so weak as to continue to want a love that never existed, especially after knowing what he had done to me." Reason groaned and dropped her face into the palms of her hands.

"Your reaction to your dream had nothing to do vith veakness. For a very long time Villiam had a control over you that vould see you take the blame for being beaten and belittled, and lead you to assume blame for vhat vas his own... reckless approach to life." Daleel paused, waiting, scrutinizing Reason. "Do you understand? Do you see that your dreams vere a lingering consequence of your experience vith Villiam, and that your conditioned mind vas repeating old familiar habits? He had no love for you, but you vere still struggling to accept this truth."

Reason peeked above her fingers at Daleel. "It seems like something I should've figured out for myself. I feel so stupid."

"Again, you judge yourself. Is this useful? Instead, learn from the experience and then give yourself some long overdue love and kindness." Daleel became silent, patiently giving Reason time to absorb his words and to respond.

Reason had not thought about loving herself as she had loved others. "Give myself love and kindness? It's not so easy," she said sullenly. She wanted very much to believe that loving herself would be easy, but she believed that to do so, she would first have to forgive herself for all of her poor decisions and mistakes. But she was not sure if she deserved forgiveness. In time, she had thought that forgiveness for William seemed a possibility, no matter how impossible it seemed now, but for herself, forgiveness seemed unlikely. "Since my experience with William, I've been very afraid of losing control over my life like I did back then with him. And it's hard for me to imagine forgiving myself for losing control in the first place, for giving it up as I did. He had all the power because I gave it to him." Reason shrugged her shoulders. "For many years my goal was to get that power back and to keep it. As a child, I was quite a little perfectionist, and after William, I figured it couldn't hurt to think like that again. You know, do it right. Keep it right. Keep everyone pleased and safe. But living life like that is exhausting..."

"It is the fear of losing control that is exhausting. The fear itself causes constant anxiety. Every vonce in a vhile you may feel moments vhen your fear is quieted, but not for long, never for long. Tell me, vhat does being a perfectionist mean to you?"

She thought she knew, but now she was not so sure. "Well," she said, "it's about wanting everything to be just right, and it's about... well, not getting it wrong."

Daleel nodded as if in partial agreement. "Perfection is a desire for certainty in a vorld that is alvays going to be full of the opposite. Trying to predict and manage the future is futile, but a perfectionist strives to do so anyvay. And vhen they realize they cannot do so, vell then, they fret and obsess about it. It is no surprise that you are tired."

Reason had never thought of her need for control in this way, but Daleel was right. She had worried constantly. "But what can I do to stop it? What can I do to change?"

"Learn how to let go of an unrealistic vay of living. Vhen you let go, and vhen you realize you cannot control vhat is naturally out of your control, you can let go of fear and by doing so, let go of anxiety. And vhen you do, vhat do you think vill replace your fear and anxiety?"

"Something good, I assume. But I'm not sure how to just let go."

"Vell, tell me. Do you think you can make an uncertain vorld certain?"

"No, I don't."

"Vell then, you must concede. You must understand that you can take responsibility for your choices in life, but that the future vill be vhat it vill be. Set yourself free. Let go of the need for control and let go of fear. That, my dear, is your power."

"But what about the feelings I had after dreaming about William? How do I let go of my shame?" Reason shook her head and lowered it. "I get how my need for control has kept me living in a state of fear... a different kind of fear than when I was with William, but just as stifling. But I can't help still feeling that shame, and I worry about how other people will judge me for those thoughts and desires."

"You have spent much time contemplating these dreams of Villiam, and the feelings incited by them. You have held on to these feelings, to judge them as bad, and to see them as a sign of veakness. By doing so, you have given yourself a life sentence of shame." He paused. "Your desires and your hopes in life are yours to change. The approval or disapproval of others is not. Your freedom lies in letting go of vhat you cannot change. Accept the fact that you, and I, and everyvon else are imperfect, and you vill know peace."

Outside the tent, the wind moaned. Reason pushed her fingers into the sand, finding it surprisingly cool to the touch. Thinking about what Daleel had taught her, she felt lighter somehow. *Let go.* At last, she genuinely felt the burden of her shame lifting, as if a bit of darkness had pulled away from her body, leaving space for some healing light to get in. "Thank you," she whispered. "I've been so consumed with one way of thinking, with one way of being, that I had forgotten what it felt like to breathe with ease, and to feel free." She drew her knees to her chest and wrapped her arms about them.

Daleel stood, rising with some of the unsteadiness of the elderly. Reason watched, wondering if she should assist him, but she decided he had been managing many years without her, and to help him now seemed almost patronizing. Rising to stand beside him, she asked, "Are we going somewhere?"

"Soon vee travel. But now I must rest." Daleel skillfully used his walking stick to maneuver three blankets into a bed on the sand floor. Then he quietly lay down and was soon asleep.

Reason moved to the tent window and stared incredulously at Giabella—so big, beautiful, and extraordinary. High up, the sky had deepened into a dark blue. Nearer the horizon, a band of blue-tinted mauve was pooling into a long, pale pink strip.

As the desert cooled into the night, Reason made her own bed, and soon she too was asleep, warmed by the thick blankets and by her newly found sense of freedom.

11

a free mind

❝ Do you think you can simply sleep?"

"Yes. I do."

"I forbid you!" Reason's eyes blinked open. "You are weak. I am strong!" Reason writhed and moaned. "I have you now. I HAVE YOU NOW!" shouted Pain. Reason gasped.

Go away! Go away! Go away!

"Don't waste precious time on worthless demands, my pet. I am here to stay. Oh my, but don't you look puzzled. Let me remind you I hold all the power!" Reason's eyes opened wide, shifting from side to side, feverishly searching for a way out. "We've been together for ages, you and I. You have been stubborn, and infuriating, but not anymore, foolish creature. NOT ANYMORE!"

Pain descended, hot on Reason's skin. She tried to cry out but could manage only an anguished moan. From above, she saw a light. And within this wavering spray of white, a face developed. "Do not fear," came the sound of a woman's voice. "Do not fight what is not your enemy. Look for stillness and you will find it. See Pain for what it is, a means to release."

Pain smashed through the image. Reason felt a heavy weight pressing on her chest. She grabbed at the bedsheets, her fingers finding an object. She seized it in desperation. Small, hard, and round—for the briefest of moments—the object was familiar and comforting. She became still. The face reappeared. And a moment before darkness took her, she saw clearly the features of a beautiful, auburn-haired woman.

CB ∞

Reeling from her nightmare, Reason looked wildly about. Silver light spilled in through the tent windows. Daleel's bedding was there, but he was not. The details of the nightmare still fresh, she pushed her fingers into the sand floor to test its reality. *I'm here. Not there with that... thing!* In her free hand, she saw she held the mindfulness bean. "Daleel!" she shouted.

A soft shuffling announced his approach before he pushed the flaps of the tent aside. "My dear girl, vhat troubles you? You are trembling," said Daleel, moving to her side.

"I had an awful nightmare. It seemed so real!" Reason glanced about as if the dark presence in her nightmare might be lurking inside the tent.

Daleel lit a lamp—its dancing flame causing shadows to flit and flicker across his face. "Vhat did you dream?" He passed the lamp to Reason and then lowered himself to the ground. He had changed his clothes and now wore an ankle-length garment with side splits and pants.

"It terrified me. I was trapped, pinned down by something. I was in a bed, I think. And in terrible pain—burning throughout my body— screaming inside my head." Reason winced at the vividness of the memory and then carefully placed the lamp on the ground.

"Tell me more," said Daleel, his walking stick resting atop his crossed legs.

"I couldn't move or speak. I tried to scream, but my mouth wouldn't open. I felt paralyzed, desperate to get away, and..."

"And vhat, my child?"

"*The pain*, it seemed... alive, like a vicious animal in the room!"

"Vhat could you see?"

"I'm not sure..."

"Take your time."

"Not very much. The room was dark. Everything was blurry, yet somehow familiar. I'm pretty sure I was in a bed... you know, like a hospital bed. Everything was still, except for the pain which raged inside my body while also, somehow... hovering over me. Oh... Wait... Something else..." Reason closed her eyes, concentrating.

"Vhat, Reason? Vhat else did you see?"

"I saw a woman! Well, I saw the hazy shape of a woman's face. She had long red hair, and her voice was lovely, gentle, and caring."

"She spoke to you?"

"Yes... Yes, she did. She helped me! She told me that pain was not my enemy. She told me to stop fighting it. She said to look for stillness. Stillness, of all things! I remember how impossible I thought that would be. Then she told me that pain was a means to release." It delighted Reason to remember the woman's message.

"Excellent advice."

"Pardon?"

"The voman gave you excellent advice."

"Maybe so, but Daleel, the pain was stronger. It broke through the vision of the woman, and as it closed in and began to... to engulf me, I..." Reason stared incredulously at the mindfulness bean in her palm. She was certain that she had safely tucked it away inside her satchel when she had prepared to sleep. "The bean... in my dream, I found it under the bedsheets. I think it saved me."

"Ah, the mindfulness bean," said Daleel, nodding approvingly.

"You know about it?"

"Of course. It vill serve you vell." His voice rose in pitch, seeming to emphasize his belief in her good fortune.

"So, it was the bean that saved me?"

"My child, avareness is vhat saved you."

"How's that?"

"In your dream, do you remember the exact moment vhen you recognized the bean?"

"I do. Despite the agony, in that moment my mind quieted. I became calm all over. My body too. At that moment, I felt at peace, and I saw where I was. And I saw her face!" Elated to remember the details of the woman's face, Reason brightened, but then she frowned.

"Vhat is it? You look troubled."

"I just had it. I remembered everything, but now... I can't remember anymore. I can't see her face, or where I was. It's all gone. I mean, I knew where I was, as if I had been in that place for a long time. And when I recognized the place, I felt as if I lived there, in the dream, and not here... with you. But here I am, and it's all become so confusing. I can remember only the emotion attached to the memory and nothing more, no images."

"The answers vill come in time, my child. Vhat is most important is vhat you have learned from the experience."

"Yes... in time," Reason considered.

"Tell me, vhat more did you discover about pain?" asked Daleel, urging Reason on.

Reason felt increasingly confused. Her thoughts were becoming more and more muddled. *Is this what's real?* She looked around at the tent walls, the ceiling, the sand floor. *Is this desert world the dream?* She looked at her hands, turned them over, and then pinched her arm and laughed. She laughed until it hurt, her laughter winding down fitfully. And when it stopped altogether, Reason wondered why she had laughed at all, and immediately cried. Daleel watched her, letting her find her way back to calm. He was very tolerant; she thought as she wiped away her tears.

"I'm so overwhelmed by this whole experience. I feel... punchy and troubled by the crazy feeling that the nightmare was somehow real."

"The senses are persvuasive, and at times they can overvhelm. Let them be. Let their mysteries unfold vhen they may. Now," Daleel patted his knees, "tell me more about the pain."

"It was horrible and frightening. It was vicious, coursing through my body, overpowering my ability to think. It seemed intent on destroying me." Reason shuddered at the memory.

"Did you feel as if pain vas trying to... control you?" Daleel had taken up his walking stick.

"Yes!"

"And so vhat did you do?"

"What could I do?"

Daleel merely waited.

"I tried to move, tried to see where I was, tried to get away!"

"And vhat did you achieve?"

"Not much. I couldn't move. I felt powerless and I couldn't seem to fight back."

"And if you believed you could fight back, vhat vould you do?"

"I would get angry. I would push through it. I..."

"Yes, go on," said Daleel.

But Reason suddenly felt that she had no suitable answer. "I thought I knew what I would do, but the idea of fighting pain seems kind of ridiculous. It was much stronger than me. Maybe I just needed to give in to it," she said glumly.

"Ah, but vould you know the difference between conceding defeat to pain and consenting to accept it? The difference is a subtle but important shift in perception. If you could make that distinction, you might find that, through acceptance, you could change your perception of pain altogether," Daleel offered.

Reason sighed, feeling overwhelmed and inadequate. She closed her eyes, trying to concentrate, but giving in to self-doubt and impatience, she said, "That sounds lovely, but how could I possibly accept that kind of pain? It was killing me! It was an evil thing! "

"You think so?"

"What?" she asked in disbelief. "If you had felt it like I did, you would know that it was evil."

"Vhat did the pain feel like? Tell me more about that."

"Well... it was awful... burning... like acid on my skin. Pain attacked me, ruthlessly crushing me so that I could hardly breathe. I was terrified. It ached and stabbed icy-cold to my bones. Pain was in more than my body. It was in my head, wearing me down—killing me!"

"Vhat if you imagine that pain is not evil, and that it is instead, good? And answer the same question: Vhat did the pain feel like?"

"But that's ridiculous."

Daleel waited, his features softened by the calm of steadfast patience and understanding.

"Fine," said Reason grimly. "I felt it... soothe me..." But she faltered, believing the exercise to be pointless, and glanced suspiciously at Daleel. "This is absurd!"

"Go on, Reason. Try again."

Reason pushed aside her exasperation and doubt. Thinking that no harm could come from trying, she surrendered to the exercise. "Pain was soothing... like a soft tingling on my skin," she began. "It held me, gently rocking me so that I could relax. I felt safe. It caressed and flowed, warm to my bones. Pain was in more than my body... it was in my head, lifting me up—reviving me."

Reason's wide eyes showed wonder and unexpected amazement. Surprised by her own words, she became emotional, tears forming. "Where'd that come from? I feel... remarkably different," she whispered. "But how's that possible? They're only words." She looked at Daleel.

"A change in perception can do marvelous things, especially vhen spoken, and particularly vhen you hear your own voice recite your spirit's vishes."

"Recite my spirit's wishes? They're only words, Daleel, and not how it was. The pain did not feel good, far from it. Although now, I feel moved by pretending that being subjected to Pain was... a positive experience."

"If you must judge pain, vhy choose evil over good?"

"It seems impossible for me to judge pain as good."

"Vhy?"

"I'd be faking it."

"So, you choose to feel pain as a bad experience. And you believe that that experience is real?"

"I don't feel as if I have a choice."

"You alvays have a choice, my dear, even in your dreams. Choosing to think of pain as good, and how that makes you feel, may seem an absurd exercise, but the exercise is no more absurd than choosing to think of pain as evil, and how that makes you feel. And vhatever choice you make, it is important to know that the vay you feel is because of a perception, an interpretation, a limited representation. And although the experience is temporary, it has its consequences." He passed Reason his walking stick. "Let us try another exercise. Please, describe the stick."

160

Reason gave Daleel a curious glance and then examined the long piece of wood. She held it upright. "Okay. Well, it's lightweight, but seems strong. It's a blond wood of some sort. It's a bit twisted but straight enough to use as a walking stick. I guess it's about five feet long, and it's smooth to the touch." She looked at Daleel, wondering if she had said enough.

"You have described many of the stick's characteristics. But it is also old, chipped, and veakened from use. Crudely made it becomes slippery vhen vet. And it is also a veapon. So, is it good or evil?" He reached for the stick and Reason gave it to him.

"I suppose it could be both."

"Ah, yes, and vee might consider that to be closer to the truth. But maybe the stick is neither. Vhy label it as more than it is? It is a piece of vood, no?"

"Well, yes, I guess ultimately it is a piece of wood. And making that distinction about good and evil is easy to do with a thing like a piece of wood, but with pain..."

Daleel waved two crooked fingers, asking for silence. "It makes no difference vhat the object of observation is to the act of observation itself. You can learn to vatch pain. No labeling. Just vatching. You see, vith the mind confined by the limitations of labeling, a thing like pain, for example, is often judged to be more than it is, and often seen to be evil. But pain is a sensation. Nothing more. Nothing less. Judging it to be more than it is, leads to delusion. And delusion deceives the senses and the mind." Daleel held the piece of wood over his head like a spear, then lowering it, held it in his upturned, flattened palms and presented like a gift. "Look at the piece of vood. Refrain from labeling it. Just vatch it and good and evil vill cease to be. You can vatch pain in the same vay. Do so vith the avareness of a free mind. A free mind is neither deluded nor deceived."

Reason listened with keen interest. She was quite fond of Daleel and his kindness and ease. But she was struggling to understand. "A free mind? But how do I achieve a free mind when caught in the throes of pain? I don't think that I can reduce pain to a harmless sensation. It's not a thing like a piece of wood. I don't think that I can feel it hurt me without forming some kind of opinion about it."

"Ah, vell, at first you might choose to test your perception by befriending pain, rather than fearing it. There is some usefulness in that. But a free mind lets go completely, letting go of the need to judge. Through avareness, even vhile in the throes of pain, a free mind can take notice of the sensation—free of opinion. It can sit vith any sensation that arises. A free mind is a present mind."

"But how do I break the habit of judging pain... of judging everything? I've been doing so my whole life. I don't even notice anymore. I just do it. I'm not sure that I know how to stop. What if I fail? What if I..."

"Pain, like any other sensation, can lead to insightful contemplation... to stillness, and ultimately, to freedom from suffering." Reason scrunched up her face in doubt. Daleel smiled and then held his large hand in the air, his palm near to her face. "Look at my hand," he said. "Vhen your mind vanders, and you notice it has, bring it back to vatching my hand." They sat this way for some time, and when Daleel finally lowered his hand and spoke again, Reason felt relaxed and revitalized. Daleel continued. "You can break the habit of constant judgment, and find release from suffering, by cultivating the art of observation. Vatch your breath in the same vay you vatched my hand. A breath comes in. A breath goes out. Thoughts vill come. Thoughts vill go. Notice them and then let your focus return to the breath. Be patient. Trust yourself. Practise often, and old habits can reform." Daleel breathed deeply, thoughtfully, and then prepared to stand. He looked back at Reason. "The time has come for us to move on and for you to locate your next marker."

The markers! I forgot! Reason slid her feet into her sandals and pushed herself up from the soft floor. Pocketing the bean, she picked up the satchel and tucked the journal inside. Daleel walked from the tent and Reason hurried out behind him. The night air was cold. She shivered.

"You vill find a spare blanket on the camel. Vear it over your shoulders."

"We're riding the camels?"

"Yes, my dear."

Reason was becoming quite comfortable with the remarkable ways of this extraordinary place and its wise and gracious guides. She felt assured that she would be safe. She followed Daleel's instructions, free of concern and feeling confident that all would be well.

CS ⁂

The animals stood one behind the other, tied together by a braided rope. The leading camel responded to Daleel's approach and command, and calmly kneeled, its knobby-kneed legs bending on one side, and then the other, its large head tilting back. When the camel's rump was on the ground, Daleel climbed on and settled onto a blanket on the animal's back. Reason watched as he leaned back, and then left, and then right, as the beast rose to its feet. "Come," he said, waving her to the camel tied behind his.

"I'm a little nervous..."

"She has had many passengers. You are just vone more."

Reason approached the animal tentatively, its thick coat of hair the color of the desert sand. Thicker hair grew on its neck and hung down from its throat, hump, and shoulders. Its long eyelashes and bushy eyebrows moved lazily over big eyes fixed on her. The camel bleated, and Reason laughed. "Well, hello to you too!" she said.

With an obedient gentleness, the beast lowered itself. Reason climbed up and onto a richly colored blanket draped across its back. At the base of the animal's neck was a thick, curved leather handle. She grabbed it, holding on with both hands.

Various trinkets, tools, and other ornaments of exotic opulence adorned the camel's neck and hung down the sides over its large, curvy rump. They swayed and clinked together as the animal moved. Fully upright, it stood at least six feet at its shoulder and taller at its hump, and to Reason, the ground seemed a long way down.

Daleel made a soft clicking sound and Reason's camel lurched forward. She held on, squeezing her legs against the animal's body. As it walked, the camel's front and back legs on one side moved forward together—and the legs on the opposite side followed with the next step. This side-to-side action created a swaying movement that was difficult to settle into. Soon, Reason's pant legs had climbed her calves—and stayed there for the duration of the ride.

The rope tying the two animals together swayed in time with their pace and gait. Daleel and Reason rode in silence, moving through the darkened desert in single file at a leisurely pace. The beauty of the starry night sky, with Giabella fading into the wee hours of the morning, seemed to encourage the riders, and Reason soon fell into the cadence of her thoughts. *Why did I have that nightmare? It seemed remarkably real.* Shaking her head at the notion, she thought about Daleel's counsel on the perception of pain. *Can pain really lead me to something meaningful?* Pain, she was discovering, could be a guide, and not just a menace as she had believed until now. *Can I truly achieve a free mind and find release from suffering?* She looked ahead at the slow swaying motion of Daleel's back and shoulders, and the fluttering of his headdress, watching the hypnotic movement for a long while. And then, in the calm and stillness of the desert night, she began noticing her thoughts, choosing to let them come and go, avoiding any attachment. Relaxed and hopeful, she looked up and, for a long time, studied the stars. *What comes next?*

Soon dawn washed the desert in a hazy white light. And as they trudged on, Reason watched the rump of Daleel's camel as it moved in a slow, steady rhythm. And then she watched the flat leathery pads of its wide feet as they drew a narrow trailing path in the sand. Suddenly, Daleel raised his hand. The camels halted. Turning his head, he spoke. "Soon vee come to a place vhere you and I must part vays."

Part ways! "What? It's too soon, Daleel! I'm learning so much from you. I want to learn more." She had thought that both Edward and Ruby had also left her too abruptly. *And now Daleel?*

"You vill be fine," said Daleel. "Think of our parting as practice in letting go." He turned away, and on hearing his command, the camels resumed the trek.

The riders carried on in silence; the sun rising steadily in a cream-colored sky, the air warming. In the distance, two objects gradually came into view, shimmering in the early light. Reason shaded her eyes in an attempt to make out what they were. When she was finally close enough to recognize the objects standing abreast in the desert, she laughed aloud. Sunshine gleamed off the stark white surfaces of two very large, framed doors. They jutted out from the sand and stood alone—with no structure around them.

At Daleel's command, the animals halted. His camel lowered, and he dismounted. Reason's camel kneeled, and Daleel helped her to the ground. Her camel stood tall and noble. She touched the base of its neck. "Thank you, my friend." Then turning and pointing at the doors, she said, "Here, in the middle of a desert? Leading to where?"

"Portals," he said. "Vone for me. The other for you. You must locate your next marker to pass through."

"My marker, yes. I'd almost forgotten. What if I can't find it?" Reason looked about. "There's nothing here but desert."

"Pay attention, my child. The marker vill reveal itself and vhen it does, you vill have all that you need to cross through."

Reason circled each door. Neither one appeared to lead anywhere at all. "How does this work?" she asked, running her fingers along the frame of the nearest door.

"Like this." Daleel opened a door. He moved to the animals and grasped the reins of the leading camel. All three moved in single file through the giant-sized doorway, and as they moved through, Reason could see only desert on the other side. From the far side, Daleel gave her a nod and then pushed the door closed.

She stared at the closed door, expecting it to open again, but nothing happened. The wind wailed and whipped the loose strands of her hair about her face. She felt her panic level rising. *Breathe, Reason. Breathe.* She walked to the door that Daleel had used and peered around it. Nothing to see. No Daleel. No camels. Nothing but desert. She reached for the door handle and readied herself, and for the briefest of moments, she felt the solid firmness of the porcelain, but the handle simply disappeared... and so did the door. Reason

165

stumbled backwards and sat awkwardly, panic flip-flopping in the pit of her stomach. On hands and knees, she scrambled to the remaining door and reached for its handle. *Locked!* She dropped her chin to her chest and groaned, frustrated by the idea of being further tested by the scorching sun. She looked about in desperation, the scene extraordinarily isolating. Dismayed, Reason tried the handle again. It would not budge. She bumped her body into the door, only to find that it was solid and unmovable. On her knees, she fought for calm.

Pay attention. The marker will reveal itself. She took the satchel from her shoulder and dumped out its contents. Her journal landed at the foot of the door. Pulling the mindfulness bean from her pocket, she stared at it. *Nothing. No result. Not this time.* She tucked the bean safely away and sat with her back against the door, looking again at the journal. The end of a yellow tassel peeked out from the book. *What's that?* She grabbed the journal and opened it. The tassel was attached to a bookmark—a bookmark which she recognized. It had been a gift from her mother and decorated with tiny yellow flowers clustered into diamond shapes. Reason tried the door again. Still locked. She pulled the bookmark from her journal and turned it over to find a long, flat key stuck to the back. *Reveal itself indeed!* She eased the key from its place and, with great anticipation, inserted it into the door lock. It met with no resistance. She turned the key to the left and with a sharp click, the door unlocked. Taking a deep breath, Reason stood, and with one last glance at the desert, she pushed the door open all the way.

12

the woman in the mask

The view through the open door was confusing and disheartening. Beyond it, Reason saw only desert. She reached over the threshold and felt nothing but sweltering desert air. *Have I done something wrong? What did I miss?* Heavy with fatigue and expecting little, she snatched up the satchel and stepped through.

The bright light of the desert went dark. The air became still and cool. Reason smelled cedar and candle wax. In the unexpected silence, she listened to the loud, uneven rhythm of her breathing. And as her eyes adjusted to the dark, she saw she was standing in one corner of a large barnlike structure.

Around the perimeter of the rustic space, eight lit candelabras hung from long chains that disappeared into a high black void. The candlelight illuminated eight gold pedestals. The pedestals sat directly below each of the hanging fixtures, and on each pedestal was a glass vase of royal-blue, white, and emerald-green flowers. Each of the flower arrangements served as a backdrop to a petite, café-style table and two chairs.

Central to the space, in dark shadow and set in rows like church pews, four groupings of low-backed benches faced the center. The complete scene reminded Reason of a theatre stage—deathly quiet and impossibly still, waiting for the actors to bring it to life.

Opposite her, a white light suddenly spilled in through two narrow, side-by-side stained glass windows. Reason shielded her eyes. The glass mosaics lit up brilliantly and together, the design they created seemed somehow familiar. She tried to place it, but she felt peculiar, as if she had lifted from the ground and was now floating nearer to the windows. And yet as quickly as the odd sensation began,

167

it stopped, and Reason found that she was staring at the windows from where she stood—vaguely wondering about the image that they had portrayed.

As she watched dust particles twirling lazily within the two milky columns of light, out of the silence the thumping of a drumbeat began—a deep four-stroke rhythm: bong, bong, bong, bong. Awakened from her trance, Reason looked for the source of the sound, and as she glanced about the room, she started upon seeing a woman sitting on one of the benches. Cupping a hand to her mouth, Reason stifled a squeal. *Where'd she come from?*

The woman sat facing the windows and appeared to be formally dressed. Reason moved toward her, but when the drumbeat abruptly stopped, Reason stopped too.

The woman wore a small, feathered hat with her hair pinned up beneath. The elegant hat plunged at a sharp angle on her down-turned head. Reason wanted to call out to the woman, to announce her presence, but the tranquility of the church-like atmosphere kept her silent. She watched the mysterious woman, waiting for her to speak, but the woman remained eerily still and quiet. *Is she praying?* Reason waited.

The columns of light reached well over the woman's head, stretching across the large room. Reason's gaze followed the twin beams to where they landed on a small table. On the table was a sheet of paper. Reason tiptoed toward it, stealing glances at the woman as she went. She picked up the piece of paper, its edges uneven and fuzzy. She looked once more at the woman and then back at the paper:

Welcome, Friend.
Please Find Your Name
in the Soul Box.

The surface of the empty table blurred, the air above it wavering and swirling. A long narrow box materialized. Reason reached out tentatively, touching the black box with one finger, pulling her hand

REASONS | Sherry denBoer

back, afraid that the box might simply disappear as other things had—but it did not. She carefully removed the lid. A tidy row of file-sized cards filled the box from end to end.

Flipping through the first few cards, Reason discovered that each one contained a name, and the names were alphabetized. She looked back at the woman who still sat motionlessly, her head still bowed. Returning her attention to the box, Reason searched through the succession of cards—looking for the letter R. Many names flashed by. Quinton, Rachel, Raymond... Rea. And there it was, Reason. Pausing, both delighted and nervous, she pulled the card from the box, turned it over, and read:

> *Many souls have passed through*
> *this place of peace and tranquility.*
> *All souls are welcome—*
> *each one protected by*
> *its own lifelong Guardian.*
> *Your soul's Guardian is the*
> *Woman in the Mask.*

Many souls have been here? Reason turned, scanning the shadowy interior of the barn, half expecting to see these other souls, but she saw no one other than the mysterious woman. She sighed, wondering what might happen next. *Should I go to her? Should I call out from here? Should I...*

"Welcome Reason," said the woman without warning, still having not moved a muscle. So still was she that Reason wondered if someone else had spoken. "Don't be shy." Her voice was soft, and pleasing, flowing across the room as if in song. "No need to stay way over there," she said.

"Well, I... I guess I was waiting," Reason said hesitantly.

"Waiting? Well then, with time to wait, there is time to awaken," the woman offered.

"Awaken?"

"To wait is to pause. Pausing creates a wonderful opportunity for stillness of mind and body. And stillness awakens the senses—allowing the soul to breathe, and simply to be."

"Be where?"

"Wherever you are. Fully present." The woman answered with a frankness that seemed to suggest that Reason should already know.

"I understand the significance of being present. You're not the first person to talk to me about being in the here and now. But with my incredibly limited experience, I don't know if I'm... well... doing it right," said Reason, edging closer to the woman. "My thoughts get in the way no matter what I do."

"Being is not something that you do. Being is a state, a fact of... existing," said the woman, finally raising her head. "This place is one of my favorite places to be. Stop, Reason, right there where you are. Pause, be still, and observe." Reason stood still and held her breath. "Breathe," said the woman knowingly. Reason breathed. "Notice your senses, all of them, one by one. Listen to the sounds. See the details. Be fully present."

"I'll give it a try, but my thoughts always get in the way," said Reason.

"There is no need to strive to be. Observe your thoughts as you observe your surroundings. Notice a thought when it arises. Give it purposeful attention. And then let it go. Release it like a balloon from your hand. Let it float away," replied the woman in her gentle, flowing tone.

Reason was unconvinced that she could let her thoughts go so easily. They always seemed to be excessive or running wild, but she was determined to try. She began by looking at her feet. *Yes, those are your feet.... balloon. Let it go.* She focused on the hard wooden surface of the floor, feeling its flat firmness beneath the soles of her sandals. *What is this place? Balloon. A church? Balloon.* Her gaze drifted to the grain in the wood, not naming what she saw, trying only to see it. Like tiny tributaries, streaks of red, cream, light brown, and black ran through the wood-planked flooring—meandering rivers of color becoming richer as Reason examined them. *How vivid...* The wavy lines of color seemed to rise from the floor as if they intended to flow right into her. She noticed the heaviness of her limbs, the softness of her muscles, and even her beating heart and the blood flowing through her veins. She closed her eyes and listened; the silence alive with potential. A hushed, calming strength seemed to fill Reason with renewed energy. She smiled, feeling whole, and opened her eyes. The room seemed suddenly ablaze with detail, the candelabras glowing luminously, the flowers filling the air with their fresh floral scent.

The invigorating experience made Reason feel she had only now fully awakened. Reveling in her relaxed bliss, she walked toward the woman, stopping near her, wanting to see her face but instead, from behind, watching the gentle rise and fall of the woman's shoulders. Reason waited, alert and calm. And when she finally spoke, even the sound of her own voice seemed more alive. "Everything here seems so... brilliant," she marveled.

"The vibrancy that you feel, the energy that feeds you now... it has always existed," said the woman. "You make the ordinary extraordinary just be noticing. To experience the true nature of anything, you must be fully present. It's not magic. It's a natural and pure awareness. Please, come, sit," said the woman, gesturing to the bench behind her.

Reason sat and got a first glimpse of the woman's mask. Glistening gold, with ruby-red half-smiling lips, the mask followed the contours of the woman's face, concealing the soft curves of her forehead, jaw, and chin. Jeweled earrings hung from the woman's ears, the blood-red of the dangling gems matching the color of her hair.

Thunder rolled nearby and then crackled overhead. Reason started at the sound. The woman in the mask did not react. Reason remembered the card she held. She put it before the mask and asked, "Have you been expecting me?" Lightning flashed from behind the stained glass windows. Reason glanced there, noticing that the image that had been visible in the mosaic before was now unrecognizable.

"You and I have met before," answered the woman.

171

Reason watched the woman's profile, intrigued by the mask, watching it move ever so slightly as the woman spoke. The thought that they had met before was shocking. "How's that possible? Where?"

"You will remember," answered the woman, "when you most need to." Reason sat back, disappointed. The old wooden bench groaned. "Please, may I see your bookmark?" asked the woman, reaching her hand over her shoulder, long pearlescent nails peeking through the intricate black-laced stitching of her glove.

My bookmark. Reason reached into her satchel, retrieved the bookmark, examined it for a moment, and then placed it in the woman's hand. "Here," she said.

"Splendid," said the woman, holding the bookmark above the mask.

The drumbeat resumed. "Where's that sound coming from?" asked Reason, looking about.

"Tell me," asked the woman, "have you seen the image on your bookmark here, in the Sanctuary?"

Reason furrowed her brow. The drumbeat stopped. *Sanctuary?* The thought of a haven was comforting.

The woman held the bookmark like a torch. Reason looked at it. She could describe the design, but she had never given it much thought or looked closely at its details. She knew the image was cheerful, with all of those little yellow flowers, and she remembered it fondly. Her mother, who had been an avid reader, had passed on her passion to Reason, and the bookmark symbolized their shared love of books. Thinking of her mother now, Reason saw her as she had appeared at the end of a good day, her legs curled up on the living room couch, a book in her hands. Reason loved how serene her mother had looked in those moments, her head bowed under the late-evening lamplight, her fingers seeking and finding the corner of a page, grasping it, waiting, then turning the page over. Reason loved the crisp crackling of the turning page. To her, it was the sound of quiet intimacy and a peaceful home.

Smiling at the memory of her mother, Reason answered, "No. I haven't. Why would I?" But her expression quickly changed. "Wait! I feel... something... different... about the image. Something more. Something important—as if the image is connected to me... somehow associated with who I am. But that sounds crazy." She laughed. "And yet, it feels important. Like it has a special meaning for me. And yes! I think I have seen it here. But where? I can't remember where..." Reason looked about. Her eyes widened. She slid to the edge of her seat. "Yes! I saw it when I was standing back there..." She pointed toward the table of cards, but it had disappeared. "Where'd the table and box go?"

"An empty box does no good here. It will reappear when it is full again. Focus on the image. Tell me more about it. Tell me where you saw it?"

Empty? But there were so many names.

"The image," coaxed the woman, "do you remember where you saw it?"

Yes. Reason leaned forward, feeling excited and on the edge of an important discovery. "I saw it when the bright light first shone through the stained glass windows. And when I saw the flowers depicted in the windows, I think... I think that I... floated out of my body! The sensation was as if I had left my body standing back there." She pointed to where the table used to be. "And I, well, more like an essence of me, floated to the window. How strange a feeling it was..." Reason clasped her hands together, concentrating, trying to hold on to the sensation of drifting free of her body before the impression faded altogether. "When the light was shining at its brightest, I remember that the mosaic pattern was the same as the picture on my bookmark. I saw it for only a very brief moment. And then, just like that, I was back in my body, and I... well, I promptly forgot."

The woman slid to the end of her bench and her new position gave Reason a chance to take in her full attire. She wore a deep-purple, cropped jacket over a blue-tinged blouse. A large sapphire and topaz brooch glimmered in the flickering candlelight, clasping the blouse closed at her throat. Wrapped about her waist, she wore a wide, blue satin sash, and from beneath it, her purple skirt flowed to the floor—a spray of tiny blue dots embellishing its wide hem. "The presence of your image in the windows confirms that all is as it is meant to be," she said with a hint of satisfaction. "The image is a reoccurring marker along your life's path."

"A sign of some type?"

"Whenever the image appears in your life, its presence verifies that you are where you are supposed to be, no matter what your circumstances are at the time. Now and then, you may sense the image, and maybe even see it, or hear it, as you have heard it here in the beating of the drum. Sometimes you may even feel its presence as a shiver from the core of your being, but after today you will no longer remember its significance. The image of tiny yellow flowers in a string of diamond shapes has been unique to you since before you were born." The woman paused and sighed. That tiny sound, and her lowered head, made her appear momentarily nostalgic. "On a quiet winter evening," she said, "with you growing in her belly, your mother was given a bracelet in celebration of your approaching birth."

"Oh, I remember that bracelet," Reason said with shining eyes, emotion rising in a sentimental rush. "She kept it in a jewelry box on her dresser. I was always sort of fascinated with it—a pretty chain of yellow-flowered diamonds. I used to try it on in secret." Reason twisted her wrist as if the bracelet was there.

The woman nodded but said nothing. She raised her chin and moved her head as if she was scanning the room. Reason watched her, captivated. Then as abruptly as the woman had looked away, she returned her attention to Reason, her voice lowered. "This image," she said, moving the bookmark to her lap, "has followed you to adulthood and will be with you always." Again, she turned away, this time tilting her head as if she were listening to a faraway sound. Then bringing a gloved finger to the eerily still lips of the mask, she whispered, "Shhh." Reason sat rock still. She heard nothing. The woman remained alert. Anxiously, Reason looked into the dark stillness of the room. "The time for you to face fear is quickly nearing," said the woman with sudden urgency. She spoke in a low, ominous tone—

moving to face Reason head on—the sudden full view of the mask surprisingly alarming.

"What?" Reason clenched her fists, speaking more loudly than she had intended. "What does *that* mean?"

"You are the storyteller," answered the woman, her voice now softened, her tone tender. "Only you know what lies ahead. Only you can face the fear that confines you."

Reason knew that she was approaching an appalling episode in her story of her time with William. She wondered if the retelling of this event was the source of the fear that she must face. She felt anxious about revisiting the dreadful incident, and still sorely unprepared to reveal the horrible details to another person.

"Others have passed through this Sanctuary," the woman said as if buying Reason time. "Many of them have been as hesitant as you. But the mystery of this amazing place will guide you, as it did the others." She gestured into the room. "And yet, no matter how extraordinary its powers, the Sanctuary alone cannot release you from your burdens. Only you can do so, by truthfully telling your story." The woman put both hands on the back of her bench and leaned into them—the mask seeming to float toward Reason. "Trust is the key. Trust that by facing fear you can leave it behind and replace it with love." She lifted her arms and fanned them into the room as if presenting it. Reason looked in the direction of her gesture. "Many have come here before you and have moved on. However, some have been here a very long time, struggling to trust and to believe. There, look." She pointed across the room. Reason looked. She saw nothing, but the hair on her arms stood on end. She watched the woman's hand waving into the emptiness. "Relax. Breathe. Trust," said the woman, the soft singing tone of her voice pleasantly hypnotizing.

Reason closed her eyes. *Trust.* She inhaled slowly, and when she opened her eyes, to her astonishment, the space had become filled with ghostly forms and strange voices—murmuring, echoing, and circling. Mostly, the magical wraithlike figures flew about with an almost fanatical fluidity, but some hovered still, hanging limp as if they slumbered. And as Reason looked on transfixed, some of the figures raced toward the windows. Once there, they appeared to scrutinize the design in the stained glass. Then, one by one, they scattered, flying away from the windows and back into the room—where some of the group faded away completely.

A sudden draft swept Reason's hair about her face. She turned and saw beside her a quivering, ethereal form. It floated a few feet above the bench. Curious and unafraid, Reason stayed perfectly still. The creature darted nearer to her. Spellbound, she stared at its pallid, wavering face. *I think it's smiling!* Reason held her breath, fearing that the tiniest of movements might scare it away. The ghostly figure suddenly wrapped itself about her, its embrace soft and warm. But the contact was fleeting. The entity pulled away, ascended, halted, peered down, and then dashed into the darkness above. Reason laughed with delight.

"Amazing! Did you see how it embraced me? What is it? What are they?" Reason glanced about the room, rising from her seat and then sitting just as quickly. "Why can I suddenly see them? Can they all see me? This one sure did. Did you see how it looked at me?" Reason looked at the woman and then peered into the room, eyes gleaming. Together, they watched the swirling fog of otherworldly creatures, Reason in awe, the woman at ease. More of the forms gathered at the stained glass windows where they blended into a large pulsating white energy, hovering momentarily, and then scattering. Reason heard whispering, and sometimes full voices, the utterances fragmented, at once close, and then distant, and in diverse languages. Every so often a faint whisper, a wild giggle, a mournful wail, or a shrill rush of laughter burst from the bustle and whizzed by.

"These," said the woman in the mask, "are sentient energies just like you, and a few are like me."

"Like us how?"

"Some are here taking part in their own journeys, telling their own stories. Others are here as Guardians. Look there, by the windows." The woman pointed to a cloud of entities. "Each one recognizes its individual sign, as you did. The stained glass windows will show a different image to each observer." The woman looked directly at Reason, her eyes dark, glinting pools of black. "What we are witnessing is a timeless creation, one that has collected over the ages. Not all of the beings that you see in this creation are experiencing the Sanctuary at the same time. And they are mostly unaware of one another, that is until permitted a few minutes of observation as you are now, or like the one who discovered you and is indeed here at the same time. But even the idea that both of you are here at the same time is an illusion, as that being exists in its own dimension, a dimension that has only momentarily intersected with yours."

The woman moved her head from side to side, and the ghostly images vanished. The room was again still—and deathly quiet. Minutes passed and for some time, the woman looked once more as if she were in prayer. Reason wanted to speak, but the woman's deliberate and prolonged silence was too profound to interrupt. When the woman finally clasped her gloved hands and then stood, Reason breathed with relief. "Where did they go?" she asked.

"A few are still here." The woman gazed into the shadows. Reason looked too, but saw nothing. "Their presence is not always detectable."

"Do all beings come here to this Sanctuary?

"Not all souls journey to *this* place," replied the woman, pushing her shoulders back and holding her lace-covered hands flat against the straight line of her sash. "Many Sanctuaries exist, just as many paths lead to each of them." She waved one hand in the air. "Whatever the Sanctuary, each being's sign is revealed. Its revelation is earned and happens only once in a lifetime. Your ability to find your way is what has led you here to meet me. I do not create your path, but I can make subtle suggestions along the way, suggestions that you may or may not notice or heed. And although you are not aware of my presence, I am near you always. I am the record keeper of all that you do. I protect your truth. You may never see me again, nor remember who I am, but I, and the image of your sign, will remain in your subconscious always."

"I don't know what to say. This experience is wonderful and intense, and humbling. I always wanted to believe in Guardians, but if

I'm being truthful, I never did. But here you are!" Reason shook her head in wonder. "All of this, it's... remarkable! And the image. A sign of my very own. That's a pleasant surprise and... comforting, a kind of safety net. But I don't understand what good is going to come from a subconscious memory of an image or of you, my Guardian." Reason frowned in frustration. "I understand so very little. I feel as if I'm wandering through some wacky wonderland here, trying my best to find my way, trying to make sense out of... everything." Reason's frown turned into a melancholy smile. "I've been searching madly, no... achingly, for an ultimate purpose to my life... and to all of this... creation. Is there some greater power that has a plan? A plan for me? I mean, otherwise, why do I have a Guardian? Why do I have a unique image?" She glanced at the stained glass windows and then back at the unsettling impassivity of the mask. "Why am I really here? Some plan must exist, right? A plan that created this place and created me and you?" She tapped her fingertips together, gathering her thoughts. "And that nightmare I had... was it an omen? Was it a warning? About me dying? That's it, isn't it?" She held her hands to her head as if to keep her thoughts in order. "I must be nearing some kind of end. Maybe even the end of my life? Right?" She glanced at the woman, pausing for the briefest of moments before continuing. "This journey, my time here...," Reason waved her arm to indicate the Sanctuary, "it's about the end of my existence, isn't it? Well, if that's the truth, then... fine, let's get on with it." She sat up straight, as if sitting taller might make her stronger and wiser. "When will it happen? How will I die? I'm not afraid of death. Really, I'm not." She sat back, suddenly exhausted. "But I am tired. Tired of dealing with the shame of my life. And despite all of this," she sighed and reached out to the woman in the mask, stopping shy of touching her, "despite all of this, and having you as my Guardian, I still feel so much pain and anguish, and I'm still ashamed about my time with William. So please, tell me, before I die, will I experience much more pain and shame? Is it true that I can be released from suffering? All I've ever wanted was... peace." She sighed at the floor; her expression weary. "That's all. Peace." Then, alarmed, she grabbed the edge of her seat. "What if I don't know what to do when I'm faced with fear?"

"Do not fret so," answered the woman. "You are here now, in this Sanctuary, precisely because of the choices that you have made so far in your journey. The opportunities ahead are endless. The potential outcomes are many. Perhaps there is no end at all. Perhaps the end and the beginning exist timelessly, like the subtle pause between breaths, not wholly joined, yet never truly separate." In the candlelight, the woman's mask glistened as if made of porcelain. "The peace that you long for is waiting." In a slow, reverent manner, she slid her fingertips along the smooth, rounded edge of her bench. "Most of the souls that visit this Sanctuary are searching for forgiveness, as are you. But to achieve it, you must first acknowledge, and then accept *all* of the choices that you have made during your life. There can be no exceptions. On the other side of acceptance is peace."

Reason's shoulders dropped and she groaned. "I hear your message. I understand the words that you are using, but... that kind of acceptance seems almost impossible for me. I don't know how to just... completely let go of the shame that comes from the choices I've made. I don't know how to accept some of my biggest mistakes. So," Reason sighed, "I might wait forever for that peace."

The mask shifted as if moved by a smile beneath it. "Think of your journey like that of a skipping stone," said the woman.

"A skipping stone?" laughed Reason with surprise and skepticism. The woman stood. She walked across the Sanctuary, the hem of her skirt flaring above ankle-high boots. She stopped near one of the suspended candelabras, the light falling onto the shiny swaying fabric of her dress in bouncing gold ribbons.

"A being is propelled into the current of life much like a skipping stone thrown onto water," replied the woman, curling the fingers of one hand over the fingers of the other and bringing both hands to her chest. The mask turned and faced the shadows. Seconds passed with another long period of quiet. Reason waited. The woman began speaking before she turned back. "Moving through space and time, a being races along its path, acceptance and peace often trailing behind like wisps of air in a perpetual chase." Again, she turned away and seemed to scan the room. Reason looked too. All was still and quiet and unremarkable. "And like the skipping stone when it touches the water," continued the woman, "a being experiences critical moments in life, moments of either great joy or sorrow, and then its fast pace slows. In these moments, when time seems suspended, acceptance and peace advance and begin to catch up." She paused, raised her hand, and listened to the sounds in the room. Reason heard nothing. "With enough critical experiences," she continued, "...moments that cultivate profound awareness and clarity... a being can attain full acceptance and lasting peace. And eventually," she said, her voice hushed but unwavering, "as it is the inevitable destiny of the stone to pass through the water... the being will also transition. The certainty of this transition is nothing to be afraid of."

Gracefully, she lowered her arms, holding them rounded like a ballerina, her hands in front of her hips, fingers almost touching. Again, she looked away. Reason watched her, heard her make a little sound, a quiet, resigned sigh before she resumed speaking. "For some beings, the intervals between critical moments are periods of slumber and dulled senses. But for others, these intervals are wonderful opportunities for awakening, understanding, and regrowth." She took two quick steps closer to Reason, her skirt swooshing, the candlelight forming a halo around her head. And then she went silent.

Reason frowned, finding it difficult to remain passive when faced with such persistent and unsettling behavior. She was about to ask the woman why she kept looking away and what she was listening for, but with a hushed and startling urgency, the woman spoke first. "Contemplate the critical moments in your own life, Reason. And you'll discover that you have already achieved a great deal of acceptance. And when your journey finally winds down, do not fear the moment of transition. That moment of change will be one when you are most awake and filled with profound clarity."

She held her arms forward as if offering Reason her grace. "The moment of transition will be peaceful, and when it happens, like the stone having found a resting place in the calm at the bottom of the lake, you will wait peacefully until the natural current of life lifts you, and brings you once more to shore."

Then the woman gathered up her skirt and hurried to Reason. Letting the satiny folds drop, she bent forward and plucked up Reason's hand. The mask hovered forebodingly. Reason gasped and instinctively leaned backward, but the woman held on. "Love, my dear, is overflowing from the hand that created you. Allow the knowledge of this great love to conquer your fear." And then with a darting glance over her shoulder, she cried, "Go to your story. GO NOW!"

CB EO

Reason awoke in relatively good spirits, and to a pleasingly sunny morning. And in a rare moment of ease, she moved through her routine without the undermining thoughts of William's arrival. A few weeks of stimulating study and a welcome flurry of social occasions had made Reason's life feel almost normal.

The unsettling news had come in a note taped to her locker, and despite her knowing William's arrival was likely, when it happened, it instantly destroyed any sense of optimistic normality she had achieved. Snatching the paper from her locker, she read its message:

HE'S COMING IN TWO WEEKS.

Reason had neither seen nor heard from the cowboy in over a month, but she recognized his handwriting. And in a matter of seconds, all the speculation was over and William was on his way. She had expected to feel crushed by the news of William's arrival, but despite her fear, to some extent, she felt oddly grounded. Now, she thought, "I can get on with the business of dealing with the situation."

The two weeks passed in a blur. And when the actual day arrived, Reason stayed home from school, huddled in her bed, periodically checking the lock on her apartment door. She stayed home for the second day, too. On the third day, she ventured out, but strictly to her classes. By the end of the week, she had established a new routine of hypervigilance, intensely inspecting her surroundings, and avoiding being alone. Her paranoia made her imagine she was seeing William on every corner. She slept little, flinching at any unusual sound, trying to suppress her fear of what William might do when he found her.

One day, in a moment of heightened anxiety, Reason stood in the college atrium, lost in thought. *Should I tell someone? Who? A friend? A teacher? He'll hurt whoever tries to help me. No one knows what he's capable of... no one.* She felt terribly alone and helpless.

"Hey? Whadaya say? Reason? You in there?"

Someone grabbed her shoulder. She spun around, primed to fight.

"Whoa! I'm *a friendly!*" said Eddie, towering over her, a grin spread across his long, narrow face. He laughed, teasingly messing up her hair. But seeing her look of alarm, he stopped. "What's up? You look scared or something."

Reason forced a smile. "Do I? Nah, Eddie. I'm just tired. You surprised me, that's all."

Eddie put his arm around Reason. He was much taller than her, and like his girlfriend, Edie (pronounced Eedee), he was a swimmer with wide athletic shoulders. He and Edie looked alike and were often mistaken for brother and sister. Their similar names were a source of humor for Reason and her friends. Together, the couple was known around campus as "The Eds."

Reason smiled at Eddie, but she was feeling miserable and stuck in an awful muck of uncertainty. Her situation weighed heavily. Looking up at him, she wished she could tell him the truth, but she was certain that she would not. She would not risk putting him in danger. He made a goofy face and stuck out his tongue, getting her to laugh. "So, are you in?" he asked. "It's a Genesis tribute band. It'll be kick-ass! Meet us there?"

"Okay," said Reason, giving in. "Save me a seat."

CS &O

William stopped cold when he spotted Reason. Squinting, he slipped out of sight, moved behind a nearby column, and watched her. Looking down into the atrium, he had an unobstructed view. He tensed when Reason smiled up at a tall man who had his arm wrapped about her waist.

CＳ ＢＯ

On the way to meet her friends for the Genesis tribute concert, Reason saw two unusual looking men. They stood on the corner of an intersection, handing out pamphlets. Short and stocky, they appeared to be twins. They each had curly, shoulder-length, ginger-colored hair. To avoid them, Reason tucked in behind a group of girls walking just ahead of her. But the two men easily waded through the girls, and waving bright yellow leaflets in the air, addressed her directly. She stared quizzically at the two pamphlets held before her. One displayed a brown arrow facing down and the other a green arrow facing up. "Sorry, guys, but I've got no money to spare," she said, smiling weakly.

"We don't want your money," said one of the men.

"Just a moment of your time," said the other.

She tried to shake them off, but they doggedly followed alongside.

"Do you know that we have given you a wonderful opportunity?" asked one.

She ignored them. They were talking nonsense, and she wanted none of what they were selling.

"Stop and look! You... you dropped something," said the other.

Yeah, sure I did.

"Stop and see! You'll be glad that you did!" they said in unison.

Despite quickening her step, the two men kept pace, and one seemed to thrust a handful of pamphlets at her. His legs were short and, in trying to keep up, he had broken into a near jog. Reason suppressed a smile. She stopped walking, prepared to tell the little man to leave her alone. "Listen, I don't have any money to give you and..." He was holding a handful of cash towards her. She blinked at the money. "What are you doing? That's not mine. Wish it was, but it's not," she said.

"Oh, but it is. It's surely yours. And we know you must have worked hard to earn it."

"No. Really, it's not mine, guys. If you found it, you keep it."

"It's no good to us. Besides, it's yours. We're sure that it is. Take it." He shook the cash and then thrust the compact bundle at her.

"Are you serious? It's not my money. What do you really want?" she asked, pushing his hand away and walking again.

"We only want to give you what you need and deserve," said one, keeping step.

"That's all we want, and nothing else. Nothing else at all," said the other from behind.

"But it's not *my money,*" Reason insisted, stopping again, confused and shaking her head.

"We do not need this money. We want you to have it. Take it," said the little man, pushing the cash into Reason's hand. She grabbed it before the bundle could tumble to the sidewalk.

"Why? It's not mine!" A single fifty-dollar bill managed to come loose and float to the ground. Reason bent to retrieve it. When she stood again, the two men were gone. She searched the crowded sidewalk and then moved into the entryway of a storefront and discreetly counted the money. *It's hundreds!* Reason leaned against the store's display window, momentarily overcome. In disbelief, she returned to the sidewalk and searched again. The men had disappeared. She glanced again at the cash clutched in her hand. *This is freaking crazy.*

Tucked in with the money, she had found a business card. On the front of the black card was an image of a red telephone. On the flip side was one sentence:

TRUST YOURSELF TO FIND A SOUND PATH.

Reason read the sentence aloud, perplexed, but happy. She split the bundle of cash into two smaller folds and tucked each one, and the business card, into the front pockets of her jeans. The bundles flattened out nicely, virtually invisible. One last time, she scanned the area for the two strange men, but they had mysteriously vanished.

Giving up the search, she turned and walked the last block to the club, a rare, hopeful smile forming on her face.

13

the stickman

S ince William's arrival, Reason had become nervous about being outside of her apartment—at any time of the day—but especially before ten o'clock at night, the hour of William's curfew.

Once inside the nightclub where her friends were waiting, she felt safer. Reason knew that William's probation prohibited him from entering the bar, any bar, and that the time of his curfew was nearing.

Reeking of cigarette smoke and beer, the club was a popular establishment, a college hangout known for cheap drinks and live bands. Just inside the door, a girl danced alone to the thump, thump, thump of the music. From behind, the girl's blond, waist-long hair bounced and swayed. She appeared to be half drunk, lost in the music, and was blocking the way ahead. Reason patiently shuffled along behind her, waiting for an opportunity to move past. The building quivered and pulsated, the blaring music vibrating in the floor beneath her feet.

When Reason finally maneuvered past the dancing girl and moved into the large open area beyond the entrance corridor, she saw Eddie. He stood and waved her over. Snaking through the filling chairs and tables, she joined her friends near the dance floor—a rectangular patch of parquet flooring that separated the tables from the stage.

Once in her seat, Reason scrutinized the room. Soon, people would pack the club—every available space filled, but for the time being, with an unobstructed view of the entrance and the long stand-up bar, she could keep a lookout from where she sat.

"Reason!" yelled Edie across the table. "Glad you made it!" Edie gave Reason the thumbs up, poured a beer from a large pitcher, and slid the glass toward Reason.

"Happy to be here," shouted Reason. "Been here long?" she asked, taking a sip of the beer which was unsurprisingly warm and a little flat.

"Got here about an hour ago. We ate. You?"

"Yeah, before I left home."

Jan, who sat beside Edie, leaned in, cupped a hand to the side of her mouth, and yelled, "Seven-dollar cover charge. They're coming around the tables to collect." She held up seven fingers. "We get a ticket for some kind of door prize. Draw happens before the last set." Reason automatically felt the folds of cash through the fabric of her jeans. She had wanted to tell her friends about the money, but how she had come to have it seemed too weird, too unbelievable. She kept quiet. She watched as Eddie stood, took Jan by the hand, and pulled her to the empty dance floor. Edie laughed, encouraging Eddie on, and then she jumped up from the table, beer in hand, and joined them.

Reason looked at her friends who still sat at the table. With the music booming, Tommy, Rob, and Deb all sat too far from Reason for easy conversation. She did not mind. She was happy to sit back, listen, and watch. She looked over the room for the umpteenth time. The barstools were steadily filling, the patrons settling in. She recognized none of them. "What time is it?" she shouted at Rob.

"What?" he yelled back while drumming the table to the beat of the music.

"What-time-is-it?" she mouthed, patting her wrist.

"Nine-fifteen," Rob mouthed back.

Unable to relax fully until ten o'clock, Reason remained alert. "Got a smoke?" she yelled at Deb, making the letter V with two fingers and tapping them against her lips. Deb pushed a red pack of Du Maurier and a lighter across the table. Reason smiled at her friends. They shared so many things: cigarettes, clothing, music tapes, study notes, food, advice, tears, and laughter. But she wondered if they all kept secrets as she did. She drew a cigarette from the pack, lighting it as one song ended and a new one started.

Reason smoked and watched the band's roadies as they marched single file to the stage and then spread out. They moved about checking cables, adjusting microphone stands, and arranging instruments. As they worked, a band member sauntered onto the stage, garnering a yelp from the growing crowd. He picked up an electric guitar and strummed it once. The notes exploded from the speakers set on either side of the stage. Reason watched the young guitar player as he lowered the instrument back onto its stand and walked off stage without once looking at the audience.

"Start playing already!" yelled a patron sitting at an adjacent table. One obnoxious drunk always spoils the mood, thought Reason. She sat back and watched the crowd.

Finally, all the band members strolled onto the stage, each one picking up an instrument except for the lead singer, who stopped and posed at the microphone front and center. They all looked angry, as if someone had interrupted them during an argument, and still too irritated, they avoided each other's gaze. "Check one, two, three," said the singer, a casual laziness in his stance, his head lowered, his lips pressed to the microphone. He wore bell-bottomed jeans and a tight-fitting, scooped-necked t-shirt. His curly brown hair, parted in the middle, hung well below his shoulders.

To either side of the stage, large stacked speakers hummed and quivered as the musicians strummed and fine-tuned their guitars. Stage lights flickered on and swung up and then down. They rotated, streaming smoke-filled beams of red, blue, and pink. Ready for the music, Reason sipped her beer and leaned forward. But after one song, the band members huddled, and then with a quick, "Sorry folks. Sound issue. Back soon," they left the stage. The restless audience booed, and the DJ returned to the business of spinning vinyl. Reason scanned the crowd, feeling a little less anxious as the time ticked closer to ten.

"It's your turn, Reason!" Eddie towered over her, holding out his hand.

"Nah, Eddie. Not yet. I'll dance... but later... when the band is back."

"I'll hold you to that," he yelled with a toothy smile.

Reason laughed and pushed him away. He bent down and shouted into her ear, "It's good to see you laugh!" She smiled at him, feeling content. Surrounded by her friends, she found their innocence comforting. It reassured her that life could be simple and good. And their friendship made her feel somewhat normal.

As Eddie began making his way back to the dance floor, Reason turned to look at the entrance corridor. People were still filing into what had become standing room only. Bright lights popped on above the bar. Aimed at the stage, they lit it in a dazzling white. Reason shaded her eyes. The crowd lining the bar had become one dark silhouette of jostling heads and bodies. She could no longer distinguish one person from another. Stony-faced, she yelled at Tommy, "I'm going to the washroom."

In the back corridor, Reason passed a wall-mounted payphone. The clear panels on either side of the sticker-plastered phone were covered in ripped, faded advertisements, and two chains dangled slack where a phonebook and yellow-pages had once hung. She reached into her pocket, checking for loose change. *Just in case.* A lineup had formed at the woman's washroom. When her turn came, she pulled open the bathroom door and held it ajar, waiting until she could squeeze inside.

The DJ once again announced the band. The crowd whistled and shouted. From inside the toilet stall, Reason heard the band launch into a cover of one of her favorite Genesis songs. Singing along, she moved to the sink and washed her hands, inspecting her image in the mirror.

Outside the washroom, a sea of people met her. She jostled her way back to the table, where she found that her dancing friends had returned. She sat, singing along with the band. Edie rested her head on Eddie's shoulder. Eddie caught Reason watching and gave her a friendly wink. The world shrank down into that moment. Reason was happy, and sitting there watching Eddie and Edie, she smiled at having recognized her happiness. A few minutes later, and five minutes before ten o'clock, as her friends pushed their way to the dance floor once again, she started for the bar. Before she had moved very far, she heard Eddie shouting, "I'm holding you to that dance, Reason!" She laughed and gave him a dismissive wave.

The clock above the bar finally showed ten o'clock. From where she stood, she eyed the corridor. Before long, five more minutes had passed. She kept the entrance in view. When the clock read ten minutes past ten, Reason relaxed a little. She pushed her slight frame through the wall of bodies and held her cash so that the bartender could see it. A tall college boy on her right stepped out of the way, letting her get closer. "Squeeze in," he shouted.

"Thanks," she mouthed.

"What's your drink?" he hollered at the top of her head.

"Nothing special," she shouted back, not wanting his attention.

"Can I buy you that nothin' special?" he persisted, leaning against her.

"Thanks, but no," she said, smiling weakly and turning her back on him.

"Ah, come on..." she heard him say, his voice trailing off.

Reason disliked exchanges like this—often struggling to find the right and firm words to fend off these types of unwanted advances. Then she felt a hand on her back, pressing between her shoulder blades. She shrugged it off. "Listen," she yelled without looking up. "Thanks, but I'm here with my friends. I'm hanging out with them tonight."

The bartender leaned in. "What'll you have?" he shouted, wiping the bar and placing a paper coaster in front of her.

"Budweiser, please," she shouted.

As Reason watched the bartender move away, someone bumped her from behind. She ignored the jolt. The person bumped into her again. *Ah, come on buddy, enough already.* She turned to give a more direct answer.

The lit stage shone brilliantly from behind him, his blond hair a mess as if he had jumped from bed and run out the door. His face was mostly a dark shadow, but Reason knew well enough who it was. The man staring back at her was William. She had little time to register his presence before he had clasped his hand to the back of her neck and yanked her close to his face. "Time to go," he yelled, his pupils wildly dilated.

When the bartender returned with Reason's drink, new faces had filled the spot where she had been.

 C3 &0

As Reason opened her eyes—the tail end of a scream shattered like breaking glass inside her head. Confused, lying on a hard surface, she stared unblinkingly at a wall rising just inches from her face. She could smell smoke. For a few perplexing seconds, she remained completely still. In a daze, she reached forward and touched the wall. And then, in a sudden burst of adrenaline, she recognized where she was. She bolted up, paralyzed by what she saw.

The Sanctuary lay in ruins—roofless and crumbling. Its walls still stood, but as jagged shards, with only one still standing at its original height—tilting outward and heavily marred by long cracks and gaping holes.

Thick, green, velvety moss spread across the leftover surfaces of the ruined building as if the Sanctuary had been in a state of decline for hundreds of years. The candelabras and the pedestals, the benches, the tables and chairs, all lay strewn about, stained and broken, covered in the dark green moss, like the decaying artifacts of a sunken ship. A piece of milky glass lay on the floor beside Reason. She reached down and picked it up—a jagged shard from one of the shattered vases—the flowers long dead.

Above, dark clouds bruised a pale-grey sky. Reason kept her gaze on them, trying to think, frantic to understand. A loud explosion shattered the silence. It rattled the loose contents of the Sanctuary and shook the ground. She leapt from the bench, scrambled through the debris, and huddled at the base of the tallest wall. The air was disturbingly hot. She edged her way along the wall and peeked around it, her heart pounding. Before her, vast devastation unfolded—violent and grotesque. Stunned, Reason gaped at the smoking remnants of a burning city.

Another blast ignited, knocking her to the ground. She rushed back to the safety of the wall and looked in the direction of the explosion. Blocks away, a thick, black column of smoke slithered into the sky. Eyes wild, she watched as a massive structure near the rising smoke collapsed into an already raging fire. More fires burned. They seemed to burn everywhere, bright bursts of orange in the deepening blue-grey of dusk. And in every direction, pillars of smoke coiled high into the sky. Scorched flakes of ash fell like snow and created a yellow pall that hung over the wounded land—the falling ash covering the torn and pitted surfaces of the Sanctuary in a dirty grey fuzz.

Reason searched the battered landscape for any sign of life. Thunder clapped overhead. She shuddered. Lightning slashed the darkening sky. A foul odor permeated the air, seeping sickly sweet— the putrid scent of death.

Reason searched for shelter or escape, but everything was in ruin or burning. She gaped at the battered remains of a high-rise tower, its one remaining wall a broken bone jutting up through the torn skin of the city. On the far side of the destroyed buildings and roadways, beyond the ruins of the tower, stood a sooty, broken forest—a sprawling mass of black, branchless spikes all leaning in one direction and piercing a low-lying, muddy fog.

Reason crouched, terrified, clasping her hands to her head. *What's happening?* She heard a heavy, pulsating buzzing and raised her head to listen. The sound grew steadily louder. In the frame of the ruined Sanctuary walls, through the pasty veil of falling ash, she watched the sky, staring in horror as a darkened patch began to swirl.

The spinning sky formed a dark, gaping mouth that began sucking in the clouds nearest to it. The swirling mass, centered above the ruins of the Sanctuary, squealed, its chilling wail rising in pitch. The noise grew deafening. Reason screamed, unable to hear her own terror. She sank to the ground. *What do I do? What do I do?*

Panicking, she jumped up and ran mindlessly—stumbling and then falling over a treacherous mound of debris. Struggling to her feet, she rushed to the ragged remains of the closest wall. Horror-stricken, open-mouthed, and eyes wide, she watched the shrieking vortex above as it suctioned the pale ash from the landscape. Overwhelmed by fear, Reason collapsed into a dazed shock and heard the horrifying clamor as if from a faraway place.

Another explosion lifted her off the ground and then flung her back down. She slid a small distance, her breath escaping in a series of grunts. An object hit her head. She reached for the spot of impact. Before she could touch it, all went black.

CB ED

Reason blinked. Her head hurt. Lying on her back, she saw the indistinct lines of a dark ceiling. Grimacing at the sharp bits that poked into her body from head to toe, with the tips of her fingers she felt at her sides, and then lifted her head. *Tree branches!* She struggled to her feet, dizzy, head throbbing. With a trembling hand, she reached out and touched the tangled branches of the tunnel wall. A pulsating hum began. *What have I done?*

A deep, staccato laugh echoed down the tunnel. Reason yelped and clamped her hand to her mouth, breathing as shallowly as she could manage, willing herself to be quiet. She stared into the tunnel, the curving structure massive, rising to well beyond her height, the retreating wall long, and seemingly endless.

The wall was a dense layering of entangled tree branches. Again, Reason reached out and touched the rough, twisted pieces of wood—jerking her hand back in horror, glancing about anxiously. In one direction, the tunnel continued a long way before it curved and she could see no further. In the other direction, near to where she stood, the hollow of the tunnel disappeared into a dirty, yellowish fog. As she watched, the fog rippled violently and then eased into a stagnant, simmering soup.

Light suddenly shot in through the tunnel wall. Reason groaned. The many slices of light created a matrix of crisscrossing lines within the eerie darkness of the tunnel. She pressed her face to the wall and peered through, seeing only a thin horizontal strip of yellow. *Is that the outside?* The beams of light went dark. Reason again heard the distinct, blood-curdling chuckle. She spun around and shouted, "Wh-who's there?"

"RUN!" screamed a disembodied male voice, guttural, gravelly, and frightening.

Reason stood braced against the wall.

"I SAID RUN!" roared the voice.

She jumped and shrieked, looked both ways, and chose the long, curved length of the tunnel over the short distance that led into the dense wall of fog. She ran hysterically, running to save her life. The hum intensified. The evil voice laughed with delight. Cursing, Reason ran as fast as she could, trying not to trip on the uneven surface of the tunnel, her breath coming in short bursts. She rounded the long curve and saw a circle of light off in the distance. She raced for it, her lungs stinging, her throat dry. Sharp branches dug into the soles of her sandals. Twice she lost her footing and tumbled, but she raced on, frantic to get to the opening.

The squealing whine of the tunnel ceased; the unexpected silence was dramatic. The rasp of Reason's labored breathing filled the unsettling stillness. She staggered to a stop and, gasping for air, glanced back at the section of tunnel she had fled. It stood empty, but at any second, she felt certain that something wicked and terrifying would round the bend. She had run less than half the distance to the light ahead. The tunnel was unnervingly quiet and still. Her eyes glued to the long bend behind her, anticipating some horrible creature stalking her, waiting to pounce, she summoned her courage and yelled, "Where are you? What do you want with me?"

"I am everywhere!" said the voice from within the wall by her head. "I am right here behind you." Reason screamed and fell away from the wall, twirling around, eyes searching wildly.

"Wh-who are you?" she stammered.

"Your new best friend," chuckled the voice.

Thin horizontal twigs in the wall wriggled and shifted and created the shape of lips and a chin, the chin rising and falling mechanically as it spoke. Reason recoiled at the peculiar sight, aghast and

194

trembling. "What do you want from me?" she managed, backing away from the aberration.

"Your company, sweet thing. Where are you going, child? There's no way out." The twig mouth jiggled up and down as the thing chuckled.

"What do you want with my... my company?" she asked, attempting to keep the thing in the wall occupied while she frantically tried to think of how to escape. But before she could think of what to do, the twigs and branches in the wall quivered and rippled, squeaked and snapped, and around the talking twig mouth, the figure of a gigantic Stickman took shape. It stood stooped within the curve of the wall, towering over Reason, and then it laughed with maniacal contempt. She gaped at it, terror-stricken. Then it ran, seeming to run within the wall itself, back the way Reason had come, clickety-click, clickety-clack, clickety-clickety-click-clack.

Her eyes flicked to the opening in the tunnel ahead and then back to the blind curve. *Do something! Shit! Think! Think!* As if the thing in the wall could hear her thoughts, it snickered in the distance. She shrieked and again started toward the light, willing it to be her way out. The smell of burning debris reached her as she neared the opening, the odor familiar, the stink of the ruined Sanctuary and the lifeless landscape. *Please, please be more than that. Be an exit!* As she neared it, the circle of light grew large, becoming an enormous gaping hole. She slowed, edging closer. Beyond the opening, far below and for as far as she could see, spread the charred city and its forest of dead trees. She dropped to her knees, moaning, the stench overwhelming. From behind her, the thing cackled. Close to tears, Reason crawled to the edge and, shaking with fear, peered over. A hazy yellow fog drifted below in long wispy lines. And below it, she saw only devastation. Distraught, she crawled away from the edge. *What do I do?* Reason cast about desperately and suddenly remembered the Raven. "RAVEN!" she screamed. "RAVEN, COME TO ME! COME NOW!"

"Craw, Craw," called the bird, the sound distant. She searched the smoky sky above the ruined city. "RAVEN!" she yelled, feeling a twinge of hope. Staggering up, again she heard the bird's call, this time coming from behind, from inside the tunnel. She turned and walked a few cautious steps. "Raven?" The bird answered, its call muted and coming to her from within the tunnel wall. In frustration, Reason slapped at the wall, scraping her palms, too immersed in fear to feel the pain. She listened and waited. Minutes passed. If the bird was still calling to her, she could no longer hear it.

Anger mixed with Reason's fear, and fueled by this new emotion, she hollered into the tunnel, "Screw you! Go ahead! Feed on my fear! But I won't always be afraid of you. I won't!" She sank in despair; in truth feeling as if her fear would never abate. "What do you want from me?" she said weakly into her hands. A giggle trickled toward her from around the bend. She stood, wrapped her arms about herself, and began the terrifying walk back. Reaching into her pocket, she clamped her hand around the mindfulness bean. *Mindfulness saved me before.* Reason brought her focus to the bean, but the voice in the tunnel let out a blood-curdling howl that dropped her to her knees. She stayed there, shaking, and as if to provoke her, the pulsating hum of the tunnel resumed, low and menacing.

Amid her panic and fear, Reason suddenly experienced an odd moment—a tiny miracle that, for a breath, broke her panic. As if from inside her head, she heard a woman's voice solemnly stressing, "Trust yourself." She looked up from where she crouched, confused, but for a moment calmed. Where the voice had come from, and what it had said, did little to change her situation, but it stirred her into action. She sat up straight, pulled her knees to her chest, kept her arms wrapped about them, and began trying to remember where she had been before the tunnel had taken her. *Where was I in the telling of my story?* She searched her memory for the moment that had transported her into the madness of the tunnel. *The club. I was at the club. I was in the bathroom. I went to the bar...*

A clickety-click-click startled her from her deliberations, the creepy sound coming from around the bend of the tunnel. Reason scrambled to her feet. *Do something, idiot! Do something!* She stood paralyzed with fear. *Move!* Her legs remained rigid and motionless.

She willed herself to move back towards the fog, pulling herself along the wall, terrified to touch it, but needing its sturdiness to steady her steps. Persevering, she worked her way back along the curve. *You can do this. You can do this.* Holding her breath and trembling, she edged around the long bend.

Reason saw no sign of the thing, but ahead, where the thick yellow fog had been, a solid brick wall now blocked the way. Her heart sank. Her stomach did flip-flops. *Is there no way out? No way at all?* With wild, terrified eyes, she searched the walls for the thing.

"Welcome back!" it snickered, applying emphasis on the sound of the hard k. Its voice seemed to come at her from everywhere. She swallowed hard; her mouth impossibly parched.

In a hideous display of slithering lines and swelling bulges, the thing was suddenly in the wall opposite her—and on the move. It slid up and across the ceiling and then down in a rush, halting in the wall beside her. She screamed, stumbled away—and was summarily stopped by the brick wall. "Oh my, you are feisty," the thing tittered. "We're going to have such a fabulous time together!"

Aghast, Reason watched as a horrendously long bark-bare branch reached out from the wall and flexed what appeared to be six twisted-twig fingers. Following it, with a frightening series of squealing, snapping and clacking, the whole creature emerged. It stretched and twisted its skeletal body, shook its gangly legs, and waggled its long arms. And perched atop its giant head, a tangle of leafless branches formed the shape of a crude top hat.

Finally, the thing settled and its gaze fell on Reason. It stooped toward her, standing between her and the open end of the tunnel. She flinched, whimpered, and turned away. "Look at me," it demanded. A creepy ball of blackened branches formed its round head—its eyes, eyebrows, nose and mouth crawling about the surface of its face as it squirmed with angry impatience.

Like a puppet on strings, the Stickman moved with awkward, jerky effort. Reason backed away and spun around—staring in debilitating panic at the brick wall. Behind her, the Stickman laughed, mocking her. She clenched her fists and turned to face the thing.

Staggering backwards, feeling for the brick, she pressed her back against it. The Stickman tilted its big head back and laughed, its mouth, eyes, and eyebrows all wriggling and squirming spastically. "Too bad about that brick wall, huh?" it said with delight, riveting its gaze on Reason. "Don't feel too badly. Many have run away from the fog. You're not too stupid, just *as* stupid." It planted its ghoulish hands onto the hard, pointy ridges of its hips. "But had you chosen the fog," it snickered, bending down to her, "you might've found an exit, dearie. Tisk, tisk, such a darn shame... because there's no chance of that now. No chance at all!" It leaned its lanky stick frame backwards and howled.

"What do you want from me?" Reason cried, attempting defiance, her voice betraying her. The thing lurched towards her. She flinched. It laughed.

"I told you already. Your company is what I want. From now, until eternity!" It clapped its hands together, clack, clack, clack.

Fuck! "You can't keep me here..."

"Oh yes, dearie, I can!" The thing paced a few inches away from her, clunk-clunk, clunk-clunk—its six-toed feet never quite landing squarely on the curved floor. Reason shuddered, feeling nauseated. The Stickman grinned and rubbed its gnarly hands together, holding them high near its chin. "Look," it said, pointing a skeletal finger towards the bend in the tunnel. "Time to play," it added in a high-pitched squeal. Reason twitched with fright.

In the formerly empty tunnel, she saw two twig chairs, one giant-sized, the other her size. The chairs sat facing one another, and in-between them stood a tall lectern. "Quiz time!" shrieked the Stickman, click-clunking its way toward the giant chair. It sat and with exaggerated flare, adjusted its top hat and crossed one leg over the other. "Come," it ordered in a slow and sinister drawl. Reason could not make herself move. "COME!" yelled the Stickman. She jumped and, on trembling limbs, lurched towards the chairs. "Sit," it said. She sat. The Stickman sat before her, looming, and then in a cacophony of squeaks and squeals, it bent down towards her, its ugly face coming too close. She turned her head to the side. A sharp object poked at her chin. Reason recoiled at its touch, but the Stickman gripped her by the chin and forced her face towards its own. "That's better," it said in a creepy low purr. She stared at its enormous face, tractor tire large, its eyes, nose, and mouth moving about convulsively, and settling into an expression of lusty greed.

Suddenly frowning, the Stickman squinted, furrowed its woody eyebrows, sat back in its throne, and declared, "Here are the rules. I ask the questions. You answer them." It feigned surprise by pressing its skeletal hand over an o-shaped mouth, and then bared a pair of fangs and hissed, "That's it! One rule!" Reason shrank back in her chair. "If," counseled the Stickman in mock stateliness, "you answer a question correctly, I will grant you a step toward freedom." Its mouth closed, its lips horizontal lines, its eyes reduced to beady dots. Then it uncrossed its legs and lunged forward. "But," it shouted, "if you answer incorrectly, which you will..." it pointed a crooked finger within a terrifying inch of Reason's eye, "then I get to change you." She could not control her trembling. The Stickman mocked her, lifting its long arms in the air, splaying its fingers, and faking a tremor, clickity-click-click. Then planting its hands on its knee, one atop the other, it twisted its stick frame into a feminine sideways pose, looked over its shoulder at Reason, and chirped, "For every wrong answer, I pick any part of you I desire, and I change it." Then displaying a toothy grin of sharp pointy teeth, it spun around, bent down, and poked at her cheek, its eyes big dark circles, its eyebrows raised.

"Change me how?" Reason moaned, working hard not to bolt from her chair.

Its eyes on her, the Stickman pointed over its shoulder, and as it did, the branches there parted, sliding open to reveal a large window. Inside, Reason saw three twig figures, small ones, much closer to her size. One sat cross-legged on the floor with its head bowed. The other two seemed in animated conversation, but as soon as they saw her, all three scrambled to the window and banged on it, their muted shouts too faint for her to understand. As they pounded the glass and shouted, the wall slid shut, silencing their cries. *Oh God...*

"How do you like my humble collection? We shall all have so much fun together!" said the Stickman, greedily drumming its fingers together. Reason made to jump from her chair, but the Stickman's large hand hit her square on the shoulder, slamming her back down. "No," it hissed. "No more wasting time." Her fear was as formidable as the creature bearing down on her, suffocating her, making her dumb.

"Question number one." The Stickman reached into a rickety twig bin hanging from the lectern. It rolled its stick fingers around in the bin, tickety-click, tickety-click, tickety-click, and then pulled out a tiny twig. With great flair, it raised the twig into the air. "Multiple-choice!" it shouted. Reason gripped the arms of her chair, terrified. "Where," it tilted its round head toward her, "was," it put a crooked finger to its skinny chest, "I," it smiled repulsively, "born?" The Stickman snapped its mouth shut and stared down at Reason's upturned face.

"Ho-How can I possibly know that?" she stammered.

It swept its face down to hers and scowled. "A, born *here*, or B, born *there*?"

Reason tried to sound brave and indignant. "You're forcing me to guess!"

The Stickman peered down at her and shook its head dismissively. "Answer the question. You have thirty seconds."

"It's not a fair question."

"Answer," the Stickman insisted, examining its non-existent fingernails.

"But I can't possibly know!" Reason squirmed in her seat.

"Was... I... born here... or there?" it drawled.

"What if I don't give you an answer?" she challenged, running out of things to say.

"No answer," it sneered, "is a wrong answer." Its voice rose in pitch. "Here? Or, there?" Smiling in a wide and devious grin, its twiggy lips rippled and its twig eyebrows moved into a deep V. Reason's mind was blank. She looked around, searching for a clue, wishing that the whole horrid affair was actually some kind of nightmare, one from which she could will herself to awake. "Ten seconds," the Stickman warned, giggling. "Seven, six, five." It stood. "Four, three..." Reason gawked at it, fear gutting her. "Two."

"Here!" she screamed. "You were born here!"

The Stickman stopped laughing and sat down with a thud. A bell rang from somewhere nearby—boing-bong, boing-bong. It turned its head at the sound, stamped its feet, and then glared at Reason. "Lucky guess," it barked.

14

the inquisition

T he Stickman put a finger to its pursed lips and tapped—click, click, click. A devious smile spread across its wide, ugly face. Its eyes, two mildly angled lines, squinted angrily at Reason. She held her breath. "Well now," it said hungrily. And then it rose from its chair.

Reason's muscles twitched with fear. She watched anxiously as the Stickman paced back and forth—his lanky frame creepy and daunting. It swung its thin arms in a wide-sweeping gesture and clasped its twig hands behind its long skeletal torso. Reason suppressed an urge to scream. It looked at her from over its shoulder. "Question number two," it sneered.

"Wait!" she shouted. "I..." The Stickman twirled around, its eyebrows two short lines raised high, its twig lips forming the shape of a small letter o. "Uh...," Reason stammered, struggling for some way to delay. "Wh-what's...?" she stuttered, her voice a hoarse, trembling whisper. The Stickman lowered its eyebrows suspiciously. "What's... your name? Yes. What's your name?" she asked in a rush, hoping that any question would do.

The Stickman lumbered across the short distance between them and then lunged. Reason gasped and leaned as far back in her chair as was possible. The wood creaked and moaned. The branches dug into her back. "My naaaame?" the Stickman asked impatiently, its voice rising in pitch.

"Yes," Reason yelled in panicked defiance. "You never told me. So... so... you should tell me your name, don't you think?"

The Stickman slammed its hands onto the arms of her chair. She screamed. Its fingers spread wide—its sharp talons curling into the gaps between the branches. The chair arms pushed outward as the

Stickman's enormous face moved within an inch of Reason's. She whimpered. It smelled like something long dead. "Let's say my name is Misery," the Stickman growled, twisting its mouth into a jagged hideousness. She cringed at the repulsive face; the black eyes devoid of depth. "And dearie," it continued, "Misery *loves* company." It lifted its hands from her chair, slapped them back down, and then thrust itself into a standing position. "Question number TWO!" it barked, returning to its chair.

"But...," cried Reason.

"NO!" the Stickman thundered, balling its hands into fists and stamping its feet in childlike frustration.

"But I heard a bell!" she retorted. The Stickman frowned. "I heard a bell," she repeated. "When I answered the first question correctly, I heard a bell. Why did it toll? What did it mean?" The Stickman leapt from its chair and stood rigidly tall, its top hat nearly touching the tunnel ceiling.

Reason watched as the monstrous creature spun around and appeared to examine the wall behind its chair. Then it let out a tiny squeal and scuttled away from the spot. It seemed to be frightened, its eyes wide black circles, its hands clinging to the round rim of its flat-topped hat as it paced somewhat hysterically and mumbled to itself. The bell, thought Reason, is something that it fears. She leaned forward in her chair, straining to hear the ringing again.

"Impossible. Simply impossible," the Stickman mumbled. "One question. Only one question answered correctly. No more. That's all. Only one...," it grumbled, nodding decisively, seeming to have reached some sort of conclusion. Turning to Reason, it shouted angrily, "QUESTION NUMBER TWO!"

Petrified, Reason watched as the Stickman, who seemed to have found a renewed confidence, marched back to its chair. It sat and stayed quiet for agonizing minutes—its head bowed, its thick twig brows furrowed. Reason edged forward in her chair. The Stickman opened its eyes wide and glared at her. She started and sat back.

Lifting its head until it sat rigidly straight and tall, the Stickman laid its long arms on the arms of its chair and splayed its talon-like fingers—an evil king on his throne, leering at Reason. "When was I born?" it asked, raising a gnarled finger as if to say, "There's more. Wait." Reason waited, terrified—watching as a slow, torturous grin slid across the Stickman's face. And then as it crossed one gangly leg awkwardly over the other, it said, "Was I born *then* or *now*?"

"What do you mean?" Reason asked, desperate to delay further.

"Then?" It bent forward. "Or now?" It opened its lips into a garish smile, baring large, dirty, piano-key teeth.

Reason shrank as far back as the chair would allow. *Think, damn it... think!*

"You have thirty seconds, dearie," oozed the Stickman, ending the statement with a prolonged, gurgling growl. Reason sat forward, frantic to escape, but the Stickman put its pointy finger to her chest and shoved her back into her chair. "Twenty-five seconds," it warned menacingly, its evil grin dividing its large, round face in half.

Feeling helpless, Reason shivered and tried to focus. She turned away from the Stickman, searching the empty tunnel for a clue. Remembering the three desperate stick figures behind the wall, her eyes widened. *If they exist, and this thing created them, then it must have been born before now! Yes! It must have been born then!* "THEN!" she shouted. "YOU WERE BORN THEN!" Wild-eyed and gripping her chair, she watched the Stickman's hideous face, waiting for a response. The repulsive creature stopped smiling. *I'm right! I'm right!* She wanted to shout for joy, and in her eagerness, ignored a faint tingle in her hand. She watched the Stickman for more signs of dismay. But then it smiled. And as it grinned at her, the tingling in her hand grew stronger. The Stickman laughed. Gloomy doubt weakened Reason's excitement. She looked at her hand, frowning in confusion as the tingling sensation grew into a stinging pain. She jerked her hand into the air, gaping at it, a burning sensation spreading through her fingers.

Grabbing at her wrist, Reason grimaced in pain. The Stickman threw her a look of mock pity. "No, my little pet," it said with melodramatic flair, "I was not born *then*." Bending down until its face was inches from hers, it sneered, "Because of you, dearie... because of you and your beautiful, abundant fear, I was created *now*. I am reborn over and over and strengthened each time fear overcomes one of you weak, pitiful creatures."

Raging pain shot from Reason's wrist to her fingers and into the bones of her hand. She watched helplessly as her tortured hand closed into a fist, opened, and then cramped into the shape of a mangled claw. The Stickman watched too—laughing, howling, clutching at its non-existent belly with its lanky arms and long, twisted fingers. Mortified, Reason moaned and tore her gaze away from her painfully cramping hand to gape at her captor. But the Stickman merely pointed to her and shouted, "And it begins!" Aghast, she looked about in wild panic. The Stickman bent down for a better look. "Don't miss a thing, dearie. The best part comes next!" The skin on the back of her hand stretched thin and then split. Leaping from her chair, Reason shrieked hysterically. "It's a beautiful thing!" exclaimed the Stickman.

Delirious with pain, Reason gagged when the glistening pink flesh started to fall in sloppy chunks from the bones of her hand. In short, shrill bursts, she began screaming at the visible skeleton of her hand. And then, feeling faint, she dropped to her knees and retched.

As she watched, the grisly wound at her wrist spontaneously healed. Groaning and breathless, she glanced at the Stickman, desperate for the agony to stop. But the exposed bones of her hand blackened and in a series of stomach-turning crackling, splitting, and snapping, they lengthened hideously. Panic-stricken, Reason cried out, "MAKE IT STOP! AAARGH!" But the unbearable pain cut her appeals short.

In hysterics, she bolted, stumbling on the uneven floor, fleeing madly, clutching her injured hand to her chest. But the insufferable pain was too much; it forced her once more to her knees. She crumpled in utter despair—and then fainted.

Some moments later, Reason awoke with her face pressed against the jagged floor of the tunnel. Through her semi-consciousness, she heard the Stickman's voice seeping from the very spot in the floor against which her ear was pressed. "Something bothering you, my prize?" She recoiled and clambered away. The pain that had surged through her ruined hand was now a slow pulsating ache that climbed her arm and then dissipated at her shoulder. The thing that was now her hand hung heavy and unfeeling at her side. In shock, she grimaced at the mass of twisted twigs monstrously appended to the flesh at her wrist. They formed a small, flat palm with appallingly long, skeletal fingers. The sharp-pointed fingers hung crooked and limp. Reason turned away from the nauseating sight.

Clicking and clacking, the Stickman stepped out from within the wall. It crossed one foot over the other and leaned against the curved structure—delighted with its victory, gloating. "And *that* is just the beginning!" It laughed a spastic bout of fitful giggles before bending forward and snarling, "The next change will be far more substantial."

Dear God, help me! "Raven, are you there?" Reason uttered weakly, turning away from the Stickman, fighting back her tears. "Where are you?" In answer to her desperate plea, the bird's faint call reached her from somewhere afar. "Craw, Craw." Reason gasped, raised her gaze, and listened. The bird called again, sounding closer. She rose to her knees and laughed crazily, blinking through tear-filled eyes. The Raven's beak suddenly protruded from the nearby wall, and then vanished. Reason cried out and scrambled to the spot. The glorious beak popped through again, and again it disappeared. "RAVEN!" she screamed, frantically peering into the ragged cracks in the wall. The Stickman shoved her aside, lurched closer to the tunnel wall, and struck it with an open hand. Again the bird's beak protruded, and again it vanished. As the Raven's beak appeared and disappeared repeatedly, Reason shrieked in excited expectation. The Stickman growled, and with its lanky limbs positioned at awkward wide angles, slapped repeatedly at the tunnel wall, targeting the bird's beak.

To Reason's horror, despite its ungainliness, the Stickman's aim was amazingly accurate. After much too short a battle, the bird's beak ceased to show. "No!" screamed Reason. "Come back! Come back!" She raced to the wall and peered through, seeing nothing but blackness. Groaning, she slumped to the floor in anguish.

"Pesky creature," said the Stickman, straightening to its full height, grunting its displeasure and giving the wall one last kick. "Question number three! And no more delays!" it blurted, wagging a long, crooked finger in Reason's face, returning to its chair, sitting down with a heavy clunk, which caused wood shavings to fall to the floor by its feet. For a moment it stared unhappily at the slivers and chips of wood, and then it kicked at them before returning its attention to Reason. "Sit," it ordered.

Reason grimaced at her transformed hand. And as she moved to her chair, her twig fingers twitched—and then the entire wooden hand came to life. She squealed in disgust. Knotted and ugly, her transformed fingers curled, straightened, and then banged and scraped against one another. She lifted the appalling extremity with her good hand, and, wincing, placed it on the arm of her chair. The contact produced a series of vibrations that spread into the soft tissues of her wrist and forearm. She groaned and turned away from the chilling sight, and amid her wretchedness, and with vehement distaste, she addressed the Stickman. "*You said...* that if I answered a question correctly, you would grant me a step closer to my freedom."

With surprise and irritation, the Stickman scowled at Reason. "I suppose I did," it conceded begrudgingly, and then it glared at the floor. "Rules, rules, damned rules," it muttered to itself.

"Well," Reason persisted angrily, "I answered the first question correctly."

"You did," it agreed, and frowned.

"You're stalling," she retorted, moving to the edge of her seat.

"I am?" it answered with mock surprise, shrugging its skeletal shoulders.

"You owe me for that correct answer," she persevered.

The Stickman pouted, lowered its broad shoulders in a dramatic slouch, and huffed. "Fine," it sulked.

Reason allowed herself a glimmer of hope.

"You'll never pull it off, dearie," the Stickman spewed.

"Pull what off?" She tried to sound unruffled.

The Stickman scowled and raised its hand as if to strike her. Reason tensed and shielded her head with her good hand. But no blow came. When she looked back at the Stickman, it sat facing her with its gigantic twig hand still raised above its head. But the hand was not aimed at Reason. Instead, the Stickman was reaching for something on the wall near to it, something it appeared reluctant to look at directly.

A wooden lever had materialized, protruding from the wall beside the creature's head. As Reason anxiously watched and waited, the Stickman's hand found the lever, grasped it, and then immediately let go. After two more fumbling attempts, finally, the Stickman held on. And when it did—as if to compose itself—it became noticeably grim and sat rigidly still, its hideous head bowed. Then, with fiendish hostility, it pulled the lever down.

A loud hiss escaped from the wall, and with it, a long horizontal crack appeared. The crack grew; steadily opening. The Stickman whimpered. Out from the opening rolled a thick wooden shelf. On the shelf sat an enormous metal machine. The shelf, with its odd machine, rolled out until it was more than a third of the way into the tunnel—and then it locked into place with a jiggle and a clank. Reason scanned the apparatus—a long metal contraption with a large, yawning mouth. The Stickman shuddered, squinting at the machine.

It terrifies him! What is it? What is it?

"Question number three," the Stickman announced, shifting in its chair, leaning away from the contraption.

"Wait!" cried Reason. *"What is that?"* she asked, pointing at the machine. "Is it important to my freedom? What is it? WHAT IS IT?" she insisted. Summoning her courage, she stood from her chair, straining to see more of the shiny gold machine that might turn out to be her only ally. Standing on her toes, Reason saw a spiral-shaped blade peeking out of the mouth of the machine. And from the top of the device, protruding chimney-like, was a rectangular chute. The blade and the entire machine glistened glossy and new as if it had never been used.

"Sit back down!" ordered the Stickman with noticeable urgency.

"It's a wood chipper!" Reason exclaimed, relishing her discovery.

The Stickman raised its hand, its twig fingers clawing at the air before clamping down on the machine to push the shiny gold mechanism away. But the device did not budge, and Reason felt another flickering of hope. She glanced at her changed hand and winced. "How many questions must I answer?"

The Stickman stared at her, its eyes two beady, dark circles, its wooden eyebrows drawn together, its mouth a straight line, sour and mean. "Three," it spat.

"Three?" she repeated.

"I will not say so again!"

"So, if I answer *two* correctly...?"

"ENOUGH!" it roared.

Fearing the Stickman's rage, Reason fell silent and watched as it balled its hands into awkward fists—its long, sharp fingers sticking out at odd angles. It slammed its fists onto the arms of its chair; pale grey clouds of dust burst outward. The Stickman moaned and muttered absurdly. Reason waited. It turned and faced her, a deep growl seeping from its terrifying scowl. She looked away. "Question number three," it repeated, its voice contemptuously hushed. Reason clenched her jaw, willing herself to persevere. "*How* was I created?" the Stickman snarled, lowering its large round face towards hers. Reason leaned back in her chair, squeezing her eyes shut. The Stickman tapped the pointy tip of its finger against her wooden hand. The contact was painful. She shrieked. The Stickman laughed with delight, sat back in its chair, and became abruptly and unnervingly quiet. Reason looked up at its slumped, intimidating form, revulsion distorting its twiggy mouth into a jagged line. Glowering down at her, it asked, "Was I created *up* or *down*?" It growled savagely, baring a mouthful of sharp teeth.

Reason brightened. "What?" she asked.

The Stickman frowned. In the distance, a bell rang, a faint but recognizable sound—boing, bong. Agitated, the Stickman looked about with two quick turns of its head, once to the left and once to the right. And then it growled, "Was I born up or down? I will not repeat the question again!"

Reason suddenly thought of Mr. Up and Mr. Down, considering their arrows, striving to remember what she had learned from the two operators in training. *It can't be a coincidence, can it? They must know where I am.* She remembered Ruby's advice: "Learn to be mindful and you will never regret it. It just may save your life!" At that moment, the walls of the tunnel changed color, darkening from grey to brown. The Stickman's eyes widened, and it groaned. *Brown is down!* Eager to give her answer, Reason stood, her heavy wooden hand dropping to her side. "You were born..." The tunnel walls brightened to an emerald green. *Green is up, but...* Puzzled, Reason closed her mouth and gaped. She watched nervously as the tunnel walls fluctuated rapidly between brown and green. Over and over again, they flickered between the two colors. The bell tolled in the distance, and despite her uncertainty, the ringing seemed to encourage her. But the tunnel walls dimmed, once more becoming a dismal grey. The Stickman laughed uncertainly. Reason was stymied.

With a venomous smile, the Stickman oozed a gurgling, throaty growl before reluctantly tearing its gaze from Reason and peering into the tunnel. Reason sensed that it was nervous and watched it with keen interest. Finally, it turned back to her and then startled her by leaping from its chair. But before the Stickman had taken four strides, an unseen force yanked it up and off its feet and flung it back onto its arboreal throne. At that moment, Reason was certain that the Stickman was in some kind of trouble. Squealing, it balled its hands into bulky fists and beat them against its head. Then, glaring at Reason, it bellowed, "ANSWER THE QUESTION!"

Reason opened her mouth, faltering, terrified of answering incorrectly. *Up or down? Up or down? Brown is down. Green is up. Which one? Which one?* As if from nowhere, the jovial giggles of Mr. Up and Mr. Down suddenly filled the tunnel. The Stickman started and clasped its hands to the rim of its top hat. "Up? Down? Is that you?" yelled Reason, sitting forward in her chair. But the sound of their merry giggling faded and then stopped completely. The

Stickman growled long and deep, its mouth a rippling dark blotch. From within the tunnel wall sprang a racket of crackling and snapping as the entwined branches separated. As they disentangled, they scrambled to form a new pattern. The Stickman watched the spectacle in utter distress. Reason watched with hopeful anticipation. The branches formed the shape of an upward pointing arrow. Reason felt a surge of joy. But then the arrow flip-flopped, suddenly pointing down. *Which one? Which one?*

"ANSWER THE QUESTION! YOUR TIME IS UP!" screamed the Stickman.

The fingers on Reason's good hand began to tingle. She cringed at them, shook them, and then peered at the tunnel wall, biting her bottom lip, searching for the answer. The arrow on the wall flipped again, pointing up once more, and then it flipped again, and again, continuing to flip faster and faster, over and over, until finally, mid flip, it disappeared altogether. And the moment the arrow vanished, the answer revealed itself to Reason. She burst from her chair. "The answer is neither! You were born neither up nor down. You were born here and now, but neither up nor down." The words flew from her. "You were born here and now because of my fear and worry! I created you! I can destroy you!" Reason jumped with joy, certain of her answer. This time the bell rang with earsplitting force. BOING, BONG, BOING, BONG, BOING, BONG.

The Stickman unleashed a terrifying scream, but Reason did not waver. She recognized with overwhelming relief that she was free of fear. "I'm right! I know it! I feel it!" she shouted in wild delight. And as if to confirm her success, the tunnel wall opened to the stick people behind the glass. The glass shattered and all three instantly transformed into their human form, gleefully unashamed of their nakedness. As Reason watched, the two men and one woman looked at themselves—examining their bodies—peering into the palms of their hands, laughing and shouting. They ran to one another and huddled in a hug.

Panicking, the Stickman bellowed and tried to flee, but remained somehow mysteriously confined to its chair.

Reason felt the heavy weight of her injured hand lift. She watched with mounting glee as her stick fingers seemed to vanish and her flesh and bone hand swiftly and painlessly mended itself. The three released prisoners ran to her. "Thank you! Bless You! Run!" they yelled, racing past her into the depths of the tunnel and around the bend.

The bell continued to toll ominously—as if warning of some impending doom. Adding to the racket, the Stickman bawled as the machine beside it came to life—rumbling, vibrating, juddering the structure that held it.

The Stickman tried in vain to escape from its chair, and then suddenly it ceased to struggle and turned its gaze to Reason—its brows dark smudges raised high above large round eyes, its mouth a slash. "It's not possible! I..." But before it could utter another word, the machine sucked the Stickman's head into its glistening mouth. A high-pitched wail flooded the tunnel, and from the machine's long glossy chute, wood chips sailed in a far-reaching arc.

And just like that, with the long torso and limbs following the head, the Stickman vanished, the bell went silent, and the tunnel became quiet and still. Reason kicked at the pile of sawdust on the tunnel floor—giddy with relief. Then she pivoted and bolted after the other three, hearing their voices faintly ahead, somewhere beyond the curve.

Rounding the bend, she saw that the three people stood perched at the very edge of the opening. They appeared to be talking animatedly, arguing even. The woman was shouting at the taller of the two men and pointing to the opening.

"Hey!" cried Reason. All three turned to face her, but before she could say more, the woman turned and leapt from the tunnel. Reason screamed and stopped running. The shorter of the two men gave her an anxious glance and then followed the woman over the edge. The tall man looked from Reason to the opening and back to Reason. "What are you doing? Don't!" she yelled, instinctively reaching out for him. But the distance between them was too great. The man turned away, hesitated, then raised his arms and jumped.

Reason once again approached the end of the tunnel and the familiar stench rose to greet her. She crept to the edge. The jumpers were nowhere to be seen. An inferno still blazed below. She groaned and moved away, fighting back tears. *Why? I don't understand. Why jump?* She slumped to the tunnel floor. A sudden pecking sound caused her to look up. "Raven?" she called. "Is that you?"

"Craw, craw," came the faint call from the other side of the wall.

Reason rose to her knees. Near her, the branches of the tunnel wall shifted, creating the shape of the letter T, followed by the letter R. Soon a string of letters spelled: TRUST YOURSELF TO FIND A SOUND PATH. Reason said the phrase, shaping the words soundlessly. She thought of the woman and the two men, closing her eyes, visualizing them. She saw the woman gesturing toward the opening, and suddenly Reason saw the entire scene very differently. The man and the woman had not been arguing. No. The woman had been encouraging the tall man to jump, coaxing him on. She had been trying to persuade him that jumping was the right thing to do. The woman had been happy and smiling. To the tall man, she had shouted with glee, "It's okay. This is the way. We're free. We're leaving." But he had been afraid, terrified of jumping. "I don't blame him!" Reason shouted into her hands.

She stood and turned to face the opening. Taking a deep breath, eyes forward, Reason walked to the edge. Blazing fires roared below. Ahead, lightning sliced through the smoke-filled sky. Thunder boomed and crackled. "Trust," she whispered, focusing on her breath. The outward sounds faded away. Opening the palms of her hands to the sky, she leapt from the tunnel of fear and worry.

CB EO

Reason felt featherlight as if she was floating on a cloud, not falling at all. When she felt a hand gently take hold of her own, she opened her eyes. Floating alongside her was a beautiful woman. Hand in hand, they ascended through a white mist. *The woman from my dream* thought Reason from within her hazy calm. The woman's pale-grey eyes seemed to reach for Reason's soul as her long red hair floated toward Reason's face. "We're rising, not falling," said Reason dreamily. The woman smiled, the fingers of her free hand brushing Reason's cheek.

"You've done well, Reason," she praised in a gentle and curiously familiar voice. Reason reached out and felt the woman's hair. Silky-soft, it slipped through her fingers. She opened her mouth to speak, but the woman continued, "You've faced your fear here in this world. You've calmed your worries. And by doing so, you've released yourself from their grasp. Feel your freedom."

Reason watched the woman's red lips as they moved, fascinated by them. "Feel my freedom," she said distractedly, hearing her own voice from a faraway place.

"Yes, my dear Reason, you have met your fear and conquered it. You are rising from it. Remember this moment. Remember what it feels like."

What it feels like... Reason let her eyes drift closed and relaxed into the ease of the moment, feeling it fully. She felt weightless and carefree, safe, strong, and free. She opened her eyes, ready to share her feelings with the beautiful woman with the scarlet lips and the long, flowing auburn hair.

15

a piece of the light

66 Freedom from fear. Yes. I feel... Wait. Where is she?" Reason opened her eyes wide—for a moment, stunned and perplexed. "I was saying something. I was..." Her thoughts became muddled, and nearly blinded by the glaring white lights of the club, she felt disoriented as if awakening from a dream.

"I don't give a shit!" yelled William into her face.

At the very moment Reason had seen William, she had experienced a sudden and vivid vision. In it she had been with a beautiful woman, flying or floating, the experience seeming very real. But in reality, she was still in the noisy club, facing William, the images of her vision swiftly fading. She blinked in puzzlement.

William yanked her off her feet. She tried to escape his grip, but he had hoisted her very nearly onto his shoulder. She swung at him with her one free arm. Held as she was, her fist made weak contact. She shouted in protest, but her cries blended in with the chaotic clamor of the club.

To her dismay, the bright lights flashed strobe-like, increasing the frenzied confusion. Reason pulled at William's hair, trying to make him loosen his grasp. He only squeezed harder, holding her so tightly that she thought she might faint. She clawed at him, her fingers just catching the fabric of his shirt. She pushed against his bouncing shoulder, trying to break free, but he swung his arm up from behind and hit her squarely in the temple. She went limp, staring vacantly at the sea of people flashing by.

Groggy, slowly recovering, she began to kick and thrash and then shriek hysterically—frantic that no one seemed to notice her dilemma. Halfway down the entrance corridor, Reason got a foot to the floor, but it only bounced and dragged. She tried grabbing at the people rushing by and got a handful of fabric, but then it was gone. "Hey, what the fuck?" someone shouted, but no one came to her aid.

Outside, William flung her to the sidewalk. In the muggy night, she scrambled to her feet and faced him defiantly. "William," she began. With the back of his hand, he slapped her across the face. She staggered back; one hand pressed to her stinging cheek.

"Shut the fuck up," he snapped.

A stranger approached, walking on the far side of the street. As the man neared, William looked about unflinchingly and then spotted a metal pipe lying near the club entrance. He rushed to pick it up. Reason sprang into action too and lunged for the pipe. But William easily shoved her aside and, snatching up the short piece of pipe, swung it up and around, and held it menacingly toward the advancing stranger.

"Miss? Are you okay?" called the stranger, speaking with a middle-eastern accent, moving cautiously, crossing the street towards them.

"It's OK. I mean, I'm OK. I... I mean you should go... just go," urged Reason, afraid that William would hurt the stranger. She waved the man on, watching him watch her, seeing him observe her shaking. The stranger studied Reason, and then looked at William, who, wielding the pipe, stepped toward him. But the stranger seemed unconcerned and moved closer.

"Fuck-off, asshole," barked William, poised to attack.

The stranger stopped. He looked from Reason to William, and then back at Reason. "Please," she pleaded, gesturing for the man to stay away, panicking that William would attack him. "I'm fine. Really, I am. Please, just go. He'll hurt you. He doesn't care. Please go." Reason was terrified for the man. She knew William's rage. The stranger did not. Unable to bear the idea of someone else being hurt because of her stupid decision to come to the club, again, she frantically waved the man on. He seemed quite old, with white hair and a gentle way about him. She watched him as he looked both ways along the darkened street and then back at her, making eye contact.

He seemed to look at her with recognition and compassion, as a father might look at his child.

William swore and stepped toward the man, but the stranger merely raised his hand and kept his gaze on Reason. He held his arm out straight, palm out, and aimed at William, gesturing for him to stop. With a look of confused surprise, William stopped.

"As you vish; I vill not interfere," said the stranger. And then, although his lips never moved, Reason felt certain that she heard him say, "I could not do so even if you vanted me to. I am here to tell you to be brave, child. And to tell you, you are never truly alone." And with that, he turned and walked away. She wanted to call out to him. Instead, Reason simply watched the stranger move farther down the sidewalk.

Be brave.

William came alive. He looked at the pipe in his hand, staring at it as if he did not know how he had come to be holding it—and then he tossed it away.

Next to the nightclub was a large parking lot. At this time of the night, it contained only a small scattering of cars. William pushed Reason toward the shadows and isolation of this lot. She stole a glance over her shoulder at the stranger, catching a last glimpse of him. William shoved her from behind, forcing her around the corner of the building. But in that brief glance, Reason had seen that the stranger had stopped walking and stood facing her. In his hands, he held aloft a long staff—the staff glimmering white against the darkness of the night.

The sight intrigued Reason, and she wanted to see more, but William pushed her against the side wall of the nightclub and pressed his body against hers. With one hand clamped on the top of her head and the other against her throat, he forced a kiss. She groaned and tried to turn her face away, but he had her head firmly pinned. She held her breath and closed her lips tightly. William pulled away. "Fuck you," he hissed.

He planted his hands on the wall at either side of her head. She stood rigidly still, cringing as he reached to her face and then slid the loose strands of her long hair to behind her ears. "Don't fuck with me, Reason. I've had a lot of time to think about this night, this entire night. I've got it all planned out." He slapped his palms against the wall and then leaned in and licked her cheek. "Time to move," he said, pulling her from the wall and pushing her deeper into the lot.

"Why are you doing this, William? You know you can change your mind. Right now, before you go any further. It's over. We're over. You know this. You don't want me." As Reason spoke, she eyed the parking lot, fearing its seclusion and dark shadows, searching for some escape.

William's answer was to hit her in the small of her back. She stumbled to a kneeling position on the hard asphalt, his breath heavy behind her. She knew his contempt. With painstaking care, she stood.

"Why am I fucking doing this?" he hissed, poking Reason between her shoulder blades. "Because you need reminding that we're not done. Not yet." He made the shape of a gun and put his fingers to Reason's temple. "No matter where you are and no matter what," he sneered, "no matter where we go in our fucking lives, you're mine until I say otherwise." Reason took a small step away from his poking finger, but William grabbed her by the shoulder and squeezed. Suddenly more angry than afraid, Reason stood tall and denied him his thrill of making her flinch. "When you least expect me, I'll find you and fuck you up." He moved quickly, coming in front of her. "Fuck-you-up," he repeated, poking Reason in the forehead with each word. And then he pressed his lips to her ear. "Now let's go have us some fun." Reason's mind raced as she fought hard not to panic.

A tall, solitary street lamp stood beacon-like in the parking lot, its light falling in a pale-white cone onto the black pavement. Within the light, hundreds of insects flew, batting their tiny-winged bodies against one another. Reason thought that she could hear the whine of the electricity and the tiny popping sounds of the insects bouncing off the glass bulb. Despite the hideousness of the sight, she felt oddly comforted by the plight of the insects—their chaotic fight for survival—their striving so relentlessly for a piece of the light. Watching them, she experienced an intense urge to run, to fight for a piece of her own light. Turning fast, she darted around William and doubled back. But her mad dash was short-lived. William grabbed her by her hair and the waist of her jeans and yanked her to the ground.

"Fuck you!" he cursed into the back of her head. "Where do you think you're going? Huh?" With a fist full of her hair, he pulled her head back and spat in her face. "Get the fuck up."

Reason winced and carefully stood—grit embedded in the palms of her hands and the thin flesh of her forearms. "Let me go, William. Let me go." She despised the pleading, wanting instead to fight. But she knew better. He jerked her head back, making it difficult for her to swallow, and with his free hand, held her by her throat and applied pressure.

"The sound of your fucking voice pisses me off," he muttered.

Ignoring his order for silence, Reason opened her mouth to plead further. But William moved his hand from her throat to her mouth and covered both it and her nose. Her eyes widened. She became still, calming herself to calm him. His hand was hot and sweaty. And when it became clear that he was in no rush to move it, she picked at his fingers, trying to pry them open.

Determined to survive, Reason went limp, and William, unable to hold her, released his grip. She fell away onto her knees, gasping for air. William planted his foot on her back and pushed her flat to the ground. "Don't fuck with me, Reason. I'm warning you. This night is about what I want."

At that moment, trembling violently, Reason's hatred for William momentarily surpassed her fear. She lay still, sucking in the hot night air, her cheekbone pressed against the blacktop. *Stay calm. Stay calm.* William removed his foot from her back and kneeled beside her, pressing his hand into her buttocks. He held his hand there for a moment, and then pushed off her to stand up. "Get up," he ordered, kicking her in the thigh. Mouth parched, hands burning, she stood.

From the direction of the nightclub came a momentary burst of incoherent shouts and some drunken laughter. A siren wailed in the distance. But no one was coming to help. And Reason knew that cutting through the parking lot was a shortcut to the halfway house.

And she knew that if the halfway house was their destination, on the way they would walk through a large desolate park and then down a short side street of old, rundown row houses. Her fear intensified.

Once in the park, William grabbed the waist of Reason's jeans and dragged her to a solitary picnic table under a giant willow. In the humid night air, the long branches of the big tree hung still and low to the ground, concealing both Reason and William, and the table. Through the thin gaps in the branches, she squinted at the dark purple grounds of the park, the seclusion terrifying—her chances for escape dwindling.

"Sit," said William. Reason glanced at the bench seat and stayed where she stood. "Sit the fuck down," he growled, shoving her into the thin, hard edge of the picnic table. She sat and held her arms out protectively. "Look at you. What are those for?" laughed William, slapping at her hands. She lowered them to the table and glanced about anxiously. William sprang at her and grabbed her by her wrists. "You've been fucking around with that asshole from college, haven't you?"

"What?" Reason asked incredulously. "Let go of me! I haven't been with anyone. But it doesn't matter. We're not together... you and me. We're not together!" she said defiantly.

"You're a fucking liar," he snapped, releasing her wrists and raising his hand.

Reason crossed her arms above her head. But William backed off, choosing instead to laugh at her. Soon he went quiet, watching her from a few feet away.

In the distance, a car passed—a low rumbling that penetrated the unnerving silence. Reason watched William nervously. He grinned at her and reached into his jean's pocket, pulling out a cigarette pack, retrieving a stubby homemade cigarette. He stepped toward the picnic table. She slid a small distance along the bench, increasing the space between them. He looked at his cigarette and then lit it, the smoke swirling lazily in the still, humid air. When he looked at her again, Reason lowered her gaze and gripped the bench seat. Her fingers discovered a name carved into the wood, and with one trembling finger, she anxiously began tracing the letters: S—h—e... "Tell me about that asshole. Who is he?" barked William.

"What? Who are you talking about?" Genuinely unsure of whom he was asking about, Reason shook her head and dared to glance at William.

"Don't play games with me, you little shit. Who the fuck is the tall, skinny asshole who had his arms around you? I was there. I saw you and him in the main hall. You're a fucking liar." He dropped his cigarette and ground it out with the heel of his shoe.

"You were at the college?" Reason heard herself speak, but the sound came to her as the voice of a stranger.

William pounced, grabbing her by her chin. "It doesn't matter where the fuck I've been. That skinny asshole can have my fucking leftovers." He let go of Reason's chin and back-handed the side of her head.

Tall? Skinny? Who? Who? Eddie? Eddie! Oh, Eddie, are you out there somewhere looking for me? Her head buzzing, Reason glanced at the moon showing through a gap in the branches, and then back at William. "That was Eddie, but..." She lowered her head, waiting for the blow. None came. She continued. "He's a friend. He has a girlfriend. Friends hug, William. A hug means nothing but a greeting between good friends."

Reason suddenly felt furious, and the intensity of her rage set her in motion. On impulse, she stood and flung herself at William, catching him off guard. Grunting, he lost his footing and stumbled backwards. Together they tumbled clumsily through the dangling foliage—Reason falling on top of him, hitting her chin against his knee, biting her tongue. She winced but kept going, pushing away. But he grabbed her arm—his hand sliding down the soft fabric of her blouse until it found her thumb and gripped onto it. Reason screamed, spinning around, chopping at William's hand until he let go. She fell backwards, frantic to escape, scrambling away crab-like. He crawled after her, rising like a sprinter from all fours, clamping his hand onto her ankle. She yelled out as he began climbing atop of her, grabbing her arm, then her hair, yanking her head forward. Reason let out a garbled scream and wrenched her head free—ignoring the hot sting at her scalp. Pushing away with all her might, she scrambled to her feet, turned from William, and ran. He grabbed at her, but lost his balance and fell. For a few desperate and promising seconds, Reason ran free. But William tackled her and her legs buckled. She fell awkwardly, hitting her head on the ground. Blotchy white lights filled her vision. The world went dim, dimmer still, and then altogether black.

When Reason came to, she lay on her side in the same spot that he had tackled her. She spat dirt from her mouth and rolled onto her back. William, who had been squatting behind her, stood and straddled her, lit cigarette in hand. He put his foot on her belly. Reason grabbed at the toe of his shoe, the heavy rubber sole pressing the metal of her belt buckle into the soft skin of her abdomen. "Bitch," he sneered, removing his foot and holding it in the air above her head. She covered her face and rolled onto her side. William laughed and dropped his cigarette. It bounced off of her cheek. He kicked her. She yelped and curled her body reflexively, moaning. Squatting, William leaned over her and grabbed her wrists, forcing her arms open. He rolled her onto her back and kicked her legs flat. Her screams did little as he pushed her hands to the ground at either side of her head and dropped his body onto hers. Pinned under his full weight, Reason struggled to breathe. William pressed his lips to hers. She wrenched her head to the side and his mouth slithered across her face. He pulled away and punched at her chin. She stopped moving—the sound of her racing heart exploding in her head. "Stay still!" he hissed before kissing her again.

Reason groaned, squeezing her eyes shut. William moved one hand to the top of her head and the other to her chin. In the vice-like grip, he pressed his lips hard onto hers. Her top lip became pinched and then split—the metallic taste of blood soon spreading between their tongues. He moved his hand from her head to her thigh, his fingers groping between her legs. She screamed a smothered cry for mercy.

Slurred drunken voices drifted into the stillness of the park. William raised his head, clamping a hand over Reason's mouth. She groped at it, picking at his fingers, trying to pry them loose. His gaze followed the sound of the voices as they receded into the sticky heat of the night. But their sound was enough to get him moving. He pushed up and off her and stood. She gasped for air. "Get the fuck up," he ordered.

Reason rolled over and then climbed to her feet—dirt and blades of grass sticking to her skin and clothes. She scanned the park with desperate hope, but saw no one and closed her eyes in misery. William pulled her toward him, his breath hot on her face. "I fucking said don't fuck around, Reason. You dying won't bother me. Not one bit. It'll only take a second to kill you, and if that happens, it'll be your own fault. So, don't yell and don't run. If you do, I'll catch you and I'll hurt you. I'll hurt you bad. You owe me this night and I'm going to have it."

William reached for Reason's throat and curled his fingers around her necklace. "I hate this fucking thing," he spewed. She felt the chain dig into her neck and then break. In the silver-blue light of the moon, the necklace flew through the air, its pendant in the lead. The fine chain seemed to hover momentarily as if magically held by the night sky, and then it fell, disappearing. She let out a tiny squeal, feeling the biting sting of its loss.

Reason knew that her situation was extremely dire. Frantic, she hid her fear, wearing a stony face as her armor. She had known similar scenes with William in the past, but this time was different. This time, he was acting out a vicious promise to himself. This time there would be no talking him down, no defending herself until he had calmed. This time he was taking his revenge, and she, terrified of being severely injured or killed, found herself once more stunned into submission.

Gripping her by the wrist, William led Reason away, every so often yanking her closer to his side. In desperation, she hunted for an opportunity to escape but saw only dark, empty alleyways between the buildings bordering the park.

Beyond the park, they moved past a few poorly kept row houses. She thought about trying to run to the door of one of these houses, but their torn curtains, cracked windows, garbage-strewn front porches, and unkempt lawns discouraged her. The closer they came to the halfway house, the more her panic grew. Unknowingly, she had quickened her pace. "Slow down," barked William, squeezing her wrist so tightly, the tiny pearl button at the cuff of her blouse pressed painfully into her wrist. He spun her around to face him. "And stop looking around," he warned, his stare glassy and wild, his pupils large, the bright blue of his eyes now black pools of hate. "We're gonna have such a good time," he whispered ominously. Then grinning garishly, he threw her wrist away as if it were suddenly too offensive to hold, and stepping behind her, shoved her ahead.

α β

A plain-clothed officer stepped out from the front passenger seat of a large grey sedan. He opened the rear door and moved out of the way. McKenzie leapt out.

"Five minutes," the officer cautioned, not bothering to look at McKenzie.

"I know, I know," McKenzie answered, more concerned about how late he was than the officer's warning. The police officer closed the car door, turned, and leaned against it to wait.

Eddie opened the nightclub door just as McKenzie reached for it. Windowless and opening outwards, the door banged against McKenzie's hand. "Sorry, man," offered Eddie. McKenzie took little notice of the collision, and less of Eddie as the two crossed paths, one racing inside the club to find Reason, and the other going outside to look for her. But Reason was far away by then—shivering fearfully at the bottom of the metal fire escape that led to the second floor of the halfway house.

As they navigated the jostling crowds of the club, McKenzie and Eddie passed by each other once more during their searches that night. Eddie eventually gave up and went back to the dance floor, thinking that Reason must be somewhere in the crowded club and that he had simply missed her. He fully expected to find her sitting at their table as the night continued. McKenzie, having searched hurriedly in the few minutes he had been granted, had also given up, resorting to leaving a message for Reason with the busy and apathetic bartender. His hastily scribbled message read: "William is on the hunt. Knows you're here. House not supervised. Hide." And then, after one more lingering glance about the room, McKenzie reluctantly returned to the police car to be transported to a nearby drug rehabilitation center.

CS &O

Mumbling a desperate prayer, Reason climbed the ladder with William following close behind her—the hard edges of the narrow metal rungs digging into the soft soles of her shoes. *God help me. Keep me calm. Keep me strong.* At the top of the ladder, an open-grid metal landing extended to her right. She climbed onto the platform and stood staring down at her feet, feeling as if they belonged to someone else.

"Welcome home," snickered William.

In the yellow light of a street lamp, shivering despite the awful heat, Reason studied the details of the fire escape and peered nervously at her surroundings. From where she stood, she saw a large gap, then the roof of the house next door, and the hard, cracked pavement of the parking lot far below.

William pushed her toward a large square window, its bottom half propped open by an orange pop can. Cracked and peeling paint covered the window's wide ledge, which sat level with her thigh. Reason felt sick knowing that the window led from the spaciousness of the night into the oppressive shadows of the house. She peered in from where she stood, seeing little. William reached past her, removed the empty pop can, and, making little noise, pushed the window open fully.

"Get in," he ordered.

"Please. Don't do this," she pleaded.

He responded by grabbing a handful of her hair and pulling her toward the opening. "Be quiet, or I'll fucking make you," he hissed, his spittle spraying her face.

Reason felt a crazed twinge of hope at the notion of needing to be quiet. *How badly can he hurt me if he expects quiet?* William shoved her from behind. She crawled in through the large opening and stepped onto an unmade single bed. To her right was a second bed, its bedding untouched. She looked about anxiously, wired with adrenaline, desperate to survive.

The room's dull, steel-grey walls blended into a grey, path-worn, wall-to-wall carpet. Thin curtains hung at the window, tied to one side with a black shoelace. At the foot of the bed upon which Reason crouched was a small table, and beyond that, a closed bedroom door. Beside the door stood an olive-green dresser with a lit desk lamp bent over a stack of magazines. Another small black metal lamp, perched atop a green plastic milk crate beside the second bed, lit the far back corner of the room. And beside the crate, also on the floor, was an open can of Coke.

William put the orange pop can back in its place and lowered the window. He moved across the room to the bedroom door and put his ear against it, listening for a moment before opening the door a crack and peering into the slit of light. Reason clenched her fists. Without making a sound, William closed the door. He turned, smiled, and walked towards her. She stiffened and held her breath, readying herself. He stood looking down at her and then offered her his hand. She stared at it, unsure of what to do.

"Take my hand, Ray," he whispered, using his nickname for her.

Reason did nothing. William reached down and gently took her hand. He pulled her up and drew her in close, wrapping his arms around her. "You smell nice," he whispered, standing beside the bed while she kneeled on it. They stayed this way for some minutes, motionless and quiet—until Reason began to tremble. William held her tighter. She groaned, terrified. He kissed her on her neck, lingering there. She tried to raise her arms, but he had them pinned to her sides. She whimpered as a shiver slithered across her skin.

"Let me go," she pleaded.

William grabbed a fist full of her hair and yanked her head back. She tried to be quiet, but a small squeal escaped. He forced her head up and forward, and with his fist, struck her in the forehead. She fell limp onto the bed. Dazed, she felt his hands grope her and then turn her over—her body and limbs impossibly heavy. He pushed her face into the mattress and then lay atop her.

"Do I need to use these?" he whispered, his breath hot in her ear, his weight heavy on her back. He reached beneath the bed, and then twisting her head so that she could see, pushed a clear plastic bag close to her face. She could not understand what it was at first, just a blurry thing smelling vaguely of pot. Then something hard hit her cheek, and when William pulled the bag away, she could see a roll of duct tape inside. He dumped the tape onto the bed, along with what looked like a dark rag, but was a single sock. "Do I?" he insisted, shoving the sock into her mouth. Unable to shake her head, Reason could only groan. William pulled the sock away. "What?" he asked.

"No," she mouthed, desperate for air.

"You sure?" he hissed, threatening to put the sock back into her mouth.

Reason clamped her eyes shut, feeling intensely ashamed of answering so quickly and for the weakness it implied. "Please. I can't breathe," she pleaded, her voice squeezed and weak.

"You get loud and I'll shove this back in your mouth and tape it to your fucking face," he said, dangling the sock before her.

William stood. "Take off your shoes. Swallow this," he ordered. Reason did not move. "Turn over—stand up—take off your shoes—and take this." With a socked foot, he kicked the mattress. She did not remember him removing his shoes and did not want to remove her own. Reluctantly, she stood, turning with methodical care, feeling dizzy, keeping her gaze on the floor in full defensive survival mode. "Look at me," he insisted, holding a tiny plastic bag with four hits of acid clinging to the clear plastic like tiny bits of confetti.

"Please, no drugs," she whispered, pushing the bag away.

William laughed, removed two hits from the bag, and licked them from his fingers. He moved to Reason, his face inches from hers. "Swallow," he hissed through clenched teeth, holding two more hits of acid between his fingers. She shook her head. William forced the drug into her mouth and reflexively she bit down. When he yanked his fingers away, the hits of acid stuck to the inside of her upper lip. William swore, looked at his hand, and shook it. His attention elsewhere, she swiped the teeny pieces of paper from her lip and wiped them onto the back of her jeans.

"You're such a fucking bitch!" spat William, punching Reason above her right temple. She stumbled against the bed and then crumpled to the floor. The room spun.

God help me. Where is everybody? Asleep? Gone? Is there no one... William hoisted Reason up from the floor and dropped her back onto the disheveled bed. She blinked woozily through the strands of her hair, trying in mounting anguish to push his hands away as they grappled with her jeans. Flipping her over, William planted his hand on her head and pressed her face into the foul-smelling bed sheets. She wrestled her head to the side, gasping for air. His fingers slid across her face, stopping to cover both her nose and mouth. When she squealed into the hot flesh of his hand, he responded by applying more pressure.

With William's weight heavy on her back, and unable to breathe, Reason slipped in and out of consciousness, trying to stay awake. But soon the darkness fully engulfed her, and when she awoke sometime later, she was groggy and nauseated. She moaned wearily. She was lying on her stomach, her head hanging off the foot of the narrow bed, her neck stiff and sore. One of her arms lay beneath her, the other stretched out from her side. She was naked from the waist down—her blouse scrunched up beneath her throat—a thin bed sheet covering the back of her head. Momentarily confused, she stared blankly at unfamiliar carpet. But from between her legs, a burning pain soon leached into her consciousness. She stiffened, stifling her anguish.

Is he asleep? Am I alone? Afraid to move, Reason uncurled the fingers of her free hand and cautiously slid her other arm out from beneath her aching body. A faint brushing noise sounded from somewhere behind her. She held her breath and lay agonizingly still. Wretched seconds passed. The muted brushing started up again, and despite her discomfort and exposure, Reason stayed still and listened. She knew that if she was to escape, she needed at first to be cautious and patient. The sound stopped, started, stopped, and started again. *Is it outside? No. It's near me… definitely near me.* She raised her head.

"Don't fucking move!" said William in a low, trembling voice.

Reason gasped audibly. The brushing sound became faster and more intense, and she could now hear William's breathing, heavy and uneven. *Oh, God! He's masturbating!* William was indeed masturbating. He was standing above and behind Reason and stroking himself. The realization shocked and disgusted her. She rose to her knees and grabbed at the bedsheet, covering her nakedness. And as she did, a noise at the door caused them both to start. In restrained, quick bursts, someone was rapping on the door. William swore and turned his attention from Reason to the sound. He did not move, but he listened. The door snapped open an inch. Hall light entered the small, dim room, focusing a narrow beam of light on a small decal stuck to the side of the dresser—a strip of tiny yellow flowers clustered into diamond shapes.

"William?" said a low, raspy male voice.

"Fucking timing," uttered William angrily.

The two men whispered at the door. The raspy-voiced man made a low, growling noise and then asked, "She in there?"

"She's here," answered William matter-of-factly.

"Let me see her."

The intruder pushed against the door, opening it another couple of inches before William used his body as a block. "Not yet," he hissed into the crack of light.

"When?" asked the man impatiently, his chubby fingers finding the inside face of the door.

Reason sprang into action. She dropped the bedsheet and scrambled to the propped-up window, struggling to lift it. It moved easily for three or four inches and then jammed. Frantic to escape, she wriggled through the small opening anyway. Her blouse caught on the framework and tore, but she kept going. Her shoulders cleared and when they did, Reason dared to hope for a hysterical second that she might actually get out. But William grabbed her from behind and pulled her back into the room. She yelped and grabbed at the window frame, but it easily slipped from her fingers. The back of her head struck the bottom edge of the raised window. The glass rattled. William hauled her up and away from the opening, and suddenly his hand covered her mouth. Her eyes moved wildly, her breath straining through her nose. She grabbed at his fingers. He squeezed so tightly they slipped into her mouth. She tried to bite him, but he pulled his fingers clear and hit her squarely in the face. She grunted and slumped—dizzy and queasy. William's hands slid around her throat. "Stupid bitch," he sneered, his voice hoarse. "You stupid, stupid bitch." Letting go of her neck, he shoved her down onto the bed and blocked the window with his body.

Reason lay still for many minutes, momentarily stunned, then hauled herself up. Sitting on the bed, she pleaded, knowing that her words were likely useless, but she was distraught and terrified and unable to remain quiet. "Please, William. Stop. Don't do this. You've had your revenge. Let me..."

He lunged at her, punching her in the stomach. She folded—her mouth agape in a silent scream. William hit her again, this time on the side of the head. *Oh God, please let me live. Let me live!* Reason tried in vain to block his punches, but the blows rapidly alternated between her head and torso. While she gagged and gasped for breath, he grabbed the loose bed sheet, pulled it over her head, and twisted the thin fabric around her neck. Reason screamed a strangled, frantic shriek. In a desperate attempt to make him think she had fainted, she went limp, collapsing on the bed. The pressure around her throat released, but in a fit of full-fledged rage, William continued to hit her—pummeling her on the backs of her legs and her buttocks until he grew tired. And as she lay heaving and groaning, and creeping into a fetal position, he shuffled to the dresser, where he stood disheveled, wild-eyed, and panting.

"Sit up," he said, breathless and brutally impatient. Reason could not breathe, let alone sit up. "Sit the fuck up or I'll fucking kill you right fucking now." She struggled unsuccessfully to lift herself. William lunged at her and yanked her up by her arm. "You're a stupid fucking bitch. This is your fault. All of this is your fucking fault. Like always. You ask for it. You're a stupid, selfish cunt. You piss me off on purpose and you know you do. It's like you want it. It's like you like it. Do you like it? Do you? I think you do. I think you're turned on by it. You're as cold as ice, you fucking bitch." William shot Reason a savage glare, made a low throaty snarling sound, and then threw himself onto the bed beside her.

She did not move. She had become a rock—a cold, lifeless, pitiful rock. *As cold as ice...*

"Don't try that again, Reason. You know I fucking mean what I say. Understand?" William's voice slithered to her core.

Suddenly the bedroom door opened wide. Light fanned into the darkened room. Then the door closed with a click. "I'm not waitin' anymore," said the man with the raspy voice. "I did what you wanted. Been keepin' watch all this damn time. They ain't even down there. They musta gone out or somethin'."

William stood with his back to Reason. "Fuck. Okay. But remember... look at me. I said look at me." William gave the fat man an abrupt shove. The man looked beyond William and stared at Reason, a grin spreading across his fleshy features, exposing large, nicotine-stained teeth. William shoved him again and then moved to block his view. "Remember, you can get as close as you want, but don't touch her." The fat man strained to see around William. "Did you hear me, asshole?"

"Yeah, yeah... I heard you for fuck's sake."

William stepped to the side and gestured dismissively for the man to get on with it. The big man moved hungrily to the bedside. Reason dragged her battered body along the damp surface of the small bed until her back hit the wall. Grimacing, she pulled her knees up tight to her body and arranged her hands in an attempt to cover her nakedness. The bedsheet lay crumpled on the floor, her jeans sprawled alongside it. Reason had never experienced such suffocating vulnerability. She felt sickened by it—and ravaged by hatred, disgust, and unbridled fear.

As Reason lay like a rag doll—weak and bloodied—listening stonily to a few cars passing on the street, William raped her while the fat man watched and masturbated. At one point, the fat man waddled on his knees to the side of the bed and stared into Reason's face, panting and groping himself. Her eyes closed, she could feel his hot, rancid breath blowing the loose strands of her hair.

Numbed, she drifted in and out of consciousness. When the fat man was finally finished, he remained sitting on the floor with his chin resting on the bed, watching her. Finally, mercifully, he raised himself in an awkward display of ungainliness and flopped onto the other bed. His rolling snore soon filled the room.

William, who would leave Reason's limp body every so often, could not stand still. He was too high and energized, and paced the room restlessly. At one point, he sat at the foot of the bed and stared at his hands, his legs bouncing rapidly. Reason took this opportunity to peer over the edge of the bed for her jeans, but they were no longer in sight. *Oh God. Oh God. Please get me out of here. Please help me. Let me live. Where are my fucking jeans?*

William sighed. Then he stood, pulled on his jeans, and walked out of the room—leaving the door ajar and turning to his right. Reason heard a strong stream of urine. She moved as quickly as her sore, torn body would allow and searched for her jeans. Seconds later William returned, shut the door, and stood with his back against it. Reason clutched her jeans with trembling hands, pushing the denim into her lap. William did not appear to notice. He swiped the back of his hand across his mouth and then crawled along the bed toward her. She held her breath, but he moved beyond her and raised the window fully. A faint glimmer of hope shimmied in her gut. "Move over. Get away from the window," he ordered.

He squeezed his body between her and the open window and lit a cigarette. The smoke curled, hovering blue in the stillness of the scorching night. The hair on their bare arms touched. William leaned his head back against the wall and exhaled a series of smoke rings. He turned his gaze to the window and stayed that way, the cigarette burning un-smoked and soon dropping forward between his slackened fingers. A dog barked in the distance. William jerked awake and then stared down at his cigarette.

"I have to go to the bathroom," Reason said quietly. William said nothing and did nothing. Eyes forward, Reason sat uncomfortably still. She opened her mouth to repeat the statement, but William put his hand on her upper thigh. He flinched, noticeably surprised by the feel of the soft denim. He grabbed hold of her jeans and attempted to pull them from her lap, but she held on. *Good God, have mercy.* William let go and stood up from the bed. He moved to an alarm clock used as a paperweight on a pile of papers on the floor, turned it towards him, and read the time. Cream-colored digits flipped to 3:57.

"Put your jeans on," he said in an eerily quiet voice. Reason did so eagerly, pulling the fabric delicately over her cuts and bruises as William watched. Her jeans on, she did her best to straighten her blouse before moving her injured body gingerly along the bed, every muscle protesting. William opened the bedroom door and peered out. He turned to Reason and jerked his head toward the door. She stood—cautiously—painstakingly. He moved towards her. She cringed and put her hands out defensively. He took her by her elbow and pulled her to the door.

"Go quietly and leave the door open."

William's room was at the back corner of the large house. A wide corridor ran from his bedroom door to the opposite side of the house—dark brown carpet running the full length. Ahead in the hallway, Reason saw three doors, all of them open, the rooms seemingly empty. To her left, a long, narrow hallway led to a steep staircase. An exit sign hung from the ceiling above the stairs. She stared at it. It seemed very far away.

"Go to the fucking bathroom," William hissed, pushing her over the threshold. She walked unsteadily, holding the wall, shuffling into the washroom. And despite his order, she shut the door and moved to lock it. It had no lock.

Reason groaned at the door handle, waiting for William to open the door. But nothing happened. Clutching herself, she looked at a piece of paper taped to the back of the door, the tape yellowed and peeling. On the paper, a typed message read: "No guests allowed anywhere on the premises. Drugs prohibited." In red marker across the notice someone had written, "Catch me if you can pig."

Reason turned from the door. A garishly bright light hung above the bathroom sink, accentuating the grey dreariness of the walls. A small window sat perched above the toilet. Reason moved to it, but it was far too small and two stories above the ground. Despairingly, she put her hands to her face and felt crusted blood and bulging flesh. She looked to the ceiling and opened her mouth in a silent scream.

William's knuckles rapped on the door. Reason started, moved to the toilet, and flushed it. She stood helplessly in front of the stained porcelain bowl, staring at the water as it swirled and rushed away. The bathroom door opened a crack. "I'm not finished," she managed, hopelessly desperate and pushing the door closed. Wounded and exhausted, but driven by a desire to survive, she labored to calm herself. Bending forward and balling her hands into fists, she thumped them softly against her bruised thighs. She thought of the stairs out in the hall—too far away—and William was too close. She would have to get out through the bedroom window and down the fire escape. She would have to endure, be patient, and wait for the right opportunity. She would have to think only of her survival—stay alert, awake, and focused.

Reason opened the bathroom door. William pulled her out and pushed her along the wall and back into the bedroom. She crawled onto the bed and edged close to the window. He had left it open. She looked at the sky. The moon and the stars had disappeared.

The bedsheets lay damp and crumpled on the floor, and William kicked at them. "It's so fucking hot," he complained. Reason sat with her knees pulled close to her chest, the flat folds of cash in her jean pockets miraculously undiscovered. She glanced at Will and then again at the open window, thinking briefly about the money. If she could ever escape this horrible house, the money might allow her to get far away.

"I've been thinking, Ray. You and me, we could've been good together. You screwed that up. But it's me that says when we end, not you. You get that, right? I can get better girls than you. Already have. You should see 'em, fucking tits and ass so much better than yours." Reason knew better than to reply. She stared at her hands. William looked at the sleeping fat man and then walked to his bed and gave him a nudge with his foot. "Stop your fucking snoring." The fat man's snore ceased. He smacked his lips in his sleep and rolled over, snorting and mumbling. The bedsheets moved with him, wrapping around his large body and exposing his bare backside. Reason looked away.

Please God. Give me a chance. I can be better. Please help me survive this.

William walked toward her and put his hand to the zipper of his jeans. Reason's heart sank. "The night is not over," he sneered.

"Please, William. Please, let me go."

"Shut up."

"What will happen to you if I'm found here? You'll go back to jail, right?" Reason was banking on William's fatigue to outweigh his hate, and for his narcissistic need for self-preservation to kick in. "You'll go back to jail, William," she insisted, slurring her words through fattened lips.

"Shut the fuck up," he snapped, sitting down close beside her, elbowing her in the ribs, and then pushing her head into the wall and holding it there. "I'm thinking only about continuing everything I've been waiting to do to you. Do you know how long I've been waiting? Do you know how long while you've been whoring yourself around town? Huh? Do you know? Do you?" He slid his free hand across her chest and then lowered his head to her breasts. Reason pushed at his head and tried to slide away. He jerked her forward, thrust her down, and drove her face into the bedding. Unable to breathe, panic rushed in and she shrieked into the mattress. With one hand holding her head, William wrestled with her jeans. Reason kicked and wriggled, trying to force him off her. Suddenly a dull thud sounded somewhere in the house. William leaned his full weight on her and pressed his lips to her ear. "I'll hunt you down. Remember that. Say nothing. I'll always find you. I'll find your fucking family. That's easy. Never forget what I'm capable of doing to you—or them."

Reason was interested only in air. She grabbed at William's hand, trying to pry his fingers from the back of her head. Another thud sounded from the hallway, louder and closer. William released his hold on her. He moved from the bed to the door and listened. Sucking in air, Reason looked at the open window, her back to William. She heard the bedroom door open and then shut. Then she heard William's voice coming from the other side of the closed door. Heart racing, she clambered out through the window and scrambled down the fire escape—not looking back—running for her life.

16

sullivan

S louched on the bathroom floor, favoring her right hip and elbow, Reason carefully leaned forward, and pausing, caught her breath. Moving with meticulous care, she began pushing and pulling the damp, balled-up facecloth across the smooth surface of the tile. With each stroke, she labored to erase the memory of William's probing hands, the heat of his rancid breath, the stink of his sweat-soaked skin. But overcome with exhaustion, she slumped and stopped. Then groaning, she squinted at the soiled floor, trying to focus on the drying remnants of vomit staining its stark whiteness. Starting up again, each of her movements painful and controlled, she wiped and scrubbed, striving to wash away the filth and the memories.

Moaning, supporting herself against the cold, outer edge of the tub, she struggled to her feet. Then shuffling to the washbasin and avoiding looking in the mirror, she pushed the stiff rubber plug into the rusty drain—and then rested. Sighing, her gaze fixed on the basin, she turned on the taps. With great care, Reason washed—the water turning pink in the sink. Shuddering, overcome by a perverse self-loathing, she dug her thumb deep into the softened soap and let the bar slide from her fingers. Her shame and the pain of her bruised and torn skin taunted her—both blatant reminders of the attack.

At the sound of shuffling footsteps, she grimaced and glanced at the closed bathroom door. The walking halted. "You in there, Reason?" asked her college roommate, her voice sleepy and muffled.

"Yeah," Reason managed, her voice thin.

"You gonna be long?" Reason stayed quiet, desperate for solitude, stalling. "Okay, whatever," said the loudly yawning girl. "No probs. I'll go downstairs. Musta been quite the party," she teased. Reason

237

groaned and leaned against the door, listening to the footsteps receding.

Soon water was running through the pipes in the bathroom below. She relaxed, unrolled a large bath towel, and spread it out on the freshly cleaned floor. Carefully wrapping another towel about her battered body, and using one more for a makeshift pillow, she lay down.

Reason welcomed the hollowness growing within her. She wanted it to consume her—to make her go numb. She sank into its stiff embrace and waited to be alone in the house.

CB ED

"Yoo-hoo," taunted Pain, impatient and restless.

Reason moaned.

"Yoo-freaking-hoo," cried Pain into her bones. She jerked awake. "You didn't really think that we'd ended our relationship, did you, foolish creature?"

Reason took a moment to respond. "I didn't, but the thing is... I don't fear you anymore." She smiled despite her physical discomfort. "I've no need, anymore, to fight you. You're not my enemy. I finally see you for what you truly are... a path, a path to love. As you've always been."

"What nonsense are you spewing now?" scoffed Pain, running its sharp daggers up and down her spine.

Reason breathed into the pulsing ache, and allowed herself a brief smile. "You're my friend," she said plainly, soothed by her new understanding.

"What?" Pain asked in disbelief.

"Despite how you may appear to treat me, you are not my enemy," said Reason. "You're my friend and you've taught me valuable lessons. You have freed me from petty cares. I used to think it ridiculous that you could become a positive influence. I didn't understand. But now *I feel the truth*—the glorious and simple truth."

"Don't be absurd," said Pain, but the thrust of its daggers had weakened.

"You're not as mean as you pretend to be," offered Reason. Pain became uncharacteristically quiet. Moments passed as the setting sun caused the late-evening shadows to climb the somber walls of the hospital room.

"What lessons could I have possibly taught you other than to obey me?" asked Pain suspiciously.

"Well, my friend, you've taught me about resilience, and because of your persistence, I've learned that I am strong—really strong. Your constant company has caused me to slow down, to move with care, to pay attention to my thoughts, and because of these things, I've become a more patient and tolerant person." Reason paused and sank back into the softness of the mattress. "And you've taught me to be grateful. Grateful for the smallest of things and for all the years of my life, for the highs *and* the lows, and... for all the love that has come my way." Laying her arms at her sides, Reason turned her palms upwards, shook her head, and smiled. "Being thoroughly stripped of all control over my own life has made room deep within me, room for hope and calm to grow. Your constant company has taught me the value of my vulnerability." She clasped her hands together. "You've reminded me of the impermanence of all things. It's such a relief to accept the fleetingness of... well, of everything, including me. And because of you," she sighed contentedly, "I've learned I'm just as I'm meant to be. I am what I am and I'm finally unburdened of the desire to be anything different." Pain skimmed across Reason's brow—a quick, prickly heat. Reason unclasped her hands and laid them palms down on her chest. "You've been difficult and exasperating, but our troubled relationship has been meaningful. Because of you, I'm experiencing my life as I did when I was a young child; I am fearless and fully present." Pain pulsed timidly at Reason's temples. "I can feel you," she said. "I know you'll never leave me. I've accepted you for what you are, just as I've accepted myself for what I am."

"So...," Pain faltered.

"Yes?" encouraged Reason.

"We are actually friends?"

239

"We are," said Reason with a smile. "We no longer need to fight. We never need to do that again."

"I'm not sure that I know how to be so... placid. It's not in my nature."

"Don't change a thing. I've accepted you just as you are."

Pain hummed, and by the time the evening's shadows had fully consumed the room, Reason had fallen asleep.

ଔ ଓ

Except for the ordinary creaking of its old bones, the house was quiet—providing Reason with a desperately needed refuge. She lay awake on the bathroom floor, wearily observing the simple details of the small room.

She gazed up at the bathroom ceiling, its flat greyness asking nothing of her—an empty slate. Waiting to have the house to herself, she surrendered to the endless tedium of passing time. The ceiling directly above took on a strange new expansiveness, a blank canvas that a person could, if she only made the effort, change to whatever she desired. The unexpected thought fostered the faintest sense of hope in Reason. She blinked—and stirred—and wondered if her life could be a blank slate too, one that she could still change for the better. *Is a better life still possible? Even for screwed-up me?* She moaned, and then with painstaking care, lifted her knees from the floor and flexed her fingers—every part of her body wounded and suffering.

Bit by bit, Reason pulled herself up until she could stand—catching an unwelcome glimpse of her face in the mirror. The bruised lids of her swollen eye had partially separated, and behind the opening slit of bulging flesh sat a blood-red eyeball. She turned from the ugliness, put her ear to the door, and listened. "You out there?" she asked, her mouth dry, her tongue thick. The house remained quiet. She cracked open the bathroom door. Only the steadfast ticking of a wall clock greeted her. She stepped into the hall.

ଔ ଓ

"Do you feel your freedom?" asked a faint voice.

Reason opened her eyes to a cloudless blue sky. She turned her head. She was lying on a gently sloped hill teeming with blue daisies with soft pink centers. She sat up—relieved at having survived the revisiting of her horrific ordeal with William. The contrast between her agony in the halfway house and the tranquility of this new scene did little to tame her wildly beating heart. She reminded herself several times that she was safe.

Suddenly she noticed a feverish panting, and jumping to her feet, spun to face the sound. A golden-blond Dachshund stood staring up at her, its tiny tail wagging at a furious pace. The dog stood only twelve inches high, its short hair shimmering in the bright sunlight. Its cylindrical body, held aloft by short, powerful legs, was considerably longer than its slim, slightly curved tail.

The Dachshund peered up at her, its brown eyes wide, friendly and twinkling. At the end of its long muzzle, its lips parted— unexpectedly giving the dog an oddly human-like smile. Reason smiled back. The dog's eyes darted away from her, and then back, its brow wriggling as if it was working hard to be patient. She stepped towards it, bending and offering her hand. The dog's long-hanging ears lifted at the sight of her outstretched arm. It closed its mouth decisively and waddled towards her.

"Hey, little guy. What's your name?"

The Dachshund allowed Reason to pat it, wagging its tail approvingly. Using its short legs to propel its long body backwards, it yelped two short airy bursts and lifted its front legs off the ground, bucking like a wee horse. A small metal tag dangled from a band around its neck. Reason read the inscription:

Sullivan:
Guide for the Garden of Lost and Found.

"Well hello, Sullivan," said Reason with a grin. The dog sneezed, its long snout dipping reflexively. Then it turned and ran down a footpath—a thin brown line that meandered through the sprawling

241

meadow. "Okay then!" said Reason. "Where are we going, little fella?" Sullivan stopped, turned back, barked twice, and then resumed running along the path.

The footpath led to a field of tall grasses with large, white feathery plumes that swayed in the breeze and arched well over their heads. Buzzing insects and tiny pink butterflies flitted everywhere. Captivated by the natural beauty, and calmed by the serenity of the flowing grasses, Reason felt safe and lighter than air.

"Do you feel your freedom?" said a woman's voice from behind.

Reason spun around, recognizing the voice of the woman in the mask. "It's you!" she exclaimed. The woman smiled, her mask gone, her somber attire exchanged for a flowing, pale yellow dress, her wavy auburn hair let loose about her shoulders. She watched Reason with compassionate, pale-grey eyes. "You saved me," said Reason. The woman barely nodded. "I knew it. It was you that saved me when I jumped from the tunnel. And I've seen you in my dreams. Please, will you tell me your name?"

The woman took Reason's hands into her own. "My name is Macy. And you, my dear, found your own way. Now tell me, do you *feel* your freedom?"

The question filled Reason with wonder. "I do! I *do* feel my freedom," she remarked, spurred on by a feeling of absolute certainty.

Macy nodded encouragingly. "And what does it feel like?"

Sullivan scampered to the hem of Macy's dress, turned a tight circle, and then settled at her feet.

"I feel unburdened... as if I'm floating free of the weight of fear. I feel a new sense of wellness, and I now know for certain that my life is fine just as it is... that, really, it always has been. I can see everything clearly for the first time. I'm finally... awake, and I can feel the strength of my own spirit. So, no matter what the future holds. I am content. I feel... ageless."

"Splendid," said Macy approvingly, releasing Reason's hands and taking a small step backward.

Reason sank into her heels, feeling the ground beneath her feet to hold on to the blissful moment. "I almost feel as if I know who I am without a body, as if I've no substance at all, but am alive and thriving. I feel connected to everything, no longer a frightened, separate being. I feel whole." She lingered in her contentment, and when Reason returned her attention to Macy, she was gone and Sullivan was again poised and ready to lead the way. Turning a full circle, Reason nodded, unshaken by Macy's vanishing, somehow knowing that she would always be nearby.

With a quiet woof, Sullivan trotted ahead along the path, and with a new sense of buoyancy in her step, Reason happily followed. Despite being odd companions, they traveled in amiable silence.

The dog took them to where the towering grasses shortened to knee height, and ahead, the edge of a dense forest appeared. When they entered the forest, long shafts of dusty brilliance shone through the treetops and birds chirped spiritedly. A short way into the woods, Sullivan stopped at an enormous oak, its trunk cloaked in a stunning display of velvety moss. The moss grew emerald-green at the foot of the tree and deepened into a purply plum as it climbed and extended to the tips of the highest branches. Sullivan showed keen interest at the base of the tree, sniffing and pawing.

"Something there?" Reason bent down, patting the dog's head.

Sullivan barked and backed away from the tree. He turned in a tight circle and then lay down. Reason ran her fingers over the moss at the base of the tree and found a piece of rolled parchment. "What's this?" she asked, pulling the scroll out from a crevice in the moss-covered bark.

The tiny wax seal on the scroll was stamped with the imprint of a telephone. Reason recognized the old-style, wedge-shaped phone. She broke the seal, uncurled the scroll, and read aloud:

YOU ARE NEARING THE GARDEN OF LOST AND FOUND. PERMISSION TO ENTER IS GRANTED BY THE TREE OF KNOWLEDGE. TO GAIN PERMISSION, YOU MUST PASS A TEST. SHOULD YOU FAIL, OR THE TREE DETECTS DECEIT OR DOUBT IN YOUR ANSWER, ITS COAT OF MOSS WILL SHRIVEL AND TURN BLACK.

> THIS UNFORTUNATE RESULT WILL MEAN THAT YOU
> MUST REVISIT YOUR STORY. HOWEVER, SHOULD
> YOUR ANSWER PLEASE THE TREE, IT WILL GRANT
> YOU ENTRY.
>
> HERE IS YOUR TEST:
>
> PROVE THAT YOU HAVE LEARNED THE TRUE
> NATURE OF SHAME. YOU MAY BEGIN.

Reason's smile faded. Sullivan prodded her, using his long snout to nudge her away from the great tree. As she turned, she saw a purple beanbag chair set in the footpath along which they had just traveled. Beside the chair was a red phone. Reason picked up the phone and put the handset to her ear. "Hello?"

"Hello," answered a familiar voice.

"Ruby!" cried Reason.

Sullivan lay down, sighing human-like, lowering his head to the ground.

"Well now, you sound happy," observed Ruby.

"I am Ruby. I am!"

"We knew you could do it. We knew you would find your way." Through the phone, Reason heard the giggles of Mr. Up and Mr. Down. She nodded happily and sat in the purple chair. The wind swelled and rustled the towering treetops, showering her in whirling bits of foliage. "And now, my dearest Reason, it's time for you to tell me what you've learned since we last talked about shame. Tell me, and you will have told the tree."

Reason straightened her shoulders. "I'll give it a try, Ruby," she replied, warily eyeing the tree. Patches of blue peeked through its great swaying bows, and high above in its branches perched a brilliant pink bird. Reason watched as the bird swooped down and alighted nearby, its head twitching and tilting as if the little creature was studying her. It skipped sideways, moving along a branch, coming closer, singing two short, high-pitched trills. She smiled, and the bird effortlessly lifted from its perch and darted away. "The power of the smallest of creatures..." she murmured. She stood from the chair, phone in hand, and walked a few steps in the direction the little bird had taken.

"What's that?" asked Ruby.

"I was just watching a pretty little bird and thinking that we humans can so misjudge the power of the little things. But I think the little things can have an enormous influence on us." Ruby remained quiet. Reason continued, "I guess shame is a bit like that... deceptively powerful. Because through revisiting my story, I've learned how shame influenced so many of the decisions I made. It seemed to serve one purpose in my life: to isolate me from others. Shame is insidious. It's sneaky, making you think that you somehow need it. So, you hang onto it and keep it as your dirty little secret, because hiding it is easier than facing it... and that's what I did. I hid it." Reason walked a little way along the narrow path, her head bowed in introspection. "But not anymore." She lifted her gaze. "Now, life feels right, Ruby. It really does. So different from before when I was... trapped in the grip of shame, withdrawing from people, believing that I deserved to be alone." Reason ran her fingers through her hair. "For a long time, I thought I was less than most other people because I believed that I'd forever lost my dignity... and my worth. But now... now I understand the truth about shame. I know that over time it led me to a place so empty, that in that nothingness, in that place so stripped of... distraction—I found grace... *my grace.*" Reason breathed in the cool forest air—slowly, deeply—feeling wholly satisfied and content. And as if talking to herself, she whispered, "Through shame, I found my grace."

"Bravo!" laughed Ruby.

"Thank you! And, Ruby, it's wonderful to be free—to feel spacious and at peace." Reason beamed. "I owe this understanding to you and Edward, and Daleel, and Macy, and..."

"You owe us nothing. The discovery is all yours. You, my dear, did all the work. If it were anyone else's creation, then you would still be blind to your own grace. As guides, we provide you with gentle suggestions. That is all."

"Well, thank you, anyway! Because I feel amazing. I feel vast and meaningful as if I'm an extension of the space that surrounds me." Reason swept her hand in a wide arc and laughed gayly. "It's a wonderful feeling."

The Tree of Knowledge quivered. Its coat of colorful moss shimmered and a white fog billowed at the base of the trunk. The fog climbed, spreading to the tips of the tallest branches. Filled with twinkling specs of light, the fog folded and swirled and the sparkly bits rained down. And by the time all of the shiny bits had dropped the full length of the magnificent tree, its moss had turned a lustrous white. Reason laughed, confident that this transformation was a good sign.

Sullivan turned from the tree and faced Reason, eyes watchful, ears alert.

"Ruby, if only you could see the tree!" said Reason in awe.

"I know, my dear, I know," praised Ruby.

"It's so beautiful!" whispered Reason, her heart overflowing with wonder and joy.

"You inspired the tree's transformation," offered Ruby. "Now go. Go to the garden. Sullivan will lead you."

"Ruby?"

"Yes, my dear?"

"Thank you for everything. Thank you for lifting me up and guiding me with such... absolute love and kindness."

"You are welcome. I have very much enjoyed being a witness to your important rite of passage. Off you go now; follow Sullivan. He has something very special to show you."

Reason looked at the little dog. "You do, little guy? But what about you, Ruby? Will I see you again?" But Ruby did not answer, and the purple beanbag chair had vanished. Reason put the phone on the ground and it, too, disappeared. She turned back to the tree and, for a moment, marveled at its beauty. Then she slipped the piece of parchment inside her satchel and readied herself for what might lie ahead. "OK, little guy. Where to next?" she asked in a hurry, running after the dog.

A constant breeze rustled the forest leaves, stirred the blue-tinged bows of the coniferous trees, and scattered bits of debris about the ground. In frequent gusts, the wind blew in from afar and rose to a magnificent crescendo over their heads. Reason enjoyed the powerful intensity of the wind, and with jubilant satisfaction, she glanced again and again at the swaying treetops. With each mighty upsurge, large, orange-winged birds swooped down from the canopy and darted about the two travelers, returning to the settling treetops once the blustery winds had quieted.

As they approached the outer edge of the forest, hazy shafts of pink-tinged light filtered into the cool-blue shade below. Sullivan ran out from the shadows and Reason followed, stepping into the warm light of a setting sun.

"Grrwoof, grrwoof," barked the dog. He spun around, sat for the blink of an eye, ran ahead a short distance, and then stopped again to wait for Reason to catch up.

In the open, the air was hot and humid and the wind had mysteriously tapered to a soft breeze. Ahead, the sun hung scarlet on the horizon, its fiery glow diffusing orange and pink in the woolly white fluff of the clouds. Between the travelers and the horizon, widely spaced, low-lying mountains rose from a sea of lush, colorful gardens. Coursing toward the mountains, long rivers flowed, reflecting the beautiful brilliance of the sky. And at the base of the grassy knoll upon which Reason stood, one of these rivers lapped against a marshy shore.

"Grrwoof, grrwoof," barked Sullivan, tugging at her pant leg, urging her forward.

"OK little guy, OK..."

The dog led them to a red canoe at the river's edge. Large blue butterflies flitted about the small boat, and as Reason approached it, a few of the butterflies alighted on pale yellow water lilies floating close to shore. Reason spied something gleaming inside the canoe, and recognizing the sapphire and topaz seedling from Ruby's greenhouse, carefully retrieved it. Holding the delicate plantlet at eye level, she pondered aloud, "What do I do with this precious thing?"

"You take it to the heart of the garden," said a male voice with a faint British accent.

Reason started and spun around. "Who's there?" she asked, eyeing the edge of the forest.

"Me," said Sullivan.

Reason gawked at the little dog. "You speak?" she marveled.

"I do indeed," said the dog, his voice deep and commanding, more fitting of a lion.

"Why not speak sooner?"

"I didn't feel the need."

"And you do now?"

"I do, because I need your help to get into the boat. Give me a boost, will you?" said Sullivan, waddling to the water's edge and sniffing. "I don't like the water. I don't swim. Well, I try, but I always seem to sink. I can't be fabulous at everything."

"Sure, right," laughed Reason, shaking her head in amusement. "OK then, into the canoe we go." She lowered Sullivan into the middle of the boat.

"The stern please," requested Sullivan with a hint of pompous indignance. Reason put the little dog at the rear of the boat and then she stepped in and kneeled facing him, her back resting against the front seat. Inside the wedge of the bow, she had noticed a small bag.

"What's in the bag?" she asked.

"Lunch," said Sullivan. "The garden is a long way off. We have a bit of a paddle. Well, you paddle. I navigate. I have a nose for these things. It may appear as if we can travel straight ahead from here, but we must avoid sandbars, animal nests, and the occasional whirlpool. Nothing is terribly dangerous, more of a nuisance. We'll picnic by the bluebells under the light of the moon, the halfway mark."

Following Sullivan's gaze, Reason looked down the river. Off in the distance was an enormous expanse of purplish-blue. "Whirlpools? That sounds dangerous."

"The rocks and crevices below the water cause the whirlpools. Down there," said Sullivan, peering into the water, "the faster currents cause sinkholes to occur spontaneously. But they are small sinkholes and the whirlpools are relatively harmless. But if we get stuck in one, we'll have trouble getting to the heart of the garden. And at the heart is where items lost," Sullivan paused, cocked his head, and looked at Reason, "...can be found."

Where items lost can be found? "And this," said Reason, sweeping her arm over the scene and then using the paddle to push the canoe from shore, "is the Garden of Lost and Found? It's beautiful." Her fingers lingered on the gold chain at her neck. "Is there something there for me?" she asked.

"Well, of course, there is," said Sullivan matter-of-factly.

With a growing sense of anticipation, Reason leaned forward and then glanced back at the retreating shoreline. The butterflies had formed a long, twisting line, and briefly, they followed the canoe. Then they dispersed in a rush and ascended like sparks into the evening sky. Sullivan stood facing her, looking past her, his nose held high. She turned back and began the journey, dipping the paddle at a steady pace, water droplets falling from its rounded tip in long bands and riffling the silvery-smooth surface of the water.

As the sun retreated, it left behind a purply grey, star-speckled splendor above. For a while, Reason watched the sky—her arms rising and falling, lifting and pulling. She looked at her hands, noticing that her slender young fingers showed signs of age. The aging process did not concern her. Instead, Reason wondered if she had learned enough from her experience here in this extraordinary world to use her remaining time wisely. And she wondered if she had been suitably grateful for the life that she had lived so far. Deep in the sensation of the movement of her arms, and the rise and fall of her paddle, she experienced a profound sense of timelessness—feeling connected to the whole of the universe. She felt eternal, and the feeling seemed remarkably familiar, one that she had always known. A noise plucked her from her musings. She looked toward the sound, a familiar tinkling in the distant sky. Reason could not yet see them, but she could hear their approach. "Sullivan," she cried, "it's the dragonflies! They're coming!" Sullivan wagged his tail and sniffed the air.

In the distance, a shimmering light moved across the sky, a long thin twinkling line that became wider and flew higher as it neared. Riveted, Reason laid the paddle across the canoe and watched the spectacle. "Can anything be as beautiful as this?" she mused. They watched in silence as the dragonflies flew overhead, clinking and chinking. Once they had passed, they circled, and then gradually lowered and disappeared into the low lushness of the far garden.

"Right on time, as always," said Sullivan with obvious pride.

"Is there one in that group for me?" Reason asked, holding her breath in eager anticipation.

"Why yes, Reason. No doubt it has spotted you. You will meet soon enough. But if you don't pay attention now, we might never get there. Look out!"

Reason felt the pull of the whirlpool before she could react to its drag. Swoosh went the back end of the canoe, the churning water drawing the boat in backwards. She leaned forward, bracing herself, and paddled hard against the pull. Her heart raced, but she did not have to take more than a few determined strokes to get free of the eddying water.

"Well done, Reason! Well done!" cheered Sullivan. Reason drew the canoe further away from the trap of whirling water. "All is good. All is good. From here on, there ought not to be further distractions. Look. Do you see the beach ahead? We will lunch there." Safely away from the whirlpool and calmed by Sullivan's good cheer, Reason relaxed and steered the canoe toward a patch of beach glowing white in the distance.

C3 80

"Tell me something, Sullivan," said Reason, having finished a delicious meal of mango, cheese biscuits, olives, and blueberry-mint tea.

"If I can, I will," said Sullivan amiably.

"When we move from one state to another, say from being sad to being happy, or from being young to being old—a point exists, an exact point just before the shift occurs, just before we become less of one and more of the other." Reason squeezed her eyes shut, concentrating. "At that precise point... are we both things equally, or are we neither?" Waiting for an answer, she started packing the leftover food and then paused to look at Sullivan.

The dog thumped his tiny tail on the soft sandy beach and then stood. "Good thing I can talk," he said with a lift of his ears and a cocking of his head. "Good question, Reason. Very good indeed. You have a thought-provoking imagination. Can we be both states at the same time, or are we neither?" repeated Sullivan, taking a few steps and then sitting again. "Let's imagine the question this way: let us think of a moving vehicle, an automobile... on a steep hill. It climbs and climbs until the center of the car reaches the crest of the highest point of the hill. There, its front end is closer to going down than its rear, but as a whole, the vehicle is neither moving up nor down. I would suggest that it is in a state of balance."

A state of balance. Hmmm. "Yes, the precise midpoint may be a perfect state of balance. I like that Sullivan. I like that idea a lot. But obviously, a car doesn't have the ability to reason. It's a thing. It can't *sense* balance. But humans are thinking and feeling beings. We just might be able to sense that perfect state of balance." She lowered her head, shaking it thoughtfully. "Even so, we won't likely understand it. We won't understand where or what we are..."

"Why do you care?" asked Sullivan shrewdly.

"Well, because I want to know if it's possible to be aware of both states of being simultaneously... as if... as if some portion of each state is recognizable at the same time, and the link that connects them is noticeable too. Because that possibility makes me think that it's conceivable for a person to sense more than one life experience at a time... with no feeling of separation between one and the other. And that sense of connection could be, as you suggest, a perceptible state of balance. Right?" Reason sighed at the complexity of what she was trying to both comprehend and explain.

"Maybe so. But why must you know this now?"

"Well, I've been feeling something, something that I can't exactly figure out, let alone describe."

"Try. I am a good listener," said Sullivan.

Reason glanced at the sky where a single, light violet moon hung serenely. "I've been feeling a sort of coming together... of all of my parts, as if all of my life experiences have somehow converged... as if I'm experiencing that place of perfect balance. Everything is connected, and as crazy as this might sound, I can sense my future too. I can't see it, but I feel it. And I know that no matter what it holds, I fully accept what is ahead." Reason opened her hands and examined them. "It's almost as if I can see and feel *all* of me... *all* of my ages through time. It's as if I can see every moment of my life right here in my palms. I see and feel my hands as a child, small and delicate, pudgy and fresh. I see and feel my hands in my youth, strong and slender. I see and feel my hands of today, a little tired, a little worn... and I feel each age equally, as if each one is me, right here, right now. It's as if that state of balance was waiting for me to sense it. And more than that," Reason paused, focusing, "I sense that I've lived more... well, more *lives* than I can remember."

"Then you have your answer," said Sullivan.

"I do?"

"Sometimes no words can suitably express what is unfamiliar to one's usual state of being. But do not fret. Sometimes, it is best just to feel without judging the feeling. Let it be. Right now, you are fully present. You are whole." Sullivan gave Reason his best human-like smile. "Every being has the chance to realize this natural state."

Reason could not fully grasp what she was sensing. But the experience felt real and otherwise effortless, so she surrendered to it, feeling euphoric and limitless. In her moment of surrender, a pulsating light radiated from the belly of the canoe. "Look at that," she said, pointing to the boat. "What's happening to the little plant?"

From the trembling leaves of the seedling, bright shards of blue and yellow sputtered and spit, and then, in a burst of swirling color, they shot high into the sky.

17

the budding

With the straps of the knapsack clutched between his teeth, Sullivan dragged the small bag to the canoe and dropped it in the sand. "The changing plantlet means it is time for us to continue," he said. From the floor of the canoe, bright shards of light continued to dance in spectacular arcs and sprays. Sullivan stood on his hind legs, his paws on the gunwale, his nails clicking against the hard surface. "To my seat, please," he requested.

Reason hoisted him into the boat. Then she pushed it from shore and jumped in herself. "Sullivan," she ventured, taking her seat and readying the paddle, "tell me more about the plantlet. Ruby told me that the seedlings are grown for the Garden of Lost and Found, but what is their purpose?"

Before the dog could answer, a familiar cry sounded from somewhere above in the speckled night sky. "Craw, craw!"

"Raven?" wondered Reason aloud, looking up in surprise and searching among the stars.

"Craw, craw!" came the cry again.

Reason soon saw the bird. It flew in slow, spiraling circles, a black silhouette passing in front of the moon and descending toward the canoe.

"Woof, woof," barked Sullivan, tail wagging in cheerful anticipation.

"Raven!" shouted Reason, thrilled to see her faithful friend.

As it neared, the Raven's wings extended with the wingtips splayed and curving inward. And with its wedge-shaped tail fanned and forward, and its talons spread, in a rush of dark plumage the bird landed on a cross thwart between Reason and the dog. Reason gasped.

Stunning and stately, the Raven stood tall and impressive, blinking slowly, its thin-filmed eyelids meeting in the middle of a dark grey stare fixed upon Reason. Under the pinkish light of the moon, its sleek coat of blue-black feathers shimmered oily slick, with smaller, downier plumage edging over the long bridge of its dark bill. The Raven's abrupt and powerful presence had rendered Reason speechless. She sat straight and still and stared in surprise until the great bird stamped its feet and broke the spell. On its right ankle, it wore a metal band embossed with tiny yellow flowers—the flowers clustered in diamond shapes and trailing point to point.

When the Raven flapped its wings, Reason started and looked imploringly at Sullivan. But the dog cocked his head as if to say, "Your story, not mine." Reason looked back at the bird and shrugged her shoulders. "Hello?" she whispered. "Do you speak?" The Raven remained impossibly still... and silent.

"The Raven speaks, Reason, but we cannot understand the language that she uses," offered Sullivan.

"Then how will I communicate with...?" Reason paused. "Her? The Raven is a she? Well, that's..." But the sudden sound of music, a beautiful sweeping melody, some kind of wind instrument—soft, breezy notes cascading down from above and lingering hauntingly about the canoe, silenced her.

With the sound of the music, the Raven stirred, raising her beak to the sky and producing a low and rapid knocking sound. Then she fanned her wings, drawing in one while leaving the other extended toward Reason. Reason instinctively reached for the outstretched wing, and as she did, thin spikes of blue and gold burst from the plantlet, two luminous lines of color mingling and twirling about them. And when the tips of Reason's fingers touched the Raven's wingtip, the lines of blue and gold shot high into the sky. The Raven seemed to watch them ascend. High above, a brilliant white light appeared, and descended toward the boat. And where Reason's fingers touched the bird, the white light penetrated, flowing like molten lava, spreading into the bird's body, neck, and head.

Wholly engulfed in a fiery white, the Raven cried out triumphantly. The music rose to a crescendo and then halted. The bright white light extinguished. And before Reason, the Raven, in all of her splendor and glorious radiance, stood transformed—her feathers now brilliant white.

"Splendid!" exclaimed Sullivan, standing and bucking, his tail wagging feverishly.

The Raven's dark grey eyes had become pools of violet-blue. And as the bird stared at Reason, cocking her magnificent head one way and then the other, her gaze both noble and tender, Reason felt safe and calm—and dearly loved. And when the Raven's brilliant white wings powerfully buffeted the air, and she lifted from the canoe, Reason watched in wondrous silence. As the snowy-white Raven soared into the blackness above, the bird shared her victorious cry, "Craw, Craw! Craw, Craw!"

"What just happened?" asked Reason in a hushed voice, still enthralled by the exhilarating power of what had just occurred. "She's so beautiful!" She turned to Sullivan. "Where's she going? Is this goodbye?"

"That, it is," said Sullivan.

Reason turned back to watch the bird. "She might be the most beautiful creature I've ever seen. But I don't understand. What happened, Sullivan? Why did she change from black to white?" Reason watched the Raven until her white glow vanished.

"She changed because you succeeded in your rite of passage. When you touched her, she too progressed, a transition that is very like an angel receiving her wings."

"She did so much for me," said Reason with impassioned gratitude. "She led me here to this extraordinary place." Reason raised the paddle and held it over her head. "Thank you, Raven!" she shouted, and then added quietly, "Thank you for showing me the way." And turning to Sullivan, "Will I ever see her again?"

"One never knows," answered the dog, his gaze to the sky, his tail twitching.

"Look!" said Reason. "The plantlet! Is it changing too?" The seedling was trembling. A cloud of fog had settled about it. Thin ribbons of gold moved within the cloud and swirled about the small plant's tiny leaves.

"The seedling is as it should be, as you shall soon understand," said Sullivan. "A little more patience is all that you need. But now, Reason, we must continue our journey."

Reason glanced at the sky once more and then lowered the paddle into the water. "Sullivan," she said, "please tell me more about the plantlet. What is its full purpose?"

"You. Its purpose is you. We created it for you and you will plant it."

"Oh! Somewhere nearby?" Reason asked, brimming with childlike excitement.

"You will plant it in the heart of the garden, where your dragonfly awaits." Reason smiled at the thought of the dragonfly, and as she paddled, she imagined the pleasant task of planting the seedling.

Interrupting her musings, the water under the canoe became lighter and more transparent, as if it was being lit from below. And all at once, Reason could see exotic sea creatures, large whale-like beasts with long tapered snouts, fluttering tails, and massive bodies. They swam effortlessly beside and beneath the canoe, and among them, darting in large synchronized groups, were several schools of much smaller fish. "What's that?" gasped Reason, pointing to one of the impressive creatures as it coasted a few feet below the surface, and very near the boat.

"That beast is a guardian of the river. It protects the garden. Many others like it swim these waters as scouts, and if need be, warriors. Thus far, we have incurred no threat that calls for unleashing their great powers. But we are comforted by their presence, nevertheless." Sullivan paused, and despite his small stature, he looked noble. "The plantlets, Reason, are essential to the survival of the garden. And the garden is integral to the survival of our world." Reason looked at the plantlet, its delicate leaves quivering inside its tiny lustrous cloud. "The plant's life cycle begins with a seed. It will grow into a mature plant and make new seeds, and then the next life cycle will begin. The seed is remarkable because it is both the beginning and the end. When you plant your seedling, you will continue this extraordinary cycle and create new seedlings for other beings that will come our way." Sullivan looked at the moon. Reason did too. "During a maroon moon, we'll harvest the excess mature plants and use them for food, medicine, and energy. So, you see, my dear, the Garden of Lost and Found is both a source for and a consequence of our way of life. It sustains us and aids us in our ability to escort souls like you to their journey's end."

"Journey's end? That sounds... important... and maybe even a bit alarming." For a brief moment, Reason wondered what would become of her at her *journey's end*—but then she pushed the thought away and pointed into the river. "The protection provided by these creatures is comforting. I feel safe here." She looked at Sullivan. "The purpose of the plantlet is remarkable. And the maroon moon, well, it sounds beautiful. Will you tell me more about it?"

"The maroon moon is magnificent," said Sullivan proudly, his snout high, his ears perked. "Its color, that wonderfully regal, brown-tinged purplish-red, is a symbol of strength and courage. Its presence in the sky marks our harvesting season, a celebrated time, and in this world, a critical stage in the cycle of life.

"Is tonight's moon the start of a maroon moon?" asked Reason, pointing her paddle skyward.

"We experience many moons. Tonight's moon is not a maroon moon. We call it Sweet Sarahja, named after the child who first discovered it. She spotted it long ago. You, Reason, remind me of her."

"Sah-rah-jah," whispered Reason, and then, "I do?"

Sullivan looked contemplative, as if caught up in the emotion of a bittersweet memory. "She was younger than you, but she arrived here after experiences similar to yours."

Reason shook her head at the thought of the young girl's struggles, and for a short while, contemplated the reflection of the moon quivering on the surface of the water. When she spoke again, she sounded distracted, as if still caught up in her wondering. "How... did she discover it?"

"Many believe that this moon was created for Sweet Sarahja, because no matter how many eyes were on the sky that night, it was not until she raised her gaze, that the violet moon became visible to us all."

"A strange, but... pleasant story. It feels like a story of hope. I wonder if I might discover something new in the night sky." Reason looked up, but her smile faded. She turned to Sullivan. "But what about this *journey's end* you mentioned? What's that all about?"

"No need to worry, Reason. Everything will be fine. It already is. We all have an end to our journey. And some even say that from there, the adventure continues."

His explanation was brief, but Sullivan's confidence reassured Reason. She paddled on, carefree and peaceful, wondering if Sweet Sarahja had been a passenger in, or had maybe even paddled this very canoe. Every so often Reason scanned the sky ahead, but no new celestial body revealed itself.

In the distance, a shoreline of light pink glowed against the darkness. And beyond the rosy glow, a white glimmer pulsed low in the night sky, likely where the dragonflies had landed. "Should I take us to that beach I see ahead?" asked Reason.

"No," answered Sullivan formally, his snout raised, his ears perked. "We must enter the heart of the garden through The Grand Archway. Head to the beach and follow the shoreline to the right. There, the archway will be revealed."

Reason moved them forward and was soon paddling along a curving shoreline. And when she neared the end of the long bend, the night sky lit up. High above the boat, a ceiling of white shone brilliantly. Long bands of light unraveled and fell from the brilliance above, spinning and twirling like party streamers—plunging toward the canoe. Before the whirling threads of light reached the water, they halted, frozen in place. Reason opened her mouth to speak. But the hovering spirals of light quivered, and moved again, flying in all directions and then coming together and weaving into a beautiful and intricate motif. With the tips of her fingers absentmindedly pressed to her lips, Reason was awestruck. And as the structure began to billow and then ascend, she laughed—watching as the glowing spectacle eventually settled into place and became still; illuminating everything in a beautiful gleaming radiance, the exquisite canopy of light extended far into the garden beyond.

"Behold!" announced Sullivan with obvious pride. "The Grand Archway of the Garden of Lost and Found!"

"It's wonderful!" said Reason with a shiver of excitement. "What do we do now?" The dazzling spectacle of the archway swooshed and swirled, and on the rippling surface of the river, it danced in a blur of stippled, flickering light.

"Straight ahead," said Sullivan. "We simply paddle straight ahead."

Reason paddled with a slow and steady stroke, frequently glancing at the kaleidoscope of light above, her eyes shining with delight when the complete structure occasionally rippled end to end. And ahead where the river ended, when a tree came into view she gasped with eager expectation. Like the Tree of Knowledge, this one was tall and shimmering white. "It's so incredibly beautiful," she whispered, her expression radiant.

The waterway gradually narrowed until its banks were almost within reach of Reason's paddle, and eventually, the canoe came to rest on a sandy bar. Reason lifted Sullivan to the ground. Side by side, they stood on a beach scattered with small clusters of marsh marigolds and tall slender patches of silvery-blue ferns. Reason scooped up a handful of sand. Despite it being well past sunset, the sand was warm and its pearlescent grains slipped through her fingers like fine slivers of silver silk.

Overhead, the archway had stopped moving, its once active threads of light now fixed into a strikingly intricate pattern. "What now?" asked Reason, her gaze again fixed on the spectacle above.

259

"We wait."

"We wait?"

"We wait."

"What are we waiting for?" she asked, lifting the plantlet from the canoe and holding it at eye level. The small gold-streaked cloud billowed and then settled, and the seedling's tiny leaves seemed to tilt upward as if drawn to the light of the archway above. Reason looked from the plantlet to Sullivan, waiting for an answer. But the dog paid her no attention. He appeared to be listening intently, his ears on alert, his head cocked. Reason listened too and followed Sullivan's gaze. And just as she thought she heard a faint tinkling, and closed her eyes to listen more intently, the dog tore off across the beach, the sand forming a low-flying wake behind him. Before Reason could react, Sullivan disappeared down a narrow pathway flanked by tall white flowers. "Wait!" she cried, holding the plantlet close to her chest and running after him.

On either side of the trail, wispy, white petals formed large, cup-shaped blooms that swayed back and forth above Reason's head—and made it impossible to see more than a few yards ahead on the path. She pressed on, the tinkling becoming louder. Ahead, Sullivan barked, and Reason emerged from the footpath. Before her sprawled a vast landscape of low rolling hills and shallow valleys. The land shimmered and sparkled as if a giant treasure chest had burst open and spilled its glittery contents. And atop the tallest hill, yet another glorious tree stood tall and stately—a royal guardian keeping vigil over the crown jewels, and pink like The Tree of New Beginnings under which Reason had found her necklace in what seemed like a lifetime ago.

Sullivan sat close by, facing acres of mature plants, their glistening blooms, the sparkling contents of the spilled treasure chest. And hovering above it all, flew the source of the tinkling: hundreds of dragonflies moving in an enormous circle. One dragonfly separated from the others. It flew down to Sullivan, and then to Reason zooming in, hovering mere inches from her face. She gasped and then laughed, recognizing the heart-shaped markings on the tip of the insect's tail.

"Sullivan!" she cried. "This is the same dragonfly I saw when I was with Ruby. Seems so long ago now, but look at it. It's the same one!" The dragonfly darted from Reason to the dog and then back to her. It lingered briefly, hovering near her face, and then zipped away and disappeared into the swarm above. "No!" she hollered.

"Don't worry. It will return!" yelled Sullivan, his voice trailing behind as he ran ahead, scampering between two rows of plants. Beside a large patch of newly planted seedlings, Sullivan stopped. He stood in a small clearing of undisturbed soil. Then he sniffed the ground, walked in a tight circle, sniffed again, and sat. "Here," he said. Reason looked questioningly at the dog, and then curiously at the ground in front of him.

The dragonfly reappeared and landed on the rich black soil in front of Sullivan. Its wings twitched and trembled and then dropped toward the ground as the creature settled. Sullivan lowered his long snout and their dark noses met. When the dog pulled away, a tiny flash of pale blue light sparked between them. The spark quickly spread high and wide and surrounded them both, and then it encompassed Reason too. The dragonfly lifted from the soil, flew about Reason, and then settled on her arm. She laughed with pleasure and surprise.

With a quiet "woof", Sullivan took a few steps backwards, and then jumped forward and began tearing at the black soil.

"What are you digging for?" Reason asked, peering over the dog's laboring shoulders.

Sullivan's nails soon grazed the surface of something hard. "There," he said, backing away from his newly dug hole, looking up at Reason with a glint in his eyes, dark bits of soil peppering his blond snout. "What was lost—is now found," he stated happily. Reason bent toward the peculiar object which Sullivan had partially uncovered. "Well?" coaxed the dog. "It's yours. You may retrieve it." The dragonfly lifted from Reason's arm and hovered beside her.

Putting the plantlet on the ground, she brushed loose dirt from the object in the hole and pried it free—finding a small, tear-shaped container with scalloped edges and pale pink striping. Lifting it to eye level, Reason held the pretty container in the flat of her palm. "Looks a bit like a seashell," she mused, running her fingers over its gritty exterior.

"Look inside," urged Sullivan.

Reason clicked the lid open. This gentle action caused the shell-like object to release a soft, airy sound reminiscent of a human sigh. Reason's skin tingled at the uncanny sound, and she paused.

"Well, what do you see?" asked Sullivan.

Eyes glistening, Reason reached in and reclaimed her long-lost locket, lingering for some seconds in the pleasant sensation of holding it again after so many years. She turned it over in her hand and ran her fingers across the yellow flowers clustered in a tiny diamond shape engraved on the back. And inside, exactly as she remembered, she found a tiny piece of white heather. Carefully removing the dried flower, she read the locket's inscription:

If ever you fear solitude, trust in Love.
Always with you, Mom & Dad

Reason felt a swelling in her chest—as if love itself had taken a human form and wrapped itself about her. She swiveled to face Sullivan. "I swear, that just now, I felt my parents' presence!" She looked around in wonder. "I felt the full strength of their love. I felt it as if that love was a physical entity right here, right now!" She looked at Sullivan, her eyes shining brightly. "The feeling was familiar but so much larger than I remember, and... pure. I don't remember feeling their love quite like this when they were alive."

Tail thumping, Sullivan moved closer to Reason. "Do you remember what Ruby told you about the significance of the dragonfly?"

"I think so." Reason looked for the magical flying creature and, as if on cue, it swooped down and landed on her shoulder. "She told me

262

that the dragonfly represents change. If I remember correctly, she said that it signifies a transition from illusion to clarity." Reason smiled at the memory and the meaning of the words.

"That's right," said Sullivan. "And do you feel that you have experienced such a change?"

"I think I have. Yes! Because thinking of my parents' love... before now, I never understood its depth. I mean, they were my parents, they were supposed to love me, and to love each other. But because of those years when they fought so often, and because of how I viewed them, and the negative view I believed they held of me as a teenager... and the bleak way I viewed myself... I stopped trusting in love. I felt separate from it. But now I understand. I understand that it's precisely love that's linking all of us together, forever." Reason held her locket tightly, her eyes bright with the clarity that comes with complete understanding. "All of us... my parents, my siblings, and all the generations that came before, we're all connected by a continuous, everlasting chain of creation—and by love—the beginning of it all. And because of this unbreakable connection, no matter what we think about our life experience or about the people in it... no one is forsaken. No one is forgotten, or lost, or ever really gone." Reason looked at Sullivan, beaming, energized by her new understanding. "I know now that despite everything that has happened in my life, and despite what I thought about my parents, or what they thought about each other, or about me... love has always been real and present. Even in my bleakest moments, I've never been alone." Reason wiped away her tears. "For such a long time, I couldn't see the truth. I couldn't *feel* it. But now... my inherent connection to all of creation and therefore, to love itself, is abundantly clear." She turned to Sullivan and sighed happily. "I am a creation of love—an ancient love—the original love. *I am love*. We all are."

"Well done, my friend, well done," said Sullivan cheerfully.

Reason returned her locket to its chain and fastened the necklace about her neck. "Ruby also said that the dragonfly celebrates the soul's advancement." She touched her locket. "I can feel how my new understanding has changed me." She pressed her palm to her heart. "I can feel an incredible sense of calm and... belonging."

"We are all destined to reconnect to one thing, Reason, and that thing... is love," said Sullivan. "Each of us is the creation of love—a love that has no bounds. And in this way, we are forever linked." He sat and thumped his tail. "Love is the purpose of life." Raising his snout and cocking his head, he added, "The truth is always accessible, always waiting to be discovered."

Reason's eyes grew wide. "Look, Sullivan. The plantlet. It's grown a flower!"

"Ah yes," said Sullivan. "Because it too has transformed." He nosed the little plant toward the hole he had dug. "And the time has come for you to plant it."

Reason lifted the seedling from the ground. The cloud of fog had disappeared and now a pale blue bud hung like a tiny bell from the plant's thin stalk. Reason peeled away the thin casing from around the roots and then lowered the plantlet into the hole. She pushed soil close to the stem, covered the roots, and gently pressed the damp dirt flat. Smiling, she turned to Sullivan. But the little dog had vanished. "Sullivan?" she whispered, knowing that there would be no answer.

At that moment, the swarm of dragonflies swooped up and away, forming an iridescent line that spiraled high into the night sky. Reason's dragonfly lifted from her shoulder, hovered before her, and then followed. She listened until she could no longer hear the magical tinkling.

She brought her fingertip to the tiny blue bud and wondered what could come next in this extraordinary world. Then, like a calling only she could hear, some sixth sense caused her to look up. High above, the stars twinkled. And then they flared brightly, and one by one fell from the sky.

18

the meeting place

When Reason's feet left the ground, she focused her gaze on the newly planted seedling until it disappeared, and all that remained below were slivers of bright light plunging into the darkness. Then, clutching her found locket, she looked up. High above, a speck of red appeared, a fiery brilliance among the plummeting flashes of white. Propelled by some mysterious energy, Reason raced towards the glowing patch of red, and despite the rush of movement, all was quiet. The red glow grew larger. As she came upon it, Reason raised her arms above her head in a thrilling surge of excitement.

ΩΘ ΣΟ

"Is she awake?"

"Soon, I think."

Reason opened her eyes, squinted, and cupped her hand to her forehead. From a cloudless sky came the piercing cries of seagulls, and in the hot air wafted the tangy, fishy scent of the ocean. She sat up. Waves swelled and crashed to shore. A long curl of white-capped water rolled in, folded, spilled and spread, and nearly touched her splayed fingers. When the wave withdrew, Reason climbed to her feet. Small, smooth stones pushed into the thin soles of her sandals while the loose strands of her long hair fluttered about her face.

She looked both ways along the beach, seeing no one. Shading her eyes, she watched the circling birds, then looked out to sea, and then again, at the long stretch of beach. This time, two figures moved in the distance. They appeared to be walking towards her, and when one of them raised a hand as if to greet her, Reason waved back. Cool water slid across her feet, catching her by surprise. She watched as her feet sank into the wet sand and as the frothy water rushed away. When she looked once more along the beach, the two figures suddenly stood alongside her. Startled by their unexpected proximity, she took a step back.

The two identical creatures towered over Reason, their tall statures imposing, but the gentle expressions on their faces kept her unfazed. Smiling, nodding at each other and then at Reason, the creatures appeared to be genderless—each with androgynous facial features and white, braided hair, long plaits twisted together and tied high atop their heads. Side by side, they stood regal and impressive— their long white robes falling to the ground and fluttering sinuously. They stood in silence, watching Reason as if waiting for her to be the first to act or to speak. But then they turned, looked at one another, and nodded with what appeared to be some sort of shared understanding. They brushed each other's fingertips and then turned back to Reason—their large, green eyes calm and penetrating. Tattooed on each of their foreheads were small gold letters: *"Whatever*

we sow," on the forehead of one, and, *"So shall we reap,"* on the forehead of the other.

"I am Radia," said the creature to Reason's right, its voice soft and soothing. Then, reaching out with long, webbed fingers, it took hold of her hand.

"And I am Ekabi," said the other.

Radia released Reason's hand, and together the two creatures turned and walked away—their long gowns skimming across the stones and rippling with hypnotic fluidity. After a short distance, the creatures stopped, faced one another, and then together gestured for Reason to move between them. She took a step forward, but halted at the sudden appearance of a structure beyond the two of them. A gazebo now sat by the water's edge, where moments before the beach had been empty. The building looked serene and inviting, but sat enclosed in an enormous, glistening bubble.

"We present to you, The Meeting Place," said Radia. "Come. Sit."

266

"Yes, come and sit with us," added Ekabi.

The two creatures seemed to glide away, and then they sat side by side on a low ridge bordering the beach. Beyond them, a field of tall, arching grasses stretched well into the distance. Reason glanced at the gazebo and then joined the two mysterious creatures, taking her seat in the space between them. "The Meeting Place? What is it for?" she asked, gesturing toward the gazebo.

"You will know soon enough," said Ekabi, the slightest hint of a smile forming on the creature's narrow, brown-skinned face.

"Before you can visit The Meeting Place, you must find forgiveness," said Radia.

Forgiveness? Reason stared straight ahead. A small flock of pink-winged seagulls had gathered on the shore, and with their heads tucked into puffed and ruffling feathers, they basked in the lingering warmth of the setting sun. "Who's left to forgive?" she asked. "I don't feel angry. I'm not hurt anymore. I've accepted all that has happened in my life, everything and everyone." Reason ran her fingers through her hair. "I don't judge people, not anymore. I no longer live in fear." She smiled. "No more fear. And I've forgiven everyone, including William." Satisfied with her reasoning and her answer, she looked from one creature to the other and waited.

"We shall see," said Radia, blond locks glistening.

"Yes. We shall see," repeated Ekabi in a tone that seemed to suggest doubt.

"You don't believe me," Reason stated boldly. "I forgive him. I do. I know he was horribly abusive, but I'm finished condemning him. If there's to be a judgment on William, it won't come from me. Not anymore." Reason sat up straighter as if doing so might bolster her argument. "Forever, it seemed, I was afraid. And for many years I wished he could be locked up forever. Or worse, I sometimes wished that he was dead. Other times, I'd wonder if he married, or had become a father. I used to hate the thought that he might actually be some child's father. And at night, when thoughts of him kept me awake, I'd wonder if he had hurt anyone else." She watched a single seagull float on the wind high above the waves. "But I've changed.

William has no more power over me and those thoughts have completely ended." She pulled her hair into a ponytail, held it there momentarily, and then let it loose. "And yet there is something..."

"Yes?" pressed Radia, surprising Reason by magically appearing in front of her, blocking her view of the ocean.

"Well," started Reason in earnest, "although I know for sure, up here," she tapped her head, "that I've forgiven William, I don't *feel it*." She placed her palm on her belly. "I don't feel it here, in my gut. And I think maybe I should be able to feel something. Something real and momentous... like a profound sense of relief and... freedom."

"By recognizing that you have more to learn, you are well on your way to discovering the truth," said Ekabi, motioning for Reason to continue.

"Maybe," said Reason with a sigh, "because there is one nagging feeling that I can't shake."

"Go on," said Ekabi.

"For all the time I was being hurt by William, I never once thought about reporting him. At first, I was focused on survival. And later, for the longest time on trying to prove to my family that I could be better, stronger, smarter." Reason clasped her hands together and then laid them flat on her lap. "Then," she added gloomily, "almost a decade later when a friend suggested I could still bring charges against William, I chose not to." She bowed her head. "I had lost so many memories. I could no longer piece together the events to make sense out of my story and I was afraid that no one would believe me." Reason sighed. "I had waited so long to tell it." She shrugged in dismay. "I didn't know how I'd explain why I had stayed with William while he was abusive."

For a few moments, no one spoke, and then Reason decisively leaned forward. She looked ahead at the ocean waves, nodding, coming to a new understanding. "But since being here in this magical world, I've come to realize that I stayed with him because I was desperately trying to normalize the relationship, to make it somehow stable and... loving." She slouched, sighed, and frowned. "But I can't shake the fact that when I finally broke from William, it never occurred to me that by pressing charges, I might've saved other women from harm—if even just one. And *that* is what troubles me." She paused, glancing at the sky where wispy grey clouds fanned far toward the horizon, and beyond them, thicker, darker clouds were forming. "So... yes... there it is, the truth—and the truth is... I've yet to forgive myself."

"And yet now you can do just that, forgive yourself," offered Radia. "And put an end to the restrictive nature of such self-judgment."

"Yes," said Ekabi. "And to help yourself further, when you think of William, wish him well."

"What?" Reason laughed, furrowing her brow in doubt. "Wish him well?"

Ekabi fanned both hands, palms up, webbed fingers long and glossy. "Wish him well because he, too, needs healing. Pay attention. Change the intention of your thoughts, and you will regain all the power that you lost. And when that happens, your heart will be open to the full promise of forgiveness."

Radia nodded in agreement and judiciously added, "You may feel that your decision not to report the abuse was one of your own free will, a decision unique to the moment you made it. But the truth is, you came to that decision for many reasons—reasons strung together like beads on a string, a string that reaches far into your past, so far back it is quite impossible to define the beginning. So, you see, to dwell on past choices is not useful. *Now* is important. *Now* is what you know for sure. And now, you have a decision to make. You must choose between pride or humility. Only one will lead you to the truth. And the truth will help you recognize who and what you are." The creature paused, its expression noble, sober, and knowing. "In order to make use of The Meeting Place, you must choose. The Meeting Place is a place of reconciliation, one that requires full forgiveness—a way of being that one cannot pretend. You must commit fully."

"Tell us, what do you choose?" asked Ekabi.

The correct choice seemed obvious, but Reason understood that to commit wholly, she must not just voice an answer, she must believe. The weight of her decision seemed enormous, life's happiness hanging in the balance. The ocean rumbled and roared, the sound of its surging waves seeming to have increased threefold. But in the powerful rhythm, Reason heard Ruby's voice: "Where do you fit in the curriculum of your life?" Reason smiled, inspired by the pleasant memory. "Wait," Ruby had said. "Wait until you remember." At the time, Reason could not imagine what she was expected to remember. The idea had seemed mysterious and locked out of reach. An incoming wave climbed, raced towards the beach, and then spilled onto the pebbly shore. *I am grace. I fit everywhere.* "I remember," Reason exclaimed. "I feel it! I know the feeling of forgiveness! It's unconditional love! And the feeling is familiar... because... well, because I was born this way. I was born good, without guilt... and free. I understand now. I understand that I've lived every bit of my life to find the truth of what I am." She grinned at the creatures; her eyes bright with joy. "I am grace and I fit everywhere."

The bubble surrounding The Meeting Place quivered and then burst, and the small building appeared to breathe, its walls expanding and then settling. Reason began walking towards it, drawn to the peace and tranquility of the quaint structure, absently moving her necklace from outside her t-shirt to inside against her skin.

Shiny, blue-tinged vines trailed from the gazebo's thatched roof, swaying lazily in the breeze—a slow, hypnotic dance. A narrow sand path led to a staircase that climbed into the center of the structure. Reason stepped onto the path. But appearing from nowhere, both creatures blocked her way.

"Oh!" she said, trying to see past them. "Can't I go in?"

"You can, and you will, but we must caution you," said Ekabi.

"Caution me?"

"You will soon be the teacher," said Radia.

"Me? A teacher?"

"You will soon meet with a very important student," said Ekabi.

"Who? What am I to teach?"

The two shared a knowing glance.

"Who is it? Who's my student?" prodded Reason.

270

"You will see soon enough," answered Radia.

"And when you do, you will know what the lesson is to be," offered Ekabi. And with that said, the two creatures moved aside.

The round structure appeared empty. Reason edged forward mindfully, matching her breathing to the restful rhythm of the rolling waves. She climbed with care, and with each step gained a better view of the inside. When her sightline became level with the gazebo floor, she paused—the only movement, the soft sweeping of the vines.

The structure was empty. She moved inside. A cushioned bench-seat followed the full length of the perimeter wall, and with the gazebo's open sides, she could see in all directions. She walked to the ocean side. Dusk was settling, and a low ceiling of dark clouds now veiled the sun. On the horizon where the clouds thinned, silver light plunged in wide, angled rays and pierced the smooth, even surface of the black sea.

Reason all at once felt drowsy—the swaying vines, the warm salty breeze, the ebb and flow of the ocean combining gloriously and lulling her toward sleep. Sitting on the bench, she leaned her head against the wall of the gazebo, and gazed out the opposite side. And the moment before she drifted off, she smiled, content, grateful, and free.

 G3 80

Opening the bathroom door, Reason found the hallway exceptionally warm and oddly breezy. Stepping into it, her bare feet met with an uneven surface; a gust of wind blew her hair about her face, and the cries of seagulls screeched overhead. She blinked, mouth agape, stunned by what appeared to be a setting sun and an endless expanse of rolling water. Just ahead, a seagull splashed into a breaking wave. Reason took a hesitant step forward—the stimulating scene transpiring before her, both beautiful and confusing.

A wave spilled across the beach, rushing towards her, and when she looked down at the water spreading across the smooth stones and nearing her bare feet, she saw she was wearing a long, green gown. "What?" she whispered, running her fingers over the long silky sleeves, and then pushing the soft material up above her elbows. Her cuts and bruises had disappeared. Reaching down, Reason pulled the long gown up above her knees—the skin there also clear. Still clutching the fabric near the hem of the fancy dress, she raised her chin and took a step back, her eyes darting here and there. A structure near the water's edge caught her eye. Puzzled, but drawn to the small, round building, she let the satiny fabric slip from her fingers and began walking toward the gazebo.

The surging and rumbling of the ocean came to her as if she was in a trance—the sounds muted and soothing. She entered the small structure in a subdued, dreamy state of mind. Nearing the top of the stairs, she stopped. A person lay motionless on the bench inside. "Hello?" she dared to utter, stepping inside. The person did not stir. Reason moved closer. "Hello? Can you hear me?" Reaching out tentatively, she touched the person's shoulder and straightaway a woman rolled over and sat up. Reason gasped and took a step back.

"Oh!" said the woman on the bench, for an instant her expression wild, but quickly turning jubilant. "You look wonderful, so young and... pretty."

Reason forced herself to speak. "Wh-who are you? You look... well... you look like me! Older, but definitely and very weirdly me! What's happening? I'm dreaming, right? Right?" She turned left and then right, searching for anything that might help to make sense of this strange and unsettling predicament.

"They told me I'd be meeting an important person. I never dreamed that it would be you," said the older woman in obvious delight. "It seems that you're to be my student."

"Who are you?" managed Reason.

"I'm you; just older."

"What...?" Young Reason reached out to steady herself against the gazebo wall. "This is all very peculiar," she whispered.

"But meeting like this is marvelous," answered the older woman, removing her sandals and swinging her feet up onto the bench.

"Well... it's making me crazy," said younger Reason, grimacing at the quiver in her voice. "How old are you, anyway?"

"I'm thirty—," started older Reason.

"Really?" blurted the younger one, impulsively interrupting her older self. "That seems old," she added in an incredulous whisper, remembering that just a few short hours before she had believed that she might die.

"Yeah, I know what you mean," said her older self with a knowing half-smile.

Both women laughed, reflective and wistful, surprising each other with laughter so similar it caused the younger of the two to go silent. After a moment, young Reason sighed. "Maybe seeing you or, uh, me... so much older... is... a good thing... a good sign." Then wrinkling her brow, she added, "Maybe it means that I don't die anytime soon." She paused, her expression self-conscious and then indignant. "Tell me," she briskly asked, "do I make smarter decisions when I'm as old as you?"

"I've forgotten how angry I was at your age," said older Reason patiently. "And how much I hated myself... but you should know that I'm fully acquainted with the choices you've made so far. I know all about what you've been thinking. I know what you've been doing... and feeling. I know what you fear. I know all about you. And I know you are more than what you think. I don't judge you. I..."

"Why I am here?" blurted young Reason defiantly—aware that beneath her angst something else was growing, something different, something she was not at all sure she trusted—something that felt a little like belonging. She ran her hand through the swinging vines— the long, thin lines of greenery cool to the touch. "I mean... being here sort of feels right. As if this is where I'm supposed to be..." She raised her face to the sun. "I feel so... alive. As if I'm more myself here than anywhere else in my life so far." She looked out at the ocean swells. "It all looks and smells so real." She breathed deeply and then frowned. "But I know that I'm dreaming. This is not real, not my actual life, nothing like the hell that I'm really living."

Reason studied her younger self, reliving, bit by bit, the ugliness and confusion she had felt during that time of her life. Even so, she thought, the experience of The Meeting Place had given her a tremendous opportunity. Calm, invigorated, and inspired, she knew

273

that by being here at The Meeting Place, her younger self had been granted an extraordinary chance—the wonderful and unexpected opportunity to go beyond survival and to thrive. And perhaps her young self could do so without having to experience the intrusive, emotional setbacks that Reason herself had faced. She turned to her young companion and with great care and compassion said, "I know where you've just come from."

Young Reason's glance was brief but clearly dismayed. She sat down heavily, pulling her knees to her chest. "I guess you probably do," she muttered, her mood sour, her mouth a thin line.

"Yes, and..."

"And you must have a string of regrets," lamented young Reason, her tone harsh, her stare hardened by too many years of self-condemnation and disappointment.

"That's a fair enough assumption," answered older Reason. "But here's a surprise. No, I don't. I've made mistakes, but I have no regrets."

Young Reason showed surprise, the hard lines softening. But her eyes revealed a deep distrust. "What you *really* mean is that you made a shit load of stupid mistakes when you were my age."

Older Reason shrugged her shoulders. "Yes, then. And other times, too. We work with what we know at the time," she said. "But we grow, and many of us become stronger and better at finding our way. We face our challenges, and if we're lucky, we learn from them. And bit by bit, we fill an imaginary toolbox with the necessary tools of life."

"Seems my toolbox is pretty much empty," said young Reason, looking away.

"I guarantee you that it is not." Reason watched her younger self huff in disagreement. "You are very hard on yourself," she said solemnly. "I know because I've lived the life you're living now." She sat forward. "William has had control over you for a very long time. For years he has kept you isolated, separating you from the people that mattered the most, the people that cared. That separation and isolation, among other things, has narrowed your way of thinking and feeling."

274

"I don't know," said young Reason dismissively. "That sounds like psychobabble. And an excuse."

"An excuse for what?"

"To cover up what a fool I've been." Young Reason's voice had faded, along with any thread of confidence she might have gained.

"A fool? You've made some errors in judgment. Some of them big. But a fool? No, you're not a fool. You're human, Reason. You trusted William, and he betrayed you." Reason sat back. She thought about the lesson she was expected to teach, and it was a lesson that she now knew with certainty that she could teach without reservation. "Think," she said. "Think about what it means to be a fool. It pretty much means to be senseless, unable to perceive anything... to live without purpose or meaning. But the opposite applies to you. You are no fool. You are smart and aware. And despite your current circumstances, you are quite able to find purpose and to recognize your worth."

Young Reason smiled.

"I've made you smile," said older Reason.

"It's just that... being here with you is so strange. Really strange. You're me. But then again, you're not. You can't be me. Because... here I am." Young Reason raised her hands in exasperation. "For some unknown reason, I feel I belong here in this strange place, but I don't know. As I said, this *dream* is really weird. And shit, if you *are* me, you're much more composed than I could ever hope to be."

"That's not true. I'm composed because, in this... dream world, I've learned how to create and maintain calmness of mind, a skill that you can learn too."

"Calmness of mind?" Young Reason lowered her gaze and shook her head, resisting the idea. "A tool for your toolbox, no doubt," she snickered. "And how did you manage to learn that?"

"It's a long story, too long to tell. And besides, I'd like for us to focus on you."

"Sure. Why not? After all, you're the teacher."

"Do you understand how completely William cut you off from your life? From the life that you knew before him?"

"What he did doesn't matter, because I am responsible, to blame for all of it, including being cut off from family and friends." She looked at her hands, and balling them into fists, pushed them into her lap. "And the beatings... the violence. I can't stop thinking that I could've stopped it all if I'd just been... stronger and smarter."

"Full understanding takes time, Reason. But I'm here as proof that your life will soon make sense to you. You're going to be okay. More than okay. You are going to succeed."

"How's that possible? Everything is so fucked up. No matter how I try to move on, I seem to keep finding myself in some kind of trouble."

"Your trouble has been William. And I repeat, you are much too harsh on yourself."

"I'm *harsh* on myself because I *blame* myself."

"Healing is not about placing blame," offered Reason, watching her younger self rest her head against the wall and stare despondently at the gazebo ceiling. "It's fine to be accountable for the choices you've made. Otherwise, you give away the power you need for change. But you must also remember that you deserve the good things that life offers. You're a loving person. Feel that love. Because if you focus, as you are currently, on the feeling of shame, it'll steal your peace of mind and destroy your spirit."

"Peace of mind? What's that?" scoffed young Reason.

"Peace of mind is what you'll find when you reject the shame."

"And what about the pain? How do I reject that?"

"You don't."

"No? Right. Why do that? Because pain is so much fun?" quipped young Reason cynically.

"Instead of rejecting pain, accept it, because pain is a teacher too. It teaches you to be humble, patient, and grateful. The hollow emptiness you feel inside is just space created by pain. Space for change. Space for letting go. Space for love. For that reason alone pain is your friend."

"You're crazy. Pain is definitely not my friend."

"I know what you think you believe. I know how you feel. And I understand. I'm asking you to be open to new ideas. Peace doesn't seem possible while you're struggling to survive, but if you pay close attention to what you think, and what you feel, you can learn how to create an inner calm—and to be what you have always wanted to be. Believe that you can. Do that much, and you will soon make room in your heart for joy."

Young Reason thought about the possibility of feeling joy, genuine joy. She strolled about the gazebo, deliberately breathing in the salty ocean air. She brought a flower from the nearest vine to her nose, taking in its sweet scent, then released the flower and reached up and plucked a piece of straw from the low-hanging roof. "These details... they're very realistic," she marveled, examining the piece of straw. "I never want to wake up. But I know I will. And at any moment the cuts and bruises and suffering will all come rushing back." She turned to her older self. "What good does a dream, or whatever this is, do me?"

"I don't know how it works, Reason. I just know that somehow, someday, and in some way, this dream will benefit you."

"But my toolbox is still empty," sighed young Reason.

"Oh, but it's not. Tell me, how do you want to live your life? Do you want to carry on as you are with dulled senses and fearing each day, or do you want to recognize all that you have, be wide awake, and be the best that you can be?"

The two women looked at one another, the younger surprised and curious, but hesitant to trust, the older eager and filled with love.

"Dulled senses? I'm wide awake all the time."

"But are you really?"

"What's that supposed to mean?"

"Are you really awake? Are you truly aware and engaged moment to moment? Imagine if one day, when you're doing something ordinary like pouring a glass of water or walking down the street and... you drop dead."

"That's kind of drastic, don't you think?"

"Drastic? Maybe so, but entirely possible. So I wonder, if that happens, will you have been paying attention? Will you have been grateful for things like your ability to walk or the ground beneath your feet? Will you have been grateful for the easy availability of the fresh water, or for the effort needed to bring it to you? The possibilities are endless. And most importantly, will you have been thankful for every moment of your life until that final one?" Young Reason said nothing. She plucked a small leaf from the vine and twirled it between her fingers. "You and I," continued Reason, "we don't know what happens to us when this dream is over. All we know is right now. And when we surface from this dream, it'll be important to be paying attention at that moment too." Reason smiled; her expression joyous. "Here on this beach, I smell the salt in the air and taste it on my tongue. I am in awe of the power of the ocean. I can feel its fresh spray on my face. I feel magnificently alive, and for me, the experience fills me with joy. It's a joy I would miss if I lived lost in the grip of resentment, guilt, and shame."

Young Reason stopped twirling the tiny leaf. She laid it flat on the palm of her hand and stared at it.

"I know," said older Reason, "that for you, that horrible night with William happened mere hours ago. For me, it seems a lifetime. Still, I remember it all like it was yesterday, the stifling, sticky heat of the night, the foul smell of the room, the damp, dirty bedsheets. I remember the putrid stink of the roommate's sweat and the sound of his vulgar, breathless grunting. I remember the stains on the worn carpet, the crushing weight of William's body, the excruciating pain, the indignity. I remember the brutality of his groping hands, the foulness of his breath, moist and hot on my skin... and I remember the horror of his chilling, rage-filled words. I remember all of it, the suffocating fear... believing that I might die... feeling stupid, weak, and worthless."

Young Reason turned her face away, put her head in her hands and let loose a stifled squeal.

Reason reached out, wanting so much to hold and comfort her younger self. "But," she said firmly, pulling her hand back, "I also remember some things that were extraordinary and encouraging that night. I remember the kind man outside the club who came to help me, to help you. And despite the odds, I remember the hope he gave us—even though we couldn't understand why he cared or the importance of his presence. And the light standard in that God-forsaken parking lot... staring at it in awe, like it was calling to us. Those little insects attracted by the light, motivating us to fight for a piece of our own light... to fight to live."

Young Reason wept, her tears spilling through her fingers and darkening the fabric of her gown.

"I remember those things, because like you, my desperation to live forced me to be wide awake and engaged. And despite the horror of that night, I was fully present for those fleeting and powerful moments of hope. I'm you; you're me. I know you know what I'm talking about. That night was a living nightmare, but it also shed light on our gift of awareness. Fight for your life now, as you did then. Don't waste your gift of awareness, a gift that comes more easily to you than you realize. Embrace it. Choose to live in awe rather than in fear. Live in awe of being alive, in awe of the sky above and of the ground beneath your feet. Let awe be your guide. Use that horrible experience to grow. Choose to soar beyond it. Choose to feel the joy and beauty that life offers, a joy and beauty that you deserve."

"But how? How do I forget?" implored young Reason.

"You'll likely never forget. But you can choose to live fully, to live now, and not in that dark memory."

"But those are just words. I don't know how."

"I'll teach you how."

Young Reason shook her head and wiped at her tears. "I want to believe you. I do. But it's so hard to face today or imagine tomorrow without thinking of last night."

"This moment is the one that counts. This one, and then the next one, and then the next one after that. Reason, your life gets better. You're a good and loving person. And in your life, you will one day know genuine passion and affection. But you must trust and believe in yourself. And Reason, you will love yourself again too. And not only will you know you are deserving of this love, but you will also forgive those who've hurt you. You'll forgive yourself. I know you doubt me now, but I think you can feel the truth in my words. Hold on to *that* feeling. Keep it close to your heart, where the truth belongs."

Young Reason felt a profound sense of relief—as if the promise found in the experience of this so-called dream, and in meeting her older self, was saving her in some way. She felt a great unburdening as the despair that had haunted her for years lifted.

"And Reason?" said the older to the younger.

Young Reason waited, savoring her new sense of hope.

"William has no more power over you. You are free of him."

For a long while they sat quietly, twilight a warm golden glow on their faces, the ocean waves crashing in great throws, the gulls crying in the distance.

"Now," said older Reason, gently interrupting the comfortable silence between them, "close your eyes. Listen to my voice. Let your breath be your focus." Young Reason seemed to do so with ease. "Let your thoughts come and let them go. Don't be troubled by how many you have or what they are. Just notice them. If you linger on one, that's okay. Notice it and then imagine that you hold it in your hand. Uncurl your fingers and let it fall away. This heightened awareness is what it feels like to be wide awake and fully present." Eyes closed, both women smiled. "Feel the warm breeze on your face, the weight of your body and your limbs, the softness of your muscles." They sat listening to the ocean pour onto the pebbly beach and then leave, the little stones clattering within the retreating water. "Notice the moment just before each wave rushes back into the sea. The water flows in, holds ever-so-briefly, and then leaves—just like your breath. Follow your breath. Stay with its continuous flow. Do this as often as you can. Your breath is your anchor. With practice, you will feel calm and composed and become open to the abundance of beauty, grace, and joy that your life has to offer."

Reason opened her eyes and for a few seconds, wholly present and profoundly moved, she watched her young self. Filled with compassion and gratitude, eyes glistening, she pressed her fingers to her locket, leaned forward, and in an impassioned whisper, said, "I love you, Reason. I always have and I always will."

19

the minute man

Reason leaned against the wall, loath to move her suffering body, but longing for the comfort and privacy of her bedroom. With quiet determination, she took a deep breath, opened the bathroom door, and stepped out—frail, unsubstantial, each step strenuous, her legs impossibly heavy.

The house stood empty; the hallway quiet. Relieved, she limped down the narrow corridor and hobbled into her bedroom. There, she shut the door and rested against it.

Her bedroom was as she had left it—her discarded clothes from the day before draped across the end of the bed, her school books stacked on the side table, her shoes lined up against the wall. But everything seemed different, as if the items in the room belonged to someone else, someone with a normal, innocent life.

The small room was intolerably hot and Reason felt desperate for air. She shuffled to the window, and with considerable effort, raised it. For a few gratifying moments, she let the fresh air wash over her, and then she limped to the bed and eased her battered body down.

From the hallway came a soft, scampering sound. Wincing, Reason carefully raised herself onto her bruised elbow and listened. From outside her window, a lone dove cooed. A dog barked. A sudden strong breeze stirred the curtain. Weary, wanting only to sleep and to feel nothing—and unable to hold back her tears—she moved to lie back down. But again, a soft skittering across the wood floor outside her bedroom, and then a dull thump against her bedroom door, drew her attention. And then came a faint mew. Reason sat up. From the hallway came yet another mew, louder than the first. Curiosity piquing, she eased from the bed, staggered to the door, and opened it

282

A crumpled piece of paper shot past her feet and skipped into the bedroom—followed by a leaping kitten. The kitten, its hairs raised from head to tail, pounced on the moving target.

"Where'd you come from?" Reason bent awkwardly toward the kitten. The tiny, furry animal bounced sideways. She scooped it up. "Are you my new roommate?" she whispered, tears welling—emotions surging in response to the enormous contrast between her misery and the innocence of the kitten.

As the kitten bit at the long strands of her hair and pawed at her face, she stroked its tiny head, its wee skull hard beneath a soft layer of orange and white fuzz. With both paws the kitten batted at her hand, leaned back playfully, and then flopping forward, bit at the tips of her thumbs. "How sweet you are," she whispered.

While Reason held the kitten, it wiggled, arched its back, and then went blissfully limp, purring, its tiny heart beating fast. She placed it on the bed and then, closing the bedroom door, bent with some difficulty, and collected the ball of paper from the floor. Tucking the crumpled paper beneath the edge of her pillow, she climbed back into bed and pulled the bedsheet to her chin. The kitten jumped about her legs, chasing its tail.

"Crazy kitty," she said through a shadow of a smile.

The kitten leapt to her pillow and from beneath it, dug out the clump of paper, picking it up in its mouth, jumping onto Reason's chest, and dropping it there.

"What's so special about this thing?" asked Reason. The kitten jumped to her shoulder and then to her pillow where it settled with a flop, its warm, featherlight body pressed to the top of her head.

Reason began working loose the craggy folds in the paper, spreading it flat against her chest and running her fingers across its wrinkles. And in doing so, she curiously experienced a strange and dreamy sensation. The bedroom seemed to fill with the scent of the ocean, and Reason felt as if she had not a care in the world. In that single moment, despite the trauma of the previous hours, she suddenly felt whole and strong and safe and hopeful. The kitten purred. She sank into the bed, relaxed every muscle, and exhaling, leaned her head into the warmth of its little vibrating body. "Well, little guy, seems you've brought me some peace. I don't know who you belong to, but I'm gonna call you... Joy. You know why? Because for a minute there, I felt happy. And you know what else? For some weird reason, I think everything's gonna turn out okay." Reason rolled onto her side, moving in tiny increments. The kitten barely stirred. "I've got some money. Not a lot, but enough. Enough to make a change, to try for a new start...." The kitten purred contentedly.

A tear slid onto the bridge of Reason's nose and then dropped to the bed. "I can't explain how I know, but somehow I just know that I'm gonna be okay. I'm alive. I—am—alive. I can get through this. I can. All of it. It'll take time. Maybe a long time." Reason carefully touched her swollen upper lip. "But cuts and bruises fade. They always do. Memories... are tougher." Feeling resolute and defiant, she balled her hands into fists. "But eventually they'll fade too." She tucked her arms beneath the sheet. The kitten continued to purr. "It's gonna be bloody hard, but I'll get better, Joy. I have to. My life will go on, and if I dig in, if I work really hard, it'll get better. It has to." She tilted her head and watched the kitten, its wee eyes blinking sleepily. "Maybe I should call you Love. Wait, I'll call you Love-Joy because that's what you've brought me." Reason ran her finger from the kitten's nose to its forehead. "Please," she asked the quiet emptiness of the room, "give me strength. Help me. Help me help myself."

She lifted the piece of paper from her chest. It seemed to contain a letter, maybe a poem, and was titled "An Asking at Bedtime". Reason began reading:

Are you there? Are you listening? What do I call you? Creation? Here's the thing... I'm feeling painfully alone. I'm feeling uncertain, afraid, and restless. I can't sleep. I feel... lost. Please help me find you.

I've heard that I naturally have love within me— and if that's true, I'll have hope too. But I wonder, if I can find my way to you, will my worries and fears lose their power? Will my awe for life be restored? And... can you really love me after all that I've done? Because if you can, I will be forever grateful... and relieved.

Yes, I'm told I have love within me—a love that's not simply mine to consider but is me; This idea makes me feel... infinite—a part of the whole— connected to everything, and stronger than my troubled existence would have me believe. And for that, among other miracles, I am sincerely thankful.

Some say that you and I are the same. The same in love. They say that my life is the product of our sameness. And that makes me think that maybe, just maybe, despite my faults, I'm destined to... to spread love. And if that's true, I'm good with that.

Well, I guess that's it, but you know, if you and I ever consciously meet, I think that I'll know you at first sight—because... well, because I sense that maybe, as crazy as this sounds, we've met before. Okay, I'm feeling a bit better now. I'm feeling the resilience of love. And now... I think I can sleep.

Love, R

Reason read the letter a second time, and then a third. She, too, felt uncertain, afraid, and restless. She, too, wanted to be loved, and to believe and to belong. And she, too, wanted to sleep. "Love, R," she whispered aloud, folding the worn piece of paper, taking care to line up its edges and sharpen its creases, holding it to her chest, feeling connected to its message.

As Love-Joy slept beside her, Reason gazed out her bedroom window and pondered the letter. She did not wonder where it had come from and knew only that it soothed her. She gazed at the roof peak of the neighboring house and the vast chunk of blue above it, worrying not whether her newly found calm made sense, only caring that she felt it.

Her bedroom curtain all of a sudden billowed high above the sill, and as Reason watched, a bird landed on a wire beyond her window. "Craw, Craw," it called. She watched it lazily, her eyes fluttering toward sleep. The bird was big and beautiful and unlike any bird she had ever seen. It had an impressive and unusual coat of white feathers that shimmered brilliantly in the early morning light. As she tried to stay awake, the bird flew from the wire and landed on her sill. Spreading its great wings, it cocked its regal head to one side and seemed to lock eyes with her. Fascinated, she labored to keep her eyes open, and for a moment succeeded. But when she stirred a few minutes later and looked for the bird, it was gone. Reason thought about going to the window and searching further, but exhaustion overwhelmed her and she fell into a deep sleep.

 જી ટ્ઝ

"The time has come," said Radia.

"Yes," said Ekabi.

Reason opened her eyes to see the two creatures standing near her, and her younger self gone. Gone too were the beach, the ocean, the salty air, the hypnotic sound of the waves, and The Meeting Place. Darkness surrounded her and her companions—a pale yellow glow spotlighting them from above. Reason climbed to her feet and squinted into the blackness—but whatever existed beyond the light remained a mystery. "She's gone," she acknowledged quietly.

"Yes," said Radia

"You did well," added Ekabi. "You are a fine teacher."

Reason glowed. "The Meeting Place was incredible," she said. "To see and hear and talk with my younger self was phenomenal. To have such an opportunity... I am humbled and profoundly grateful. Thank you." She smiled, and then her expression turned doubtful. "Will she remember the dream? Or our meeting? Will she remember me?"

"She will learn from your meeting and she will experience a new sense of well-being," said Ekabi

286

"But will she remember the actual meeting?"

"She will not. But no matter what her life brings from this point on, she will never again lose her sense of self-worth. From now on a strong inner sense of dignity, insight, and serenity will be her guide," said Radia.

"Good. Very good," commented Reason, her smile jubilant. "But she won't remember meeting me?"

"She does not need to," offered Ekabi.

Reason nodded. "Okay. Okay... that makes sense, I guess." She clasped her hands over her heart. "I feel such an intense love for her."

"What you are experiencing is a pure and genuine love of self, made possible when the heart is no longer restricted by the affairs and concerns of a busy mind," said Radia. "And because you have found self-love, the love that you feel for others, and life, and all of creation—becomes simple, transparent, and everlasting."

Reason believed that she understood. Profoundly changed, she felt euphoric and expansive—limitless, really—as if she extended into the universe. "Thank you," she whispered. "Thank you."

The two creatures nodded, turned and faced one another, and once more touched fingertips. When their hands parted, the ground began to rumble and vibrate, and the floor on which they stood began to rise, carrying its three passengers into the pale light above.

"What's happening? Where are we going?" Reason asked, peering eagerly into the solemn faces of her companions.

"The Minute Man awaits," answered Ekabi.

"The Minute Man," repeated Reason quietly, untroubled by the somewhat ominous name, content to let the continuing mystery of this incredible adventure unfold as it may.

Higher and higher they went, until the floor eventually stopped alongside a narrow platform, the long ends of which vanished into the blackness beyond. A high-pitched mechanical whine approached from Reason's left. She looked in that direction. From the inky depths emerged the shiny gold nose-cone, and then the egg-shaped body, of a vehicle. The small driverless car moved slowly and dipped somewhat before coming to rest opposite her.

"From here you must travel alone," announced Radia.

"I'm not surprised," replied Reason. Despite the mysteries that lay ahead, she stood unafraid, feeling as if this whole magical adventure had been readying her for what was coming next—each daunting challenge and rewarding victory instilling in her a renewed inner strength and confidence, and a calm certainty that to face the journey's mysterious conclusion alone was altogether fitting.

The car's side door opened. When she turned to say goodbye, she was alone. With a knowing nod, Reason glanced into the surrounding darkness and then stepped into the car. Inside, a single pedestal chair occupied most of the compact interior. She sat on the soft, curved seat. The door slid shut. Then the vehicle promptly sped up, moving steadily into the blackness.

Reason brushed her hand across the velvety red fabric that lined the walls inside the car. Above her head, hundreds of pinhead-sized lights sprinkled the dark ceiling—twinkling and glittering like a cluster of stars. She was leaning forward and peering out the large, curved front window, seeing only utter blackness, when an object slid across the floor near her feet. Reaching down, Reason found a small container and held it up to the dim light. Before she could examine it, the car lurched forward and picked up speed. Ahead, a tiny white dot appeared, and as the car sped towards it, Reason tucked the found object into her satchel and held on.

The dot ahead soon became a ball of light, growing larger and brighter as the car approached. And just before the small vehicle launched into the immense, white brilliance, Reason instinctively turned away and braced herself.

Inside the light, she felt weightless, and then a fluttering in her belly as the car abruptly and quickly descended a great distance. Gradually, the speeding vehicle leveled out and soon eased to a halt—hovering quietly above a large patch of blue grass. Reason blinked in the bright light. The car door slid open. She stepped out onto a patchwork of multicolored grasses—a giant, living quilt that blanketed a vast stretch of land and ended nearby at the blunt edge of a cliff

Near the sheer drop, an enormous fire burned inside a shallow pit lined with large, smooth stones.

Behind Reason, the small car whirred in acceleration. She turned and watched it swoosh away—and vanish into the side of a mountain. When she returned her attention to the fire, someone stood beside it— a tall figure dressed in a long, pale blue cloak, and whose face hid in the shadow of an oversized hood. The mysterious figure beckoned her forward. Unafraid, confident and calm, she started walking, sensing that she was nearing the end of her amazing journey of transformation. But as she approached, the figure moved—and disappeared behind the tall wall of flames.

Reason stopped in her tracks, surprised and a little confused. As she did, in a sudden eruption of sound and color, a flock of birds flew up from beyond the edge of the cliff, hundreds of brilliant pink beaks and bright yellow wings flying in unison. The birds flew in a great sweeping arc, and then plummeting as one, they swooped around the flames and headed toward Reason. Twice they circled above her, flying low in the sky, twittering and tweeting. Then ascending, they billowed and twirled into a swirling cloud of pink and yellow. Reason smiled, exhilarated by the sudden and unexpected show. And then, in serpentine fashion, the flock spiraled downward, sailed toward the precipice, and promptly dropped out of sight.

Reason waited for the flock to reappear and when it seemed as if the birds were gone for good, she continued towards the fire. But just then, the flock came back into view—a swirl of color departing for the horizon. The large group of birds dispersed, darting this way and that, spreading like a burst of fireworks and disappearing one by one into a fleet of puffy, flat-bottomed clouds. Reason marveled at the sight, watching until the last speck of pink and yellow had vanished.

When she looked again at the fire, she discovered that a small, pink table now stood where she had last seen the hooded figure. On the table, a green envelope sat propped against some object. Reason hurried forward, and with the heat of the fire warm against her skin, reached for the envelope. Behind it was a bell. She glanced about for the stranger in the blue cloak but saw no one.

A round pillow of orange wax sealed the envelope. Reason broke the seal and removed a card with her name printed on it. Turning the card over, she read: "The Minute Man awaits." Again, she looked about for the hooded figure. Again, she saw no one. The fire popped, crackled, and hissed. Returning to the card, she continued reading:

Open the receptacle found in the
transport gondola.
In it, a message has returned.
Read it. Burn it.
Then ring the bell to summon
The Minute Man.

Reason pulled the small receptacle from her satchel, and pushing a tiny latch, released the lid. Inside, she found a neatly folded piece of paper. Unfolding the paper, she instantly recognized what it was. Incredulous, she read the familiar title aloud: "An Asking at Bedtime".

Holding the letter in her hands, Reason remembered its origin. She had been traveling to visit friends, and on the way, had met a fascinating woman on the train. Making quick and friendly acquaintance, the two had begun chatting early into the trip, their discussion soon becoming more intimate, and leading to a friendly debate about fear.

"In my experience," Reason had declared, "the world is always going to make most people afraid of something or someone... and their lives difficult. Fear is both a necessity and a curse."

"What about love?" the woman had asked. "Surely love has some say in the matter."

"True love," Reason had argued, "is meant for a few lucky ones. And in my life," she had explained, "that kind of love has been no match for fear."

"But love naturally resides in you," the woman had said.

"Not in my experience," Reason muttered, feeling strangely unprepared for such a claim.

"Yes," the woman had offered. "You are a creation of love. Therefore, my dear, *you are love.*"

"Ha!" Reason laughed. "Sounds nice, but..."

"You must take a moment to ponder this truth and to understand that love created you," interrupted the woman, her expression kind, her eyes smiling, her tone earnest. "You and the creation that created you are the same in this way, both the very fabric of love."

Reason had smiled politely, quite ready to change the topic. But the woman had taken her firmly by the arm, and smiling shrewdly, had insisted, "Learn how to understand and express your fears, my dear. Try asking. Ask for help. Learn how to help yourself. You need only to believe in love."

Standing by the roaring fire and remembering this exchange, Reason thought of it with surprise and fondness. Back then, she had been utterly skeptical, not at all sure that she even believed in any sort of all-encompassing creation, and not able to imagine a life without looking over her shoulder in fear. And yet some weeks after the encounter on the train, during a particularly lonely night when she was feeling overwhelmed with sadness and believed that she had nothing to lose, Reason had penned "An Asking at Bedtime".

The next day, while sitting on a park bench and revisiting what she had written, Reason had lost the letter. A jogger had thumped down at the other end of the bench, and startled by his sudden arrival and furtive appearance, she had risen to leave—stuffing the letter into her jacket pocket. His hands in his pockets, and his head bowed, the hood of his pale blue jacket had completely hidden the jogger's face. She had given him an anxious glance before walking away, unaware that the letter had fallen to the ground. Behind her, the jogger had casually picked up the crumpled piece of paper and slipped it into his jacket. And yet now, magically holding her letter once more, Reason marveled, because, in addition to having the letter back in her possession, she realized that the stranger on the train had been Macy—and the jogger? She glanced about for the figure in the blue, hooded cloak.

291

Reading the words that she had written so long ago, knowing how much she had learned since writing them, Reason felt that the letter had been answered. She brushed her fingers over the soft cloth feel of the old paper. *Read it. Burn it.* She nodded at the fire and then scrunched the piece of paper into a tight ball and tossed it into the flames. She felt no sense of loss. In fact, Reason felt more fulfilled than ever, her heart light and filled with love.

The bell, plain and beautiful in its simplicity, had a single letter "R" engraved near its base. Reason swung it high above her head, the wooden clapper producing a deep, soothing tone. Beside her, the huge fire was extinguished. And on the far side of the smoldering heap, stood the figure in the pale blue cloak.

20

the breeze of the soul

Reason felt odd, as if she was entering some kind of altered state, seeing the scene before her through two small eye holes—her face a mask, her body a cloak, and she, a wisp of smoke floating on a breeze.

"Welcome," said the being in the pale blue robe. "I am known as The Minute Man. Come. We have people and places to visit."

The Minute Man moved alarmingly close to the brink and then stood looking into the distance as if fixated on the view beyond the precipice. With measured steps, Reason moved alongside him and looked in that direction. Below, the vast stretch of land was relatively flat, and it contained a large body of water that met the horizon in a straight line, appearing like the blunt edge of the planet itself.

"Who are we to visit? Where are we going?" Reason asked, wary of the dizzying drop only a few feet away.

"To the present, my dear."

"I don't understand. How can that be? We're already... here, aren't we?" said Reason.

The Minute Man did not immediately answer, but when he did, his manner was cordial and relaxed. "We can agree that the present is happening now, but... it is fluid—containing depths which you've hardly begun to explore. Are you truly capable of sensing all that it offers? Look around. Are you able to describe the whole of now?"

Reason wished that she could see The Minute Man's face, but his monkish hood hung well forward—the rippling, wafting fabric seeming to have a life of its own. "I think so," she answered tentatively, looking forward, fanning her arm to indicate the vast scene. "The present is in everything I see." A flock of teal-feathered

293

birds sailed past her sightline, a streak of beautiful blue brilliance on a cream-colored backdrop. "It's in what I feel." She rubbed her hands together. "It's in the air and the sounds. And...," Reason paused, lowering her head, thinking, "I feel something else. Something more. Something deeper." Again, she looked at The Minute Man. He appeared unmoved by her description, remaining motionless and silent, his face still well hidden. About to explain further, Reason opened her mouth to speak, but in that instant, she realized her satchel was missing. She turned to look for it.

"No point in searching," stated The Minute Man plainly. "Your satchel is gone."

"But why?" asked Reason with some alarm. "What about the things I've collected?"

"Do you believe that because you no longer have possession of those articles, that they are now meaningless to you?"

"I... I don't know...," said Reason. She thought about the items in her satchel, concentrating on each one, discovering that she could imagine the cool smooth texture of the mindfulness bean, almost able to feel its solidity in the palm of her hand. She smiled, comforted by the sense of connection. Next, she thought about the bookmark, visualizing the moment when she had found it here in this magical world, its yellow tassel wavering in the hot desert breeze. And with this visualization came an instant connection with her mother. Reason felt a surge of love. The feeling was encouraging. Thinking of each item: the journal and the key, the card from the Sanctuary, the piece of parchment from The Tree of Knowledge, and the shell that had contained her locket—each seemed to reward her similarly. "No," she finally answered. "I don't feel as if the items are lost and meaningless. I feel their presence and power as strongly as ever."

"And so," said The Minute Man, "now that you know the items are not lost, and that in their absence they can still influence you, you can let them be—and tell me more about your perception of the here and now."

Reason nodded and then searched for the words to best describe what she was feeling. "The present moment has a lot to offer," she began. "So much, in fact, it seems almost impossible to take it all in. And... since being here in this... otherworld, I've learned that the present is influenced by how I see it... how I receive or reject what it offers." She scanned the landscape. "The here and now is remarkably vivid, but it also feels... nuanced—as if it has... layers."

The monastic hood moved up and down, smoothly, and just once. But with that one nod, Reason found the encouragement to continue. "Here, with you, I feel that I'm part of the present, but I also feel somewhat distanced from it... almost as if I'm both here and somewhere else at the same time. Well, that's not quite right. I know that I'm here with you. But the experience is a bit like I'm watching a movie." She looked down. "My body feels as if I'm wearing it... like... a cloak. As if the real me is light and weightless, more like the air I breathe than a dense body of flesh and blood." Reason examined her hands, turning them over, flexing her fingers, almost feeling as if she was watching them from above—as if they belonged to someone else. "It's a curious sensation. I feel a bit like an explorer making discoveries and... touching things, but I feel removed from the experience, more like an observer." She looked ahead at the sprawling land beyond the edge of the cliff, at its glistening body of water. "It's as if I'm seeing all of this from... some other layer of existence." Reason turned to The Minute Man. "Is that possible? Is it possible to experience the present as if it has layers?" She laughed with euphoric delight, sensing that she was making a new and important discovery. "Is it possible to sense more than one layer at a time? And in which one do I exist? What layer is this?" She pointed to her surroundings and turned—her body following her as if form had become mist, and she the breeze that shaped and moved it.

The Minute Man spoke with ease, his tone tender. "Try not to rush for an answer. Relax. Feel your new sense of expansiveness—and the whole of the present without the need to name what you are feeling."

Reason gave her head a little shake, choosing to let go of her need to understand fully her new sense of perception, settling into the lightness of being that she had become, and feeling an absolute absence of burden. Some seconds later, when she opened her eyes, she felt rested and at ease and sighed happily. "This place...," she fanned her arm, "it feels somehow ageless... as if being here is like being present everywhere at once."

"This is a place of beauty and serenity."

"What do you call it?"

"This, the otherworld, is called Zephyr-a-sul. It dwells within the cosmic breath that sustains the connection of all of creation. Zephyr-a-sul means Breeze of the Soul. It is a place where the soul is free to roam unrestrained. Zephyr-a-sul is a magical world where secrets are revealed and mysteries are solved."

Reason opened her mouth to speak, but The Minute Man took her by the hand and pulled her over the brink.

CR ⊗O

In the darkened hospital room, the two women exchanged a meaningful glance. One smiled somberly at the other and shook her head: no. They touched hands in passing, a simple gesture of support. The morning nurse checked and recorded the old woman's vital signs. Returning the chart to its place, she turned to look out the window. Dawn was breaking pale yellow. It was time to let the light in.

"Reason is stable," said the night nurse, having paused at the doorway. "See you tonight," she added before exiting the room.

Macy and the night nurse had made similar polite exchanges every day for the past five weeks. And on this particular morning, each believed that Reason would not live to see the end of the day. The night nurse guessed so because she had been a witness to death in palliative care for over a decade. Macy knew with certainty. She walked to the window and opened the curtains. The morning light burst into the room and fell onto Reason's face.

Standing at Reason's bedside, Macy kissed her brow and held her limp hand. "You've done well, my dear," she said, gazing lovingly at Reason's peacefully sleeping face. Then, with a knowing smile, she let her gaze drift upward.

CR ⊗O

"Can she see us up here?" Reason asked, peering down at the quiet scene below.

"No," replied The Minute Man. "But Macy can sense you. And she knows that your presence here means that you have made your way to the heart of Zephyr-a-sul—and that that achievement has allowed you to experience the wondrous essence of your soul."

Reason scrutinized the woman asleep in the hospital bed below, and in sudden astonishment, she realized that the elderly sleeping woman was the older Reason at the final stage of her life. With this revelation came an exhilarating flurry of visions, and Reason witnessed scene after scene from the old woman's long life.

"Incredible!" she whispered. "But is she... dying?"

"She is," said The Minute Man. "But while you have been on your healing journey with us, she has been your witness. She has seen your transformation, and she too has changed. Like you, she has found peace in pain, rejected shame, and realized forgiveness."

"But how?"

"She dwells in a world somewhere between life and death. From there she has watched you. She has observed each struggle, decision, revelation, and change."

"She knows of me? She knows of younger Reason too?"

"She does."

"But what good is her transformation if she's dying?"

The Minute Man put his hand on Reason's shoulder, and her visions resumed. In them, Reason saw how, like her, her elder self had become vulnerable to, and isolated by, the power of shame. And then Reason experienced the thrill of the life-changing moment when her elder self had let shame go, and having done so, how she had recently become free to experience the purest of gratitude for the simplest of pleasures. She witnessed her older self enjoying the soft, caring touch of a visiting friend. Then she saw the older woman basking in the peppery scent of the pink carnations that arrived daily to her bedside. Next, Reason watched her frail elder self smile tenderly at the attending nurse who had spent many a coffee break in Reason's room. And finally, Reason enjoyed the same enchanting pleasure that her elder self had savored while watching the setting sun glow orange-red through the bedside window.

The many parts of the older woman's life had unfolded like a movie in Reason's mind. She had seen her mother, father, brother, and sisters, and she had felt the unbreakable bond between them all, realizing that no matter where each of them was, and no matter what their differences, their connection as love was real and everlasting. And then Reason had witnessed the pivotal moment when her elder self's pain had transformed from foe to friend. Pain had become a teacher of patience, a source of gratitude, and a guide to peace. Reason had witnessed each of these moments clearly and in the span of a few quick minutes.

"Extraordinary," she uttered in hushed reverence. "To see her life in this way. To watch all of its important turning points."

"Not quite all," said The Minute Man as he gave Reason's shoulder a gentle squeeze.

"Oh, her wedding! She's married," cried Reason happily, her eyes glistening. "He seems a wonderful and caring man." She laughed with pleasure. "I saw her asking to feel this kind of love, and I can feel her joy as if it's my own. She's had a rich life, and she knows it." Reason watched as Macy arranged a pale green blanket over the frail form in the bed below. "When she dies, will her husband be okay?"

"He will. The strength of their love will sustain him."

Relieved and comforted, Reason sighed happily and asked, "So, what happens now?"

The Minute Man turned slowly, facing her, the features of his face remaining concealed within the shadowy depth of his hood. When he spoke, his voice was solemn and kind, and seemed to take on the pitch and cadence of more than one gender. "You have come to the end of your journey here. Be gladdened, because, through your resolve and honesty, you have found grace. And grace is the key to renewal and rebirth." They paused and eased even closer to Reason. "When we reveal our face, one minute will remain in your journey. But remember, you are forever connected to all of creation. In that way you are eternal." They raised both hands to the rim of their hood.

298

"Wait!" cried Reason. "Wait," she repeated more softly. "Please, let me have one last look." The Minute Man nodded in approval. Feeling no sense of fear or restraint, she drifted down toward her elder self, and observing the details of the old woman's face, she thought about her younger self and The Meeting Place—and was consumed with love. "I see you," she whispered, reaching down, the tips of her fingers coming close to touching the sleeping face. "We did it. All of us. All of us Reasons." She turned to Macy, who seemed to meet her gaze directly. "Can I give my older self something?" Reason asked The Minute Man.

"Yes, my dear, you can."

Reason unfastened the chain from around her neck and, holding it above the bed, let it go. But before she could see if it landed, she found herself back above the bed and floating alongside The Minute Man.

"It is time," they said.

"I'm ready," answered Reason, feeling utterly calm.

With steady, slow-moving hands, The Minute Man removed the hood. And just as she glimpsed the face within it, a bright white light engulfed them both, and from within this radiance, Reason heard the powerful voice: "60, 59, 58..."

"Thank you... Creation," she began spontaneously. "Thank you for this remarkable journey. Thank you for every single minute of my life. And thank you for your... wisdom."

"49, 48, 47, 46, 45..."

"I am comforted to know that I'm a tiny part of your magnificence. And I am grateful to finally know this. I humbly ask that you continue to love and guide elder Reason's husband, my siblings, my friends, and... well, all living things. I don't know what will happen next but... I am ready."

"26, 25, 24, 23..."

"Because I know I am strong and... I'll gladly be a messenger of... love. Thank you for your abundant generosity. Thank you for the lessons in forgiveness." Reason listened for the intoxicating voice.

"4, 3..."

"I love you," she whispered.

ᝢ ᝣ

Muffled voices and muted sounds drifted in from the hallway. "Need a break?" asked the nurse, having returned to check in on Macy and Reason.

"No," answered Macy. "I'm fine."

"Has her husband been in this morning?"

"Yes, he's been here all night. I convinced him to get some sleep. He's resting in the family room. I expect he'll be back soon." The nurse nodded and disappeared into the hall.

Macy moved to the window and opened it. A fresh breeze blew into the stillness of the room, stirring the pages of the magazine that she had left open on the bedside table. For a moment, she watched the bustling activity on the street and then turned back to the bed. An object glittered near Reason's head. When Macy saw what it was, she smiled in recognition. She lifted the necklace from the bedding and brought it to her lips. Then she placed the chain into Reason's hand and closed her fingers around it.

"I've brought you a cup of tea," said the returning nurse.

"That's kind of you. Thank you," smiled Macy.

"During the last few weeks, you two have become quite close," said the nurse solemnly.

"We certainly have," replied Macy, her expression showing gratitude and pleasure.

"It must be very difficult for you to watch her die."

"Oh, I'm fine. Really," said Macy. "I'll miss Reason, but I'm not upset. Look at her. She is at peace." Reason breathed evenly. Her lips parted, seeming to form a faint smile.

"Yes," agreed the nurse. And pointing to a small watercolor that hung above the bed, she asked, "Is this one of her pieces?"

Macy glanced at the framed picture. "Yes," she answered. "Reason said that the gazebo is a place meant for peaceful transformation. The image came to her quite suddenly one day. She called that painting Meeting Place by the Sea." Reason lifted her hand

and splayed her fingers. Macy guided it back down by her side. "Not long now, my dear Reason. Not long."

"Well, okay dear. I'll be back in a little while," said the nurse, turning to leave as Reason's husband entered the room.

A faint sigh arose from the bed. The nurse turned back. In the silence, all three watched Reason's body rise at the chest. Her limbs stiffened and then slackened as her slight frame sank back down. She made a soft "oh" sound and raised her fingers on both hands. The fingers hung in the air briefly and then lowered. Her husband took her hand into his own and bowed his head. And when Reason released her last breath, Macy saw it hover fleetingly above the bed and then sail out the open window.

"She's gone?" asked the nurse from the doorway.

"She's gone," said Macy, watching Reason's husband bend forward to kiss his wife.

In the quiet that lingered, a nearby clock ticked, measuring time in a world without Reason. The nurse was the first to speak. "I'm so sorry for your loss. I'll go now. I'll tell the front desk." She left quietly.

As Reason's husband watched, his grief rendering him silent, Macy adjusted the bedsheets. And as she did, a small dark object fell from the folds. It dropped to the floor, and in a wide arc, rolled across the linoleum, passed over the threshold, and disappeared beyond it.

Outside the room, a child giggled. Macy moved to the doorway. In the corridor, a laughing toddler had squatted to the spot where the mindfulness bean had come to rest. Around his plump wrist, the child wore a bracelet. As Macy watched, the bracelet seemed to light up as if lit from the inside, and in the golden glow, she saw a line of turquoise squares that formed a chain along its length. The pattern flashed as diamond shapes filled with little yellow flowers—and then transformed back into a line of turquoise squares.

Macy bent down to the little boy. He giggled with delight, plucking the bean from the floor and bringing it close to his beaming face. "Well now," she said. "Hello, little one. It appears you are in need of a guardian." She reached for his hand. "Shall we find where you belong?"

☙ ❧

Along the marshy shore of the quiet summer pond, clusters of pink-flowered lily pads drank in the morning sun. And between scattered tufts of long still reeds, water spiders skittered higgledy-piggledy across the glassy surface. Suddenly, a small flat stone sailed out from the shadows of the forest. It skimmed and skipped across the tranquil water, kissing the surface several times before sinking out of sight.

Under a small tree near the shore of the pond, Reason gazed lazily at the vastness of the sky. Then, in a moment of thrilling realization, she sat up and reached for the notebook lying on the ground beside her. For a moment she stared at its blank pages, and then eager to record what she could remember, she wrote: Book title: Reasons.

In time, she stood, lingering for a few minutes, continuing to document her thoughts. And then, closing her notebook, she started down a narrow footpath toward home.

Near the far shore, a white raven flew out from a dense cluster of giant pines. "Craw! Craw!" it called. Reason stopped and looked back. She smiled at witnessing the rare bird, feeling an odd sense of recognition, but the moment of familiarity was brief. She turned and continued—while behind her, the majestic bird cleared the pond, rose high into the white-washed sky, and vanished.

☙ ❧

Deep within the forest, in a magical place where few are granted entry, Edward clasped his hands to his chest and let out a soft, contented chuckle. Then, with a glass pen, he initialed the documents that lay before him, and after a moment of reflection, filed the records chronicling Reason's journey—slipping them into a wide drawer in an old wooden filing cabinet.

Humming gleefully, he clapped his hands together, twirled around, coattails flying, walked to the middle of the library, and poured himself a steaming cup of sweet-smelling tea.

About the Author

Sherry was born in Galt, Ontario, Canada, the youngest of four children. At seven, her family moved to Burlington, Ontario, where she spent her teenage years. Out on her own by seventeen, life was no picnic. As her debut novel, REASONS is a creation formed out of the challenges Sherry faced as a young woman; and further enhanced by the lessons she learned. Although the novel draws from Sherry's life experience, it is a work of fiction.

In her early twenties, Sherry completed post-secondary education in sales and marketing. For years, she enjoyed her work as a Project Manager in both the Exhibit and Signage industries. And for twelve years, she was a partner with her husband in a sign manufacturing company.

Sherry has fond memories of her role as a business owner—but life soon saw her venture onto an alternative career path. She currently lives in Peterborough, Ontario, with her husband Robert, where she continues to pursue her writing career.

Manufactured by Amazon.ca
Bolton, ON